The

ACCIDENTAL

ALCHEMIST

DEDICATION

For my parents.

The
ACCIDENTAL
ALCHEMIST

Gigi Pandian

MIDNIGHT INK
WOODBURY, MINNESOTA

MYS
PANDI

First Edition
First Printing, 2015

Cover illustration: Hugh D'Andrade/Jennifer Vaughn Artist Agent
Cover design by Kevin Brown

Midnight Ink, an imprint of Llewellyn Worldwide Ltd.

Library of Congress Cataloging-in-Publication Data

Pandian, Gigi, 1975–
    The accidental alchemist / Gigi Pandian. — First edition.
        pages ; cm. — (Accidental alchemist ; book 1)
    ISBN 978-0-7387-4184-0 (softcover)
1. Alchemists—Fiction. 2. Gargoyles—Fiction. 3.
Murder—Investigation—Fiction. I. Title.
    PS3616.A367A65 2015
    813'.6—dc23

                                                        2014037546

Midnight Ink
Llewellyn Worldwide Ltd.
2143 Wooddale Drive
Woodbury, MN 55125-2989
www.midnightinkbooks.com

Printed in the United States of America

Acknowledgments

The following people were instrumental in making this new series come together:

My early critique readers, whose feedback helped me turn this book from a mess with promise into something I'm proud of: Brian Selfon, Nancy Adams, Sue Parman, Emberly Nesbit, Daryl Wood Gerber, Ramona DeFelice Long, Amber Foxx, and Patricia Winton. My local writer pals, who keep me sane and make this the most fun job in the world: Emberly Nesbit, Juliet Blackwell, Sophie Littlefield, Rachael Herron, Mysti Berry, Lynn Coddington, Martha White, Lisa Hughey, Adrienne Miller, Jon-David Settell, Michelle Gonzalez, and the Sisters in Crime Northern California Chapter. And my writer pals from afar, who make modern technology worth it! I don't know what I'd do without the Sisters in Crime Guppies, especially my partners in crime Kendel Lynn and Diane Vallere.

My publishing team, who made this book come to fruition: My amazing agent, Jill Marsal, for never settling for "good enough"; Terri Bischoff at Midnight Ink, for believing in this new series and being awesome all around; Nicole Nugent, for stellar editorial feedback; and the rest of the Midnight Ink team for all the work that went into producing this book.

The independent bookstores that have supported me, especially A Great Good Place for Books and Murder By The Book.

The city of Portland, Oregon, which gave me the heart of this series, and my Portland writer pals, who've made me feel like I have a second home in Portland. My coworkers, who inspire me daily and send me out into the world ready for anything, especially Catrina Roallos, the best office-mate ever. Victoria Laurie, for writing an amazing set of books I discovered while undergoing chemotherapy; those books gave me hours of enjoyment during a dark time and inspired me to try my hand at writing in this mystery subgenre.

As for my family, there are way too many thanks to list here! The short version: My mother and father, for giving me the world; Leslie Bacon, as true a sister as there ever was; and James, without whom none of this would be possible—or at least it wouldn't be nearly as fun.

And last, but definitely not least, my wonderful readers. All of you have made the last few years more amazing than I ever dreamed.

ONE

The once-beautiful Craftsman house was falling apart. Sloppily applied sections of wood covered several windows. A chunk of the roof was missing, a plastic tarp in its place to keep out the frequent Pacific Northwest rains. More exposed wall than lavender paint showed on the outer walls. And on the inside? Well, let's just say that the plumbing had seen better days—and I'm pretty sure those better days weren't any time during the previous century.

In other words: *perfect*.

At least, it was perfect for what I had in mind. I smiled as I looked at the rundown structure through the window of my trailer. Finding this house in the artsy Hawthorne neighborhood of Portland, Oregon hadn't been easy. Real estate agents had a difficult time grasping the fact that I wanted a house in complete disrepair.

It was probably my own fault, because I didn't lie to them. I told them I wasn't a professional home renovator. Nor was I a house flipper. No, I wasn't a masochist either. But I left it at that, letting them think I was a single young woman with trendy dyed-white hair and a limited budget who loved a challenge. I didn't tell them I was someone who needed a residence where doing substantial construction wouldn't raise eyebrows—that I was someone who wanted to hide in plain sight.

As soon as I'd seen the listing that a peppy young real estate agent emailed me with a healthy dose of skepticism and at least a dozen exclamation points, I knew this was the perfect house for me. I'd even found the perfect contractor, who'd come highly recommended by the real estate agent for being discreet.

The contractor wanted me on-site to make sure he was correctly executing my unique instructions, which is how I found myself moving into my new home during a furious winter storm, the day before he promised to begin work. I love the rain, but I love it most when I'm inside the warm, cozy trailer where I've lived for years, listening to the rhythmic sound of the rain tapping on the roof.

Inside the silver Airstream trailer, I bundled my coat around me and scooped up a bag of a few essentials before running the few yards to the house. Not that there was much more to move inside. I was born and raised in Massachusetts, but I'd been living out of that old trailer for a long time. Half the space in the trailer was taken up with the trinkets I sold at flea markets across the country. Most of the antique wares I'd accumulated over the years were in storage. I was waiting for a shipping company to deliver them that afternoon.

I hung my silver raincoat on a rusty hook next to the front door, then carried the bag to the kitchen. It contained my blender, a kettle and mug, a few jars of dried herbs, raw chocolate, and a bag of produce and nuts from a hearty farmer who braved the rains at the farmers market. Like I said: essentials.

The water from the kitchen's mid-century faucet ran a yellowish-brown color, but I wasn't deterred. A small sip of the water assured me it was only rust. A little extra iron would do me good. Still, I let the water run for a few minutes while I poked around the kitchen. Though it was in desperate need of cosmetic upgrades, its bones were solid. The vintage porcelain stove was functional, and it would be beautiful after a little cleaning. The pink fridge was one of the models popular in the 1950s that looked like it could have withstood a bomb blast. The best part was the window box above the sink, perfect for growing delicate herbs. My blender didn't explode when I plugged it into a socket, which was a good sign. I made a green smoothie with fresh leafy greens, an apple, avocado, mint, chocolate, and ginger.

Energizing drink in hand, I was ready to explore my new house. I'd toured it already, but that was different. Now it was *real*. A home I could make my own. I couldn't remember the last time I'd allowed myself to feel so optimistic. I was almost hopeful. Almost.

I shook out the faded curtains that covered the tall living room windows. Branches of unpruned cherry trees scraped against the windows like claws. The trees would need to be trimmed, but not too much—I liked the privacy they granted.

Floorboards creaked underfoot as I made my way up the stairs. Before I reached the second floor, a honk that played the opening notes of Beethoven's Fifth Symphony alerted me to the movers' presence. You've gotta love movers who enjoy the little things in life—and who don't ask questions about the items they're delivering. In addition to the furniture for the house and the antiques I sold online, the crates contained glass jars I didn't want anyone looking at too closely.

Within an hour, the efficient father-son team had carried the heavy furniture and crates inside, and I'd made us all a pot of mint tea with a hint of licorice. I had to scrounge up two additional mugs from my trailer; I'm not used to entertaining.

After the movers departed, I sank into the green velvet couch that had been in storage for years, enjoying the sound of the rain. The respite didn't last long. As soon as I pried open one of the crates, I knew something was wrong. *Someone had tampered with my shipping crates.*

It was the smell that hit me first. A metallic scent assaulted my senses. With the crowbar still in my hand, I examined the mess. The glass and copper antiques that had been carefully wrapped in old newspapers were now exposed. This wasn't the type of chaos that could have been created by a turbulent flight, or even damage that would have resulted from the crate being tipped on its side or placed upside down. Taking a closer look, I saw that not only had the contents been unwrapped, but the lids from several glass jars had been sloppily resealed. That's where the metallic fragrance was coming from. There could be no doubt that someone had rifled through the contents.

The strange thing was, nothing seemed to be missing. Even the jar containing a small amount of gold was there. Instead, as I removed the glassware and pushed aside the tangle of newspaper padding, I saw that something had been *added*.

A three-foot stone gargoyle stared up at me from the wreckage that used to be carefully organized antique alchemy artifacts.

Instinctively, I stepped backward. How had this statue been added to my sealed crate? And why on earth would someone do so?

I ran out the front door, but the movers had already departed. The porch sagged beneath my feet and the rickety front door banged shut behind me in the strong wind. When I turned the door handle to let myself back inside, the brass knob came off in my hand. *Be careful what you wish for, Zoe Faust.*

Thankfully, a strong shove was all the door needed to open. Back inside my new home, I returned to the crate for a closer look. The gargoyle reminded me of the stone carvings on Notre Dame in Paris. The gray creature looked similar to the famous "thinker" gargoyle, with short horns and folded wings. The main difference was that this gargoyle held an old, leather-bound book in his arms. That was odd. I would have expected any added detail to be made of stone, not this real book with leather binding. I couldn't place the type of stone used to carve the gargoyle. Granite? Sandstone? Or perhaps softer soapstone? It wasn't like any stone I'd seen. I leaned in for a closer look. There was something...

The gargoyle blinked.

My fist tensed around the crowbar. I stumbled backward, falling into the large couch.

Sprawled out on the couch, I laughed at myself. I'd seen a fair share of magic shows in my time. I knew what this gargoyle was. He was something that had been a popular attraction over a century ago: an automaton.

"You're the best-looking automaton I've ever seen," I said.

The gargoyle's shoulders moved, as if it was stretching. It was a wonderfully constructed piece. It must have been programmed to awaken when light shone on him. A good trick for the stage.

"I am no automaton," a deep voice emanating from the automaton said. He—for his voice assured me he was male—climbed out of the crate onto the hardwood floor.

I gasped and fell off the edge of the couch. *Ouch.*

I'd seen ingenious automatons created by stage magicians. None were as advanced as this one. If I were to believe my eyes, I would have sworn he was alive. But then again, technology had progressed since automatons were popular in stage shows of the 1800s. A famous example of an early automaton was The Turk, a chess-playing machine that drew huge crowds to watch him play chess against famous chess players. Automatons were a combination of technical wizardry and stage showmanship, and the most famous automatons were aided by human helpers. There was no way a person was inside the crate with this creature, so he had to be completely mechanized.

"Where are my manners?" the creature said, bowing before me. "I did not mean to startle you. Allow me to introduce myself. I am Dorian Robert-Houdin." He spoke in English with a thick French accent.

I pulled myself together and stood up. "Either I'm going crazy, or your creator had a mischievous sense of humor. Incorporating a recording of his voice—"

I broke off when the gargoyle who called himself Dorian Robert-Houdin blinked at me again. The effect was quite disconcerting. His eyelids looked like granite, but the eyes themselves were a liquidy black substance.

"I assure you," he said, "I am not a robotic automaton, nor are you going crazy."

Most people would have run screaming from the room if they saw a walking, talking gargoyle emerge from their storage crate. I admit I was surprised, but I've seen many things in my lifetime. I stood my ground and took a closer look at the creature, trying to find evidence he was an incredibly advanced robot. I didn't see any. All I saw before me was a creature that looked every bit as alive as I was. It wasn't only the wrinkles in his gray skin and the absence of visible mechanized parts—it was the spirit that showed in his eyes.

Through my shock and confusion, another emotion poked through: disappointment. It was a feeling I knew well. Portland was supposed to be my chance at a normal life. I'd been traveling for far too long. Running. I was tired. Ready to settle down. My trailer had been my sanctuary for years as I crisscrossed the country, never staying in one place for too long. But when I'd passed through Portland the previous year, the city spoke to me. It had all the elements I cared about. Plentiful greenery, an ancient river, vibrant weather, and most of all, welcoming people—many of whom I felt might be kindred spirits. Feeling instantly at home in Portland had struck me as too good to be true. Maybe it was. This was the last place on earth I expected to find a creature that wasn't supposed to exist.

"Surely you know what I am," the gargoyle continued, "*Alchemist*."

The word hit me more forcefully than a slap.

Did I mention that when I was born in Massachusetts, it was 1676? I've been around for a while. But even my many years hadn't prepared me for what I'd find in Portland.

TWO

BEING AN ALCHEMIST ISN'T as glamorous as it sounds. Turning lead into gold? It's a laborious, utterly draining process that's incredibly difficult to replicate. Living a longer life? Not without unpleasant consequences, such as outliving everyone you love and feeling the effects of years of unhealthy living.

Alchemy means different things to different people, but at its core it's about transformation that strives to achieve perfection. It's a personal journey that involves transforming yourself as you transform plants or metals. Finding the philosopher's stone to create gold and the Elixir of Life to live forever are the most famous goals of alchemists, but those are only two parts of a much greater whole.

It's a lonely life. Because there are so few of us who have succeeded in realizing alchemy's true potential, and because we've seen what has befallen alchemists over the centuries, we're forced to keep the extent of our alchemical transformations a secret.

It's not as bad as it was during the Salem Witch Trials, when misunderstandings had consequences much worse than hateful comments on Facebook. Society has come a long way since then, but people are still afraid of what they don't understand. The people I've met in my travels love that I can use herbs to create healthful elixirs that heal what ails them or sell them a decorative alchemical relic. But tell them about my deeper connection to plants, my ability to detect poisons, and the fact that I first did so over three hundred years ago? They'll get as far away from me as possible and probably call a psychiatrist. I've learned not to tell people the whole truth. It's better for everyone. That's why I was doubly disconcerted to have a living gargoyle standing in my new home announcing who I really was.

The creature's eyes followed me as I took a few slow steps backward and leaned against the wall, steadying my trembling legs.

"How do you know me?" I asked. "Why do you say I'm an alchemist?"

Dorian bowed again. This time his wings widened as he did so. They, too, looked visually like stone, but moved like the wings of a bird or a bat.

The rain had stopped, at least for the moment, but a strong breeze outside rustled the branches of the trees in the front yard and they again brushed against the living room windows. Standing in the shadow of the crate, Dorian cocked his head and looked at the windows, his eyes narrowed.

"You will draw the curtains," Dorian said. "Then we may speak more freely."

I kept the creature in view as I stood up to close the musty curtains. Part of me thought he'd disappear if I let him out of my sight.

"There is no need to pretend with me," he said. "Besides, you give yourself away, Alchemist. You seem rather unsurprised to find a living gargoyle in your luggage."

"You don't call falling off the couch surprised?"

"You are sitting here speaking with me," he said. "That is more than most people would do if they saw me."

"You lucked out and hid in the crate of an open-minded person."

The gargoyle rolled his eyes. Apparently it was a universal way to express exasperation. Or maybe I really was going crazy.

"Zoe," he said. "I knew your apothecary shop, Elixir, in Paris."

"My grandmother's shop?" Maybe that explained things. Well, as much as things could be explained with a talking gargoyle in one's living room. "I've got a great collection of historical alchemical supplies she left me, as you must have seen from rooting through my shipping crate. I sell things like these antiques to make a living."

"*Mon dieu,*" Dorian said. "I know that you are the same person as the young woman from a century ago you claim was your grandmother."

"That's ridiculous," I said, hoping my shaking voice didn't betray me.

"If you are not going to trust that your secret is safe with me, at least you can feed me. Do you have any food? *J'ai faim.* That crate was in transit for much longer than I imagined it would be. I apologize that this is why I searched through your belongings. I was hoping to find something to eat."

"You *eat food*?"

"But of course."

Something about the gargoyle saying how hungry he was made me realize the absurdity of the situation. I glanced around the expansive living and dining room, empty except for shipping crates, a

10

green velvet couch, a mango wood coffee table, and a oak dining table with chairs. I half-expected a Frenchman with a remote control to jump out from behind the couch and tell me this was a practical joke for a reality TV show.

"What are you?" I asked. The gargoyle was even larger that I'd originally thought. He stood three-and-a-half feet tall, two feet shorter than my five-foot-six frame, and looked every bit as real as I did.

"I would think that was evident," he said. "*Je suis un gargouille*—a gargoyle. As I said, my name is Dorian. I am no less alive than you."

The hilarity I felt a moment before drained from my body, replaced by fear.

"You're a homunculus," I whispered. I no longer cared about what I said in front of the creature, even if it meant admitting I was a practicing alchemist. Keeping my secret was now the least of my problems. Having such a creature in my home was far more dangerous than the most advanced robot—because he had a mind that was controlled from afar. A homunculus could not be deactivated or killed by anyone besides the person who created him.

There were rumors of alchemists who had succeeded in creating a homunculus—a living being created out of an inanimate object—but none of the rumors had ever been proven true. They were either stories told by men who wanted to appear more powerful than they really were, or legends created to make people fear alchemists. It couldn't be…

"My father did not think so," he said casually, as if this was a normal conversation.

"Your *father*?"

"The man who raised me and cared for me. That is what one calls a father, no?"

"Yes, but how—"

"There is much to tell, but I am hungry," he whined.

"But why are you here in the first place?" I asked. "What were you doing in my moving crate?"

"You visited Paris so briefly," Dorian Robert-Houdin answered, looking up at me. "You were there only to pack up your storage unit. That did not leave me time to speak with you about my book." He held up the antique book clutched in his clawed hands. "I assure you I am no homunculus. I have a mind of my own, you see. You have nothing to fear."

Though I wasn't sure how much better it made me feel to know that he had a mind of his own, I didn't have time to give the matter more thought. A crash sounded from the direction of the kitchen. The swinging door burst open and a scrawny boy fell to the floor.

Dorian's black liquid eyes bulged and he scampered back inside his crate.

Sprawled on the hardwood floor was a boy who looked about thirteen or fourteen years old. Curly black hair stuck to the sides of his face, messy from the earlier rain. He met my gaze as he pushed himself up. His hazel eyes resembled those of a cornered animal—defiance masking fear.

Instead of anger at the realization that he'd been spying on us from behind the swinging kitchen door, my first thought was concern. A large streak of blood covered the boy's forearm.

"You're hurt," I said.

"I'm fine," he stammered, his voice breaking as he held his bleeding arm.

"Let me get something to bandage that. Then you can tell me why you were *in my house* eavesdropping—"

"I'm fine," he repeated, "and I didn't see anything." He stood still for a second longer, then bolted back toward the swinging kitchen door.

He was fast, but Dorian was faster. The gargoyle jumped out of his crate and grabbed the boy's leg.

"Don't hurt me!" The boy tried to shake free of Dorian's grasp, but the little creature was strong.

"*Mon dieu*," Dorian said. "We are not going to hurt you. But you must give us your word of honor you will not speak of what you saw."

"I swear I won't say anything." The boy kept squirming, but Dorian's grip was unrelenting.

"What's your name?" I asked.

The boy glared at me.

"What do you think you saw?" I asked. "I was unpacking my robot—"

"Nothing," he said quickly. "I didn't see anything."

"The boy is not stupid," Dorian said. "It is evident I am no robot."

"I'm not a boy," he said, jerking his arm away. This time Dorian let go. "I'm fourteen. And I'm just leaving—"

"Let me clean your cut," I said.

"I told you, I'm fine."

"No, you're not," I said. "You're also breaking and entering."

His face paled. "You can't call the cops. This place is abandoned. I'm not doing anything wrong."

"As you can see," I said, spreading my arms and looking over the room from the velvet couch to the crates, "I'm the new owner. How did you get in?"

He looked at the floor.

"Watch him," I said to Dorian.

I poked my head into the kitchen. One of the windows had been forced open. A smear of blood covered the rusty latch.

"There's no way that window latch is sanitary," I said to the boy. "Let me clean that cut."

He crossed his arms and glowered at me, but didn't attempt to run.

"I'll be right back," I said.

I went to my trailer to find an antiseptic salve and a bandage. It took me a few minutes, and when I returned, Dorian and the boy were sitting cross-legged in front of the brick fireplace. They watched each other skeptically, apparently having reached a détente.

"Let me see your arm." I took his hand in mine.

He wore a black hoodie that was pushed up to his elbows. The blood from his cut had soaked the cuff. He winced as I cleaned the cut and applied an herbal salve of yarrow and aloe. Though the boy was scrawny, his hands were strong. His fingertips were calloused, like he played a stringed instrument. I wondered which one. I couldn't see him playing in a school orchestra, but one thing I've learned over the years is that people never fail to surprise me.

"Why did you break in?" I asked.

"I told you," he said. "This place was supposed to be abandoned. We saw the trailer in the driveway." He shrugged. "We wanted to know who would be staying in a haunted house."

Dorian rolled his little black eyes.

"Your friends are with you?" I asked. This situation kept getting worse and worse.

"They stayed down the street. None of them were brave enough …"

"You're here on a dare?"

He glared at me again. The kid seemed to have a lot of practice.

"They won't believe you, you know," I said.

A brisk knock sounded at the door.

"*Mon dieu!*" Dorian exclaimed. "What is this, *une fête*?"

"Maybe you should—"

"*Oui,*" Dorian said. But instead of getting back inside the crate, he stood next to the fireplace. After stretching his shoulders for a moment, he stood so still that I would have sworn he was a stone gargoyle, just as solid and unmoving as a garden decoration.

"Could it be your friends?" I asked the boy.

He shook his head, confusion showing on his face. "They wouldn't—"

"Police," a deep voice called out from beyond the door. "May I speak with you?"

What were the police doing at my door? I felt my pulse quicken as memories flooded back to me. I wasn't alone in my reaction. My young intruder's eyes grew wide.

The boy hovered nervously behind me as I opened the door to find a handsome man with deep brown eyes standing on my rickety porch. Instead of a police uniform, he wore dark blue jeans, a slim-fitting black sweater, and a jacket. Two kids, a boy and a girl, stood next to him.

"What can I do for you?" I asked, hoping I didn't sound as nervous as I felt.

My injured intruder groaned, slinking further behind me.

"I'm Detective Liu," the man said. "Max Liu. These two were worried about their friend Brixton. They said they saw him—" He broke off and cleared his throat.

"Let me guess," I said. "You were going to say they saw him disappear into the neighborhood haunted house." The house had been uninhabited for several years, due to a legal battle among the family of the elderly woman who'd lived here. That's how it had fallen into its current state of disrepair. I knew about the history from the real estate agent, but for everyone else in the neighborhood who saw the biggest house on the block sitting empty for unknown reasons, rumors about ghosts made perfect sense.

"Bingo." The detective raised an eyebrow at Brixton's friends.

The girl shrugged awkwardly. "Brixton said he'd be *right* back. He didn't show, so I texted him and still didn't hear back…"

"He fell and hurt his arm," I said. "He got a nasty cut and I was helping him clean it."

"He wasn't disturbing you?" Detective Liu asked as a cold wind pushed up the collar of his jacket. "Trespassing?"

"Not at all. He was simply saying hello to his new neighbor. I'm Zoe." I paused to shake his hand. In spite of the chilly air, his hand was warm. And there was something else… A faint scent of lavender wafted up from his hand, along with another plant essence I couldn't place. The overall effect was familiar and comforting. "Do you want to come in? It's getting cold out there."

"This is nothing," he said, stepping inside. "I take it you're not originally from Portland."

"I've lived in much colder places, but I always appreciate the warmth." I paused as it hit me that I hadn't seen any identification from Detective Liu. He didn't look like a typical police officer. It wasn't just the fact that he wasn't dressed like one. I've known detectives in many eras and countries. There was something different about Max Liu. He was guarded and open at the same time. Looking into his eyes as I'd shaken his hand, I had the strongest sense that he was both genuinely friendly and hiding a burdensome secret.

"You introduced yourself as 'detective,'" I added. "Isn't it a bit much to send a detective because a fourteen-year-old decided to turn off his cell phone for a few minutes?"

"I live in the neighborhood," he said. He reached into his pocket and brought out his badge. "They found me at the teashop down the street."

"I bought this place last month," I said, "and moved in today."

"Why?" the girl next to Detective Liu asked. She gaped at me, ignoring her friend who was jabbing her with his elbow. Even in ballet flats, she was several inches taller than either boy. She was beautiful, but from the way she held herself I could tell she couldn't see it. She hadn't yet figured out how to hold her long limbs gracefully.

Her friend remained silent. With a white t-shirt, leather jacket, and I'm-the-cool-silent-type expression on his face, he looked right out of a 1950s movie. But he wasn't fooling me. His inquisitive eyes betrayed a curiosity even greater than the girl's.

"I love a challenge," I said—but the words were drowned out by a crash from overhead. My body tensed. I stole a glance at Dorian, stock still as his stone self next to the fireplace. It wasn't Dorian who was upstairs.

The girl screamed. Brixton jumped. The other boy's body jerked in surprise, followed by a cringe at the fact that he hadn't played it cool.

"Should you check on whoever that is?" Max Liu asked.

"There's nobody else here," I said.

Before I'd finished speaking, the detective was already bounding up the stairs.

"Stay there," he called down to us.

"Another friend?" I asked the kids.

They shook their heads in unison.

I followed the detective up the stairs. What was going on? Was there another stowaway in my boxes?

"Miss," Detective Liu said, rushing out of the master bedroom and nearly giving me a heart attack. "You shouldn't be up here while I—"

"I know what's going on," I said, pushing past him.

He followed me as I knelt down and picked up a sheet of plywood.

"This," I said, "used to be attached to the frame of this broken window. The wind must have dislodged it."

The detective groaned.

"Sorry to have worried you, Detective," I said.

"Max," he said. "Since we've caught a rogue piece of plywood together, I think you can call me Max."

"Sorry, Max." I tried to ignore the effect Max's voice was having on me as I wrestled the piece of wood back into the window frame. The thin wood had warped and refused to stay in place.

"You're *living here* already?"

"I've got a repairman coming first thing in the morning to fix up the place."

Brixton and his friends appeared in the doorway.

"False alarm," I said.

"The house moved on its own?" the girl asked. "Spooky."

"Not really." I held up the warped piece of wood.

"Come on, Veronica," Max said. "We should leave our new neighbor in peace to fix up her house."

"Good luck," Veronica said, a timid smile on her face.

I smiled back at her. My smile was genuine, but I was also wondering what to do about Brixton. I couldn't have him telling Max Liu about Dorian after they left. Brixton knew he could get in trouble if I told the detective he'd broken in. I had the bloody latch to prove it. Was that enough? I wasn't into taking chances.

"I know the place needs a lot of work," I said. "That's why I was so grateful that Brixton offered to help me weed the yard. Isn't that right, Brixton?"

Brixton had a sudden coughing fit.

"Tomorrow after school?" I said, patting him on the back.

Brixton looked from me to the detective and nodded. How had a fourteen-year-old cultivated such a wary look?

A gargoyle, a hoodlum, and a detective. And I'd been in my new home for less than a day.

THREE

"They're gone," I said. I ran my hands through my short white hair, wondering what I'd gotten myself into. I needed to keep an eye on Brixton to make sure he didn't start talking about things nobody would believe. When I turned to face Dorian, he had already uncurled himself from his stiff perch at the fireplace.

"You have good instincts, Alchemist," he said. "The boy does not wish you to press charges, so he will help you and not tell anyone what he saw of me."

"I hope so."

"Do you always worry this much?"

"You aren't worried?"

He gave a Gallic shrug. "I have hidden from people since the day I was brought to life by my father. It was a mistake, you see. He did not know what he was doing."

"What do you mean he—"

"I have learned," he continued, ignoring my half-formed question, "that people discount what they do not wish to believe. We can run, Zoe Faust, but we cannot truly hide. You are only fooling yourself if you believe you can control those around you. The boy may tell his friends. There is nothing you can do about that. But rest assured, they will not believe him. They will think he has an overactive imagination."

And here I was thinking that the day couldn't get any weirder. The gargoyle's words reminded me of my mentor, the alchemist Nicolas Flamel. Nicolas and his wife Perenelle discovered the secret of eternal life in the fifteenth century, as well as how to turn lead into gold, but they were wise enough to know the world wasn't ready for their secrets. They donated huge sums of gold to charity before "dying" of old age in Paris. In truth, they faked their deaths to avoid scrutiny, living their lives in the shadows after their official deaths, only revealing their true identities to alchemists like me. I wished I hadn't run from them during a difficult period of my life. I had never been able to find them again.

"I have but one question," Dorian said. "Why is everyone speaking English?"

"Why wouldn't we be speaking English? You're speaking English."

"You spoke to me first. You were speaking English. It was only polite that I reply in the language you spoke."

"You know you're in Portland, Oregon."

Dorian's snout twitched. His granite mouth opened but no sound came out. "Oregon?" he said finally. "You left *France*?"

"Where did you think my shipping crates were going?"

21

"I did not have time to find out! I wanted your assistance, but I could not approach you when you were with others. Your assistant turned her back for but a moment when packing. That is when I climbed into this crate. I could not ask her where it was being sent. *Mon dieu*, this explains why the journey took so many days!"

His wings flapped in a single violent motion. Though the movement was fluid, as if the gray wings were thick feathers, the tip of his wing clipped the edge of the fireplace, sending a chunk of brick crumbling to the floor. He closed his eyes and squared his shoulders, folding his wings back to their resting place.

"*Je suis désolé*," he said. "I am sorry. I have control of myself now. I simply do not understand why anyone would leave France! But you are a grown woman who can do as she pleases."

"A grown woman who didn't expect to find a gargoyle in her living room in the town she thought was finally going to give her a normal life." I crossed my arms and looked down at the little Francophile.

"If you are done being maudlin," Dorian said, "we can have a more civilized conversation after we eat. What are you cooking for dinner?"

"Dinner? I was going to make myself a simple vegetable soup."

The gargoyle's black eyes darkened and widened. "*Mais non! You cannot be serious!*"

"Sorry to disappoint you. But you were also going to tell me why you're a castaway in my crate."

Dorian sighed and stretched his neck and shoulders from side to side. His movements were more controlled now. I suppose it must have been rather cramped in my shipping crate. "If I finish explaining about my book," he said, "you will feed me a real meal?"

"That's rather presumptuous for a castaway."

He stopped stretching and locked intensely on my gaze. "Please?"

How could one say no to a polite gargoyle? Especially if that was the only way to get this curious creature to tell me how he knew I was an alchemist and why he had traveled across the world to show me the worn book he clutched.

"All right," I agreed. "We'll make dinner, then you'll tell me all about this book of yours as well as how you found me."

"You drive a hard bargain, Alchemist," he said, narrowing his eyes at me. The pupils of his eyes looked more like glass than stone. A fluid, moving glass. He extended his clawed right hand.

I reached out to shake it. His hand was cool, but didn't feel like stone. It was a little bit rougher than human skin, but malleable in the same way.

"You have ham?" he asked.

"Ham?"

"Yes, the cured meat. Made from a pig—"

"I know what *ham* is," I said. "No, I don't have any ham."

"Bacon, then," Dorian said.

"No bacon."

"*Mon dieu!*"

"You only eat pork products?" I asked. This gargoyle was making me more and more curious.

"Of course I eat more than ham and bacon." Dorian sniffled, his little snout moving side to side. "But with a ham hock or a slice of bacon as a base starter, and a few herbs, I can create a masterpiece, regardless of the other ingredients you have available."

"I see," I said, unsure of what else one could say to that. A talking gargoyle was standing in my living room lecturing me about cooking. Even for me, this was pretty weird. "I'm a vegan."

"*Pardon?*"

"I eat a wide range of plant-based foods, but I don't eat animal products."

Dorian swore in French and shook his head. "You at least have basic supplies?"

"Fresh winter vegetables and a few herbs are in the kitchen already, and cooking pans, oils, and more herbs and spices are in my trailer outside."

I went to my trailer to retrieve a portion of my kitchen bounty, from a hanging bunch of dried cayenne peppers to newly ground garlic powder in a glass jar, which I carried inside using a copper saucepan. I've always been aware of the link between food and health, but didn't always treat my own body as well as I treated the people I healed. It wasn't until recently—a little over a hundred years ago—that I felt worthy of taking care of myself. I kept my cooking simple, but used pure, healthful ingredients.

Dorian conceded the high quality of my home-prepared dried herbs and infused oils, after which he banished me from the kitchen. I sat down on the couch with his book on my lap, hoping my instincts were right to trust him in the kitchen. I wondered if the smoke detectors had batteries.

Looking at the book more closely for the first time, the title gave me pause. This was an alchemy book. Translated from Latin, *Non Degenera Alchemia* would be *Not Untrue Alchemy*. What a strange title. What was the point of the double negative? Why wasn't it simply *True Alchemy*?

It took me a few minutes before I could bring myself to open the book. I hadn't practiced alchemy in years. I hadn't been ready. Not after what had happened.

I breathed in a scent I knew well as I opened the book. I work with lots of old books, but in spite of the familiar scent of its binding—seventeenth-century calf-skin, I guessed—this one held unfamiliar secrets. I carefully flipped through a few pages. The title was in Latin, as was some of the text inside, but it didn't look like the alchemy I'd studied. It also included something similar to the coded images used by alchemists, but these symbols weren't quite like any I'd seen before. In the many woodcut illustrations in the book, the necks of the birds twisted to the left to an unnatural degree that reminded me of something seen in a horror movie. I shivered and shut the book. A woody scent wafted up to my nostrils as I did so.

I had excelled in spagyrics, also known as plant alchemy, which uses alchemical techniques to extract the healing properties of herbs rather than the precious properties of metals. The general idea behind all types of alchemy is the same: transforming a substance into something greater than its original whole by making the corruptible into something pure.

I feared I was beyond my depth here. I closed my eyes and clutched the gold locket I wore around my neck. The locket I always kept close to me yet hadn't opened in many years. I hadn't even wanted to *think* about practicing alchemy for decades. Not since Ambrose.

Stop it, Zoe. It wasn't your fault.

I repeated my mantra of that past century a few times before opening the book again. Pushing all thoughts of Ambrose to the back of my mind, I tried to focus on the calligraphy of the title page. I wasn't sure where to start. Many of my old alchemy books were packed in the shipping crates. It would take some time to locate what I needed. For the time being, I took a cursory look at how the book was organized and snapped a few photos of interesting pages with my cell phone. As I did so, I became more certain than ever that this wasn't alchemy. The illustrations resembled alchemical symbolism only superficially, as if the person making the illustrations had never studied it. Perhaps that explained the convoluted title.

I wasn't sure how long I'd been absorbed in *Not Untrue Alchemy* when a heavenly aroma wafted out from the kitchen. Sage, rosemary, and onions. Dorian carried a hot casserole dish from the kitchen and set it down on a cork matt on the solid oak table. He ran back to the kitchen for the plates and utensils I'd brought inside earlier.

"You made this with what I had in the house?" I asked, my eyes wide and my mouth watering.

He grinned proudly. "Butternut squash roasted in olive oil with onions, sage, and a hint of rosemary. The sauce is lemon tahini, with cayenne-infused salt and toasted pumpkin seeds sprinkled on top. The fat from the sesame seeds used to make the tahini fools the senses into thinking there is a ham base."

"This is amazing," I said.

Dorian ate quickly but with refinement, serving himself a second helping before I was halfway through eating my first. I ate slowly, savoring the exquisite flavors. With the same ingredients I was planning on using to create a simple meal, Dorian had created a feast.

"*Pardon,*" he said after a small burp.

"That meal was incredible," I said.

"*C'est rien,*" he said. "It was nothing. I would have made something better if I was not so hungry."

"I haven't eaten such a gourmet meal in ages," I said.

"You will help me with my book?" he said, looking across the table expectantly.

"You haven't told me exactly what you need done with it, re-member? If you're looking for a translator, I'm not the best person."

"*Mais oui!*" he said. "Now that we have satisfied our earthly needs, we may discuss practical business." He scrambled off his chair and returned a moment later with the book I'd left on the couch.

"You are an alchemist. You can help me not only translate my book, but *decipher* it."

"I'm sorry to disappoint you," I said. "Especially after you traveled all this way. But this isn't an alchemy book."

"You are correct it is not a normal one," Dorian said, "but there are alchemy tenets inside. The philosopher's stone, Alkahest, recipes with the three essential ingredients of mercury, sulfur, and salt. It is all here. It is the same principles for creating an Elixir of Life, no?"

"Yes, but that doesn't mean—"

"I," Dorian said, cutting me off, "was once stone. This book is what brought me to life."

I stared across the table at the gargoyle. "That's not possible."

The philosopher's stone was the alchemical creation that en-abled both the transformation of eternal life and the creation of gold. But it wasn't something that could be used to bring an inani-mate object to life. There was a natural order to things. Steps that had to be taken both outwardly and inwardly—planetary align-ments, clockwise rotations, separating and rejoining elements in the proper order, connecting yourself to the processes.

"The secret to immortality is personal," I continued, "not some-thing that can be granted to inanimate objects. Even if stories of the homunculus were true, it's a transformation that doesn't give a per-sonality, a soul, or a mind of your own—meaning it can't possibly be what happened to you. I'm glad you're alive"—and I really was;

the little creature was growing on me, especially after that meal—
"but books can't achieve that kind of transformation."

"Yet here I am before you," Dorian said. "*Regardez.* I am telling you, this is no normal book. I know about you. I know you can do this."

"What do you mean you *know about me*?"

"There is something strange about this book. A secret that you, of all people, would wish to know."

"Why me?"

He sighed. It was a slow, sad, movement. "I saw what you were doing nearly eighty years ago, after you closed your shop, Elixir."

"How could you?" But as I spoke the words, I knew.

"I was there," Dorian said, "when you were nearly discovered. You, as the woman you claim to be your grandmother, were called in by *un Commandant* to help with a strange occurrence at a manor outside of the city."

I nodded slowly. I remembered it well. I was in bad shape, emotionally, at the time. It's why I shut the shop for good and returned home to the U.S., buying a brand-new 1942 Chevy pickup truck, followed a few years later by an Airstream trailer. The truck and trailer allowed me to keep running.

"You may recall," he said, "that the estate had gargoyles. I had been brought to life some years before, and had come to know Paris and its surrounding areas well. I would often hide as stone, as I was that day."

"You were there," I whispered. "Watching."

"I see it as clearly on your face now as I could see it then. You do not feel as if you belong. You never have."

It was so close to the truth that sadness overcame me. Dorian must have known that feeling, too. He was a gargoyle. In the shadows. Always watching, but never able to join in.

"It was *you* who saved me from being discovered that day," I said, staring at the little creature and seeing him in a new light. "You created the distraction by throwing pebbles off the roof, stopping me from telling the French police the truth about how I solved the puzzling crime, giving me time to think it through." On that day eighty years before, I was recovering from an experience that had left me shaken and prone to acting without thinking. I would have been discovered had it not been for my anonymous savior who created a commotion on the roof.

He shrugged. "We are alike, you and I. I have suffered the same fate. Of course I would do what I could once I realized what you were. I do not believe you understand more about why you are alive than I do. Alchemy is about one true thing, no? Yet it is not that simple. This book can help explain it. *To both of us.*"

We stared at each other for several seconds before my phone chirped the soothing sound of a sandpiper.

Dorian shook his head. "Americans," he mumbled. "Never silencing their phones during meals." He tossed his napkin on the table and began to clear the plates.

I saw my contractor's name on the phone's screen and picked up. "Mr. Macraith."

"Eight in the morning work for you to get started? I like to get an early start on the day." His voice was gravely, as I remembered, but even rougher than in our previous conversations. I hoped the jack-of-all-trades handyman was up for the large job I'd given him.

"That works," I said. "Thanks again for scheduling something on such short notice. I'm eager to get started fixing up this place."

"Until then." He clicked off.

Dorian cleaned the dishes while I spread out on the dining table with his book and a cup of chamomile tea. Dorian wouldn't tell me more about the strange tenets in the book. "Simply have a look," he said.

Now that I knew how we'd crossed paths before, how could I say no?

The fact that this wasn't a straightforward alchemy book made it easier to focus. It allowed me to avoid dwelling on the old memories of alchemy that were trying to push their way to the front of my mind. I thought it had been long enough that I was ready for anything. I didn't want to be wrong.

I spent a short time searching for information online, before realizing that was a dead end. I then turned to unpacking my crates in search of alchemy books that might be helpful, but I wasn't hopeful. I already knew what was in those books, and I doubted they could help me. But it had been a long time since I'd opened those books. I wondered what I would find if I reacquainted myself with their secrets.

I fell asleep at the table with one of my alchemy books resting under my head. Not a good position to sleep in if you happen to like moving your neck without searing pain.

I woke up at dawn. My body is so attuned to planetary shifts that I wake up with the sun, even when it's a cloud-covered day and I've slept for only a few hours in an upright position. Since it was wintertime, shortly after the start of the new year, it was a few minutes after seven o'clock.

I saw no sign of Dorian, even after a thorough search of the house.

After taking an alternatively freezing cold and scorching shower that made me glad Charles Macraith would be arriving soon, I made myself a breakfast smoothie of blended fruits and vegetables. There was still no sign of Dorian. I hadn't asked him where he slept—or even *if* he slept—so I wasn't sure where else to look. He'd taken care of himself without being discovered before he met me, so I told myself not to worry. Perhaps he hadn't liked my suggestion that he return to the shipping crate while the contractor worked on the house, and had hidden elsewhere.

I had a little time before our scheduled meeting time, so I set out on a walk. Dorian's meal and my morning juice had used up most of what I'd bought the day before, so I stopped at a small market to buy fresh produce.

Though I'm attuned to plants and planets, I don't have an inner compass. I got turned around rather badly and didn't arrive back at my new house until shortly after eight o'clock.

I walked up the narrow path overgrown with weeds, feeling the stillness of the day. I loved how the house was centrally located but at the same time set back from the street, giving me the privacy I liked. I didn't see anyone waiting for me on the raised porch in front of the house. I was wondering when Charles Macraith would show up, when I realized he wouldn't.

Not alive.

Lying on the ground in front of the rickety porch was the prostrate body of my contractor. The acrid scent of poison overwhelmed the fragrant oranges that dropped from my hand as I knelt over his dead body.

FOUR

IN THE HOURS FOLLOWING the death of Charles Macraith, I was back in 1692. Between the whiff of poison and the suspicion directed at me by well-dressed men in positions of power, I was transported back to my first experience with death, when I was sixteen years old and the Salem Witch Trials were going strong.

I felt an irrational sense of panic rise within me. Though I had no connection to the murder, I knew firsthand how easy it was for innocent people to get caught up in hysteria. A false answer is often easier than a complicated truth. Even if it destroys the innocent.

The uniforms were different today, as were the formal attitudes about innocence before guilt proven beyond a reasonable doubt. But people were still fallible, victims of their own minds trying to make sense of things. And death was the same. A tiny amount of the right poisonous plant extract could fell a healthy man in his prime.

I knew little of Charles Macraith beyond the facts that he was a man of few words, a skilled home renovator who charged a rate I could afford, and that he had only recently returned to work after an injury sustained on the job. How had he come to die on my front porch?

As soon as I was certain he was dead, I didn't touch anything else. I also stopped myself from entering the house to look for Dorian. After a few frantic moments of calling Dorian's name and getting no response, I gave up and called the police from my cell phone.

That was how I came to be waiting at the police station to talk to a detective while my new home was roped off as a crime scene.

Three people, with expressions ranging from curt to eager-to-please, told me I was welcome to help myself to coffee. All of them registered shock or confusion when I said I didn't drink coffee. This was apparently the wrong town for such admissions.

"Sorry to keep you waiting," a friendly voice said. It wasn't the tone of the voice itself that was friendly, I realized, but my positive association with it. How odd for me to have had that reaction. It was the detective who had visited my house the previous night.

"Hello again," he continued. Unlike the night before, he was now dressed in a charcoal gray suit and tie. Both were cut narrowly, matching his frame.

"Detective Liu."

"And you're Zoe Faust. Interesting last name."

"It's an old family name," I said, answering with a partial truth. Unlike Zoe, the name Faust wasn't one I had been born with, but it was a name I felt a connection to on many levels. Johann Faust was an alchemist who lived in the early sixteenth century and died during an alchemical experiment. The Faust most people think of when they hear the name is the character in the play by Goethe—

the man who sells his soul to the Devil. The Puritan preachers of my childhood in Salem Village spoke unrelentingly of the Devil, and as a child, he was as real to me as anything in this world. Once I realized what I had become, Faust felt a fitting name to assume.

"You okay?" Detective Liu grimaced at his own question. "Sorry, dumb question after what you saw today. Did anyone offer you coffee?"

"I'm not a coffee person."

He took a moment to look at me before answering. "You and I may be the only two people in Portland who feel that way." He stopped speaking as he glanced at a commotion taking place at the other side of the floor. "C'mon, let's talk somewhere quieter."

"Small world," I said as we walked through the large station.

"I'm here because I'd already been over to your house—" He paused as we reached a door, which he held open for me.

We entered what I assumed was an interrogation room. He hadn't read me my Miranda rights, so I wasn't going to jump to the conclusion that I was a suspect. *Breathe, Zoe.*

"You've had quite a day." He set a bottle of water in front of me.

"This wasn't what I was expecting the second day at my new home."

"Where'd you move here from?"

"You saw the trailer in my driveway? I've been living out of it for a few years. Traveling around. I wanted to see the country."

"Taking some time to see the world after college?"

"Something like that," I said. "But I didn't go to college." It was true. I had never earned a formal degree. I'd studied with some brilliant scholars in the United States, Europe, and Asia, but couldn't risk the records that would be created if I had applied for a formal degree. It was easier to stay out of sight as much as possible.

34

Modern technology and the Internet were a mixed blessing. At first it seemed like it would make it impossible to keep one's identity a secret. But with a little bit of effort, one could be even more anonymous online than in real life. That was true of my shop Elixir, now an online store where I didn't have to stand behind a counter to greet customers.

I had shown the police my Massachusetts drivers license that listed my age as twenty-eight years old. According to official documents, I was the child of an American mother who looked remarkably like me and also bore a strong resemblance to my French grandmother. People often commented on the uncanny resemblance, but nobody ever suspected that we were the same person.

"So." Max rested his elbows on the table. "How did you know Charles Macraith?"

I looked at the ceiling. Low and confining. "The real estate agent recommended him to me. I only had money to buy a fixer-upper, but I really wanted a house. I've been traveling so long ..." Longer than I could say. "Sorry. I'm tired. I haven't finished unpacking yet. I didn't sleep well in the new place. I'm usually on my second cup of tea by now."

"I won't keep you long."

"I don't know what else I can tell you. I have no idea who would poison him."

Max Liu's body jerked back. "Who said anything about poison?"

"The smell. It was obvious." I thought back on the awful sight of Charles Macraith's still form on my porch. I hadn't detected anything that anyone familiar with herbalism wouldn't have sensed, had I? I tried to think about that moment. The scent was fleeting. Familiar fragrances mingled with unfamiliar essences. What exactly *had* I detected?

The intensity of his eyes grew as he sat back and studied me in silence. "It was obvious?" he repeated with an intonation that said it was anything but that. His strong reaction faded as quickly as it had surfaced, and he was once again calm in the seat across from me.

"Maybe it wasn't as strong by the time the authorities arrived," I suggested.

He nodded slowly, but the skepticism in his expression was apparent.

"I've studied some herbalism," I said. "I've always been a natural with plants. I grow herbs, dry them, and cook with them. I have a good sense of smell." God, why wouldn't I shut up? I wanted him to believe me. I knew my innocence would be proven, but it was more than that. I hated the way he was now looking at me.

"You want to start over? Tell me what happened at your house this morning?"

My mouth was dry, but before my hand touched the bottle of water, I stopped. Fingerprints. He wanted my fingerprints. I breathed deeply and swallowed.

"I went on a walk," I said, "and got turned around on my way home. Charles Macraith had already arrived when I came through the gate. He must have been waiting for me on the porch when someone found him and poisoned—"

I closed my eyes and thought back on what I remembered. I hadn't imagined the scent of poison. But I should have seen signs in addition to the smell. Many poisons would have resulted in the victim vomiting, but not all poisons had that effect. I tried to think back…

"You didn't find him robbing your house?" Detective Liu asked.

My eyes popped open. Many of the items I'd taken out of storage were valuable antiques that were my livelihood.

"I didn't give him a key," I said. "He was meeting me on the porch." I groaned and put my face in my hands. "The door knob," I said. "It broke off yesterday. What was stolen?"

Max Liu's expression shifted from detached to confused.

"You didn't go inside?"

"Why would I have done that? A man was dead and I had no idea anyone had been inside my house." My house with my living gargoyle. "Wait. I've been unpacking. It's a mess. How do you know anything was stolen?"

"Broken glass and an antique book with ripped pages. Didn't look like something you would have done yourself. Uh, you don't look very well. I'll be right back."

I nodded, my head spinning. The faint voices coming from outside the room weren't the voices of rational police officers but the voices of an angry mob. I wasn't inside a rather pleasant modern-day police station, but in a grimy cell awaiting trial.

When the door opened, I snapped back to the present. Detective Liu set a steaming mug of tea down in front of me.

"Chinese privet," I said as the steam reached my nostrils. "For calming the nerves of someone who's stressed out. That's the scent you had on your hands, along with lavender, last night."

He sighed. "You weren't lying about smelling a poison, were you?"

"You didn't bring me this tea to help my nerves, did you? It was a test."

"Can't it be both?"

"Why would I have made up that I smelled poison?"

He ran a hand through his black hair. "Could you tell what it was?"

I shook my head. "It wasn't something I could identify. It was harsh. Toxic. I'm trying to think what would help narrow it down."

"We'll run a tox screen."

I knew that toxicology wasn't magic. It wasn't as simple as testing blood for "poison." You had to know what you were looking for and run a specific test to find it. When it was a new science about a century ago, it did seem rather like magic, working backward to detect a particular poison inside the complex human body.

"You don't want the tea?" he said.

"I'm all right. It smells wonderful though."

He watched me for a moment before speaking. "We already have your fingerprints from your house, you know," he said. "It had been cleaned before you moved in and it looks like only you and Brixton touched the doors and windows without gloves since then. Computer databases are a wonderful thing for expediency. I know you're not in the system."

I laughed nervously. "Guess I watch too much television." As part of being careful with my identity, I'd never held a job that required fingerprinting. I took a sip of the tea.

"Where did you get this?" I asked. "It's incredible."

"I grow it in my backyard."

"You made this yourself?"

"Yeah, I learned about it from my grandmother." It wasn't exactly a smile on his face when he spoke, but his face softened when he spoke of her. "She and my grandfather were apothecaries in China. That's what they were called back then."

I wished we'd met under other circumstances. I wanted to ask him about his garden, about this tea, and about his grandmother, but it was a ridiculous thought at that moment. A man was dead, I had possibly been robbed of all of my possessions, and my new, unbelievable friend was nowhere to be found.

"Have I given you enough information to narrow down the poison?"

"We don't need more information about what you thought you smelled."

"What do you mean *thought* I smelled?"

"We don't need to run a tox screen to know what happened."

"You're saying you already know what poisoned him? Then why ask me all these questions? To gauge my reaction?" I mentally kicked myself. He wasn't a genuinely nice guy. He'd been playing "good cop" to get at what I knew.

"That's not what I'm saying," Detective Liu said. "Charles Macraith didn't die of poisoning."

My hand clamped over my mouth. "He's not dead?" How could I have been wrong? No, there was no way I had been mistaken. I'd seen more dead bodies in my lifetime than I liked to think about.

"You misunderstand me," he said. "I don't know what you're trying to do by misleading us with talk of poisons, but we'll find out. Charles Macraith wasn't poisoned. He was stabbed. That's what killed him."

FIVE

I WAS FREE TO leave the police station. After I was dismissed by Detective Liu, a uniformed officer drove me home to look around the house to see what had been stolen.

On the short drive, I thought more about what the detective had said. Charles Macraith *hadn't been poisoned*. How was that possible? I was sure I'd smelled poison and that it was coming from his body. I was rusty, though. I hadn't honed in on the poison as precisely as I should have.

But I wasn't wrong.

Not only was I letting down a dead man who deserved justice, but the most interesting man I'd met in ages thought I was both crazy and a suspect who was lying about something. Zoe Faust, crazy murder suspect. *Ugh.*

"You okay?" the officer asked, glancing at me as he merged onto the Hawthorne Bridge.

Whoops, I must have said "ugh" out loud.

"I'm fine. Just rattled."

He nodded and turned his attention back to the road.

Portland was a city of bridges. My new house was on the east side of the Willamette River. Downtown Portland, where my district's police station was located, was west of the river. The Hawthorne Bridge was one of many bridges that connected the city. As we drove across the river, I looked over the water and the bridges to the north. Cars, bikes, and people made their way across the city as if nothing had happened.

When we stepped out of the police car in my driveway, the wind whipping around us was so strong that it rattled the front windows, making me jumpy as we walked up to the house.

"You're *living here*?" the officer asked.

I followed his gaze to the tarp that covered half the roof.

"It's a fixer-upper."

"I'll say."

I wasn't permitted to retrieve anything inside the house, but in order to determine whether theft was a motive, I was able to walk through it to inventory what was missing.

I had unpacked only a few of the items in the crates. Most were valuable books and items related to alchemy that I sold online. After I'd closed the bricks-and-mortar location of my shop in Paris nearly a century ago, I catalogued the antiques that I left in a storage unit in Paris. Once the Internet created an online marketplace, I hired an assistant living in Paris who could ship items to buyers when an online purchase was made. My website's inventory was small because it consisted of collectors' items rather than a high volume of low-price trinkets.

Now that I had a house, I was planning on converting the attic into a business office and storing items myself, which was why I'd brought the contents of my storage unit here to Portland. High on Charles's to-do list for my new house was making sure it was secure. Keeping everything on site was supposed to make my life *simple*. Now it looked like I'd achieved the opposite effect, my carefully preserved items ransacked and drawing the attention of the authorities.

Many years ago, I used to make a living selling dried herbs and herbal remedies, before I gave up practicing alchemy. Herbalism wasn't the same thing as alchemy, but the processes overlapped enough that creating herbal remedies reminded me too much of my old life. My life with Ambrose.

In the modern age of regulations, it was also simpler to sell secondhand items. It was easy to accumulate desirable objects, which I began to do when I realized that many of the utilitarian items I'd once used were considered "antiques." I didn't think of it as a career. I didn't have to sell much. Compound interest is a wonderful thing. Even though I was awful at turning lead into gold, I knew how to open a bank account. A small amount of money over a hundred years adds up. Still, I hadn't ever cared much about money, spending more of it on others in need than on myself. While I'd been living in Albuquerque the previous year, I gave an anonymous donation to a family who had befriended me when I was new to town, after they were badly injured in a car accident. Most of my remaining savings had gone into buying the house and moving. The little bit I had left over was meant to pay for fixing up the house. Maybe it wasn't such a bad idea to try to get better at turning lead into gold. I sighed and turned my attention back to the task of inventorying the items at the house.

The thief hadn't spent much time rooting through the crates, but most of the items I had already removed were gone. Five original alchemical manuscripts, two alembics used in the Court of Rudolph II, and a portrait of Isaac Newton, an alchemist better known for his more mainstream scientific discoveries. A few items remained, but it looked like that was because they had broken. Shattered glass covered the floor, along with the brittle, torn pages of a fifteenth-century book on alchemy.

Two items that weren't mine were also missing. Dorian was gone. And so was his book.

Had Dorian gone in search of his missing book? Or had he been taken himself? The shiver I felt creep up my spine wasn't from the drafty front door.

I gave the officer a list of the missing items—except for the last two. I couldn't very well tell the police about a half-living half-stone gargoyle, and I didn't know the provenance of Dorian's book. For all I knew it could have been stolen, either by Dorian or at some point in the past. I had taken a few photos of it with my phone, but I was hesitant to give the police the full details about the book. I first had to find out what had happened to Dorian. *Where was he?*

I assured the officer I could stay in my trailer until they were done with the crime scene. He left me in the overgrown front yard, the wind swirling around me.

I'd been living out of my trailer for long enough that I'd made it a home. A tiny home, but one that was free of the prying eyes of the outside world. I unlocked the door of my sanctuary, the 150-square-foot Airstream trailer. I'd spent years slowly customizing it. In spite of the madness going on around me, stepping into the trailer lifted my spirits.

Along the back window, I kept a small herb garden. The potted plants lived in trays that I could move between the inside of the trailer and the outside world—I even had a sill on the side of the trailer to set the planter box. The only danger was remembering to bring it inside if I was going to move the trailer. I had only made that mistake twice. Well, maybe three times.

My current winter mix consisted of cottage rosemary, lemon thyme, sage, shiso, chervil, Mediterranean oregano, and aloe, all growing out of clay pots in the long wooden planter. Rounding out the mix were two larger containers of mint varieties that needed more space. Spearmint and lemon balm flanked the rack of fresh herb pots, their tendrils wrapped around the wooden planter box. The mint would have easily overtaken the other plants if I hadn't used some leaves daily. A sweet, minty scent filled the trailer.

The plants were arm's length from a tiny kitchenette. I kept my cooking simple, so building out the kitchen wasn't necessary. It was the plant ingredients themselves I cared about, which is what I made space for. In a nook next to the kitchen was an area I kept dark with an added curtain. That's where I hung dried herbs next to a custom-carved wooden shelf full of herb-infused oils, tinctures, and salts.

Underneath a narrow couch that converted into a bed, drawers slid out to reveal the less expensive alchemical items I sold at flea markets in my travels across the U.S., including a full drawer of vintage European and Americana postcards—a reliable bestseller. Finishing out the trailer interior was a modern, though minute, bathroom. I had grown up without indoor plumbing, so in spite of its size and lack of water pressure, it felt luxurious.

Conspicuously absent was space for alchemical transformations. That was the point. I hadn't wanted any reminder of practicing alchemy. Getting involved in it had been an accident to begin with. And discovering the Elixir of Life? The biggest accident of all. I hadn't done it for myself. I had been trying to help my brother and I hadn't understood what I'd done. But it didn't matter. It was too late.

"Zoe?" a young voice called out, pulling me back to the present. "You in there?"

I opened the door of the trailer. Brixton stood in the tall grass, a backpack on his back. Of course. I had told him to come over after school to weed the garden, which now seemed completely unimportant. Not twenty feet behind him stood the crime scene tape.

"I don't know if you've heard," I said, jumping down from the trailer's front door.

"The murder," he said with a shrug. "Yeah, I heard. Everyone heard."

"I'm not going to press charges for you letting yourself into my house," I said. "You don't have to do any weeding. But what you *think* you saw—"

"The gargoyle," he said matter-of-factly. "Where is he?"

I opened my mouth to protest, but thought better of it. "Why aren't your friends here?" I asked instead. "Surely they'd want to see a walking, talking gargoyle."

He glared at me.

"They didn't believe you, huh?" I said. So Dorian had been right about that.

"I looked up alchemy. Is that how you brought a piece of stone to life?"

What had I gotten myself into? "Brixton, I don't think it's a good idea for you to be here."

"We could go inside. So nobody overhears us. That's what you're worried about, right?"

"No. Well, yes. But mainly it's that you shouldn't be at a crime scene. I'm sure your mom wouldn't want you here."

"She knows I'm coming over. Can we go inside or what?"

"You may have noticed the crime scene tape. I can't even go inside myself."

"I meant your trailer. You live here, right? I used to live in one with my mom. Ours wasn't nearly this nice. It's starting to rain. You going to let me in?"

"A little rain never hurt anyone."

"I want to see the gargoyle."

"He's not inside."

"Where is he?"

"He's not my pet. I don't have him on a leash—"

"You mean he's gone?"

Two women walking past slowed down as they passed the front gate. With the large yard, they were far enough away they couldn't hear what we were saying, but Brixton was right. This was a conversation that would be better without prying eyes.

"Come on in," I said.

"Wicked," he said as he stepped inside, apparently forgetting about Dorian. "Can I see the philosopher's stone? Is it over here in the corner?" he pulled back the curtain keeping my dried herbs and infused oils in the dark.

"You did some research."

"Can I see it?"

"What do you think it does?"

"Makes gold. And makes you immortal."

"You think I'm immortal?"

He gave me a look that only a teenager can. The equivalent of rolling the eyes but without moving a muscle.

46

I could have told him that although I'd lived for centuries, I could die almost as easily as anyone else. I had mostly stopped aging, so I wasn't likely to die of an old-age-related condition, but I could be killed by anything else that would kill a person, such as disease or violence. Therefore I wasn't exactly immortal. I hadn't even entirely stopped aging. The white hair that everyone thought was so stylishly dyed was my true hair color.

Instead of explaining all that to Brixton, I gave him the simple version: "I'm not immortal."

"If you don't have the philosopher's stone, what about Alkahest?" He looked around the trailer.

"The universal solvent? Why do you ask about that?" Asking about the famous philosopher's stone, I understood. But Alkahest? It wasn't an element popularized in books or movies.

"It's the part of alchemy I looked up online that didn't make any sense at all. If it dissolves *everything*, then how would you keep it? I mean, wouldn't it, like burn through anything you tried to keep it in? Wouldn't it even burn through the earth, destroying the world?"

"Good point. Maybe that's why I've never encountered it." The theories asserted about how to make Alkahest were dubious. I'd seen recipes that called for ingredients including blood, sweat, and worms. "Not everything you read online is true, you know."

Again with the eye roll.

"I'm good with plants like these herbs," I said, pointing at my beloved herb garden. "I can transform them into a lot of things, like the salve I used on your arm. That's what makes me an alchemist. I don't make gold. And I don't bring stone gargoyles to life."

"So," Brixton said, making himself comfortable on the long seat in the living area. "You think the gargoyle did it?"

"Feet," I said automatically, knocking his sneakers off the cushions. "Did what?"

"Killed Charles. Because he didn't want to be discovered."

I stared at Brixton. The kid was right. Dorian took not being discovered seriously. *Very* seriously. My pulse quickened as Brixton's words sunk in. I felt my heartbeat so strongly in my ears that I could barely hear what Brixton was saying. It was like that damn story by Poe. Though I wasn't guilty of murder myself, it might have been done because of me.

Why hadn't I thought of it before? I knew why. Because I liked the little creature. A misfit, like me. And he'd helped me in Paris years ago … hadn't he? How would he have known about that if he hadn't been there? And he couldn't go around killing anyone who saw him. He was the one who'd pointed out that nobody would believe Brixton. The gargoyle wouldn't have turned violent … would he?

"Earth to Zoe," Brixton said.

"It doesn't fit," I said, shaking my head.

Brixton shrugged. "At least you didn't say *oh he's such a nice guy, he would never have done it*. I hate it when they say that on TV."

"This isn't TV."

"Are you always this much of a downer?"

"A man was killed."

"Yeah, I liked him."

"You knew Charles Macraith?"

"He came around the teashop. He didn't talk much, but he used to help me with my homework sometimes."

"Teashop?" I wondered if it could be the same place I'd visited when I'd fallen in love with this neighborhood. The welcoming café was one of the main reasons I'd felt so at home here.

"Yeah, Blue's teashop. That's where I know Detective Liu from, too. Hey, are those chili peppers floating in that bottle?" He jumped up and pulled back the half-closed curtain that shaded my nook of herbs. He lifted a glass jar of sesame oil infused with peppers. "Wicked. I love spicy food. Did you make all this stuff? Is that lemon balm and pineapple sage floating in these other bottles?"

"How on earth did you recognize those?"

He shrugged. "Blue loves wildcrafting. She taught me about what that meant and about finding plants in their natural habitats. She harvests herbs for her teas and other stuff."

I hadn't met many wildcrafters. Under other circumstances I would have asked him more about it. But now, I had more pressing matters to deal with. "You were telling me about Charles Macraith visiting the teashop."

"Yeah, nobody had anything against him." Brixton set the bottle back on the shelf and looked right at me. "That gargoyle of yours is the only logical explanation for why he's dead."

SIX

BRIXTON OFFERED TO LIVE up to his end of the bargain and weed the yard, but the rain pelting on the roof of the trailer assured me there wouldn't be any gardening that day. Brixton had heard the rain too. I wondered if he'd have made such a generous offer if there was any chance I would have taken him up on it. He was a smart kid. I sent him home with a clear conscience, but as I watched him ride off on his bike, I wondered if I had been too trusting.

I could see the crime scene tape on my porch from the window of the trailer. Also in view was the tarp covering a huge section of my roof. It swayed in the strong winds but looked like it was holding firm. I had no idea where Dorian could be. I didn't know if I'd lost his alchemy-that-wasn't-alchemy book or if he'd taken it with him. Brixton's assumption about Dorian couldn't be right. It couldn't be.

In spite of the rain, I needed to walk and clear my head. I grabbed my silver raincoat and headed out.

Portlanders weren't afraid of a little rain. Or even a lot of it. Hawthorne Boulevard was packed. Locals poured out of organic restaurants, coffee shops, and an annex of Powell's Books. I stopped in a café and ordered an orange and pomegranate salad. It was good but didn't compete with Dorian's cooking. I looked out into the nighttime downpour. *Where was he?*

That night, I feel asleep to the sound of the wind whispering to the rain, but woke up a few hours later with an irate gargoyle standing over me.

"*Ou est mon livre*!?" Dorian screamed. "Where is my book!?"

The trailer was nearly pitch black. Dorian hadn't turned on a light, but I knew his voice and smelled his fruity breath close to my face. Could he see in the dark? I sat up abruptly at the thought, accidentally head-butting his snout. I hadn't realized he was *that* close to me.

"*Merde*," he mumbled, hopping down from the edge of the bed as I flipped on a light.

"Where have you been?" I asked as Dorian's claw snagged the blanket and pulled it to the floor along with him. Luckily I was fully covered by my white cotton nightgown. I'd had it handmade by a seamstress in North Carolina several years ago, based on a pattern from the previous century. Seventeenth-century women had to wear scratchy, heavy, and overall burdensome clothing, but the night clothes from the Victorian era were the most comfortable I'd ever encountered.

"This city," Dorian said, rubbing his snout, "she has a different lunar cycle than Paris. I did not realize the sun would rise an hour earlier. I was not yet close to the house when day began."

"You had to hide."

He nodded and sniffed. "I could not return without being seen."

"I've been worried. I'm glad you're safe." I thought about what Brixton had suggested about Dorian, but pushed it from my mind. Besides the fact that I had already grown quite fond of Dorian, I wasn't lying to myself that it didn't make any sense for him to have killed the handyman.

"I hid in one of the forests. There were many to choose from. I chose one that had wild blueberries and blackberries."

"I don't think they're technically forests—" I began. I don't know why I said such an inane thing, except that I wasn't at my best after being woken up after midnight by a furious creature who smelled like wild berries and could see in the dark.

"What has happened?" Dorian asked. "When night returned, I found my way back. *Mais* … there is blood at the door and the bright strips of plastic that say 'police line do not cross.' When I went inside—"

"You *crossed the police line*?"

"I thought my book was inside."

I groaned and rubbed my eyes.

"Yet my book was not there," Dorian continued. "Last night you fell asleep at the table with your head on the pages. I did not wish to disturb you. Dorian Robert-Houdin is a gentleman."

I stood up and looked around the trailer. The bedside lamp cast stark shadows, but illuminated the whole interior. The door was closed, as I'd left it.

Locked.

"Dorian … How did you get in here?"

His throat rumbled. I couldn't tell if he was growling or attempting to imitate an awkward cough. He held up his clawed fingers. "Better than lock picks."

"You *broke in*?"

"My father was a great magician. He taught me many things."

I groaned again and sat back down on the bed. I'm no good at being awake in the middle of the night. When the sun disappears and the plants sleep, I feel myself drawn to sleep as well.

"Robert-Houdin," I said in my foggy state. "Wait. That name. Your father was Jean Eugène Robert-Houdin, the famous French stage magician!"

"*Oui*, I told you this."

"You told me *your* first name, not his."

"There is no other Robert-Houdin. He joined his surname with his wife's. Quite unheard-of at the time."

"He was an alchemist?"

I knew of the French stage magician who was a huge sensation in the mid-1800s. I had once seen him perform on stage. He was talented, performing feats that seemed like magic to sold-out theater audiences. I had believed, then, that he was simply a skilled stage magician. He was, after all, such a master magician that he was asked by the French government to avert a military crisis in Algeria by showing French magic to be more powerful than that of local tribal leaders. The history books had recorded Jean Eugène Robert-Houdin's feats as illusions, skillful tricks performed by a master showman. But now I had to wonder—had he used real magic?

"He was no alchemist," Dorian said. "Yet he was the one who brought me to life."

"That doesn't make sense."

"He did not understand what the book was capable of." He shook his head. "I was meant to be a prop in a stage show. The book is filled with lyrical passages of text. He found them quite theatrical. But he never considered the power in the pages from which he read. I will show you. Where is the book?"

"Dorian, we need to talk. About a lot of things."

"Yes, I agree. I do not see my book. You have put it away?"

His little black eyes looked at me so expectantly that I hated to tell him what had transpired.

"I'm sorry," I began. "The book is gone."

"*Pardon?* I must not understand your English; I am nearly fluent, yet—"

"The man who was going to fix and secure the house was killed this morning. That was the blood you saw."

"*Je suis desolé.* But what does his death have to do with my book?"

"When he was killed," I said slowly, "the house was also burglarized. Your book was one of the things stolen."

Dorian's eyes grew wide. His stony shoulders tensed and his wings flew out from his sides, knocking over my pot of chervil with one wing and scraping a gash into a wood panel with the other. The pot shattered as it hit the floor.

"You let someone steal *my* book?" His body shook, adding additional gashes to the wooden wall paneling surrounding him. Even after seeing how his wing had chipped the fireplace, I hadn't realized just how strong and heavy they were.

"We'll get it back. The police are investigating."

"You told *the police* about my alchemy book?"

"Not about your book in particular. And of course not about you. Or me, for that matter. Many of my rare books were stolen." My head felt heavy at the reminder of everything that had been lost in the past day. In addition to losing much of my livelihood, I'd lost a book that didn't belong to me, and a man had lost his life.

"You knew how valuable my book was. How could you have let this happen?"

"There was no reason for it to happen!" I said, struggling to keep the heavy feeling in my head from turning into a massive headache. I got myself a small glass of water and added a few drops of peppermint oil to stimulate my senses and wake me up; Dorian glared at me as I did so. "It must have been a crime of opportunity. Charles Macraith was killed, and the person who killed him saw items that looked valuable and grabbed them. The police think they were in a hurry."

"You were not there? How could you not be there?" Dorian stamped his clawed feet like a toddler throwing a tantrum. I would have offered him some tea to calm his nerves except that my kettle was inside the house beyond the crime scene tape.

"*Nobody knew* we had valuable books inside the house. There was no reason to think I couldn't go on a short walk to buy some food before Charles was due at the house. But you're right. When I couldn't find you, I shouldn't have left your valuable book alone. I'm so very sorry, Dorian."

Dorian's wings collapsed back to their usual resting place at his sides. "I understand your desire to buy food," he said, "yet leaving the book unattended was unwise. Someone had to have known about it."

"*Someone?*" Was there more going on here than he'd told me? "Do you have a particular person in mind?"

"I do not know! This is why I came to you!" His wings vibrated, but didn't fly out.

"Does anyone know you came here to see me and get my help?" I asked.

"No. It is not possible."

"Then how—"

"I do not know!"

"Then why do you think this is about your book?" Now that I was a little more awake and coherent, I was beginning to realize that there may have been more going on than a crime of opportunity. "Tell me more about this book."

Dorian's snout flared, but he remained mute.

"What," I said, "aren't you telling me?"

Dorian's shoulders slumped. He sat down next to me on the edge of the bed. "I did not lie to you."

"I didn't say you did. But you didn't tell me everything either."

"I did not think you would believe me."

"You're a living gargoyle and I'm an alchemist who was born over three hundred years ago, but you didn't think I'd believe you about a book?"

"It is for that exact reason that you could not know," he said. "I thought it would be easier for you to solve the riddle of my book without already having a particular outcome in mind. If a scientist thinks he knows what the result will be, it prejudices the study."

"I understand," I said. "But I'm so far from understanding what's going on that you need to tell me everything you can."

"Now that the book is gone, it does not matter." His wings crumpled like a wilting flower as he shook his head.

"The book isn't entirely gone." I lifted my cell phone from the side table, tapped a couple keys, and handed it to Dorian. "Take a look. I took photos of some of the more interesting pages of the book."

"Zoe Faust, I take back what I was thinking about you."

I thought it wise not to ask what he was thinking about me. "Thank you," I said. "I think."

"I might have a chance yet."

"A chance at what?"

"I am dying," Dorian said. "This book is the only way to save me."

SEVEN

"My body," Dorian said, "is slowly turning back into stone. You might say this is the natural state of things, for us all to die. But this is not a natural death. When I turn to stone, I do not sleep. I will be awake but forever trapped in this stone shell."

"Oh, Dorian—"

He held up a clawed hand. "I did not wish to speak of it. It makes it more the truth. Now that the book has been stolen—" He broke off and shook his head.

"Why is this happening now? What changed?"

"I do not know. If I had known this would happen, I would have sought you out before now. Now that I am here, you can help me by deciphering the remaining pages of the book. Perhaps there are answers in the pages you found interesting enough to photograph."

"Maybe, but I need to understand more—"

"Yet I know very little." His words were clipped. "This is why I have come to you."

I felt the weight of his words sink in. He was putting so much faith in me, and I didn't know if I would be able to help. But I had to try.

"You know more than you think you do," I said. "Tell me about the transformation. The day Jean Eugène Robert-Houdin brought you to life."

"I do not remember the moment," he said, his voice softening. "It is a blur, as they say. I will tell you the story told to me by my father. He had been given a great gift from his friend, the architect Eugène Viollet-le-Duc, who was restoring the cathedral of Notre Dame de Paris. Father's friend had fanciful plans for the cathedral, including a balcony of stone chimeras. Unlike the water spout gargoyles along the sides of the cathedral, his stone carvings had personality. I was one of his prototypes. I was not large enough, though. Because my father collected many items for his stage performances, Viollet-le-Duc thought he would appreciate this carving—and he was correct."

"That's amazing," I said, thinking of the gallery of gargoyles at Notre Dame I had climbed many times. When I had first seen Dorian, he reminded me of one of the gargoyles there. Now I knew why.

"My father created mechanized automatons. He was planning on building an automaton based on my stone carving. He had already retired to Saint-Gervais and was working on his memoirs, but his mind was restless. He wished to continue innovating for the stage. The idea for his new illusion was to read from an ancient alchemy book, at which point the automaton would begin to move— the illusion of coming to life." Dorian closed his eyes and paused.

"I know it must be difficult to talk about this, but it will help me understand what happened to you."

Dorian nodded. "As my father built his clockwork automaton, he placed the stone prototype—me—on stage, to practice. He was not very good at reading Latin. He practiced again and again so the words would sound dramatic for his audience. One day, he pronounced the words properly. This is the day I came to life."

"If I'd known what was happening to you, I could have read the Latin out loud to rejuvenate you."

Dorian shook his head. "I have already tried this. *Tristement*, it is not that simple. That is why I need you."

"Where did your father get the book?"

"This," Dorian said sadly, "I do not know."

"You must know something."

"What I know is that my father found stage magic accidentally. He had ordered two books on his vocation, clockmaking. In their place, he received books on magic. It is for this reason that he always collected an assortment of books. The more happenstance, the better. Friends and well-wishers knew this of him. Many people gave him strange books. There is no way to trace the origins of *Non Degenera Alchemia*."

"He didn't remember who gave it to him?"

"If he did, he did not tell me. I did not give the book much thought for many years. Only when my body began to change did I realize my life continued to be tied to the book. I can read and write in many languages, but have never studied alchemy. This secret language of alchemists is a mystery to me. You, Zoe Faust, are the one person I knew of who could help me."

In spite of my desire to know more, that was all he could tell me. I was also about to fall over. I needed sleep. I wasn't built to be awake in the middle of the night. I'm so attuned to the sun that simply staying awake at night is challenging.

Dorian cleaned up the broken pot of chervil and told me to get some sleep, saying I looked like I needed it. He assured me he would pay more attention to Portland's sunrise, then disappeared into the darkness. The sadness on his face before he headed out into the night lingered in my mind. Was he really dying? Could I help? Even if we had the book back, I didn't know what I could do as an out-of-practice alchemist who didn't speak whatever coded language the book was written in. But he had been right the night before. He and I were two outcasts who didn't understand what had happened to us. I didn't want to let him down—or to lose him.

———

As always, I awoke with the sun. In spite of my fatigue, I had tossed and turned for several hours. Yawning, I pulled open the trailer curtains, thin muslin from Egypt that assured privacy on the inside but let in natural light from the outside.

With my blender stuck in the roped-off house, I couldn't start the day with a smoothie of fruits and vegetables. As the sun rose, I ate dried heirloom apples and wild blueberries with a handful of walnuts, and drank a large glass of water with lemon essence. The familiar flavors and hydrating water helped calm my nerves after Dorian's upsetting revelation.

I tucked my legs under me and sat in the window in the direction of the sunrise, thinking over the strange events of the last two days. If it hadn't been for the scratches running across the panels near my bed and the broken pot in my herb garden, I might have been able to believe Dorian's presence the previous night had been a dream.

Was Charles Macraith's death a result of his own life catching up with him at my front door? He was, after all, known for being "discreet," a word with an added meaning that hadn't occurred to me when the real estate agent gave me his card. Or was his death a consequence of someone in search of Dorian's book, an unintended casualty because he was in the wrong place at the wrong time? Whatever was going on, Dorian and I were right in the middle of it.

I scrolled through the photographs of Dorian's book I had on my phone. I stopped on an image of the earth being engulfed in flames. That pretty much summed up how I was feeling about my life.

After my night, I needed a calming cup of tea to think straight and decide what to do about Dorian's dilemma. Since I couldn't make tea without my kettle, I went in search of the teashop Brixton had mentioned. Brixton hadn't referred to it by name, but if it was the same teashop I'd visited, it would be easy to find. I remembered it had a large weeping fig tree growing in the midst of the tables.

After a quick shower using my trailer's nearly depleted water supplies, I slipped on custom-made gray wool slacks and cream cashmere sweater, and grabbed my silver raincoat. I've never gotten the hang of wearing off-the-rack clothes. How do people wear clothes that aren't made specifically to fit their unique shape? Tailored clothes weren't always considered the luxury item they are today. It was simply how things were done. Once mass-produced clothes were a reality, that's what felt like a luxury to people. There's certainly the instant gratification from seeing something you like and taking it home with you, but it doesn't compare.

I found Blue Sky Teas on Hawthorne Boulevard, several blocks from my house. From the sidewalk, I could see it was the same teashop I remembered. Beyond the tall glass windows, the familiar weeping fig tree filled the welcoming space without dominating it. The plaque above the teashop's bright orange door read: "'There is no trouble so great or grave that cannot be diminished by a nice cup of tea.' —Bernard-Paul Heroux.'"

It was a few minutes before 7:30 and a woman with wild gray hair was turning a hand-painted wooden sign from "closed" to "open." She caught my eye and smiled.

The storefront was narrow, but as I stepped inside, I felt as if I'd set foot in an expansive forest. The ceiling was taller than the width of the shop. Mosaic tiles covered the floor except for a spot in the center of the shop where a live weeping fig tree with gnarled roots grew out of a three-foot circle. The branches stretched up to the curved ceiling, which was painted the color of a deep blue sky with wispy white clouds. As long as I didn't stare directly at it, it felt like real sky hanging above me—minus the fickle Pacific Northwest weather. Eight tables lined the walls, their tops made of solid redwood with the tree rings showing. The walls were unadorned, as I remembered, except now one corner held a framed photo of a young red-haired woman. The picture was surrounded by cards and dried flowers, including fragrant lavender.

Walking through to the counter, located at the back, a cacophony of scents washed over me, but in a pleasing rather than overwhelming way. I could pick out many of the scents—mint, jasmine, honeysuckle, cinnamon—while many of the herbs blended together. Breathing in the fragrance of the teashop had an immediate effect on calming my nerves. I wasn't exactly relaxed, but poking through my apprehension was the same feeling of hope I'd had when I first visited Portland. I wanted desperately to grab hold of the feeling and not let it go.

"I'm glad I opened early today," the gray-haired woman said. "Zoe, right? Brixton mentioned you."

"You must be Blue," I said. "He mentioned you too." I hadn't recognized her until the scent of jasmine triggered my memory. It was the same woman who'd been here the previous year when I bought the best cup of lemon ginger tea I'd ever tasted. If I recalled, her secret ingredients were fresh turmeric and a hint of cayenne.

Though not classically beautiful, here in her element she was radiant. She wore no makeup, but her round cheeks had a natural glow. Curly hair more gray than brown swept halfway down her back, falling on the simple white blouse she wore over faded jeans. She stood behind the counter, a steaming cup of jasmine green tea in her hands.

"Blue Sky," she said, setting down her cup of tea and offering me her hand. "And yes, that's really my name."

"I wasn't going to ask. It suits you."

"Thanks for not pressing charges against Brixton. His mom lets him run wild, but he's a good kid. Anything you'd like, it's on the house."

"That's not necessary. He didn't do any harm. I was going to have him help weed my yard, but then ..."

"Charles," Blue finished for me. "Such a shame."

"You knew him?"

"Not well. But this neighborhood is like a small town in many ways. Charles came into the shop, especially while he was off work recovering from a construction accident. He was a man of few words. I always got the feeling he was more comfortable whittling on wood than talking to people. You know—" she paused and frowned. "I don't even know where he's from. Portland is a place that gives fresh starts for a lot of people. It's what the city did for me. I didn't try to get to know him better. I wish now that I had ..."

I never knew what to say surrounding death. You'd think it would get easier, but it never does. Maybe that's a good thing. I remained silent, letting Blue have the time she needed. No platitude would help.

"I'm sorry that was your introduction to your new home," Blue continued, then snapped her fingers. "You look like a fan of cinnamon. I bet you'll like my homemade spicy chai."

"I don't do dairy," I said. "I follow a vegan diet."

"Even better. There's no milk in my chai. People often complain about that—until they taste it."

With a wink, she turned away from me to brew my chai. It gave me more time to look around the teashop. I placed my hand on the rough bark of the tree. It was old. The building must have been built around it. There was so much to love here, but now I knew there was also something to fear.

"See if you like this," Blue said, startling me from my thoughts.

The intermingling scents of cinnamon, ginger, cloves, fennel, and cardamom wafted up from the clay mug. Unlike many teashops and coffeehouses across the country, the liquid in this mug wasn't close to boiling. It was hot enough to be steaming, but cool enough to drink. Just as tea was meant to be served.

"Real Ceylon cinnamon," I said.

"I can tell you're going to keep me on my toes."

I felt an immediate sense of warmth spread through my body. "This is exactly what I needed after yesterday."

Blue smiled, the wrinkles around her friendly eyes crinkling. "You shouldn't let Brixton off the hook."

I breathed in the aromatic scent of the tea, hoping it would help me decide what to do about a lot of things. "I don't know."

"Cleaning up your yard after he broke your window is exactly what he needs." She saw the hesitation on my face. "You don't need to protect him from anything. It's unfortunate Charles's life caught up with him outside your house, but life is about moving forward. And that boy needs structure. He's been in trouble before."

"What kind of trouble?"

Blue waved off the question. "Nothing serious. Just kid stuff. But I worry."

"You sound like you know him well."

"His mom, Heather, had him when she was sixteen. I moved here when Heather was twenty and Brixton was four. What a precocious boy he was—still is."

"I noticed."

Blue smiled wryly. "For the last ten years, she's often left him at the teashop, letting me babysit. Until he was old enough to be on his own after school, he'd often sit at that table by the window and do his homework." She pointed at one of the smaller tree-ringed tabletops. "The regulars loved to help him with his homework."

"You said that in the past tense."

"He's in high school now. Old enough that he can do what he wants. Which doesn't seem to involve doing homework."

A bell chimed and an exceptionally tall young man walked in. He wasn't especially young, though he looked it to me. He must have been in his late twenties, around the same age people thought I was, which I'd never stop thinking of as young.

"Morning, Blue," he said, giving her a sad smile. "The usual."

"Coming right up."

I brought my chai to a table near the tree while Blue helped the customer, who got a tea to go in a personal travel mug. Now that my attention wasn't focused on Blue, I noticed the vast array of teas in metal jars lining several narrow shelves behind the counter.

The man smiled at me as he left with his tea. Blue came out from behind the counter and joined me at my table.

"I'm an early bird," Blue said, "so I like to get started early, even though I don't usually get many customers this early. Tea isn't the usual choice of commuters looking for a quick caffeine fix on their way to work. A lot of my teas are actually decoctions that take a while to brew."

"How long have you run this place?" I asked.

"It's why I stayed in Portland. This tree was here on the corner and was about to be cut down to build more storefronts. I was able to save it."

"I love it," I said. I wasn't just being polite. The old tree brought so much life to the shop.

"I can tell you're going to like it here. Brixton told me you moved into that haunt—I mean the house that's been sitting empty for years."

"You don't have to censor yourself. I've already heard it's known as the local haunted house."

"We're a tight-knit community. It's all well-meaning. So don't you worry about what they're saying about you."

"Wait, *what?*"

"Looks like the rush is starting," Blue said, standing up and turning her attention to four people who were walking up to the counter. "Stay and enjoy the chai."

EIGHT

I WAS IN NO hurry to get back to my trailer overlooking the crime scene. I didn't yet know how I could help Dorian, no matter how much I wanted to. I didn't have any faith I could decipher his book, especially when I was left with only the few pages I'd photographed. Furthermore, was it possible a murderer had followed him from Paris? Someone who wanted this book badly enough that they wanted to make doubly sure the person standing in their way was dead? A tingling fear crept over me as I thought about what that might mean.

I breathed in the aroma of the chai to calm my nerves. As I did so, another chilling idea occurred to me: Could the murder have something to do with *me*? Dorian wasn't the only one who had things of value in his possession.

Neither scenario made sense. Both Dorian and I lived off the grid, and we hadn't been in Portland long enough for anyone to know what we were. The murder had to be about Charles Macraith himself. It had to be. Didn't it?

With shaking hands, I looked at the photos of Dorian's book that were saved on my phone. On the screen, the images were too small to see the details, but zooming obscured the bigger picture. I preferred tangible photographs to computer screens. The only two modern inventions I adopted early were automobiles and blenders, both of which were perfected in the 1940s, as far as I was concerned. My vintage blender now sat behind the crime scene tape. Crime scene tape! I'd been so careful over the years. In two days I'd drawn more attention to myself than I had in the last two decades.

Having a nervous breakdown wasn't going to help anyone. I had to relax if I was going to make sense of any of this. Placing the phone facedown on the table, I took a beaten-up paperback from my coat pocket. One of the things I had learned the hard way was that when faced with a stressful task, it's important to take a few deep breaths before beginning. Books served as a psychological deep breath. Before I tackled the task of deciphering the pages of Dorian's book, I could give myself these few minutes to enjoy a cup of tea and a few of my favorite passages.

Living out of my trailer, I didn't have space for many books, so I owned only a few dozen favorite paperbacks. If I wanted to keep a new book, something old had to go. It was a small cost for living on the road, but a difficult one.

One of the very few purely positive things about living so long was getting to read so many books. While styles of prose changed over time and varied across different cultures, storytelling remained fundamentally the same. People have changed how they express themselves, but the human condition doesn't change, and neither does how we relate to it. Instead of making new stories unnecessary, each successful storyteller puts their own twist on a familiar tale and finds a way to connect with the readers of their time. Especially successful writers reach across time, ending up as classics.

It was fascinating to see how history created false images of famous authors after their deaths. Even the author whose book I now held in my hand, Sir Arthur Conan Doyle, was far different than popular culture would have people believe. Casual fans of Sherlock Holmes assume his creator was a scientific-minded man like his famous detective. People who study his life in more depth believe he gave up rationalism for spiritualism. Neither was the whole story. He was grieving for deceased loved ones—his wife and son, among others. It was a feeling I knew all too well. One part of his life was blown out of proportion as he sought to reconnect with those he missed dearly.

Regardless of how history documented the man, there's no arguing that his stories stood the test of time. I opened my battered copy of *The Hound of the Baskervilles.*

The teashop didn't sell coffee, but that didn't prevent it from doing a bustling business. From the moment Blue went back to the counter, people funneled into the teashop, keeping her busy. Though an assortment of pastries was available, most customers only ordered tea.

"Did you hear about the murder?" a woman whispered loudly to her friend as they stood in line.

My shoulders tensed and I felt an instinctive desire to flee. I shoved the book back into my pocket and stood up to leave.

"Oh, don't go." The voice came from the table next to mine. The older woman sat alone. She sat with her back to the wall, giving her a full view of her surroundings. "You're the one who bought the house on the hill, aren't you?"

So much for settling in quietly.

"I need to get going," I said, forcing a smile.

"Nonsense. What an awful introduction to our neighborhood you've had. Let me buy you another cup of tea."

"Thank you, but—"

"I won't take no for an answer."

She stood and swooped in on the counter. That was really the only way to describe it. She wore a blood-red shawl and timed her approach to the counter perfectly to correspond to a lull in customers. I had a moment to study her unobserved as she ordered two teas. She knew who I was, knew about Charles and his murder the previous day, and nodded at several of the people in the teashop. I guessed she spent a fair amount of her time here. Though it was difficult to discern because of her perfect makeup and rich brown hair that was pulled back into a bun, I guessed she was old enough to be retired, giving her plenty of time to spend at the teashop. She couldn't have been much taller than five feet, and I doubted she weighed a hundred pounds.

She returned a minute later with a pot of tea and two small mugs. The aroma told me it was a simple black tea, but smelled high quality and delicious.

"Olivia Strum," she said.

"Zoe Faust. And thank you for the tea." I wondered how quickly I could drink it and extricate myself. I should have known people would know who I was. With the murder fresh in everyone's minds, this wasn't how I wanted to meet people. Especially before the police had solved the crime.

Olivia leaned in. "You mustn't order the food here. Blue knows how to make the most superb tea that tastes sublime and makes you feel alive, but she couldn't cook a decent pastry if her life depended on it. She insists on making everything herself, so she can make them *healthy*." She shuddered. "Can you believe that her desserts are mostly *vegan*? Life is too short to eat inedible food because it's healthy. My nephew Sam is the one who convinced me to try the teas here. One of the few sensible suggestions he has ever made. I should also warn you Blue only accepts cash. She doesn't trust credit cards. Ah, Ivan! Come sit with us."

An unshaven middle-aged man with a newspaper tucked under his arm approached our table. I wondered how long Olivia would have gone on talking if it hadn't been for the interruption.

"This is Zoe, the woman who bought the house on the hill," Olivia said to him. "Zoe Faust, this is Ivan Danko."

He nodded politely but without smiling, then headed for the counter, pausing first at the sole photograph on the wall. Other people had done so as well, but Ivan's gaze lingered.

"Don't mind him," Olivia said. "He hates retirement. He's still getting used to it."

"What's the interest in the photograph of the young woman on the wall?" I asked. "Is she Blue's daughter?"

"Anna passed away several months ago," Olivia said. "She wasn't Blue's daughter, but she was a regular here."

"She's so young." No wonder the photograph interested customers who must have known her. I could see, now, that it was a shrine that had been set up for the poor girl. Though the death of Charles Macraith was tragic, the death of someone so young was especially devastating.

In the midst of unfamiliar faces, a familiar one came through the door. Max Liu breezed by us and headed straight for the counter. For a detective, he wasn't very observant that morning. Though he passed by quickly, I noticed the dark circles under his eyes. Only when he turned around with a cup of tea to go did he notice me.

His body gave a jerk as he stopped abruptly.

"Will you excuse us a moment?" he said to Olivia.

Being pulled aside by the police in gossip-central? Not good.

I stood and followed him outside, feeling Olivia watching me.

Max's hand brushed against my elbow as he opened the door for me. I felt a little jolt of electricity. It was a feeling I hadn't felt in years. *Get a grip, Zoe. This guy is investigating a murder—a murder he thinks I might be involved in.* What was the matter with me?

"Were you looking for me?" I asked. We stood just outside the teashop, under the blue awning that matched the painted blue sky inside.

"Stopping in on my way back to the station, but I'm glad I found you."

"You are?"

"How did you know?" he asked. Up close, I saw further evidence of sleep deprivation beyond the dark circles under his eyes. He hadn't shaved, his eyes were bloodshot, and his collar wasn't folded properly, as if he'd dressed in a hurry, or perhaps slept in his clothes.

"Know what?"

"About the poison."

"So Charles Macraith *was* poisoned in addition to being stabbed?"

He held my gaze, ignoring his tea. I could smell the faint scent of jasmine from the hole in the lid of his traveling mug.

"Do you believe what I told you or not?" I asked.

"I want to know why you thought it was poison."

"I already told you," I said. "I smelled it."

"But how did you know what you smelled was poison if you couldn't identify it?"

I took a moment before responding. How could I answer that question? The real answer was complicated—more complicated than could be explained to a detective on a Portland street corner. More complicated than could be explained in any way Max would understand, for that matter.

Ever since I was a small child, I've had more of an affinity to plants than most people. People with my gift were called "simplers." I've always been sensitive to the elements that make up plants. Their smell, texture, taste, healing properties—and their poisonous properties, too. It never seemed magical to me as a child. I still don't think of it as magic. *Natural* magic, perhaps, but not a sorcery type of magic. I wasn't born with unexplained knowledge. I merely let myself be open to my natural sensitivities, then studied to learn what the sensations I was experiencing meant.

When I was forced to flee my home with my little brother because my talents were equated with witchcraft, it was the alchemists who took me in. They were the ones who shaped my knowledge of plants, turning my natural aptitude into a skill to practice alchemy. I hadn't even heard of alchemy before an alchemist found me—or, I should say, before the alchemist found my brother Thomas. We were selling the healing tinctures I made, and the strange man assumed it was Thomas who had the aptitude for transforming plants. Thomas was more amused than I was.

"The foul smell," I said, choosing my words carefully. I was tempted to say more, but I knew it wasn't a good idea. Saying less was almost always better. I'd learned that the hard way.

"Why did your mind jump to poison, though? Did you recognize it as something specific?"

"No, not really."

"Then why didn't you think it was garbage nearby? Why did your mind jump to poison if it wasn't something you could identify."

It was a good question. But it wasn't odd that I hadn't identified the exact poison. There are many different ways plant essences can be manipulated, causing toxicity in different ways.

I glanced into the teashop. Olivia wasn't attempting to hide her interest in watching us. When she saw me look at her, she gave a little wave. The sleeve of her blouse fell to her elbow, revealing scars on her forearm. Ivan's face was hidden behind a newspaper.

"As I told you before," I said, "I work with plants. Scents fall into different general categories. I didn't know with absolute certainty it was a poisoning, but I thought I smelled a foul herbal odor. The type of thing that's suggestive of poison. Since there was a man lying at an unnatural angle who wasn't breathing, I jumped to that conclusion. Since you're asking me about it, I'm guessing I was right that he was poisoned in addition to being stabbed."

"I can't comment on an ongoing investigation."

"Then what exactly are you asking me?"

"If you happened to have ideas about the type of poison we might be dealing with…"

"Is the lab having trouble identifying the specific poison?" Though modern toxicology had come a long way, I knew it was far easier to detect damage to internal organs than it was to determine the cause.

He took a sip of his tea but didn't speak. Instead his face contorted into a pained expression.

"Are you all right?" I asked.

"It's nothing." He rubbed his lower back with his free hand, again wincing in pain. "I got hurt chasing a suspect last month. It's the stupidest thing, really. I fell through a trap door. They say you never see it coming, but *that* I truly couldn't have seen coming."

Max's cell phone beeped. He read something on the screen and put it back in his pocket. "We're done with your house. You're free to go back inside."

"Before you go, there's something I forgot." I held up my cell phone showing a picture of the cover of Dorian's book. "I have a photograph of one of the books missing from my house."

Was it just my imagination, or did Max Liu's breath catch when I showed him the photograph of *Not Untrue Alchemy*?

NINE

Even if my imagination was overactive, there was *something* going on with Dorian's book. I found the local library, but I needn't have bothered with the library card. None of the alchemy books at the library could tell me more than my own collection. These were books about alchemy, not original alchemy manuscripts. The earliest published alchemy book at the library was far too modern, from 1888. I gave up and went to the market.

When I returned home with a bag of groceries and printed photos from *Not Untrue Alchemy*, a gargoyle poked his head around the kitchen door.

"Those men," Dorian said, "I thought they would never leave."

"You hid, right?"

"*Mon dieu.* You would do me the courtesy of giving me some credit. I have been surrounded by humans for over a century. I know how to hide."

"I'm sorry. Of course you know how to take care of yourself." I set the groceries down and turned back to Dorian. "Something strange is going on here. My contractor was both poisoned *and* stabbed. And now the detective seemed to recognize your book. It's so obscure there's nothing about it on the Internet. How could he recognize it?"

"The book was never in danger until I came here! France is a much more civilized country."

"It has its charms," I agreed. "But Portland does too. As soon as I came here, I—" I stopped myself, unsure of what I wanted to say next. It would have been so easy to open up to Dorian, with his concerned eyes looking up at me. I knew he wouldn't run screaming from whatever I told him, because he was a fellow freak of nature. But I wasn't ready to tell *anyone* about my hopes for this place. Hope was a dangerous thing. If I shared it with anyone, I feared I might make it too real to take back.

Dorian didn't seem to notice that I'd stopped speaking mid-sentence. He stood on his toes on the stepping stool and tipped the bag of vegetables onto the counter. He looked up at me, holding an acorn squash in his hand. "You said you have spoken to *les flics*. What have you learned about the retrieval of my book?"

"They're looking into it."

"And before they get it back, you will translate the pages you photographed?"

"I'm working on it." I removed the short stack of 8x10 photos from my bag and set them on the counter next to the food.

Abandoning the squash, Dorian rooted through the photographs.

"I don't want you to get your hopes up," I said.

"American idioms are odd," Dorian mumbled as he looked through the photos. He stopped and looked up at me. "I have faith in you, Zoe Faust."

I smiled. Nobody had said that to me in a long time.

"I have faith you are a good alchemist," he continued. "As for a cook… What are you making for lunch?"

"I thought I'd make roasted winter vegetables with steamed greens and pecans. I have enough ingredients for both of us."

Dorian returned his attention to the bag of food, nodding to himself. "I will cook, giving you time to begin translating. This will work for now, but I will give you a shopping list of a few more ingredients for dinner—all vegan. I respect your wishes. I am a good houseguest."

I crossed my arms. This was getting ridiculous. "I've got plenty of herbs and spices in the trailer—"

"Yes, yes," he said, scribbling on a notepad I'd left on the counter. He tore off the paper and handed it to me.

"You certainly are a little gourmet," I said.

"You will buy these, yes?"

"I wish your tastes were a little less expensive."

He stared at me with a confused expression. "You are an *alchemist*," he said. "Can you not simply make more gold?"

"The thing is…" I looked away for a moment, embarrassed. "I never really got the hang of that part of alchemy." I watched as his eyes widened in horror.

"But then we could buy good wine and truffles!"

———

While Dorian cooked, I took a quick look at my email. Someone had ordered one of the rare antiques I listed for sale on Elixir's website. I knew the embossed brass medicinal container had to be *somewhere* in the crates. Until my assistant and I had packed up my inventory, the antiques had sat on shelves in a small Paris storage unit, which my assistant Agnès had visited once a week to mail items that had been purchased. One of the reasons I liked this house was that it had a large attic that would be perfect for storing my small inventory—at least it would be once I got the roof fixed. In the meantime, I would have to keep the items in crates stacked at the side of the living room. I sighed as I thought about the volume of wares I would have to root through.

I briefly contemplated ignoring the order in favor of the more pressing matter of deciphering the pages of Dorian's book, but knew I should first attend to practical tasks. Every alchemist knows that a distracted mind leads to disaster. In the back of my mind I knew that if my business failed, I'd have zero income. It wouldn't matter that I saved Dorian's life if we starved to death or were crushed beneath a crumbling house.

While I searched for the brass container, an antique from China, I kept my phone to my ear, calling locksmiths. I was hoping to find someone who could come that day. The first two I called were disorganized, realizing they couldn't make it only after I'd taken time to give them details about what I needed and told them my address. That was odd. On my third try, I found one who said he could be there later that day to change the locks and secure the broken ones.

"What are you doing?" Dorian's voice startled me. "Why are you not looking at the pages from my book?" He stood behind me, clutching a baking dish.

"One of us has to make a living and keep a roof above us."

"If you learned how to transmute gold like a proper alchemist…" Dorian mumbled under his breath as he scampered to the dining table.

The sweet scent of sugar hit my nostrils as I sat down at the table. "Where did you find the sugar?" I asked. "It can't be maple I smell."

He smiled with satisfaction. "The acorn squash is baked in caramelized onions, with a pecan puree stuffing, and lightly braised kale with garlic."

I don't know how he did it with the simple ingredients I had on hand. After another of the best meals I'd eaten in years, Dorian was clearing the dishes when there was a knock at the door.

"I wish," he said, "you were not so popular."

"The locksmith must be early."

Dorian left the remains of the stuffed acorn squash on the table and went to the fireplace, where he stood still and turned to stone. It was a disconcerting sight.

I showed the locksmith the doors where I wanted new locks along with added deadbolts. He regarded the baked squash dish with hungry eyes as we walked by the table on the way to the back door. It was easy to see what his eyes were doing—the thick black eyeliner circling his pale eyes made every expression dramatic. I'd hired a Goth locksmith. He also had a handlebar mustache with perfectly curled edges. The mustache didn't seem very Goth to me, but hey, this was Portland. Maybe he was a Goth-Hipster, a new trend I hadn't yet heard about. Or was the proper term Hipster-Goth?

Just as I was coming to understand one new trend, a new one would inevitably emerge. I had long since abandoned trying to keep up. I liked to think I wore classic clothes that never went out of style—tailored dress pants in neutral colors with simple cotton blouses in warm weather, and knitted sweaters with my beloved silver raincoat in cold climates—but I noticed that sometimes I was considered more trendy than at other times. It was language that I was better at keeping up with. Because I was forced to move around so much, I had become accustomed to picking up local languages, including a language's changing vernacular and speech patterns.

"There's plenty of food," I said. "Shall I get you a plate?"

An hour later, I felt a lot safer and I had a Goth-hipster friend for life. The locksmith was just starting out, he told me, so he lived on canned food and the occasional food truck meal. He said he hadn't eaten a meal that tasty and satisfying in ages, and was shocked to learn the meaty-textured nut stuffing didn't contain meat. I sent him home with leftovers.

As soon as he left, another visitor arrived at the door, leaving me no time to work on the pages of Dorian's book. I sighed and opened the door for Brixton.

"Where should I start?" he asked.

"I let you off the hook, remember?"

"I feel bad about breaking in. Veronica and Ethan wanted to hang out, but my mom said I should do like I promised."

There was no defiance in his expression. Where had this polite version of Brixton come from? I hesitated for a moment while I contemplated what to do about him.

"Thanks," I said. "You can get started weeding the backyard. Everything along the edges of the fence. I'll grab gloves from the trailer and show you what to do."

"The *whole fence*?"

"I thought you wanted to help."

"Yeah, I do. It's just … Nothing. It's cool. I just thought maybe you'd want to tell me more about alchemy, so I don't, like, go asking other people about it. You wouldn't want that, right?"

I doubt I had been that intelligent—or manipulative—at fourteen.

"All right," I said. "Here's your first lesson. The heart of alchemy is transformation. Something new is created based on how you transform existing elements. A perfect example is this garden. Right now it's full of weeds, but through your efforts you're going to transform it into something new."

"I've got a better example. Turning lead into gold. You said you don't, but that's what you guys do, right?"

"Some alchemists have tried to turn lead into gold, but I'm a plant alchemist."

"How did you buy this house, then?"

"I have a job, like everyone else."

"Why aren't you at work?"

"What kind of question is that? I run an online business."

"Can I see the website?"

"Maybe after you practice some alchemy in the yard." I dreaded what a fourteen-year-old would think of my outdated website.

He mumbled something under his breath, but donned the gloves I handed him and watched as I showed him how to pull weeds from the root. He had a lot to do, which would give me time to research the pages of Dorian's book.

I spread the photographs on the dining table, again struck by the fact that the images and text weren't like anything in my own alchemy books. I wished I hadn't lost touch with the alchemists I'd known. Without personal contacts, it would be close to impossible to find a real alchemist. Though there were many people who considered themselves alchemists, most were either scholars or spiritual alchemists. Neither category would understand what had happened to Dorian. And I didn't know how much time I had.

Before I could decide if I should join an Internet discussion group of alchemists, a frantic pounding sounded at the front door.

"Zoe!" Brixton yelled. "Let me in!" My newly secured doorknob shook but didn't open.

I jumped up and opened the door for him.

"I didn't mean to pry," he said, rushing past me into the house. "Really, I didn't. I was just looking for a snack."

"What's going on, Brixton?" I felt his fear. He wasn't joking around.

"Poison! I found poison in your trailer." He thrust the bottle into my hand.

I gasped, then I saw what he'd handed me. "This," I said, laughing as I let go of my tension, "isn't poison. It's asafoetida. A spice."

"No way. It smells like—"

"I know. One of its nicknames is 'Devil's Dung.'"

"It's *food*?"

"Sure is," I said, getting my laughter under control.

"Why would anyone eat this?"

"As soon as it's heated in a dish, it transforms itself and brings out the flavors of other spices. It also helps digestion."

Brixton swore. "I, uh, kind of messed up your trailer. Some bottles fell and broke when I ran out of there. Sorry."

———

While Brixton cleaned up the mess he'd made in the trailer and got back to weeding, I walked to the market to buy the items on Dorian's list. I chuckled when I got to the bottom. He'd added bacon to the list, as if I wouldn't notice. I didn't object to other people—or gargoyles, for that matter—eating whatever they wanted to. But I was a single vegan woman living alone. I had enough secrets to cover up. I wasn't going to buy animal products for my secret guest.

When I got back, a few weeds were gone, but there was no sign of Brixton in the yard or the trailer. I found him in the kitchen. Dorian was showing him how to safely light an old gas stove with a match, and Brixton was rolling his eyes as if the gargoyle was treating him like a child.

"Did you find everything on my list?" Dorian asked in an innocent voice.

"Nice try."

The two of them seemed content, chopping food for dinner, so I left the kitchen, taking the photographs from *Not Untrue Alchemy* to the dining table. The disturbing bird images again made me want to look away, but I forced myself to examine the woodcuts. The twisted, broken necks stirred a feeling of apprehension deep within me. Along with my revulsion was a flicker of recognition, but the flame quickly faded and I was left with nothing.

Coded symbols such as these allowed for secret alchemical teachings to be passed down from one generation to the next. The pelican, for example, symbolizes self-sacrifice, which is a code for distillation. But the birds in this book weren't familiar to me. Instead of elegant pelicans, crows, peacocks, and phoenixes, these birds had twisted shapes and looked more like dodos and pterodactyls.

In the past, coded messages were often publicly displayed, carved onto buildings during alchemy's heyday in the Middle Ages. The markings could describe alchemical operations, such as a dove representing the purifying transformation turning from the Black Phase to the White Phase and the phoenix representing the final alchemical operation resulting in the philosopher's stone.

But here in *Not Untrue Alchemy*, I couldn't easily identify the significance of any of the illustrations. I made out an ouroboros—a dragon eating its own tail—on one page, but the dragon's body wasn't curled in a circle to symbolize eternal re-creation as one would expect. Instead, the creature was contorted and looked as if it was writhing in pain.

Distressed shouts interrupted my thoughts.

I ran into the kitchen. Brixton clutched his hand and Dorian held a cell phone.

"He was recording me!" Dorian screamed.

I took a deep breath. And another. I now understood Brixton's apparent change of heart.

Dorian held the phone in his clawed hand. The image displayed on the screen showed a gargoyle cooking in my kitchen.

TEN

"Make the video play, Zoe." Dorian was close to shouting as he held the phone in an unsteady hand. "The touch screen of the phone does not respond to my fingers."

"It would help if you handed me the phone."

"*Non*." The grip of his clawed hand tightened around the phone. "You can make it play with the phone safely in my hand."

I glanced at Brixton, sulking in the corner of the kitchen with his arms folded, then tapped the screen of his phone in Dorian's hand. The video on the cell phone screen clearly showed the gargoyle chopping vegetables as he explained to Brixton how to use acidulated water to stop chopped vegetables from turning brown.

"Brixton," I snapped. "What did you do?"

"He scratched my hand!"

"You would not give me your phone!" Dorian said. "What could I do?"

"I'll tend to your hand, Brixton," I said, grabbing the salve I'd applied just two days before on the cut he received while breaking into the house. "But *what did you do*?"

"Nobody believed me! What was I supposed to do?"

"You don't realize what you've done." I was past anger. I was disappointed. *And scared.*

Brixton heard the change in my voice. "It's not even posted yet," he said quietly, looking down at the 1950s linoleum floor.

"You're telling the truth?"

He nodded, still not looking up at me.

My shoulders relaxed and Dorian recited a prayer of thanks in French. I had forgotten I was holding the aloe salve to treat Brixton's scratch.

Brixton watched me as I treated the wound made by Dorian's claw. "Why doesn't it sting?"

"Not everything good for you hurts."

"Thanks," he mumbled so quietly it was barely audible.

"You don't even need a bandage this time," I added.

"He would have killed me if you hadn't come in."

"He knows not what he says," Dorian said, flapping his wings in what could only be described as a huff. "I would never hurt a child."

"Only an adult who was here to fix the house," Brixton said, his voice defiant.

Dorian gasped. "You cannot think—" His head whipped between the two of us. "Zoe, you do not think I was responsible for that poor man's murder, do you? You cannot think I would do such a thing."

Before I could decide what to do about either of them, a burst of knocking sounded at the front door. *Wonderful.*

"Stay here," I said. "Both of you."

Looking out the peephole in the front door, I saw a young woman with long blond hair, several strands in messy braids woven with flowers at the ends. She held a plate of cookies in her hands. Friendly new neighbor?

"I bet it's my mom," Brixton said from behind me. "She said she wanted to thank you for not pressing charges against me. I never know if she's going to follow through on anything, so I didn't know if she'd really show up."

She knocked again. Brixton stepped past me and looked through the peephole.

"Yeah," he said. "That's her."

A quick survey of the room assured me Dorian was gone, so I opened the door. Brixton's mom's smile was powerful enough that under normal circumstances it would have brightened up a room, but at that moment it was only strong enough to make the tension bearable.

"Zoe!" Instead of handing me the platter of cookies in her hand, she set it on the floor and enveloped me in a warm hug. "Thank you for looking out for my pumpkin."

"Mom," Brixton said.

Brixton's mom let go of me and gave her son an even bigger hug. Even on the chilly overcast day, she was barefoot. She stood on her tiptoes as she hugged her son. Before letting go, she kissed his forehead, causing him to turn bright red. Even if what Blue had said was true about Brixton's mom not always being there for her son, Brixton certainly wasn't lacking in physical affection.

"I'm Heather," she said. "And these—" she paused and picked up the tray of cookies, "are my famous vegan oatmeal cookies."

"You told your mom about my being vegan?" I asked Brixton. I hadn't realized he'd paid attention to that fact. And, more importantly, I wondered what else he'd told his mom and others about me. Had he told the truth that he hadn't uploaded the video of Dorian on his phone?

Heather gave me an even bigger grin. "Brix, you didn't tell me that!"

"Um, yeah," Brixton said. "Now you two can be BFFs or something. So, can we go now?"

"I'm not a strict vegan," Heather said. "That would be tough, seeing as I don't cook much. These cookies are the one thing I do well. The dinner you're cooking smells delicious."

The scent of the food Dorian had been cooking did smell mouthwatering. He was using a common herb combination of marjoram, rosemary, and thyme to bring out the flavors of the winter vegetables. I also recognized the scent of other herbs that were transforming the dish into something greater than the sum of its parts. If I hadn't been worried about that video, I would have been a lot more curious about the meal.

When I hesitated, Brixton gave me a strange look. "Yeah, Mom," he said. "Zoe is a great cook. Isn't that right, Zoe? Because *who else* could be cooking in your kitchen?"

"That's sweet of you to say," I said through clenched teeth.

"I hope my baby isn't causing you too much trouble," Heather said.

"He's really taken to gardening, even though some stinging nettles scratched his hand. Isn't that right, Brixton?"

"Can we go, Mom? I just need to get my phone. I left it in the kitchen."

"I'll come with you," I said. "I need to check the stove. Heather, please make yourself at home in the living room. I'm still unpacking, so don't mind the mess."

Dorian wasn't hiding. Not exactly. He stood in the corner of the kitchen, unmoving. He looked exactly as he had when I first opened the crate: a sleeping stone statue. The only difference was that instead of an alchemy book in his hands, he held Brixton's cell phone.

"What the—" Brixton said with a start.

"We're alone, Dorian," I said quietly. "Brixton's mom is in the other room."

Gray stone shifted. The movement was subtle and fascinating. I hadn't been this close when his transformation from stone to life had taken place before. It was like watching an avalanche at a quarry. Granite-colored sand granules shifted in a cascading effect until stone had morphed into thick gray skin.

"No way," Brixton whispered.

Dorian rolled his head from side to side and stretched his wings. "You must delete it," he said, handing me Brixton's phone. "I cannot use the screen of the phone with my fingers. Mobile phones were much better when they had real buttons."

I found the video file and deleted it before handing the phone back to Brixton. He was still staring at Dorian. I had to push him out the kitchen door.

Once Brixton and his mom were gone, I made sure all the curtains were drawn and the doors and windows locked. I tried one of Heather's cookies. She wasn't exaggerating about how good they were. She'd used a sweet and savory combination of dried cherries and salted walnuts. I followed my nose back to the kitchen, where Dorian had resumed cooking. He stood on the stepping stool, stirring the contents of a Dutch Oven pot with a wooden spoon.

How could he be so calm after the close call?

"Dorian, what—"

"*Un moment, s'il vous plaît,*" he said, holding up his clawed index finger. He lifted a spoonful to his snout, nodded to himself, then added a shake of sea salt. He placed the lid on the pot, rested the spoon on the counter, and hopped down from the stool to face me.

"I will require," he said, "an apron and a spoon rest."

"An apron?"

"Yes, you did not appear to have one. Quite uncivilized."

"About Brixton—" I began, caught between being somber about the near-disaster of a video of Dorian going viral and the absurdity of imagining a gargoyle in my kitchen wearing a frilly apron.

"Zoe, it is done. Crisis averted. There is no sense dwelling on the unfortunate occurrence. That would only distract you from discovering the secrets of my book. I will be your personal gargoyle chef while you translate the pages from my book. That way you will have sufficient time to devote to it."

I burst out laughing. Once I started, I couldn't stop. My very own personal chef. I was laughing so hard a tear trickled down my cheek.

"*Mon amie,* you are hysterical."

"Dorian, what's going on?" I leaned back against the counter, my shoulders still shaking but getting hold of myself. "Nothing makes sense."

Dorian jumped up to sit on a free section of the counter next to me. "I do not think things make much sense once one has left France."

"Maybe that's it. The last few decades traveling across America have been a blur."

"This meal will make you feel better. It is an old recipe from the French countryside. Adapted, of course, for your veganism. But I am nothing if not a gentleman. I had no idea a cassoulet could be so decadent without pig fat."

"How did you learn how to cook?"

"From a chef."

"Who was open to teaching a gargoyle?"

"It is complicated to explain ..."

"If you hadn't noticed, I have a complicated life."

"I think the cassoulet needs more seasoning." He left his spot next to me and resumed his position on the stepping stool in front of the stove.

"You're avoiding my question."

"Give the alchemist a prize."

"I can better help you with the alchemy book if I understand your history."

He sighed. "He was blind."

"A blind chef?"

"He was not always blind."

I waited a few moments, but he didn't continue.

"The blind chef," I prompted.

"Fine, yes, all right," he said impatiently, still fussing with spices instead of looking at me. "There was a kitchen fire. This is what blinded him. He saved his staff, but was badly burned and lost his vision. He had been a successful chef who once had much power. He lived alone in a large house, where he was both lonely and angry for losing the adoration he once had. He was a friend of my father's. My father knew of fame, and he felt sorry for his friend's predicament. Since the man could not see, I was able to visit him with my father. In spite of the chef's reputation for being difficult, we got along well. Father was nearing the end of his life and did not know what would become of me. He told his friend I was 'unemployed' and that I was wary of people seeing me because I was disfigured. The lonely former chef hired me to be his live-in assistant. He previously had people delivering prepared meals to him. Upon hiring me, he ordered uncooked food to be delivered, and taught me how to cook. I took to it quite well. Before he passed away, he wrote me a reference. I became a chef for other blind people who wanted good food and companionship at home. That is what I have been doing."

"That's lovely," I said, imagining the gargoyle happily at work in the kitchens of people who had no idea of his visage. "Why didn't you want to tell me?"

He turned to face me with a wooden spoon in his hand. "You of all people, Zoe Faust, know that speaking of the past brings up unintentional memories we do not wish to remember."

ELEVEN

I woke up to the scent of coffee. *Coffee*? Why was there coffee in my house? I shot out of bed and promptly shivered. I'd sealed off the broken window as best I could, but painter's tape wasn't as robust as the fitted piece of wood. I found my thickest pair of woolen socks and crept downstairs.

"Where did you get that?" I asked, indicating the large contraption on the kitchen counter.

"I took the liberty of ordering an espresso maker. It is uncivilized that you do not have one."

"How did it get here?"

"One of the benefits of American impatience is the rapidity of express delivery. *C'est très vite.*"

"You have a credit card?"

"I am cooking for you," he said, blinking at me, "should I not receive payment of some kind?"

I sighed and rubbed my temples. "No more taking my credit card without asking, okay?"

"I did not wish to interrupt you while you studied the pages of my book. I understand alchemists do not like to be interrupted."

"Well, yes, that's true—" I broke off when I saw a French-language newspaper spread out on the table. "You also ordered *Le Monde*?"

"Yes, is it not agreeable that they offer this service outside of France?"

"Was it really urgent enough that you couldn't ask? Is this how you treated the previous people you cooked for?"

Dorian sniffed and sipped his mug of espresso. "I was homesick."

My mood softened. "Have you ever been outside France before?"

He shook his head.

"Well," I said, feeling my anger dissipating, "just be sure to ask me in the future if you want to charge anything."

"I have *l'espresso et le journal*, what else could I possibly want?"

————

After making myself my usual morning smoothie and watering the portable herb garden I'd moved into the kitchen window box, I set out for a brisk walk to clear my head before working on the pages of Dorian's book. I walked in the direction of Blue Sky Teas, thinking I'd get a cup of tea to go.

Bells chimed when I walked through the door, and Blue's voice called from the back: "Be out in a minute!"

I walked around the weeping fig tree and looked up at the painted sky. I didn't feel as comfortable in the teashop as I had before. It wasn't because of the gossip I knew would be taking place there shortly. It was something else. Something was … off.

The comforting teashop from the day before had changed. I whipped my head around, searching for the difference. I sniffed the air, wondering if Blue had accidentally burned something she was cooking. That wasn't it either. I couldn't place the source of my discomfort. All I knew was that I had to get out of there. I turned and ran out the door. I didn't stop running until I'd reached my street.

The exertion made my chest hurt. I stopped to catch my breath. What had happened back there? There was too much going on for me to think. I desperately needed to unravel the secrets of *Not Untrue Alchemy* to keep Dorian from the awful fate of being trapped in a dead stone body while his mind lived on, yet I hesitated before walking up to the house. My mind was troubled with too many thoughts that would get in the way. *What was going on at Blue's teashop? Had her words about Portland meant she was running from something? What had happened to Charles Macraith? What was Max Liu hiding? Why had someone stolen Dorian's book? Was the gargoyle capable of more than I thought?*

I turned on my heel and headed the other direction. What I needed was a long walk, far away from the distractions of my house and the teashop. Only then would I be in the right mindset to decipher the riddles of Dorian's book. I had so few of the pages that I needed all the help I could get.

In all the places I've lived, I've found the nearby places where I could walk in nature. Forests, deserts, swamps. It didn't matter where it was. What mattered was that the natural plant life surrounding me made me feel at ease. I was in my element smelling the scents of fragrant trees of the forest like pine, maple, and hickory. I could watch the plants of swamps interact with the water for hours, from wispy cattails rising from the dark waters to the duckweed floating on the surface. Even the desert begat life. Creation could come from anywhere.

I hadn't had much time to explore Portland's greenery yet. Even when I'd purchased the house, I hadn't done much exploring. That was the whole point of buying the house! To have time to settle in and explore the area's many parks, forests, arboretums, gardens, and other hidden places I didn't yet know about. I didn't know where I was going, but I was hoping that in this city of trees I'd hit a park or something similar before too long.

Sure enough, after walking a few blocks, I came to a beautiful park blanketed in trees. It turned out to be the Lone Fir Cemetery, which a plaque informed me was the oldest cemetery in Portland, dating back to 1846. What a young city this was. I walked through the serene grounds, letting my mind wander to the trees and the Gothic mausoleum I passed. The gardens and trees didn't appear to be part of a central plan, which made it all the more charming.

With my mind clear, I allowed myself to turn back to the events of the present. Only now was I able to identify what I had sensed at Blue's teashop. It was such an unexpected thing that my conscious mind hadn't put it together: the odd scent I had detected over Charles Macraith's dead body was similar to what I'd smelled at Blue Sky Teas.

I wasn't being dense or forgetful. The odor had mingled with the scents of the numerous teas in a way that made it difficult to distinguish. But here in a cemetery park full of an assortment of plants, I'd been unconsciously picking apart the mingled fragrances of the trees and winter flowers.

I had to get back to the teashop.

The sun was high overhead. I must have been walking for hours, which explained why I'd passed the same trees again and again.

When I reached Blue Sky Teas, it wasn't Blue who was behind the counter. Instead, a stunning red-headed woman greeted me with a smile that didn't reach her eyes. The deep lines and puffiness around her light green eyes didn't match the rest of her polished appearance.

"Blue had to leave early today to prepare for a houseguest," she explained. "Can I help you?"

Could she? The poisonous scent that I thought I had detected earlier was no longer there. Had Blue taken it with her? For her houseguest?

I bit back my shock and confusion, instead giving the woman behind the counter a wide smile. "I was supposed to be here earlier to bring her something for her guest," I said. "I lost track of the day. Do you have her address so I can bring it to her?"

"Oh, of course. That's very sweet of you to go out of your way."

———

I went home to get my truck, not venturing inside the house. I'd deal with Dorian's wrath later. This was more important.

Twenty minutes later, I stood outside Blue's house. The cottage was on the outskirts of Portland, in a less crowded part of the city where houses had acres of land. Blue's yard, if you could call it that, was an overgrown plot of land that might look like weeds to most people. Technically these were indeed weeds, but these were *useful* weeds. Even with a brief glance, I identified field mustard, sorrel, and wild onions. I understood why she lived here. It was a wild-crafter's dream here in her own yard.

Standing in the wild yard, I hesitated. If I gave myself time to think, I'd convince myself this was a stupid idea. If I thought Blue was going to poison someone, I should call the police. But what could I tell them? *I think I maybe smelled something strange, which I can't identify, and you'll never be able to detect it yourself, and now it's gone?* No, I had to see if I could find it on my own.

I took a deep breath and knocked on the door. The knock was met with silence. I tried the doorbell, followed by another knock. Still, nothing.

An old VW Bug was parked outside, but for all I knew she might have multiple cars. I walked to the closest window and looked inside.

The first thing I spotted beyond the half-drawn curtains made my body jolt with a mix of relief and anger. On a side table next to the window, nestled in an ornamental woven bowl, sat two of my antique alembics that had been stolen. That had to mean Dorian's book was nearby too. I was giddy with relief before the anger hit me. I was vexed not only with Blue for taking a life and my possessions, but also with myself for letting my emotions get in the way of thinking she was capable of such things.

The second thing I saw drained the anger from me, a wave of numbing cold washing over me in its place. Beyond the side table, Blue's body lay on the floor.

TWELVE

Hospitals and medicine have come a long way in the last few centuries. Plague doctors once wore beaked masks filled with straw and fragrant mint, cloves, myrrh, and rose petals thought to protect them from miasmatic bad air, and used a pointed cane to examine patients without touching them. Their frightening costumes have been immortalized in woodcuts from the seventeenth century, but in person they were even more terrifying. Imagine lying listless with fever, unable to keep down food or water, your body covered in painful boils, only to be visited not by an angelic sympathetic doctor, but by a demonic, faceless figure who poked you with a stick and told you to repent for your sins. It was an image I would never forget.

I hadn't been one of the unfortunate souls on the other end of the plague doctor's stick, but I had seen their work when I used to practice plant alchemy and was more actively engaged in making herbal remedies to heal people. Just as doctors couldn't stop the plague, healers like me were helpless to save everyone. My work wasn't enough to save the people I loved.

That was a long time ago, but hospitals still made me uncomfortable. Contagious people crammed into sickbeds with countless others had given way to the sterile hospitals of the present century. The details didn't matter. The very fact that sickness and death were such a part of life was something I'd been running from for a long time.

After seeing Blue sprawled on the floor, I dialed 911. The fire department was the first to arrive. They discovered Blue had a pulse, and the ambulance that arrived minutes later took her to the hospital. As the gurney transported her from the house to the ambulance, I knew what had happened. Wafting up from her body was a mix of scents similar to what I'd sensed earlier. Similar, but not the same. I frowned to myself, wondering what was going on.

Blue hadn't regained consciousness and was now in a coma. After the police arrived, Blue's hospital room was placed under guard. They must have thought the person who tried to kill her might try again.

I shivered in the sterile atmosphere of the hospital. I knew I should have trusted my instincts. Blue *wasn't* responsible for the murder of Charles Macraith. She was a victim herself. Why would she leave stolen items in plain sight in her house? It was as if they were meant to be found—placed there to frame her, by the same person who tried to kill her. Would Dorian's book be among the items recovered?

The tea from the hospital's café consisted of prebagged cardboard boxes of black and green teas, plus one herbal mint blend. I took the scalding paper cup from the café to the waiting room. The scent of modern abrasive chemicals was making me feel sick. I was hoping the mint tea would help calm my stomach.

A light rain gave the view from the waiting room windows a hazy appearance. It wasn't falling hard enough to see the raindrops, yet the mist gave the trees outside a surreal sheen, as if I was watching an old movie instead of experiencing it as reality.

I was caught up in my thoughts and didn't notice when Max sat down opposite me.

"You most likely saved her life," he said, "by finding her when you did."

I glanced around. Aside from me and Max, the only other people in the waiting room were two elderly women in the opposite corner. "Have you gotten any sleep?"

"I look that bad, huh?" He ran his hand through his disheveled black hair as his lips ticked up into a faint smile.

He didn't look bad at all. In fact, in his rumpled suit, a barely visible spot of tea spilled on his white dress shirt, and despite his unshaven face, I felt stirrings in me I hadn't felt in years. His sallow skin, however, suggested that he needed a good meal and a solid chunk of sleep more than what I was thinking about.

"How is she?" I asked.

"Stable. I don't know much myself, but I can tell you that much."

"What's going on, Max?"

"It's an ongoing investigation."

"Which involves me—"

"I wasn't finished. It's ongoing, and because Blue is in a coma we can't question her yet. But we found more of your stolen possessions, hidden at her house."

"You found my books?"

"Books?"

"Books were among the antiques that were stolen."

Max scrolled through the screen on his phone. "Damn."

"What is it?"

"The crew found several of the items you reported, but none of the books."

I groaned. I'd been holding out hope that it would be simple to recover Dorian's book.

"It's early in the investigation," Max said.

"What's the guard for? You really think someone is going to try to finish the job?"

Max studied my face for a moment.

"What?" I said, hoping I didn't have a chunk of kale caught between my teeth.

"Why would you think that?"

"You answer a lot of questions with another question, Detective Liu."

He sighed. "You ask a lot of questions, Ms. Faust."

"This couldn't have been an accident, if that's what you're getting at. The poison I smelled wasn't something she would have mixed by accident. Someone gave it to her."

"The poison that *only you* somehow detected."

"This again?" Now I was annoyed. "I told you, I've studied herbs enough that I'm more sensitive to this type of scent than other people."

"I don't think she ingested it accidentally either."

"Oh. You agree with me. Then what are we arguing about?"

"You're forgetting something."

"What?" I snapped. I was tired of riddles.

"Blue is a good person." He paused but held my gaze. "I don't think she took the poison accidentally—because there's a good chance she took it on purpose."

I was speechless for a few moments. "You think she was trying to kill herself? Why?"

"I've seen good people be driven to murder before. It eats them up inside."

"Wait, you mean you think *Blue* may have had something to do with the murder?" I thought back on my conversation with Blue. I remembered a kindred spirit, not a guilt-stricken woman.

Max started to say something else, but his words were drowned out by someone shouting as they ran down the hallway.

"Is this the right way? Blue!"

Max jumped up and stopped Brixton before he got close to the room with the guard.

"Hold on, kiddo."

"Where is she?" Brixton asked. His face was streaked with tears he hadn't bothered to wipe away.

A lanky man followed a few steps behind Brixton. He looked familiar, though it took me a moment to place the tall, sandy-haired young man. I'd seen him at the teashop, Blue's second customer of the day who'd gotten his tea to go.

"You can't see her right now," Max said.

Brixton tried to push past Max, who grabbed his wrist.

"Ow!" Brixton said. Max didn't release his grip.

"You drove him, Sam?" Max asked.

"I knew he'd ride his bike here if I didn't. I wanted to see her, too."

"I'll stay here," Brixton said. "I promise. Just let go of your death grip. Isn't this, like, police brutality?"

"You're fine," Max said, but at the same time he released Brixton.

"I'm Zoe," I said to the newcomer.

"Sam Strum. I'm one of Brixton's teachers."

"Who *cares*?" Brixton said, tossing his backpack to the floor and flinging himself into a chair. "Blue is lying there dying—"

"She's not really dying, is she?" Sam asked, scratching his neck. The skin was already raw. I understood the feeling of being uncomfortable in hospitals.

"She's stable," Max said. His expression was unreadable.

"Thank God." Sam rubbed his neck nervously again. "God, I hate hospitals. I spent far too much time in this place with Aunt Olivia last year."

At the mention of Olivia's name, I realized this was the nephew she said recommended the teashop to her. It had taken me a moment to make the connection, because the difference between the two was striking. While Olivia was a tiny figure, Sam stood well over six feet tall. Yet where Olivia's personality made her seem larger than her slight body, the impact of Sam's exceptional height was lessened by his slumped shoulders.

Brixton tapped his foot and glared at us. "Why can't we see Blue?"

"She's asleep, Brix," Max said, omitting the facts that Blue was in a coma and there was a police guard at her door.

Brixton glared at Max. "She'd want to see me."

"I'm sure she needs her rest," Sam said. "Let me take you home."

"I'm staying here."

"You can't stay here," Sam began.

"Why not? My mom isn't home. She's at an artist retreat. And my stepdad is away on business."

"She leaves you at home alone?" I asked.

"I was supposed to go over to Blue's house after school today. I was going to stay with her for a few days."

Max and Sam glanced at each other. So it was Brixton who was going to be Blue's houseguest.

"Can you call your mom?" Sam asked. "She'd want to come home to be with you now."

Brixton started to type a text message, but Sam elbowed him. "*Call* her," he said.

Brixton grumbled but did as he was told. He spoke quietly into the phone. I didn't hear what he was saying until he handed the phone to me. "She wants to talk to you," he said.

"Me?"

Brixton rolled his eyes and handed me the phone.

"Would it be too much trouble for Brix to stay with you for a couple of days?" Heather asked.

I walked with the phone to the other end of the waiting room. To make sure my voice wouldn't carry back to Brixton and the others, I turned to face the window. The misty rain had turned into a heavier downpour.

"Brixton is really upset," I said softly. "I think he'd like you to come home."

"Oh, Brix is a resilient kid. He said Blue's okay. He'll be fine."

"She was poisoned."

"But she's not dead or anything."

I stared at the phone. Heather was so very young. I put the phone back to my ear. "Blue has been a big part of his life since he was little, right? He's really upset. If you could come back—"

"If it's too much trouble for him to stay with you—"

"Wouldn't he feel more comfortable staying with one of his friends?"

"Have you *met* Ethan's parents? No, I don't want him staying there. And Veronica's parents don't have an extra room—and now that the kids are fourteen … If you don't want to have him stay with you, don't worry. He knows how to take care of himself. He'll be fine on his own. I'll be back in three days—"

"Hold on."

"You mean you'll do it, Zoe?"

THIRTEEN

I ADDED AN EXTRA scoop of unsweetened cocoa powder to the mixture in the blender.

"I'm not drinking that," Brixton said.

"One sip," I said, "is all I ask."

"Whatever." He skulked to the other side of the kitchen and stuffed his hands in the pockets of his jeans, then took them out and crossed his arms. Without a cell phone, he didn't seem to know what to do with his hands.

I'd driven Brixton back to my house from the hospital. Of course I wasn't letting a grieving kid stay in his house by himself. I wasn't sure how Dorian was going to react to Brixton's staying at the house for a few days, or to the new information that his book wasn't among the items recovered at Blue's house. Upon seeing us come into the house, Dorian hadn't yelled or hidden. Instead, he held up a clawed hand and simply said, "Phone." Brixton complied, handing over the device. "I will return it to you when you leave the house," Dorian told him. Brixton wouldn't be getting any more videos of the gargoyle.

I hadn't yet told Dorian that his book wasn't one of the items recovered. I knew how important it was, so I couldn't bring myself to break it to him. Brixton didn't know Dorian was dying, so I had to wait until he wouldn't hear us talking. I wasn't looking forward to that conversation.

I turned my attention back to the blender. The trick to creating a kid-friendly green smoothie is all in the chocolate. Fruits have natural sugars that sweeten a smoothie, but without chocolate, the flavor of vegetables can overpower the fruit.

In addition to the subtler flavors of cucumber and avocado, the sweetness of a large pear, and the spicy kick of a knob of ginger, I added a few leaves of light green curly kale. Kale is a winter vegetable, making it abundant at local farmers markets. As it was, it would have been a perfect smoothie for me, but I was making this for Brixton. Since meeting him earlier that week, I had seen him eat cookies and peanut butter sandwiches he had in his backpack, but I hadn't seen him eat a single vegetable. That was going to change. And he was going to like it.

To make sure it would be palatable for his taste, I added a scoop of peanut butter and instead of plain water I opted for coconut water, which was sweeter. After blending it well, I poured half of the creamy mixture into a mug and handed it to Brixton.

He took a sip and scowled at me. "What's in it?"

"You saw everything I did."

"Yeah, but this actually tastes *good*."

I smiled. "Come on, I'll show you where you can sleep."

Even with my old furniture the movers had delivered, the house was sparsely furnished. Brixton would have to settle for the small mattress I'd brought inside from my Airstream trailer, which I'd placed in the upstairs bedroom with the least leaky windows.

When we reached the top of the creaking stairs, Brixton lagged behind.

"When do we get to check on Blue?" he asked.

"I'll call and check on her. I promise I'll let you know as soon as I hear anything."

In addition to a small backpack, Brixton had a guitar with him. Maybe that would help get him out of his funk. The scuffs and stickers on the case suggested the instrument was well-loved. I'd tried out several instruments over the years, but it was the piano that spoke to me most. Not the most practical thing for someone who lived on the road. But now that I had a house… If I could solve the madness surrounding me, was I fooling myself thinking I could stay a while? From the top of the stairs, I turned to look down at the living room. It was still filled with moving crates, but I could imagine a grand piano in the corner. Such an instrument might be worth the depleting task of transmuting lead into gold.

"Why don't you bring your guitar downstairs after you get settled," I said.

"I'm not playing for you," he said.

"You don't have to."

"Whatever."

I left Brixton to unpack his small bag and found Dorian attending to the fireplace. "Both you and the boy are wearing heavy sweaters," he said, "so it must be cold inside."

"You don't feel it?"

"I feel the difference in temperature, but I do not mind it. I checked the chimney last night. It is sound. I thought we would have a fire."

"That's a great idea."

"Zoe Faust," Dorian said, "for someone who has had time to learn to lie, your face is an open book, as they say. You are keeping something from me. Is it about the woman who was found nearly dead? Is her condition more serious than you are allowing the boy to think?"

"It's about her, but not in the way that you think." I hesitated. I hated being the bearer of bad news. "Some of the items stolen from the house were found at her house."

"*Mon livre!*"

"I'm sorry," I said, "your book wasn't among the items recovered."

Dorian fired a million questions at me—or at least a dozen—none of which I knew the answer to. I was more than ready for a break from the gargoyle's interrogation when Brixton came downstairs and found us sitting in front of a blazing fire. He brought his guitar with him but wore a skeptical look on his face.

"*Est ce que tu connais 'Dame Tartine,'* Zoe?" Dorian said to me.

"Of course you'd think of that folk song. It's all about butter."

"Not only butter," Dorian said. "Also anise and raisins."

Brixton looked at us like we were crazy. But he also looked like he was itching to play the beaten-up acoustic guitar he held with a confident hand.

"If you play these chords," Dorian told Brixton, "we will sing."

Dorian and I sang the French-language verses about sweet pralines, fried croquets, and baked biscuits, with Dorian prompting Brixton when to play different chords.

"It's about a woman, Dame Tartine, who lives in a house of food," I explained. "A tartine is a French style of open-faced sandwich."

"I'm fourteen, you know," Brixton said. "Not eight."

"But the song is in French," Dorian said. "It has a very nice sound. If you learn the words, you do not have to tell your girlfriend what they mean."

"Veronica is *not* my girlfriend," Brixton said. He didn't blush when he said it, but it was interesting that he immediately thought of her when Dorian used the word. I remembered the tall, awkward girl standing on my porch earlier that week who was going to be a knockout once she grew into her own skin.

"How long have the three of you been friends?" I asked.

"Me and VCM have been best friends since we were little."

"VCM?"

"Veronica Chen-Mendoza. V or VCM for short. Anyway, Ethan moved here two years ago. Everybody wanted to be friends with him except us."

"I must have misunderstood your English," Dorian said. "Is he not your friend?"

"Me and V hated him at first. His parents are, like, uber-rich. He has everything. But then we learned he doesn't care about that stuff. He's cool."

"Why does he dress like James Dean?" I asked.

"Yeah, kinda weird, huh? He had us over to his house and showed us this movie *Rebel Without a Cause*. That's when we knew he was cool." His face clouded over. "Do you think Blue tried to kill herself? That's what people are saying."

"I honestly don't know."

"She's like a mom to me, you know? You met my mom. She acts more like Veronica's little sister than a mom sometimes. I don't know what I'd do if Blue doesn't—" He broke off and stood up, walking away from us. He wiped his face with his sleeve.

Dorian stood up. I put my hand on his arm to hold him back, giving Brixton space.

"When do we eat around here?" Brixton said after a minute. "I'm starving."

"That is the best suggestion I have heard all day," Dorian said. "Let us cook."

I followed them into the kitchen to get a glass of water.

"We begin with *mise en place*," Dorian said to Brixton. "This means putting everything you wish to use in a meal in its proper place, before you begin cooking. What shall we cook for dinner?"

While they prepared dinner in the kitchen, I sat in front of the fireplace and stared into the richly colored flames. What was I going to do about the two of them? I couldn't let either of them down.

Since the police hadn't recovered Dorian's book with the other items found at Blue's house, there was renewed urgency in deciphering the few pages I had.

I spread out the photographed pages, stopping on the one with an unsettling image of a basilisk, the creature that symbolizes the destructive fire necessary to perform transformations. As you'd normally find in an alchemical woodcut, the creature had the head of a bird and the body of a serpent. That's where the similarities ended. The tail of this serpent was contorted and wrapped in such an unexpected and disconcerting way that I was sure it had to mean something. But what that was, I had no idea. Perhaps the background setting had significance. The contorted basilisk was perched at the top of crumbled castle ruins, clinging to the one turret that remained.

My own books hadn't yet proven helpful to decipher any of the pages, so I again opened my laptop, delving deeper on the Internet for anything that might be remotely relevant. Nothing like this image seemed to exist. I typed sections of the convoluted Latin into a search, again coming up empty-handed. Read literally, the text explained how one needed to walk in the direction where one cannot see. Riddles! The alchemists always had their riddles. I had never appreciated that part of alchemy. I liked my mysteries solved, which is probably why I loved the detective fiction that came of age in the nineteenth century. Yet there was something about the riddle of these pages that tickled at my brain—as if I'd been searching in the wrong places and the answers were within me.

"Ignore the color of the soup," Dorian said, carrying a tray of three steaming bowls from the kitchen.

"What's wrong with the … oh." The creamed soup was certain shade of brown that should be reserved for a room of the house that wasn't the dining room.

"He didn't warn me," Brixton said, following Dorian out of the kitchen carrying a Dutch oven with two pot holders. "I thought using the purple carrots would be cool."

"Don't worry," I said. "I've done it myself. It's simple chemistry. Purple blended with the other vegetables gives you brown."

"The risotto is a much more palatable color," Dorian said.

As we ate, I couldn't pull my mind from *Not Untrue Alchemy*. I was missing a crucial element of deciphering the pages, making me simultaneously far away and close to unlocking the secrets in those pages.

I knew what I had to do.

There was one thing I hadn't yet tried. The more I thought about it, the more sure I was that it was the key. I could immerse myself in alchemy, doing something I hadn't done in nearly a century. I could set up my alchemy laboratory. I didn't know if I was ready, but that didn't matter. I had to be.

FOURTEEN

THE EMPTY CONCRETE BASEMENT smelled of mildew and beer. The scents alone would be distracting to the point of causing failure. I looked at the harsh light bulb suspended from the ceiling and considered my options.

Becoming an alchemist takes years of study. Learning the foundations is essential to be successful at your transformations. I was an impatient young woman when I began my alchemical studies. Nicolas Flamel had taken me in, with my brother in tow, when he received word from an acquaintance about my aptitude with plant transformations. Since alchemy, at its core, is about transformation, he had high hopes of training me to be an alchemist like him and his wife Perenelle. But my alchemical training was incomplete. I had given it up after my brother Thomas died. I was his big sister. I was supposed to take care of him, but I failed.

I shook my head at the memory, and my hand automatically flew to my gold locket. I pushed the painful thoughts from my mind and forced my hand to let go of the locket. I couldn't let myself get distracted by misfortunes that had caused me to act rashly. Though I had never completed my training, there was still a great deal I knew about alchemy. But so much time had passed. I was sure that was a big part of the reason I was having difficulty understanding Dorian's strange alchemy book. Getting back into hands-on practice would help me see what I was missing.

That was the idea, anyway.

When I'd had the foolish notion that I might have a normal life for a little while here in Portland, I thought I might be ready to practice alchemy again. Not right away, but I wanted to give myself the space I needed to see if I was ready. It's why I had wanted a house with a basement in need of renovation.

This basement was the reason I had hired Charles Macraith. Working with a contractor with a versatile set of skills who was known for keeping his mouth shut, it would have been possible for me to build the type of alchemy lab I thought I might want again. Not merely a room, but a carefully organized laboratory including a tower furnace.

Even before Dorian came into my life with his peculiar book, the reason I was drawn to practicing alchemy again was because I wanted to feel whole. Alchemy had dominated so much of my life that even though I had run from it, I couldn't escape it. But while I was running, I was also running from myself. I wondered if I needed to practice alchemy to find myself again.

My plan, when I bought this house, had been to ease myself into it. Finding a place to call home, working the land to create an edible garden of herbs and vegetables, and fixing up a working laboratory to practice alchemy. The *last* step would be creating spagyric plant transformations to heal myself both physically and psychologically.

Now that fate had forced my hand, that final step had to jump to the forefront.

I had already found the Elixir of Life, but the elixir is only a small part of alchemy. As I had explained to Brixton, alchemy is about the transformation of the impure into the pure. Transforming lead into gold. Transforming the body to free it from its bonds of mortality. Transforming the spirit into mental well-being.

I had lost sight of myself over the last century. I had been taking care of myself physically, because I could make simple healing foods without thinking. But I wasn't really living. Ever since Ambrose.

Besides my brother, Ambrose was the only person I had ever loved. After Thomas died, it was Ambrose who taught me how to live again. For a while, at least. But that, too, ended in a tragedy I didn't anticipate. Because of me, they had both died painful deaths, alone. How could I have known what Ambrose would do?

But that was all in centuries past. I had been running without looking back for long enough. I felt my gold locket again. The metal was warm from where I wore it close to my heart. The only two people I had ever loved with all my heart were gone. There was nothing I could do about that now. But I could save those I cared about in the present.

I had to have a clean workspace free from distractions before beginning an alchemical transformation. I had never shied away from hard work, so even though I couldn't build a proper lab, I could clean the basement and set up the old alchemy laboratory supplies I'd shipped from Paris. I needed to buy some new materials, but I would be able to do some simple transformations right away.

I hoped.

After I saw Brixton off to school the next morning—listening to him grumble about water torture from the malfunctioning shower—I got to work.

With a combination of vinegar and strength of will, four hours later my basement no longer smelled like a dank moldy brewery. Now it smelled like a fresh-scented brewery. A previous owner must have brewed his own beer down here. I was going to do my own brewing, but not of beer.

Now that the floor was clean, I noticed a scrape running across the center of the large room. Had someone previously built the basement into separate rooms? I thought again of the plans I had wanted Charles Macraith to execute, immediately followed by a pang of guilt. The man was dead. And I didn't know if his death was related to me.

The idea would have been easier to dismiss as paranoia if not for the reaction of other contractors I tried to hire. I was willing to settle for a handyman who could do basic repairs to the roof, broken windows, and pipes. I'd deal with real fixes later. If there was a later.

But as soon as I mentioned the address of the house, everyone I contacted gave excuses for why they couldn't come. They were booked. For how long? For the foreseeable future. They hung up without saying goodbye. One person even had a bout of shingles come on while they were talking on the phone. I knew the economy was doing better, but were they all so worried about the possibility that I was a lunatic murderer that they didn't want such a big job? *Oh.* When I thought of it like that, maybe they were being prudent. It had made the papers that Blue was under suspicion. But Blue Sky Teas was a Portland institution. I, on the other hand, was new in town. The day after I arrived, a man was not only poisoned but stabbed right outside my front door. If I didn't know me, I'd probably run away screaming.

I sighed and took a look at what I'd been able to accomplish on my own in the basement. At least it was no longer a moldy room that reeked of hops so strongly as to overwhelm the senses, I reminded myself.

I had a few more hours before Brixton was due back from school. Enough time to get started.

I've never liked the expression that something you used to do but haven't done in years is "like riding a bike." I didn't learn to ride a bike until I was over one hundred years old, shortly after the miserable contraption was invented. It was called a *velocipede* at the time. And it never came easily to me. Maybe it was because of the discomfort of those first bicycles that didn't have air-pressurized tires, giving them the nickname "bone shakers." Give me a motorcar any day. Now *that* was an invention I related to. I took to driving almost as naturally as I did to plants. I was quite disappointed when speed limits were introduced.

Setting up my alchemy lab turned out to be *exactly* like riding a bike—meaning I completely failed at picking it up again.

Though I didn't have everything I would need for a full laboratory, in theory I had enough to get started. Several glass retorts—long-necked containers that could be heated over a flame and sealed with a stopper—and other glass containers that had survived the journey, including a hermetic vase, skull cup, angel tube, spirit holder, and tomb of the dead. I never said alchemists weren't creative. I was missing an athanor—the furnace Charles Macraith was going to build into the wall below the living room fireplace—and I'd need to restock several ingredients.

When Dorian crept down the stairs to bring me a sandwich, he nearly dropped the plate when he saw me. I didn't blame him. My arms were covered in green sludge. Perhaps the consistency would have been better described as slime. If I thought my creaking old house was actually haunted, I would have sworn a ghost had vomited ectoplasm on me.

"Take a break," Dorian said. "Brixton will return from school soon. I'll keep this sandwich warm in the oven for you. "

After taking a quick, icy shower in the upstairs bathroom that needed plumbing help, I joined Dorian at the dining table. Brixton was already there, inhaling a sandwich.

"Thith ith tho good," Brixton said through a mouthful. "What ith thith?" He swallowed. "I thought Zoe didn't eat meat or cheese."

Dorian grinned and removed my roasted mushroom sandwich with truffle cream from the oven. The cream sauce was made from blended cashews, not dairy, with the mushrooms giving the sandwich its hearty "meaty" texture. It was the same thing Brixton was eating, and it was every bit as good as he said. I hadn't realized how famished I was until I took a bite of the heavenly toasted baguette sandwich.

"Can we go see Blue?" Brixton asked.

Dorian raised an eyebrow at me, then lifted another two un-toasted open-faced sandwich slices into the oven.

"Why don't you give your mom a call," I said, "while I call and see about Blue."

Brixton sat back in his chair and crossed his arms. "The gargoyle has my phone."

"*Mon dieu*," Dorian said. "You may have the phone to call your mother, but I will be watching. *N'est pas?*"

Two minutes later, we all returned to the table, disheartened. Brixton's mom hadn't asked him about Blue during their brief text message conversation. On my end, I was told that the hospital wasn't allowing visitors.

As we ate in moody silence, Dorian threw his hands into the air.

"I cannot stand this!" he said. "If you wish to eat without speaking to savor the flavors I have created, that is one thing. But this? I cannot tolerate such a maudlin mood while eating. I will at least tell you of some interesting news stories I have been reading in *Le Monde*."

"What's *Le Monde*?" Brixton asked.

"You may never have seen one of these before," Dorian said, scampering off his chair and picking up one of the folded newspapers from the far side of the table. "It is called a *newspaper*. A very civilized invention that has neither pop-up ads nor viruses."

Brixton rolled his eyes.

"Listen to this," Dorian said. "Three museums on the continent are reporting that gold pieces from their museums have been switched for fakes! None of them know how the switch was made, but the fakes are crumbling."

"What's 'the continent'?" Brixton asked.

"*Mon dieu*. The European continent. France, Spain, Italy, Portugal, Germany, Luxembourg—"

Brixton grunted a laugh. "You made up that last one."

Dorian sputtered.

"I don't think he's had geography or world history yet," I said.

"Yeah we did."

"You're not helping yourself, Brixton."

"What? I know all about local history. That what's important, isn't it? Did you know there's a wicked series of tunnels that runs under Portland? Mr. Strum took us on a field trip to the Shanghai Tunnels in his class last fall. It was pretty funny, because he had to walk hunched over the whole time; otherwise he'd smack his head on the low beams in the ceiling. He showed us all sorts of hidden areas—that was before the tunnels were boarded up even more and he couldn't take anyone back. We learned all about the history of this place. In the old days, guys who went to bars would be kidnapped and sold to ship captains. It was called Shanghaiing, since they were put on ships headed to Asia. Pretty wicked, huh?"

Dorian gave up at that point. We were done eating anyway.

It was raining again that afternoon, so instead of fitting in weeding first, I sent Brixton upstairs to do his homework, asking him to let me know if he needed any help.

"I know what we must do," Dorian said, speaking quietly so as not to be overheard.

"Brixton is only in ninth grade. It's okay that he hasn't been paying attention in class."

"Not that. I know what we must do as a next step in our investigation."

"What do you mean *our investigation*? There is no *our investigation*."

"Things are moving too slowly."

"I know. That's why I set up my lab. I think it's the last step I need to figure out the riddles of your book. I'm already beginning to remember more."

"And the specific pages from the book? You have had more success translating the pages you have?"

"It's tough without greater context, but I'm getting closer to an overall understanding—"

"It was difficult," Dorian said, "for me to shift from stone to life today." He gave one firm shake of his head. "We can no longer wait for you to see what you can accomplish with only those few pages. *We must find the book.*"

"I can't stand seeing this happen to you, but how do you propose we get it?"

"Blue Sky possessed your other stolen items. Is it not possible the police missed something? They did not know what they were looking for. We must go to Blue's house."

"It's a crime scene, Dorian."

He tapped his claws on the table. "Then we must break in."

FIFTEEN

Getting a closer look at Blue's house was a tempting thought. Tempting, but dangerous. I wasn't into danger these days. I'd had enough of it for many lifetimes.

"I'm not breaking into someone's house," I said.

"Why not?" Dorian asked.

"It being *illegal* is the first thing that springs to mind."

The gargoyle rolled his eyes. "For someone who lives outside of normal society, you have a strange concept of justice."

"I'm not talking about it being *wrong* to break in." I'd lived through the execution of enough unjust laws that "the law" wasn't high on my list of things I respected. "I'm talking about it being risky. I'm trying to stay under the radar."

He squinted at me.

"Oh," I said, "'under the radar' is an idiom that means I don't wish to be detected."

"Ah yes, I understand now. But this is not the time for an English lesson. If we wish to learn what has become of my book, there is much more we must learn of Blue, no?"

"There are other ways."

"Such as?"

"I haven't thought of them yet," I admitted.

"You know why this is so important to me." His eyes bore into me.

"I know, Dorian," I said. "I know."

———

That's how a few hours later I found myself making an energizing chocolate elixir to stay alert in the middle of the night.

"Brixton is getting ready for bed," I said as I came through the kitchen door with a coconut. After dinner I'd made a quick stop at the market for the coconut and checked on Brixton.

Dorian was finishing cleaning up the kitchen after the three-course dinner he'd cooked us—a potato mushroom soup starter, a pumpkin loaf crusted with poppy seeds as the main dish, and a bed of arugula with fennel and orange for the third course. Brixton had eaten everything except the fennel, which he refused to taste. I thought the licorice flavor of fennel would appeal to him, but not so much. He'd accepted a lot that week. I wasn't going to push.

During dinner that night, Brixton had continued to ask intelligent questions about alchemy. He was understandably confused about what was real and what wasn't, due to pop culture's treatment of alchemy that gave it magical properties. The more answers I gave him, the more questions he had. That was alchemy.

Once Dorian finished washing the dishes, he untied the apron from around his waist and hung it on the door hook. "I do not understand why we cannot make the boy a dessert and add something to it that will *help* him sleep while we are out tonight."

"I'm *not* drugging Brixton," I said emphatically.

"It would be safer."

"I draw the line at drugging a kid." I slammed a butcher's knife into the fresh young coconut, splitting the thick white husk on the first try. Two more firm pounds with the edge of the knife and I had a triangular hole in the coconut.

Cutting into a coconut is daunting if you're not used to it, but coconut was an important part of the energizing elixir that helped keep me awake when I had to be up well past dark. Being alert during the middle of the night was nearly impossible for me. My only chance at being coherent was natural sugars and fats with a little bit of caffeine.

"Now that you have successfully massacred the coconut," Dorian said, "you should place it in the fridge."

"I need to drink this before we go."

"How long does it last? We should not venture out until after midnight."

"After *midnight*?" I set down the knife. "Can't we go earlier?"

He shook his head resolutely.

———

I stayed awake by again looking through the pages of Dorian's book, this time hoping the mental preparation of setting up an alchemy lab was enough to spark further understanding.

I paused on a woodcut showing a menagerie of animals. At the bottom of the illustration, the land was covered with toads, symbolizing the First Matter. Yet even in the still illustration, the toads were clearly dead. In the sky above, bees swarmed, symbolizing purification and rebirth. The carving alluded to motion, showing the wind pushing the bees in a counterclockwise direction, pushing them toward the earth.

The stress of not understanding, while knowing what was at stake, did a decent job keeping me awake. Still, I felt myself fading. Midnight might not be a bewitching hour, but it effectively turns me into a pumpkin.

At a few minutes to midnight, I grabbed a jar of unsweetened cocoa powder from the cabinet and scooped a few tablespoons into the blender, scraped vanilla paste from a vanilla pod I kept in a glass jar, added the coconut meat and liquid from the fruit I'd split open earlier, and blended the mixture. I offered half to Dorian. He politely declined.

Before we left, I walked by Brixton's room, trying not to make too much noise on the creaking floor. I could see through the one-inch space between the door and the floor that his light was off.

We drove my truck to an isolated field near Blue's house. Dorian took my hand to lead me through the field. His eyes were able to see in the dark much better than mine, so it allowed us to move without a flashlight.

"Is that it?" I asked, pointing to a house blanketed in shadows.

"Yes," Dorian agreed, "I can see the police tape."

We had reached the edge of a growth of trees but were still at least fifty yards from the storybook cottage. I hadn't had much time to study the yard the first time I'd visited. Now that my eyes had adjusted to the moonlight, I couldn't help noticing some of the more interesting plants. Caught up in the bounty surrounding me, I lost sight of Dorian.

I whipped my head around. I didn't see him. Some of the weeds grew higher than three feet, so he could have been anywhere in the field.

"Dorian," I whispered.

He didn't answer, but I heard a click. I followed the sound. He had just opened the front door.

I hurried to the door, following Dorian inside and closing it behind us.

Unlike the wild nature of the outside of the house, the inside of the cottage was well maintained. In the kitchen, colorful hand-crafted dishes filled open cabinets. The remnants of dried herbs hung from hooks on the ceiling. The police must have taken the rest as evidence.

One thing was lacking from the house: photographs. I wondered at first if it was the police who had taken the photos as evidence, until I saw that there were a few photos on a bookshelf. One was a photo of Blue with a younger Brixton. I didn't recognize the people in the other photos, but they all had Portland backdrop. There was no evidence of Blue's life before she moved here. *The life she'd been running from.*

I took a step from the dining room bookshelf into the living room. This was the room I'd seen from the window. The room where Blue's unconscious body had been. As my foot touched the carpet, the sensation hit me like a gust of cold air. Only there were no doors or windows open.

"What is it?" Dorian asked.

"There's poison here," I murmured. I crouched down. "The glass has been removed, but some of the contents spilled onto the rug here."

"What are you doing?" Dorian exclaimed. "We are not looking for poison. We are looking for my book!"

Ignoring Dorian, I touched the moist rug and smelled my fingertips. I felt a shiver spread from my fingers to the rest of my body. Something was wrong. This wasn't a concoction infused with Blue's personal touch. More than that, *it was something reminiscent of alchemy*.

I stood up hastily, knocking over a small wooden table.

"Are you well?" Dorian asked.

"We need to get out of here."

"What is wrong?"

"This isn't something Blue created," I said. "I'm sensitive to the energies put into extracting plant essences, and Blue's energy isn't here."

"What does that mean?"

"This was no accident. And no suicide attempt."

"Who made it?"

"All I can tell from this small amount is that it was deliberate poisoning. Someone tried to kill her." I didn't say the question hanging on my lips. The question that sent a lightning-bolt shiver through me. *Was this the work of an alchemist?*

Dorian's head darted around. His eyes locked on a box of tissue across the room. He moved quickly. A few seconds later, he took my hand in his, wiping away the drops of poison with half of the tissues in the box.

I smiled at the gesture. "I can feel it through my skin because I'm attuned to it, but it's not going to poison me this way." I hesitated. "At least I don't think so." I could handle toxins, as all alchemists must if they wish to perform laboratory experiments beyond theoretical exercises. But this was different. There was something both strange and familiar about it. I tried to think what it could be, but there wasn't enough of the substance remaining.

"*Mon dieu.*"

"We need to leave so I can tell Max that Blue is innocent."

Dorian crossed his arms and glared at me. "You cannot think you are getting involved in a *police* investigation. *Les flics* cannot help us."

"It's all connected, Dorian. If we find out what happened to Blue, we find your book. Max seems like a good guy."

"You propose," Dorian said stiffly, "waking him up at two o'clock in the morning, telling him you broke into a crime scene, and explaining how you detected that Blue herself did not create the poison she ingested. You are not that careless."

My body began to shake. What was going on?

"You are ill!" Dorian said. "Do you know what poison it was you touched? Is there an antidote?"

I shook my head as I sat down on the couch and pulled a small purple blanket over me. "I'm only shivering because it's cold and it's hours past when I should be sound asleep." I silently cursed myself. Of course a poison would have a greater effect on me in the middle of the night! Like plants unfurling, I get my strength from the light. I had never before touched a poisonous substance after dark.

"But the poison?"

I shook my head again. "I can't tell what it is. There isn't enough here in the rug for me to determine what it is or who made it." There was another possibility that I hoped wasn't true. I had pushed my memories of alchemy so far to the back of my mind. Was it possible I could no longer access the knowledge?

"Your skin is pale."

"I'm fine."

"Can you walk?"

"Yes. Just give me a minute."

"*Merde*. You sit here while I search the yard for anywhere my book could be hidden."

"I told you—"

"Yes, yes. You are fine. *Mais non*. Take a nap here on the couch while I search outside. I will return shortly."

Shortly after Dorian slipped out the door, I felt myself falling asleep. I hopped up. If I went to sleep now, I wouldn't want to wake up. Instead, I pulled the blanket around me and continued searching Blue's house for anything the police might have missed. I didn't have high hopes. Now that I was certain Blue hadn't poisoned herself on purpose, it was clear she was being framed. The person framing her would have left the stolen items where they would be easily discovered. Meaning Charles Macraith's murderer must still have Dorian's book. What did they want with it? And was that all they wanted?

Dorian returned while I was finishing leafing through the books on Blue's bookshelf, which was full of books on tea, wildcrafting, meditation, plus several dozen romance novels. Dorian's expression was somber.

"I didn't find anything either," I said.

We walked back to the car in silence. The cold chilled me to the point where I began to shake again.

"What you need is a bisque to warm you up," Dorian said. "I have a container of broth in your fridge, so it will take no time to cook."

I was too cold and tired to argue. I blasted the heat on our drive back to the house. There was no rain, but the wind was whipping up leaves and bending tree branches.

At first, that's what I thought I was seeing as I approached the house. As we grew closer, I realized I was mistaken. It wasn't swaying tree branches in my yard.

Two shadowy figures were creeping up to the house.

SIXTEEN

I KILLED THE ENGINE before we reached the driveway.

"You saw the shadows too," Dorian said.

"We never should have left Brixton there alone," I said, hastily throwing off my seatbelt and reaching for the door handle. "At the very least I should have insisted you give him back his cell phone you confiscated!"

Dorian's firm hand gripped my arm. "Go. I will hide, but I will be near in case you and the boy need me."

My earlier feelings of exhaustion and cold disappeared, replaced with adrenaline as I crept up the side of the yard. What was going on? Charles Macraith was dead and Dorian's book was gone. What could the thief and murderer want with my house?

The two figures were dressed in black. Hooded sweatshirts covered the backs of their heads. One was tall and thin, the other short with an average build. Neither was very large. I had learned different schools of self-defense moves over the years, but hadn't put any into practice in decades. If I had to use any now, I might be rusty but at least I had a fighting chance.

The figures had almost reached the porch.

I followed at a distance, walking up to the house along the side of the fence rather than the main path. There was nothing shielding me from their line of sight. If they turned, they would see me. It was a risk, but I had no choice.

The porch light clicked on. I cursed under my breath. Brixton was exactly the type of kid who'd take it upon himself to investigate if he heard strange noises. That didn't surprise me. But his next move did. The front door eased open. *What was Brixton doing?*

Brixton motioned the figures inside. When the taller figure stepped forward, I caught a glimpse of the face beneath the hooded sweatshirt. It was Brixton's friend Veronica.

I couldn't see the face of the other figure, but he was the right stature to be their friend Ethan.

Confusion replaced my apprehension. I briefly considered joining them before the front door closed behind them but thought better of it. Whatever they were doing, they were unlikely to tell me about it if I asked them directly.

"Dorian," I whispered. "Are you here?"

He wasn't.

A light clicked on inside the living room. I crept to one of the large windows. The curtains were drawn, as I'd been careful to do because of Dorian. I couldn't see or hear anything.

I hurried to the back door that led to the kitchen. I opened it as quickly as I could, but it gave a shrill squeak. I stopped and waited. I heard young voices trying to whisper but failing and speaking animatedly instead. They hadn't heard me. I closed the door behind me and went to the swinging kitchen door, the exact place from which Brixton had eavesdropped on me and Dorian. Between the swinging door and the door frame, there was a half-inch gap through which I could see a section of the dining and living rooms.

"You begin with *mise en place*," a voice said.

I froze. It was *Dorian's* voice.

I peeked through the door. Dorian was nowhere in sight. Brixton was holding up a cell phone—a different model from the one Dorian had confiscated. The voice was coming from the phone.

Foiled from getting a video recording of the gargoyle, Brixton had recorded Dorian's voice.

It all made sense now. It had been far too easy to get Brixton to accept that Dorian's existence needed to be a secret. He hadn't accepted it at all. He was pretending to befriend the gargoyle so he could prove to his friends that Dorian existed.

Anger bubbled up inside me. Brixton was old enough that he should have thought about the consequences of his actions. Watching him and his friends through my hiding place, I had to stop myself from bursting through the door. Before confronting Brixton, I needed a plan.

Brixton stopped the recording. "I told you," he said to his friends.

"So what?" Ethan said. "You've got an audio recording of a guy with a French accent."

"That's why I invited you here," Brixton said. "I thought he'd be here, near the fireplace. That's where he was earlier. But he's a creature of the night. He must have gone out."

"A creature of the night?" Veronica said. "Like a vampire?"

"Yeah, except vampires aren't real. The gargoyle is real."

"So we wait," Ethan said. "I brought snacks." He spread out on the couch and tossed a bag of pretzels in gourmet packaging onto the coffee table.

Veronica tore into the bag. "No chocolate?"

"Keep it down, you guys," Brixton said. "I don't know how soundly Zoe sleeps."

My anger barely contained, I slipped out the back door and circled to the front of the house. Giving up any pretense of being quiet, I shoved my key into the door and opened it.

Veronica screamed and dropped the bag of pretzels.

"Slumber party?" I asked.

"Zoe?" Brixton croaked. "What are you—I mean, I thought you were asleep."

"I stepped out to visit a friend. Sorry, if I'd known you were going to be up, I would have left you a note."

"Sorry about your floor, Ms. Faust," Veronica said, picking up broken pretzel fragments.

"Please, call me Zoe. Don't you guys have school tomorrow?"

"Group research project, Zoe," Ethan said. He was the only one still sitting calmly. He'd made himself comfortable on the couch. He leaned forward with his elbows resting on his knees, an easy smile on his face.

"Research, huh? Anything I can help with?" I looked pointedly at Brixton.

"Uh, yeah, we're just about done."

"Since you've been working so hard, let me get you all a proper snack."

I led them to the kitchen and removed a chocolate cake from the fridge. Dorian had made it the day before while I was working in my makeshift alchemy lab. He was cooking more food than the two of us could eat and had used up most of the food in my pantry. The last of the cashews had gone into making the creamy frosting for the cake.

Veronica's eyes grew wide.

"You like dark chocolate?" I asked.

She nodded, hungrily eyeing the frosted cake. I took plates from the cabinet and let the kids cut whatever size pieces they wanted. Veronica took the largest piece, which made me smile.

"Omigod," she said, closing her eyes and savoring the mouthful. "I think this is like the best cake I've ever eaten, Ms. Faust."

Brixton took a bite of cake while sulking silently in the corner.

"So, Zoe," Ethan said, eyeing me and leaving his cake untouched, "you were out visiting a 'friend' in the middle of the night."

Veronica kicked him.

"He's a Frenchman," I said, following through on my idea to disabuse them of the notion that I had a French gargoyle in my house. "The French enjoy late dinners. I drank wine, so I had to wait a while before it was safe for me to drive home."

"You have a French boyfriend?" Veronica said. "That's so romantic! I've always wanted to go to Paris. Is he from Paris?"

"He's from Paris," I said, thinking about the other stone gargoyles carved by Eugène Viollet-le-Duc. "But he's just a friend."

"A *gargoyle*, huh?" Ethan said to Brixton.

"What's that, Ethan?" I said in my most innocent voice.

Brixton glared at me.

"Brixton," Ethan said, "was telling us all about your French friend. Weren't you, Brix?"

"Shut up and try the cake, Ethan," Brixton said.

With a smirk on his face, Ethan took a bite of cake. His expression changed. "Wow, that *is* good. Is this from Petunia's?"

"It's homemade," I said.

"Nice," Ethan said.

A creaking noise sounded.

"I'll be right back," I said. "I don't remember if I locked the front door."

I looked around and didn't see Dorian. It was probably the wind trying to get through one of the broken windows or drafty doors. I double-checked that I'd locked up. Everything seemed in place.

I paused before returning to the kitchen. I could hear Veronica speaking to the boys.

"You're such a jerk!" she said. "Calling Zoe's boyfriend a gargoyle. Is he disfigured, or just ugly? No, he couldn't be ugly. He's French."

I smiled to myself and pushed open the kitchen door.

"I love your dyed white hair," Veronica said. "The short, slanted bob is very Parisian."

"Like you'd know," Brixton said.

"This has been fun, Zoe," Ethan said. "But like you said, it's a school night. We should go."

"Thanks, Ms. Faust," Veronica said. She smiled awkwardly at me before shooting Brixton a dirty look, presumably still upset that she thought he'd come up with a nasty nickname for my romantic French boyfriend.

"Maybe we could meet your *friend* some other time," Ethan said. *Think, Zoe.* "He's shy. He's self-conscious about a nasty scar. People in America are less accepting than they are in France." *Ugh.* It was an awkward lie, but something had to be done.

"You are *such* a jerk," Veronica whispered to Brixton. He glared at me.

I held open the kitchen door. "Let me drive you home."

"They've got their bikes," Brixton said.

"They'll fit in the back of the truck."

"Um," Veronica said, "I'm not really supposed to be out this late."

"I won't wake up your parents," I promised. "We won't all fit in the cab of the truck, so Brixton, you can clean the dishes while I'm gone. We're not done. I'll be right back."

I shivered as I walked back out into the night. Now that my adrenaline had worn off, I could feel an unwelcome substance coursing through my veins.

———

After dropping off Veronica and Ethan, I found a sulking teenager and a gargoyle waiting for me in the living room. My body shook more from anger than the residual effects of the poison.

"He wouldn't let me go to bed," Brixton said. "That's child abuse."

"I thought you said you weren't a child," I said.

He glared at me.

"You betrayed us, Brixton," I said, glaring back at him. "To say I'm disappointed in you doesn't convey the gravity of what you've done. Don't you realize what could happen to Dorian if anyone found out he existed?"

Brixton didn't answer. He turned his glare from me to his feet.

"People might lock him up, caging him like an animal to study him," I continued. "Is that what you want?"

"They can't do that, can they?" Brixton asked, looking from me to Dorian. "He's, like, a real person. That's not what I—You know I don't want that."

"Do I?"

"I didn't mean anything by it! V and Ethan didn't believe me. I just wanted them to believe me."

"Do not be too hard on the boy," Dorian said. "His wish to be understood is only natural. No harm was done. I thank you for your quick-thinking explanation about a French friend."

"Can I go upstairs now?" Brixton mumbled.

"This is serious!" I ran my hands through my hair and tried to calm down. A small clump came out in my hands. It must have been the poison. Fear gripped me. Had I been affected more than I thought? I couldn't seem to shake the chill that was now covering every inch of my body. This was no place for Brixton. Why had I agreed to let him stay with me?

"I get it!" he said. "You won. Now V thinks I'm a loser who makes fun of disabled people. You can stop yelling."

"This isn't about winning! And this isn't just about Dorian. We're on your side, trying to help you."

He stopped glaring for a fraction of a second, but the expression returned a moment later. "By having my friends think I'm a jerk?"

"By finding out what happened to Blue."

"What are you talking about?"

"Why do you think I was out in the middle of the night? Do you know how hard it is for an alchemist to be awake when the sun isn't? We were investigating at Blue's house. That's what we were doing tonight."

"Really? You went to Blue's cottage?"

"Past the crime scene tape," Dorian said.

"You found something the police missed? Something that will help Blue?"

"I think so," I said. "We're working on it."

"Did you tell Detective Liu?"

I glanced at Dorian. "It's complicated."

"Everything is always complicated! Why can't people just say what they mean?"

"I wish it was that simple."

"Whatever." He stomped up the rickety stairs so hard that I half-expected one of them to break.

"Let him go," Dorian said. "He will feel calmer in the morning. Those friends of his are a good influence."

"I'm guessing you heard them say they liked your cake."

"*Oui.* If you would be so kind as to obtain oat flour, almonds, cashews, and fine quality cocoa powder, I shall fix a new chocolate dessert for Veronica tomorrow."

I eyed the gargoyle.

"We failed at locating my book," he said. "While you work in your alchemy lab and on the pages you photographed, I wish to stay busy so I do not disturb you. I know you will do what you can."

I looked from my crates stacked in the corner to the bowed stairs before turning back to Dorian's resigned eyes. I'd come to care for the creature. I didn't want him to die—or to suffer the fate worse than death that awaited him, being awake but trapped inside a body of unmoving stone.

If I was being truthful with myself, my selfish side liked having someone around with whom I could be my true self. My moral compass also didn't like the idea of someone getting away with murder and framing Blue.

All those thoughts flitted through my brain without a lot of coherency. My teeth continued to chatter in the drafty house. Between my anger, fear, chill, being awake in the middle of the night, and the poison, I was in bad shape. I was certain I would wake up with the sun, but at least I could get a few hours of sleep before then. That would help my body heal itself.

To come and go as he pleased during the night, Dorian had discovered he could use the hole in the roof that was covered with a tarp. The hole wasn't big enough for a person to get through, but the small gargoyle could easily maneuver through it and tie the tarp back into place.

I wrapped a blanket around me and went into the kitchen. To cleanse the toxins from my body after touching the unknown poison, I made myself a dandelion root tea. With the warm mug in one hand, I walked through the drafty house, making sure the doors and windows were locked. I clicked off the porch light and the other lights downstairs, pausing in front of the living room bay windows to straighten the curtains. The lights were now off inside, so nobody could see in. But I could see out.

A streetlight halfway down the block cast faint light on the front part of my yard near the street. A moving shadow caught my eye. Not only because it was the middle of the night, but because of where the figure was. It didn't appear on the sidewalk or the street; the shadow flitted across the fence inside my yard.

I gripped the edge of the curtain as my eyes followed the figure. Dorian was already outside, but this figure was the wrong shape to be Dorian. It was the shape of a human. Should I venture outside? If I did, I could see who it was, but they might be dangerous and then I'd be leaving Brixton exposed.

Before I could act, the decision was made for me. As my fingers closed more tightly over the curtain, the figure vanished. I shook my head. People don't just vanish. The person must have disappeared from my line of sight. That was all. Most of the yard was bathed in darkness.

Veronica and Ethan were safely at home, so it couldn't have been either of them. *So who—or what—was it?*

SEVENTEEN

I WOKE UP NOT with a start but with a groan. I'd slept on the living room couch. After seeing the shadow lurking around the house the previous night, I'd added an extra layer of protection to the house. I fished through my crates for a string of bells from Morocco. I separated the bells and placed them in front of the front and back doors. Several windows were effectively locked by virtue of being rusted shut, so I only tied bells to the latches of the ground floor windows that could be opened.

"What is the purpose of the bells?" a deep voice asked. "And for you sleeping on the couch?" Dorian sat in front of the fireplace a few feet away from me.

"It's creepy to find you hovering while I sleep," I said, stretching. My body ached more than I expected from the couch. It was the poison I'd touched.

"You are the one who is not in your proper bed."

"I don't like how we don't know what's going on. With Brixton staying with us, I wanted to add an extra layer of security." I omitted the fact that I'd seen someone lurking outside the house. Part of me wasn't sure I'd seen anything. The poison had affected me more than I wanted to admit.

"Why do you not call a security company?"

"I tried that already. They all said the house needs to be fixed up first. It has too many loose parts, so I'd get too many false alarms."

"*Mon dieu.*"

"Agreed. And none of the home renovators will call me back after what happened to Charles Macraith."

"How odd."

"Not really," I said. "They probably think I'm a murderer."

"*C'est vrai?*"

"Yes, unfortunately I think it's true." Though as I spoke the words, I realized it *was* strange that the people I'd called got skittish as soon as I said the address, but not for the reason I'd originally considered. Even if people didn't like the idea of working for a possible murderess, *how did they know*? It wasn't as if I was only calling contractors who frequented Blue Sky Teas or who lived in my neighborhood.

I shook off the disconcerting feeling. The murder had taken place only days ago. The address could have been reported on the news. That must have been it. Still, I couldn't shake the feeling I was missing something.

I hadn't heard any of my makeshift alarm bells during the night. Dorian followed me through the house as I checked that all of them were in place and the house was secure. I picked up the bells and put them in a basket on the mantle. Now the decorative tin bells looked like a piece of home decor, not a burglar alarm. No need to unnecessarily worry Brixton. Even though I was still mad about what he'd done, I wanted to protect him from what was going on, both physically and emotionally.

In spite of only sleeping for a few hours, my mind was alert. I watered my herb garden in the kitchen window box. The two mint varieties had grown a few inches in as many days. They liked their new home. In spite of the pressures weighing on me, so did I. After drinking a cup of lemon tea, I hopped into the shower, cursing as the water alternated between glacially cold and blisteringly hot, as usual. It did nothing for my aching muscles.

Being in the sun would help, but Brixton would be up for school shortly, so I couldn't go far. I took my laptop to the back porch to look up a few more ideas about Dorian's book. When I sat down on the rickety back steps, the sun was poking through the clouds at the same time that a light mist fell from the sky. As I hit another dead end in my research, the light rain turned into a full-blown down-pour. It was time to go inside anyway. I found Dorian and Brixton sitting at the dining table, which was covered with enough food to feed half a dozen people.

"The boy has apologized," Dorian said.

"Yeah," Brixton mumbled, speaking to the table. "It was stupid. I see that now."

"You understand you can't ever let anyone know about Dorian," I said.

Brixton's hazel eyes met mine. Instead of the defiance I had so often seen in his eyes, I saw humility. "I promise."

"*Bon*," Dorian said. "Help yourself to food, Zoe."

"Crepes?" I asked, looking at the spread of thin folded pancakes.

"*Galettes*, to be precise," Dorian said, looking up from *Le Monde*, "because they are made of buckwheat. These are a specialty from the Brittany region of France."

"You should try one, Zoe," Brixton said. "They're wicked. The filling is mushroom. I used to hate mushrooms, so I think Dorian is magic. I mean, he *is* kind of magic, right? There's no other way these would taste so good."

"I didn't think it was possible to get these so thin without an egg batter," I said, scooping one of the buckwheat crepes onto my plate.

"Silken tofu is an amazing invention," Dorian said, a pleased look on his face.

"There's tofu in here?" Brixton said, stopping mid-bite and eyeing the gooey crepe suspiciously.

"*Pardon*, I misspoke. It was not tofu used for the *galettes*. For these buckwheat crepes, I soaked freshly ground flax seeds in a warm water to replicate the properties of the egg. The tofu was used in my chocolate cake."

"There's *tofu* in the cake?" Brixton repeated.

"*Mon dieu*. Here, let me read you news for the day. The European gold thefts are spreading. There are no leads. The thieves are clever. They also have a flair for the dramatic. They continue to leave crumbling imitation-gold statues and gold dust in place of the gold items they are stealing."

The way Dorian spoke of the crumbled gold made the thefts sound much more ominous than they must have been. The little gargoyle had a flair for the dramatic himself. A sense of unease crept up my spine as he recounted the news.

"You're going to be late for school, Brixton," I said. "It's raining too hard for you to take your bike. I'll drive you to school."

On the way home after dropping Brixton off at the high school, I passed the teashop. I had expected it to be closed. Not only was it open, but people poured out into the street. Blue was in a coma, so of course people would flock to the store. I should have expected it. Morbid curiosity no longer surprised me.

People would say the right things—that they were there to support the shop and to come together to offer each other a shoulder to cry on—but I knew the truth. I'd seen the crowds that flocked to the town square back when there were public executions. When murder and mayhem could be observed at a safe distance, people wouldn't miss an opportunity to be there.

But who had opened the teashop?

Instead of driving on, I found myself pulling over and walking through the melee into the shop. I was human, too. I was curious. I suppose it was human nature drawing us all to the teashop.

It was crowded enough that nobody noticed me. Stepping into the line that was six people long, I caught a glimpse of Olivia. Though she was tiny, it was impossible to miss her in the deep red shawl draped around her shoulders. The gossip who had brought me tea now stood behind the counter, taking orders herself.

I caught snatches of conversation from various people, most of whom were talking about Blue, but a few seemed not to know who owned the teashop. They were drawn in by the presence of a crowd, and I heard them asking their friends what it was about this shop that made it so popular.

When I reached the counter, Olivia took my order before waving to a woman sitting at a table near the counter. It was the redhead I'd spoken to when she manned the counter two days before. The woman excused herself from her conversation and stepped behind the counter while Olivia made my ginger tea. Again I was struck by the fact that the woman looked like she had been crying. She covered it up well, but the signs were there.

"This place is claustrophobic," Olivia said, handing me the tea in a to-go cup. "Cora can cover while we go to the hospital to see Blue."

"Are they allowing visitors now?"

"Not that I've heard. That doesn't mean she won't feel our presence nearby. I've spent more time than I'd care to think about in the hospital. It's not the visit as much as it is knowing that someone was there to see you. I thought we could pick up some flowers for her."

"That's a lovely idea," I said, thinking I'd misjudged Olivia. "I'm surprised this place is open. I didn't know anyone else worked here."

"Sam works here part-time during the peak afternoon tea-time hours, after he's done teaching for the day." Olivia took her coat and purse from behind the counter. "It's charity, of course."

I gave her a questioning look.

"Blue doesn't really need help most of the time." She led us through the shop, maneuvering through the crowd. "When Sam and I were having trouble paying our bills, after my illness made me too sick to work, Blue offered him the job, even though it was a stretch for Blue to pay him as generously as she did."

We reached the sidewalk and Olivia kept right on talking without missing a beat. "Sam teaches during the day, so he can't be here now. It's the least I can do to help the teashop make money while Blue can't be here. Who knows what kind of medical bills she'll have. Health care costs are exorbitant these days. We can stop at the corner shop to pick out flowers. Over-priced, but quite skillfully prepared. They'd better be, at those prices! And where is your car parked?"

It took me a moment to realize she'd stopped talking.

"My car is right over here." I pointed at my truck.

Olivia frowned disapprovingly at my lovingly up-kept truck. I reminded myself to feel more charitable toward her. Underneath her faults, she was a good person, helping keep open the teashop to help Blue. Or had she opened it because she wanted everyone to gather there and gossip? I tried not to be cynical.

We picked out an assortment of white flowers that Olivia insisted upon, but let me pay for, before getting into the car.

Olivia frowned again as I revved the engine. It was in perfect condition, but wasn't as silent as modern engines. She pointed me in the direction I should drive, then shook her head as I pulled into traffic. If Olivia wasn't going to hide her feelings, I might as well take advantage of the opportunity to learn something useful.

"The police aren't telling me anything," I said. "You seem to know everyone here. You must have had people open up to you about it. What do you think is going on?" A little flattery never hurt.

Out of my peripheral vision I saw her frown change to a sly smile.

"I thought it was *you* who would know more, my dear. The Taylor boy is staying at your house, is he not?"

"Brixton?"

"And what kind of a name is that? Heather has damaged that boy in so many ways. It's too late for him."

"He's only fourteen."

"He's already been arrested for assault."

My hands tensed on the steering wheel. Blue had said he'd been in trouble before. But in trouble with the law? Assault?

"Oh, you didn't know?" Olivia's smile widened.

I was almost afraid to ask. "What happened?"

"I'll spare you the details, but he's a violent child. I thought it wise you should be warned, since you're vulnerable alone with him in that big house of yours."

"Why did you think Brixton would know what's going on? You don't seriously think he had anything to do with Charles Macraith's death?" Brixton may have been making my life difficult by trying to show the world Dorian existed, but I couldn't imagine him hurting anyone.

"I wouldn't put it past him. But that's not what I meant. That boy is always sticking his nose where it doesn't belong." Olivia paused and pointed. "Turn here."

"You were saying?" I prompted, hoping we had a little more time before we reached the hospital.

"Wisdom comes with age. You wouldn't understand this yet, dear. I've tried to counsel Brixton's mother Heather to improve herself and the life of her boy. And I tried to stop her from marrying her deadbeat husband."

"I haven't met him."

"You wouldn't have. He's never here. Some people, there's no reasoning with."

"What do you mean he's never here?"

"He disappears for long periods of time."

"And you don't know why?"

"I'm not one to gossip."

"Of course not."

"Now *Charles*," Olivia said, "he was a better father figure to Brixton. I would often see him helping the boy with his studies. He was the most sensible of the lot of them. Brixton's mother thinks my nephew Sam is a good influence, but I don't buy it. Sam was too lazy to finish a PhD. Instead of being a true historian, he's teaching history to children at the high school! That's why he can't afford a place of his own and has to live with me. What kind of message does that send? Turn again here, dear."

"Mmm hmm," I murmured, following her directions.

"I wish my friend Ivan were a better role model. Did I introduce you to him? Oh yes, the other day at the teashop. That's a man who was a scholar during his time. A prominent chemistry professor. But he doesn't take care of himself. He has health issues but won't look into finding a cure. I don't understand that man. I tell you, I don't understand any of them. *Men.*"

EIGHTEEN

AT THE HOSPITAL, WE weren't allowed to see Blue or even leave her flowers. We were told her condition hadn't changed; she was still in a coma but stable. Olivia insisted on taking the flowers home with her so the beautiful bouquet "wouldn't go to waste."

Olivia asked to be dropped off at her house, a Craftsman in an East Portland neighborhood not far from mine. Though a similar style to mine, her house was half the size, but in much better condition. Barren rose bushes lined the small yard in front of the porch. I imagined that in the springtime they would match the pink shutters. It was walking distance to Blue Sky Teas, and Olivia said she wanted to eat lunch before returning to the teashop.

"Blue's healthy pastries will be good for another day or so," she said, "but I don't enjoy the taste of sawdust."

"They can't be that bad."

"I gave you fair warning."

I was again curious about how bad Blue's cooking could possibly be, but I didn't have time to find out. Brixton would be home from school in a few hours, which gave me enough time to try another experiment in the basement. I was still holding out hope that by going through the motions my subconscious would kick in and I'd remember the important subtleties of alchemy I learned long ago, helping me see what I was missing in the coded illustrations and text of Dorian's book.

As soon as I came through the front door, planning on heading straight to the basement, I was accosted by a frantic gargoyle.

"Where were you? I was worried."

"I went to see Blue at the hospital."

"You left only to take Brixton to school. I thought you would be returning home presently."

I'd been on my own for so long that it hadn't occurred to me anyone would be worried about me. "I'm so sorry," I said. I'd been pushing people away for so long that this was a big adjustment. Attachments were too painful. But along with the pain, I'd lost sight of the joy they could bring.

He sniffed. "I used up the last of the fresh vegetables cooking us lunch. You will need to buy more food before you resume work in your alchemy lab."

"Ah," I said. "That's why you missed me."

"The provider of food is a very important role." He sniffed. "As is the chef."

With that, he returned to the kitchen. I followed behind to see what he was making. He'd cooked a fresh loaf of bread to accompany a roasted beet soup. I often made a pureed beet soup in the blender, but Dorian's stove-top version was a combination of chunks of seasoned beets and other root vegetables floating in a creamy broth. The attention to detail in the small touches in the meal assured me that Dorian's transformation back into stone wasn't progressing more quickly. We had at least a little bit of time. I hoped.

After lunch and a quick trip to the market, I took a few deep breaths and walked down the stairs to the basement.

The French cooking idea of *mise en place*, where you set up all your ingredients and tools before starting to cook a meal, also applies to alchemy. Even without a proper lab set up, it was important to locate the tools and measure the ingredients. Glass vessels, a stone mortar and pestle, herbs I'd dried myself, and pure alcohol. It wasn't much, but it would do for now.

Dorian poked his head in the door. "We are out of coconut sugar again," he said.

"Already?"

"I know you are busy. You can buy more at your earliest convenience."

That gargoyle was going to send us to the poor house. If it wasn't such a draining process, there was no question that I would have worked on turning metal into gold as my foray back into alchemy.

For now, I returned to a basic plant alchemy transformation. I used a mortar and pestle to grind the dried herb, mixing in a rhythmic, clockwise circle. As soon as I mixed the herbs and alcohol together, the concoction began to steam. That *wasn't* what was supposed to happen. I knew what must have happened. In all my efforts to clean up the basement itself, I hadn't cleaned the mortar and pestle. It was a stupid mistake. One I never would have made before. I couldn't remember what I had last ground with it. The contents of the steaming jar began to bubble.

This couldn't be good.

The mixture exploded from its glass jar, showering me with *gray* slime this time.

"*Mais non!*" a voice called out from the stairs. "What has happened?"

I wiped gray slime from my lips. "I told you not to disturb me until it was time for me to pick up Brixton from school."

"It is time. You are going to be late."

I could have sworn only thirty minutes had passed, not three hours.

"This is part of alchemy?" Dorian asked skeptically. "Turning yourself gray is correct?"

———

Half an hour later, Brixton voiced a similar question.

"What happened to you?" he asked as he climbed into the truck.

I hadn't had time to shower to get rid of all the slime. I thought I'd gotten most of it with a wet washcloth. Apparently not.

"I forgot to put the lid on the blender," I said.

"You're making *gray* smoothies now? There's no way I'm trying one of those."

Brixton knew I was using my skills in an attempt to figure out the poison used on Blue, so we could save her and clear her. But I was shielding him from the reason I was setting up a complete alchemy lab. I didn't want to burden Brixton with the knowledge that someone else was dying, and that I needed to solve the riddle of *Not Untrue Alchemy* to save Dorian's life. Worrying about Blue was enough for him.

Brixton had convinced Dorian to let him use his phone for short interludes while the gargoyle watched him, and Brixton had started calling the hospital to check on Blue's condition. That made it clear how important it was to him, because the thought of speaking to someone on the phone, rather than texting them, horrified him. He knew she was still in critical condition, still in a coma.

While Brixton devoured the desserts Dorian had been baking, I headed to the bathroom to get rid of the remaining gray slime. I was nearly as good as new when I joined Brixton and Dorian downstairs. I smiled at the sight of the two of them at the dining table.

The thick wooden table was something I'd found in the south of France in the late 1860s. It wasn't practical by any stretch of the imagination, even at the time. I knew I would only be in the village for a few years, until it was obvious I wasn't aging. I'd learned that it was easiest to live as simply as possible. The less baggage—both emotional and physical—made it easier to move on. But living without attachments also took its toll.

The local man who built the table was a true artist and also a struggling widower with four small children. I didn't have the money to pay what the table was worth, so for more than a month I went through the draining process of creating gold. By the time two full moons had come and gone, I hadn't yet transmuted enough lead into gold. I must have looked as tired as I felt, because the town took up a collection to send for a doctor to attend to me. I was so touched that I paid everyone back twofold with gold. With the renewed energy their generosity had given me, I was able to transform the largest amount of lead I'd ever turned to gold. I paid the craftsman more than he was asking for the table. It's one of the most beautiful pieces of furniture I've ever owned. I kept in touch with his daughter for many years. After I had to leave, we kept up a correspondence of letters until she passed away from old age. I would have liked to have seen her again, but there was no way I could have let her see me. The table was one of the special items I kept in my storage collection.

Brixton had an algebra textbook in front of him on the hundred-year-old table.

"Can we go visit Blue?" he asked.

"The last time I checked, they weren't allowing visitors."

"It doesn't hurt to try, right?"

"Are you done with your homework?"

"It's *math*," he said, slamming the book shut. "I suck at math."

"Um…" I began. I knew mathematics as it applied to calculating measurements and documenting chemical interactions, and also in its older and broader usage that included astronomy and physics. But I wasn't sure any of that would come in handy with algebra homework.

"Do not look at me," Dorian said, not looking up from the paperback book he was reading. "I can assist with French literature, linguistics, and the sciences, not mathematics."

"We can check on Blue," I said. "We'll figure out the math later."

"While you are out," Dorian said, "please stop by the library to get me more detective fiction novels." He gave a contented sigh and closed the Agatha Christie novel in his hands.

"I've got a whole shelf of them in the trailer," I said.

"I know. I have finished them."

"There are dozens of books."

"Yes, I never knew how entertaining such books could be. British 'penny dreadfuls' were looked down upon when I was a child."

"You," Brixton said, "were a child?"

"Of course," Dorian said. "Were you born knowing everything you know today?"

"A little baby gargoyle?" Brixton shook his head. "My life is too weird."

"I was never smaller than I am now," Dorian said, "yet I did not possess the knowledge I now have."

"I hadn't considered that," I said. "What *did* happen right after you were brought to life? Could you speak, or were you as helpless as a newborn?"

"You have not obtained another recording device?" Dorian asked Brixton.

"No way. You're helping clear Blue. You don't have to worry about me."

"I was not," Dorian said, "an infant in the traditional sense. I was neither tiny nor helpless. I spoke only Latin."

"*Only*," Brixton muttered.

I agreed with the sentiment. Nicolas Flamel had insisted I learn Latin for my alchemical studies. I hadn't taken to it nearly as well as I had to plants. But after learning the basics of Latin, other languages followed much more easily.

"You spoke Latin," I said, "because that was the language of the text that brought you to life." It made sense in an alchemical way—transformations rearrange existing elements. I wished that knowledge of the strange visual symbols included in the book had been transferred to the gargoyle as well.

"What are you two talking about?" Brixton asked.

Damn. I had spoken before thinking. I was used to keeping my own secrets, but having a gargoyle in my life was something new. But Dorian didn't seem to mind. He chuckled.

"My father's Latin was not so good," Dorian said. "It took time for us to learn to communicate and for him to teach me French."

"Your *father*," Brixton repeated.

"You have heard, of course, of the great Jean Eugène Robert-Houdin?"

Brixton stared at him blankly. "That name sounds French. I live in Oregon. So your dad's like an actor or something in France?"

Dorian's complexion didn't turn red when he was angry, but dark gray granules gathered in his cheeks when he became agitated. His face was now visibly darkening.

"He was a very famous stage magician," I said before Dorian could explode. "This was in the 1800s. He used to create mechanized illusions that were technologically much more advanced than the times."

"That's wicked," Brixton said.

Dorian's coloring returned to normal.

"I'll pick up some books for you," I said. "Come on, Brixton. Let's go check on Blue."

———

I hadn't expected the trip to the hospital to be successful, but visitors were allowed in to see her. Though Brixton was happy about this development, I wasn't so sure I was. There was still a murderer out there who had already tried to kill her once.

Blue's condition remained the same. Brixton sat with her for the twenty minutes until visiting hours were over.

"Can't you, like, *do something*?" Brixton whispered at one point. "With your alchemy? Do you have any of that Elixir of Life stuff? That should save her, right?"

"I wish it worked like that," I said. "The Elixir of Life can't be transferred between people."

I spoke the truth about the Elixir, but at the same time Brixton's words were more true than he knew. I used to be thought of as a healer. But that was centuries ago. I'd pushed those skills aside along with the painful memories I tried to keep at bay. There was no longer anything I could do for her.

Neither of us spoke on the drive to the library. Brixton stayed in the car while I selected the maximum number of books I could check out. I was only half paying attention to what I'd selected for him. I grabbed anything that fit the description of being from the Golden Age of Detective Fiction.

I handed Brixton the books to look through in the car, but he simply set the stack down at his feet. When we reached the house, he went straight up to his room and slammed the door.

"*Qu'est que sait*?" Dorian asked.

"He's worried about Blue."

I set down the stack of books on the dining table. Dorian hopped up on a chair and looked through them, nodding with approval.

"These will work," he said.

"You mean you'll enjoy them?"

He set down the book in his hand and faced me. "I did not wish to speak in front of the boy. It is my body. If I allow myself to be completely still, I begin to turn to stone. This did not used to be a problem. *Maintenant*, it is more and more difficult for me to resume my normal moving form. Even small movements, such as reading, keep my body awake. This is why I have asked for books. While you and the world sleep, I must stay awake—or I fear I may remain trapped in my stone body forever, never to return."

NINETEEN

At dawn the next morning, the house was silent. I'd like to say I knew something was wrong right away. That the house was "too still." But I didn't.

On my way downstairs, I noticed that Brixton's door was ajar. I poked my head in. The bed was empty.

"Dorian!" I called out, rushing down the stairs. "Brixton!" I opened every squealing door in the house, one of which fell off its hinge when I yanked too firmly. I even checked under the beds, holding out a false hope that they were playing a joke on me. I circled the house, thinking maybe they couldn't sleep and had gone outside to eat an early breakfast. I checked inside the trailer. They weren't there, but a strong odor was. The confusing scent rattled me until I remembered that Brixton had broken several bottles. I continued my search. My truck was parked in the driveway behind the trailer as usual. There was only one thing out of place. Brixton's bike, normally resting in a spot next to the back door, was missing.

I had once known a Native American tracker, but I had no idea how the skill was executed. I couldn't even detect a bike track leading out of my yard. I had no way to know where they'd gone. Could I have slept through the two of them being abducted? I'm a sound sleeper to start with, and I'd been exhausted.

The sound of wheels skidding echoed in the early morning stillness. I sprinted to the front door. An out-of-breath Brixton ran through the open door a second later, Dorian right behind.

"What's going on?" I asked. "Are you all right?"

Brixton bent over and breathed deeply, his gloved hands on his knees. "I think we lost him."

Dorian nodded, clicking off the living room light and peeking out the windows. "You have it?"

"What are you two talking about?" I looked between them but neither of them looked back at me. "What's happening?"

Brixton stuck his hand into the pocket of his bomber jacket and removed a small glass vial.

This couldn't be good.

"What is that?" I said.

"The poison that hurt Blue." Brixton handed the vial to Dorian. "Don't worry, it's not blood or anything. It's the liquid remains they found of whatever she drank."

"I will hide this with Zoe's other alchemy supplies," Dorian said.

"You didn't," I said. "The *police lab*? You broke into the police lab?" I sat down, not feeling so well.

"Dorian said you could learn more about the poison than the police," Brixton said. "You said you were trying to help her." When he spoke of Blue, his eyes weren't those of a jaded teenager but of a worried child.

"Brixton, this isn't a movie. You can't go around breaking into places you don't belong—especially police labs—no matter what Dorian says."

Dorian coughed indignantly. "I resent the assumption it was my idea."

"Wasn't it?"

"*Mais oui.* Of course this was my idea. But I did not wish the child to come with me."

"I'm not a child!" The outburst made him sound more like a child than usual.

"He followed me," Dorian continued, "on his bicycle."

"What?" Brixton said when I gave him a pointed look. "He told me what he was doing. Did he really think I wouldn't follow?"

"It is not my fault that he followed!" Dorian said.

This must be what it felt like to have children. I took two deep breaths to moderate my voice when I spoke. "Just tell me," I said, pausing to take another calming breath, "what happened."

"The boy could not sleep during the night," Dorian said. "I was here reading, and I made him a snack. He asked about what you and I were doing to help Blue. You did not have a large enough sample of the poison from Blue's house. He told me the police lab would have it. He knows much about this city. He knew where the lab was."

"How did you get inside?"

"It was not difficult," Dorian said, tapping his claws together.

"But there was an alarm," Brixton added.

I put my head in my hands. "Of course."

"It was a silent alarm. We didn't know—" Brixton broke off and looked to the gargoyle.

"Until the police arrived," Dorian finished.

I groaned. "How did you get away? Did they see you?"

Brixton flipped up the hood of the black hoodie he was wearing under his jacket and held up his hands. Between his shadowed face and gloved hands, even in close proximity it was difficult to identify him.

"This isn't the first time I've broken in somewhere," Brixton said. "I know what I'm doing. I'm the reason we got out of there."

"He is a very intelligent boy," Dorian chimed in.

"You're not helping, Dorian," I snapped. "How could you let him go into the lab with you?"

"He was already there! Would it not have been worse to leave him outside?"

"No," I said. "It would have been a million times better if he hadn't *broken into* a police lab."

"We're back," Brixton said. "And we got the poison. No reason to be so upset."

"*No reason?*" I said. "Do you realize you've broken the whole chain of evidence? Anything we learn from this can't be used as evidence."

I took measured breaths, trying to calm myself. I really shouldn't leave those two alone.

"Who cares about evidence?" Brixton said. "I just want you to fix Blue."

It was difficult to be blindingly angry when I knew why they were each doing it. Desperate times called for desperate measures. My exasperation faded. But only a little. "What happened when the police arrived?"

"I'd hidden my bike a little ways away," Brixton said. "We ran there and I put Dorian on the handle bars."

"The police didn't follow?"

164

"It was weird," Brixton said. "I didn't think they had seen us, but then one guy caught up. I took us through the Shanghai Tunnels to get away. My bike got beaten up going down the stairs, but Dorian was able to fix it in the dark. We stayed down there for a little while, to make sure nobody was following us. That's why we're back so late."

I hadn't noticed until now that they were both dusty. The underground tunnels explained it.

"Get cleaned up," I said. "I'll drive you to school."

"It's Saturday."

"Oh, well, then… take a shower to clean that tunnel dirt off."

"Your shower is either freezing or boiling. It's torture."

"Then let the cold and hot water run together and take a bath."

He grumbled on his way upstairs.

"Is this enough?" Dorian asked, holding up the vial.

"This is a bad idea," I said.

"Do you have a better one?"

———

Dorian cooked breakfast—brown bread fresh from the oven with wild blackberry preserves from wild blackberries he found in the woods during one of his recent nights out exploring.

"I have not yet perfected a vegan butter," he lamented. "Nut butters are not the same. I will master it yet. Dorian Robert-Houdin does not walk away from a challenge."

I had a challenge of my own to tackle. I waited until Brixton climbed into bed before getting to work on the poison.

With fear as a motivator, I was more effective in the laboratory than I'd been the day before. In a strange way, I was also happy. I had experienced some of the happiest moments of my life when Ambrose and I worked side by side.

We each worked differently—he with metals and me with plants—but we complemented each other. They talk about couples completing each other's sentences. Ambrose and I completed each other's thoughts about our alchemical transformations. If I needed a glass retort for the next phase of a process, Ambrose would hand it to me moments before I moved to get one myself. If he needed a crucible to move his creation into the fire of the athanor, I knew when he was ready for it. In alchemy, a practitioner's energy is transferred to the vessels they work with. Therefore most alchemists didn't let other alchemists touch any of the items in their labs. But with two of us, it was as if those rules didn't apply. We were so in synch that our alchemy transformed us into one. I had never felt so connected to life as I was when I was in the laboratory with Ambrose.

Remembering those moments, I found my rhythm. Like many alchemists before me, I was so caught up in the moment, so focused on the process, that I forgot I was dealing with an unknown substance. I should have been working more carefully, but I was giddy with getting back into the rhythm of alchemy. Through the distillation process, some of the liquid from the vial had turned to steam. It was too late to stop the process, or to leave the room. I breathed in the noxious fumes.

I felt myself falling. I must have been physically falling to the hard concrete at my feet, but that's not what it felt like. I was falling in slow motion, through the sky.

I knew, then, what I was feeling. The toxin in the air was the most essential metal in all of alchemy: *mercury*.

The last thought I had was that I was being killed by an alchemist.

Then everything went dark.

TWENTY

I AWOKE TO THE sharp smell of ammonia overwhelming my senses. I shot up from the cold, concrete floor, feeling like I was going to vomit. My head throbbed. The room spun around me. The light was so bright it felt like the sun was in the room with me. I pressed my eyes shut. The scent of ammonia dissipated, but the bright room kept spinning.

"Drink," a deep voice said. Cold hands pushed a glass jar to my lips.

I sipped the water. The sensation washing over me triggered a sense of familiarity. I remembered what I had been doing before passing out. *Mercury.*

"It is better?" Dorian asked.

"The air!" I said, realizing the fumes might have remained. "We need to get out of the basement."

"There is nothing in the air."

"Mercury doesn't have a scent."

"Mercury?"

"I'm sure of it."

Along with sulfur and salt, mercury is one of the three essential elements of alchemy. The dangerous one. I knew it well, having conducted many alchemical transformations using the enigmatic metal. It has a dual nature, both therapeutic and poisonous, both liquid and solid, which is why it's called the *rebis*. It's an essential ingredient for creating the philosopher's stone, but one that has also poisoned countless alchemists.

"Do you need further care?" Dorian asked.

"With the amount I ingested, I should be fine. But we need to air out the basement."

"I will take care of it."

"Be careful, Dorian."

"*Mais oui.*"

Dorian helped me up the stairs. I lay down on the couch, awake but reeling. I closed my eyes. A raw ache radiated from my shoulder and spread through my arm. I must have hurt it when I passed out.

A sharp claw poked my side. I opened my eyes. The little creature stood bending over me, his eyes wide. "I do not think you should be lying down."

"Doesn't matter," I mumbled.

He poked me again, harder this time.

"Fine." I let him pull me to a sitting position.

"This is better."

"How did you know?" I croaked.

"I heard the sound of a crash. When I came to investigate, I found you unconscious on the floor. You did not have smelling salts that I could see, therefore I took a jar of ammonia to wake you."

I smiled weakly. My body trembled.

"*D'accord*," Dorian said. "You may rest. I will watch you."

Though my body pleaded for rest, my mind raced. Now that I had ingested a stronger dose, I had a better understanding of what the poison was. But it raised even more questions. The strangest thing was, what I had told Dorian was true. Mercury didn't have the noxious scent of other poisons. It was odorless. *Then what had I smelled on Charles Macraith and Blue Sky?*

I'd let myself be confused because it wasn't poison. Not exactly.

I recognized some of the herbs from an old Chinese herbal remedy, which included mercury—but this blend had been tainted with additional substances I couldn't identify. It wasn't poison for poison's sake. And it wasn't the same mixture that had been used on Charles Macraith. It was as if someone hadn't checked for toxic contaminants in formulas that otherwise would have been harmless or even healing. I had no way of knowing if it was purposeful, or if someone had been cutting corners. Either way, coupled with mercury, it was a dangerous mix.

Front and center was mercury, but not in a high enough dose to kill anyone. In spite of my initial reaction when I realized there was mercury present, an alchemist wasn't the only explanation. There was something I was missing.

I must have dozed off. I hadn't meant to, but my body needed the rest to recover. Being attuned to natural substances makes me both stronger and weaker than the average person. Stronger when it comes to natural substances, because of my connection to plants. But weaker when it comes to unnatural additives, such as some of the toxins I'd ingested.

When I woke up, I was back in the basement. How had that happened? No, that wasn't right. This wasn't my basement. I was back in the old alchemy lab I'd shared with Ambrose. He was there, working at my side. The underground stone walls were covered with rich green ivy, so bright it was nearly fluorescent. The plant's tendrils covered not only the walls but the floor as well. As I watched, the ivy grew. The tendrils reached out like octopus arms, enveloping our glass and copper materials, even wrapping itself around Ambrose. Why wasn't he reacting? This must have been a dream, though it didn't feel like one. I was awake and sleeping at the same time. The ivy wrapped itself around my ankles. I screamed. Just before I was swallowed up by the plant, a stick poked me.

I opened my eyes. Dorian was seated cross-legged a few feet away from me. He held a hardcover book from the library in one hand and a stick in the other.

"Quit it with the poking," I said, my voice hoarse.

"You were making odd noises. Whenever a look of distress appeared on your face, I poked you. It calmed you."

"Odd noises?" The dream came back to me. It had to have been a dream, but it felt *so real*. Because it wasn't a normal dream. It was a hallucination.

"Your complexion did not change," he said, "nor your temperature. I thought it was best to let you sleep instead of dialing 9-1-1."

"Good choice," I said, stretching. Pain shot through my shoulder, but it was a surface pain, not the bone. "Oh God, what time is it?"

"Do not worry. The boy still sleeps."

I sighed. "I should call Max."

"You cannot go to the detective with the information you learned from the stolen vial. Especially since you said it was an unscented poison. How would you explain your information? This is information for us to find Blue's killer and retrieve my book."

He was right. I couldn't tell Max how I'd learned it was Chinese herbal remedies tainted with mercury and God knows what else. I

170

wasn't even sure what that meant. I was somewhat familiar with Chinese herbs, but not enough to identify the exact mixture. But I had to do something. On shaky legs, I stood up.

"You are going to the police station?" Dorian asked as I bundled in my thick wool sweater and jacket.

"I haven't figured out what I'm doing."

"Then where are you going?"

"I need to walk off the effects. You'll stay here with Brixton?"

I walked to Blue Sky Teas, taking the long way around the neighborhood. The rain was holding off, for which my roof was thankful, though clouds blanketed the sky. When I reached the main drag, the sidewalks were crowded with people going to restaurants, coffee houses, bookstores, specialty shops, or simply walking their dogs.

Olivia's friend Cora was behind the counter at the teashop when I arrived. I was unsurprised that Olivia passed off her good deed to the frazzled woman. The shop was only half-full now, a stark contrast to what I'd seen the day before. I supposed there was nothing more for people to learn. Still, even with only a few customers to deal with, Cora looked at least as distressed as she had the day before. Her red curls were pulled into a messy knot, which had fallen onto the side of her head.

Before I reached the short line, I was startled by who I saw sitting at a back table: Max Liu.

I held my locket between my fingers, took a deep breath, and walked over to him. He looked up at me but didn't offer me a seat. Two newspapers and an eBook reader filled the table, along with a teapot and teacup.

"Shouldn't you be off catching bad guys?"

"I'm on leave."

"You're *what*? Why?"

"It doesn't matter why," he said. "What matters is that right when we might have a breakthrough in the case, I'm off it."

"A breakthrough?"

"I can't talk about an ongoing investigation."

"But you said you were off the case."

"I'm sure Detective Dylan would greatly appreciate me telling the details of the case to one of the suspects."

"I'm still a suspect? I thought you said there was a breakthrough."

Max's facial features relaxed a little. He didn't smile, but his deep brown eyes softened as he looked at me. "I think he'd be wasting his time if he focuses on you."

"Thanks."

"Don't thank me." The warmth in his eyes was gone, if it had even been there to begin with. "I can't do anything about what happens from here."

The poison was in my basement. Oh, God. What if they got a search warrant?

"What's the matter?" he asked.

I shook my head. "I don't like any of this. A man was killed outside my new home and meaningful objects were stolen. I don't believe Blue did it."

"Neither do I." He sighed. "You might as well sit down." He folded the newspapers, making room on the table.

I sat across from him, not entirely sure why I'd walked up to him in the first place. I wanted to tell him what I'd learned about the poison, but hadn't yet figured out a way to do it. I also couldn't deny that I was drawn to the man. But there was something different about him today. He held himself at an emotional distance that I hadn't felt before.

172

"I feel like I should be asking you what's the matter, too. For a guy on leave, you don't look very relaxed."

He looked over my face for a moment before speaking. I felt suddenly self-conscious. I hadn't looked in a mirror since being knocked out from the tainted herbs.

"Remember how I told you how I was injured," he said, "when I fell through a trapdoor while chasing a suspect?"

I nodded.

"That wasn't all there was to the story."

"What happened?"

"That night, I discharged my weapon."

My breath caught.

"I didn't kill anyone," he said. "I've never killed anyone. But that night … It was down in the old tunnels that run beneath the city. They were built to transport supplies from ships to merchants without clogging up the streets, but many of them were used for unsavory purposes."

"The Shanghai Tunnels."

"You're learning your local history. Kidnapping able-bodied men and forcing them into indentured servitude on ships is a big part of this city's history." He paused to take a sip of his tea, wincing as he raised the cup.

"You're hurt."

"It's nothing. I've had much worse." He shifted in his chair and I noticed he was trying to keep one of his legs straight. "Last month, in those tunnels, I fell through a trapdoor—which I learned is technically a 'deadfall' when it's made for the express purpose of capturing an unsuspecting man. I wasn't careful because I didn't think it was possible—I was already below ground *in* a tunnel, but it turns out there's another level of tunnels I didn't know about."

"Didn't you have backup?"

"I hadn't waited for it. Stupid, I know. But the case was important. A girl had died." He indicated the lone photo hanging on the wall.

"You knew her?"

"We all did. Blue has created a great sense of community at the teashop. All of us who are drawn to the healing properties of tea find each other here."

"The girl who died was one of them—one of you?"

Max lowered his voice before continuing. "Anna West. A real shame. She was supposed to start college this fall. Her mother likes to spend time here now, to feel close to her. I don't see that it helps her, though." He looked toward the counter.

"The woman working the counter is her mother?" Of course. Now that I looked at the framed photo on the teashop wall, I saw the resemblance, most strikingly with the lush red hair they shared.

Max nodded.

"Anna was killed in the tunnels?" I asked quietly.

"No, it was a suicide at her home, but I suspected it was connected to the people who I was chasing in the tunnels."

"Since you were on your own when you got hurt down there, how did you get out?"

"I was lucky not to have broken any bones. I was able to get out of there myself. But I saw some strange things."

"Strange?"

"I don't know what I saw. In the darkness in those tunnels, I saw shadows … Shadows that I was convinced were monsters. That's what I shot at."

I remained silent. He must have taken my silence for skepticism.

"I know what you're thinking. The psychologist who examined me after the shooting agrees it was trauma brought on by the acute pain caused by the fall. That I had a mental break. She was loath to put me back on duty. She reluctantly agreed to it. But after what happened last night, she put me back on leave."

Oh no. Last night? I was afraid to ask. "What happened?"

"There was a break-in at the lab where we sent the poison found at Blue's house."

"You were there?" I swallowed, feeling guilt and bile rise in my throat.

"Since it was my case, I got a call. The perpetrator had already gotten away, and the first responders had lost sight of him. But from the direction I came from, I caught sight of a suspect fleeing."

My heart was beating so furiously that I was sure he would hear it. "And?"

He laughed, but it was a mirthful laugh. "I think that psychologist was right. I'm going crazy. I've had an overactive imagination ever since I was a kid. My grandmother told me the most amazing stories about what apothecaries could do. It took me way too long to stop believing in her magical stories. I don't know why I said anything in the first place. Only, doing things by the book is important to me. I know it might sound stupid to someone who's not a cop—"

"It doesn't sound stupid. It doesn't sound stupid at all."

"I've never lied on a police report," Max said. "Never."

"What did you see?"

"It was a damn monster."

I didn't know what to say. None of this made sense. He must have seen Dorian last night, without realizing what he'd seen, or even believing his own eyes. But how was it possible he'd also seen Dorian *last month*?

"What did it look like?" I asked. "The monster, I mean."

He gave me a sharp look. Did he think I was mocking him?

"I should go." He stood up, favoring his right knee.

I was too stunned on many levels to do anything as he brushed past me and headed for the door. It had to have been Dorian he saw last night. At least he hadn't seen Brixton. But what had Max seen the previous month? Dorian had only arrived in Portland this week, with my shipping crates.

Hadn't he?

TWENTY-ONE

I WAS STARTLED FROM my thoughts by two people sitting down at the table next to me. Olivia placed two steaming mugs on the tree ring table top and tossed her red shawl over her shoulder as she sat down. Ivan sat down next to her, gave me a friendly nod, and buried his scruffy, haggard face in a book with Cyrillic text.

"That poor boy," Olivia said, shaking her head as she watched Max depart.

"I don't think his injury is too bad," I said. "He'll be fine."

Olivia barked a laugh. "You are quite dense for a smart young woman."

"What do you mean?" I was fairly certain I knew what she was going to say: that Max believed I was a suspect.

"He knows."

"Knows what? I didn't have anything to do with the crimes—"

She laughed again. "Not *that*. I'm talking about your French boyfriend."

"I don't—" I began, but realized I had to keep up the lie. One little lie to protect Dorian … I should have known people beyond Brixton and his friends would hear about what I told them.

"Why would Max care if I happen to have a French friend?"

Ivan sighed and shook his head. His tired eyes and unkempt beard and hair didn't match his tailored wool suit.

"You should go after him," Olivia said with the first genuinely warm smile I'd seen.

She was right. I stood up and went after Max. When I reached the sidewalk, there was no sign of him. I closed my eyes for a moment. Running after him had been a stupid idea anyway. What would I have said to him if I'd caught up with him? Told him I wanted to push all thoughts of poison and murder from my mind and sit down with him and talk about his apothecary grandparents and the tea he grew? That was only a fantasy.

Back to reality, I hurried home. I needed to hide the stolen vial. Now that Max was on leave and a new detective on the case, there was no way I could entertain the notion of telling anyone what I'd learned. I hadn't even figured out how I was going to tell Max. Instead of knowing more, I knew *less* than I had before. I hadn't learned more about Charles Macraith. I hadn't identified the exact makeup of the poison. I hadn't gotten any closer to figuring out who had killed Charles Macraith, stolen Dorian's book, and was trying to frame Blue Sky.

The only thing I'd learned was that one of the key components of the poison was the most important element to an alchemist.

I had more questions than I knew what to do with. Had Dorian hidden out in my crate as he'd told me, only emerging when I opened the box? I believed him to be trustworthy from what I'd seen of him and from what he did for me years ago in Paris. But what other explanation was there for what Max saw? Could there be more creatures like Dorian out there? If *Not Untrue Alchemy* brought one stone carving to life, could it do the same to others?

———

It was Brixton's last day staying with me before his mom returned from her artist retreat. I was going to miss the kid, but at this point I was wondering if he would have been better off on his own these last few days.

I needed to wash away all the evidence that he and Dorian had stolen the poison. I wasn't going to destroy the liquid remaining in the vial, but it would need to be hidden somewhere safe, away from the house, until I could figure out what to do with it.

Before reaching the basement door, I was waylaid by smoke curling from underneath the kitchen door. Or rather, the room formerly known as a kitchen. It looked as if a tornado had blown through the room. Dorian wore the apron I'd picked up for him on a recent trip to the store, but that hadn't prevented his entire body from being coated in flour, which also coated large swaths of the walls and window blinds. Wisps of smoke escaped from the old oven. Nuts crunched under my shoes as I stepped into the room. And was that sweet potato on the ceiling?

"Um, Dorian?"

He turned from the stool he stood on as he mixed a bowl of frothy batter. His black eyes stood out against the white powder on his face.

"The boy is playing his guitar upstairs," he said.

"What happened here?"

"Do you know how difficult it is to make a soufflé without eggs? Who does not eat *eggs*? You know there is a family a few houses

179

over who have chickens in their backyard. It would be so simple to take the eggs during the night. You are lucky I respect your wishes."

"By destroying my kitchen?"

"You need a new oven regardless."

"What did you do to my oven?"

"I told you, I am trying to make a vegan soufflé. I almost have it!"

I couldn't imagine this gargoyle gourmet having a sinister plan and lying to me about when he arrived in Portland. Unfortunately, I didn't like the alternative any better: that there was another creature out there—and one that might not be as goodhearted as Dorian.

"I need to ask you something," I said.

"Sweet potato."

"What?"

"That is the ingredient I was hoping would make the soufflé work without eggs. Sadly, I was mistaken, thus the potato on the ceiling. I have learned that similar to what worked for the *galettes*, ground golden flax seeds in warm water or nut milk works well as an egg replacement."

"Oh. That's great. That's not what I was going to ask you."

"No?" He resumed whipping the batter with a whisk.

"When you hid out in my shipping crates, you didn't open the crate and come out before I opened the crates in my living room, did you?"

"How would I have done that?"

"You use your claws to get into all sorts of places. Like police labs."

"Yes," he said. "But not when heavy wooden boxes are stacked on top of each other in those metal containers that go on lorries. Why do you ask?"

"Just curious," I said.

He stopped mixing, setting the bowl down and jumping off his cooking stool. "You," he said, walking up to me, "should be a better liar for someone who has lived for so long."

"I didn't want to worry you unnecessarily," I said.

"I respect your privacy, but if this involves me—"

"Someone saw you last night."

"*Zut. Je suis desolé.* I did not think anyone had seen us!"

"Just you, not Brixton. It was Max. But he thinks he imagined it."

"This is good."

"No," I said. "It's not. He saw something similar last month, here in Portland."

"Last month? But I was not here."

"Exactly. So *who was*?"

"But this is impossible! I have had the book in my possession all these years. How else could there be someone like me? Especially here in Portland."

"I don't know, Dorian," I said. "I don't know."

"I shall investigate tonight."

"No. You've done enough investigating. Speaking of which, I need you to take the vial you stole far away from here. Max is off the case and there's a new detective working it. I don't know if he'll consider me a serious suspect. We need to make sure there's nothing linking us to the break-in. I'm going to clean up the vessels I used to test it, and I'll give you the vial to hide tonight."

"You are done with it?" he asked.

"It doesn't matter," I said. "But it can't stay here. You can climb somewhere that nobody will be able to get to it, but that we can get back if we need it."

"You do not yet know *who* is connected to the poison. You could try one more time."

"It doesn't work like that."

Dorian scowled. "You said the poison would help."

"It's sort of like a fingerprint," I said. "I can't detect the person who created a poison if I haven't already seen what they can do. Like how a fingerprint is meaningless unless you've got something to compare it to. The reason I could tell it wasn't Blue who mixed that particular concoction was that it didn't have her signature."

"You mean it is a process of elimination?"

"If I have already seen the way someone has put things together and the energy they have put into it, I can tell if a new substance was created by the same person. Their own unique signature. Only…"

"Only *what*?"

"If this mixture was created by someone other than the person who used it, I wouldn't be able to link it to the killer. And since it was a mix of mercury, herbs, and other substances, I don't know exactly what's going on with it."

"Why did you ask me to steal the vial, then, if it could not help?"

"I didn't ask you to!"

"You implied it. You wished me to take action where you could not."

"It wasn't for nothing," I admitted. "I'm more sure than ever that Blue is innocent and being framed. I know mercury is involved, meaning we need to be extra careful, because we don't know who we're dealing with. And now I know more about some of the ingredients that were given to Blue—" I broke off. I couldn't believe I'd been so stupid. There was a time when this type of poisoning was much more common. A time when I knew how to heal people.

"What is it?" Dorian asked.

"Wait here," I said.

"Where would I go?" He glanced around the disaster area that was my kitchen.

I ran down the basement stairs. I found the vial of poison Dorian and Brixton had stolen, still half full, and slipped it into my pocket. I rooted through my glass vessels. I knew it had to be somewhere … I'd seen the blue-tinted glass when I'd carried things downstairs. *Yes.* I found the tincture I was looking for and ran back up the stairs. It had been so long since I'd thought of it that I'd forgotten it was there.

"Here's the stolen vial," I said, handing Dorian the vial after wiping it off with a kitchen rag.

"Where are you going?"

"There's something I need to try. I'll be back soon."

———

I arrived at the hospital with a few minutes left during visiting hours. Though I was relieved that the only police officer in sight was chatting with a nurse at the far end of the hallway, I again wondered how safe Blue was. If I could get to her so easily, who else could? I was there to give her something I hoped might save her, but someone else might come with different intentions.

Blue looked so peaceful that I could have easily believed her to be asleep, if it hadn't been for the tubes and machines surrounding her. Though I knew the plastic tubes were doing her good, the sight of them still made me shudder. Doctors of the past who prescribed bloodletting and other cures always thought they were doing good. They did the best they could with what they knew.

"I don't know if you can hear me, Blue," I whispered, "but I'm sorry someone did this to you. I want to help."

I glanced over my shoulder to make sure nobody was watching, then removed the small glass jar I'd brought with me. I removed its dropper lid and put three drops through her parted lips.

It was a spagyric tincture I'd created a century ago—a mixture of plant essences in alcohol with calcinated plant ash to strengthen the effect of what would otherwise be a simple healing tonic. Tinctures last many years, but I had no idea if they lasted *that* long. I no longer knew how to create this concoction, and it was the last of the batch I'd transformed all those years ago. I had made it back when I was practicing alchemy with Ambrose, before I gave it up. Back then, I had often created healing tincture and tonics. They helped people, but they weren't miracle cures. I hadn't thought about this tincture for Blue's coma until I realized the nature of what had poisoned her body. It was something I created to help the body detoxify from a mercurial poison that was making industrial workers sick, before the effects were known to be poisonous.

A knock sounded at the door, startling me. The dropper fell from my hand and into the folds of the bedding. I couldn't see where it had gone.

Cupping the container in my hand and slipping it into my pocket, I turned to the person who'd knocked.

"Visiting hours are ending," the nurse said.

"I'll just be a minute."

"I can wait. I'm here to check her vitals."

Behind her, a police officer appeared. He frowned as he looked past the nurse into the room.

Time for a new plan. "Take care, Blue," I said, leaning over to squeeze her arm, hoping it looked like a natural affectionate gesture as I attempted to see where the dropper had fallen.

I didn't see it.

The nurse and officer stood in the doorway and watched me as I left, empty-handed.

TWENTY-TWO

BY THE TIME I reached the house, I had thought up a long list of the many horrible things that could happen if the dropper was discovered on Blue. What if my fingerprints were found on the dropper? What if they thought it was poison? My tincture wouldn't hurt her, but it was possible it wouldn't have any effect. It was a harmless plant mixture, but would modern doctors or the police realize that? Or would they think I had poisoned Blue and was trying to finish what I'd started? I was the one who'd found her lying unconscious, after all. The person who calls in something like that is automatically suspected.

Dorian was almost finished cleaning the kitchen. He was a responsible little gargoyle, I'd give him that.

"You do not look well," he said, a scouring brush in his hand.

"I'm tempted to pack up and move to Paris."

"Truly?"

"No, not really. It's just been a bad day."

"Oh." His shoulders fell.

"I'm sorry, Dorian. I didn't mean to tease you. You miss it, don't you?"

"Why do you think I have been cooking soufflés today? If I merely wished to stay awake, I would read one of the many books you kindly brought me from the library."

"You're cooking comfort food the same reason you ordered *Le Monde*," I said. "You're homesick."

He gave a Gallic shrug. "This is a strange country."

"What's been going on here isn't normal."

"I am not speaking of the murder and the theft of my book. I realize it was I who brought this upon you. For that I am truly sorry."

"You couldn't have known."

"You are a kind woman, Zoe. This is why I wonder if perhaps I should leave you and return to Paris myself."

"Are you serious? You can't leave."

"Why not?"

"We need to find out what's happening to you. Find a way to reverse the effects of whatever is killing you."

"Maybe I am meant to die this cursed death. Perhaps," he said, "it is my fate."

"I know you're French, but you don't have to be so resigned."

"I do not hear Brixton playing his guitar," he said.

"Nice try. Don't change the subject."

"I am serious. We should hear him."

I rushed upstairs. The guitar rested on Brixton's unmade bed. There was no sign of Brixton.

After searching the house and yard, I sent him a text, only to hear the beeping of a phone—coming from Dorian. The phone was in the pocket of his apron, where Dorian was keeping it to prevent Brixton from filming another video.

"Why did I agree to let him stay here?" I said. "There was a murder here, and a murderer still out there. What was I thinking?"

"Do not forget that the boy and I were also seen last night by the detective. Someone else may have seen us too."

"You're not helping."

"*Fais l'autruche?*"

"No. You're right. I don't want to bury my head in the sand like an ostrich."

"You are worried. But you must keep a calm mind."

"A calm head."

"*Exactement.*"

"His mom is picking him up tonight. He knows that. He knows he should be here. What if something has happened to him?"

"It is too early to think that."

"I hate feeling helpless." I grabbed my keys. "It's sunny for the first time this week. Maybe he and his friends are out enjoying it."

Though my little neighborhood felt much like a small town, I quickly remembered how big a city Portland was. Over half a million people lived here. And I was looking for one kid.

He wasn't at the park across the street from the high school, where I knew he sometimes liked to hang out. Checking there had been my grand idea. I wasn't sure where else to look. Was downtown Portland a draw for teenagers who lived across the river? I drove through Old Town and ended up on the main drag with Powell's Books. I doubted they would be at the bookstore.

I returned to the house shortly after dark, empty-handed. I was frantically considering options when a very dirty Brixton opened the back door with the key I'd given him.

I ran up to him and gave him a hug, a huge wave of relief washing over me.

"Are you okay?" I held him at arm's length, looking him over. Dirt covered the lower half of his face and much of his clothing. He held an odd hard hat in his hand. "What happened?"

"I'm fine. You can chill."

"What happened?"

"Nothing. I was out with Veronica and Ethan."

"You should have told me you were going out."

"My mom never asks me."

Of course not. "What were you doing?"

Brixton grinned and held up the strange hat I'd noticed. "Spelunking."

The hard hat was clean but looked decades old. A light was affixed to the top. "Where on earth did you find that?"

"Ethan found it online. He gets bored. I think the school he went to before moving here was harder. He's always buying stuff online. He found this and thought it would be perfect for the tunnels. He knew I was bummed about Blue, so he ordered us all hats so we could go out and stay busy."

I softened a little. "That was nice of him."

"Ethan's generous like that. So, um, have you learned anything else about Blue? Like with the poison Dorian and I got for you?"

"Brixton, you know you can't tell *anyone* what you did, right? Not even Veronica and Ethan."

"I'm not stupid."

"It wasn't long ago that you were trying to convince them about Dorian."

"That was two whole days ago."

Right. What was the calculation of two days in teenage years? Definitely a lot longer than what two days meant to me.

"Things are different now," Brixton said. "I know Dorian is a secret, and obviously B&E is a secret. V is great and all, but she's sort of a gossip."

Which explained how everyone knew about my "French boyfriend."

"Good," I said. "Nobody besides us knows about the breaking and entering."

"You going to tell me what you learned?"

"I was right that Blue didn't poison herself."

"You told the police?"

"There's nothing I can tell them. I told you the evidence is worthless now."

"But it should lead you to the person who did it."

"It only told me Blue didn't create it herself."

"I thought you were supposed to be good at this stuff."

"Being good at something doesn't mean it's easy."

"Then what's the point?"

"I may have found a way to counteract some of the effects of the poison."

"Really? You can cure her?"

"I don't know if it worked or not. I went to visit her in the hospital today. Visiting hours were ending, so I couldn't stay longer to see if she would wake up."

Brixton slammed the hard hat into the arm of the couch.

"It could still work," I said.

"Right." He turned away from me and wiped his eyes with his sleeve, then brushed past me to pick up the hard hat from where he'd tossed it.

"Why did you need the hat for the tunnels?" I asked. "Don't they have lights?"

"Not the ones we go to."

I was about to suggest it was a bad idea to go exploring unlit city tunnels, but stopped myself. I wasn't his mother. His mother would be here shortly. She could deal with him. Besides, the tunnels were probably a lot safer than what was going on above ground.

"Why don't you get cleaned up before your mom gets here," I said instead.

"Is the shower fixed yet?"

"I've had other things to deal with."

I chose to ignore the language he used as he dragged his feet up the stairs. Brixton would be leaving shortly, so I returned his phone to him.

A few moments later, it began to ring. "Zoe!" he called from the top of the stairs. I rushed back into the living room, expecting to find that he'd fallen through a rickety stair.

"It's Blue!" he said. "You did it! She's awake!"

"It's her on the phone?"

"Yeah." He put the phone back to his ear. "Blue, I'm here with Zoe. We're coming right over. Wait, what? *What*? No, don't go. Blue? Blue?"

"What's going on?" I asked.

He stood mute, then sank down onto the top step.

"Brixton, what's happening?"

"She's awake," he said, "and they're arresting her for murder."

TWENTY-THREE

"HOLD ON!" I SAID as Brixton rushed past me.

"We need to go!"

"No, we don't." I caught up with him before he reached the front door and put my hand on his dust-covered shoulder. "We know she's okay, which is what counts. If the police are arresting her, it's not a good idea for us to go to the hospital." I thought of the dropper of tincture left on her bed. That was one reason I wanted to stay far away from the hospital. I also didn't want Brixton to see Blue being hauled off by the police.

"I thought you cared about her too." He shrugged off my hand. "But that was a lie, wasn't it? You were just using her to help Dorian."

I stared at him.

"You thought I didn't know he's dying?" Brixton said.

"He told you?"

"He didn't have to." He glared at me. "I'm not stupid. I saw there was something wrong with him, so I asked him. You could have told me what was going on."

"I was—"

"What? Trying to *protect me?* You were trying to protect yourself. Are you going to the hospital or what?"

"We're not going," I said.

"Maybe you're not." He ran to the back door, grabbed his bike, and sped down the driveway.

I wasn't able to catch him, but I could follow. I knew where he was going. The tires of the truck screeched as I pulled out of the driveway and headed for the hospital. What I didn't count on was the fact that there was traffic. The start-and-stop traffic inched along, making me more anxious by the minute. It was Saturday evening and apparently everyone in the city of Portland had decided it was a nice night to go out.

I ran into Brixton's teacher Sam—literally—as the elevator doors opened on Blue's floor of the hospital. I nearly knocked down his tall frame in my rush to find Brixton.

"Blue is with the police," Sam said. "They won't let me see her."

"Have you seen Brixton?" I asked, catching my breath.

"He was here a few minutes ago. I assumed he was here with you. Were you parking the car while he came up?"

"He ran off without me."

He gave a sad chuckle. "He's like that."

"You said he *was* here. Does that mean he's gone?"

"I don't know where he went. He was really upset when they wouldn't let us see Blue."

"She's all right?"

"You could call it that. She seems to have made a miraculous recovery. But the police are questioning her. I heard a little bit of the conversation before they pushed us back. They're treating her like she's a suspect in her own attempted murder. I don't get it."

"Did you hear anything else?"

"Like what?"

Oh, I don't know, I thought, *like about a tincture dropper on her bed?*

"I need to look for Brixton," I said instead.

"If he left without you, I have a feeling I know where he might go."

"Where?"

"His mom is still out of town, right?"

"Until later tonight."

"Try Max Liu's house."

"The detective?"

"He's one of the few adults Brixton trusts." Sam consulted his phone and wrote down an address for me.

———

Thirty minutes later, I knocked on a red door with a gold dragon knocker.

"Have you ever thought of being a detective?" Max Liu asked as he opened his front door for me.

"I take it I was right that Brixton is here?"

"Come on in," Max said.

"Go away!" a young voice called from somewhere beyond the threshold.

Max smiled at the admonition, quickly followed by a cough to cover it up.

The exterior of the single-story house was Spanish architecture with a red-tiled roof that matched the front door. Inside, Max's house was simplicity itself. The open floor plan revealed only the barest assortment of furniture. A single white couch with a pewter-topped coffee table filled the center of the hardwood living room floor. Two large canvas paintings of scenic forests, each at least six feet high, covered one wall. The only thing out of place was Brixton's bicycle, which was propped up in the entryway.

The main room looked over both the kitchen and, through sliding glass doors, the backyard. The only items visible in the kitchen were a cast iron tea kettle resting on the gas stove and two framed photos: a colorful image of a twenty-something south Asian woman in a field of tulips, and a black-and-white photo of an older Chinese woman in front of a row of metal jars.

Though it was a moonless evening, a soft light from an outdoor lamp illuminated the backyard. I could see that the small yard held a tree, an assortment of edible herbs and plants in a row of clay pots, and a wooden bench sheltered by an awning. The bench was in the perfect position for the person sitting on it to gaze at the tree, herb garden, and sky. Right now a cranky teenager sat on the bench.

"Your house is perfect," I said, not realizing I was speaking aloud until I'd already begun.

"A lot of people ask if I've just moved in and haven't bought any 'stuff' yet."

"I don't mean to intrude, but I need to get Brixton."

Max tilted his head toward the backyard. "What did you do to him? It looks like he bathed in mud."

"I have a new appreciation for mothers."

"He's a handful, but he's a good kid."

"I know. His mom is due to pick him up at my house any time now. I'd better let her know we're running late."

"I think Brixton already took care of that."

Brixton opened the sliding doors. "My mom texted me. She's outside."

"Your stuff is still at my house. Should I bring it by your place later?"

He looked at his mud-covered shoes. I cringed when I thought about what Heather would think of my child-care abilities. "Nah," he said. "Can Dor—I mean, can me and my mom go by your place on our way home? I still have the extra key you gave me. I'll bring it back to you tomorrow."

I hesitated for a moment. Even if he was at home, Dorian was good at hiding. And even though Brixton was upset, I didn't believe he was trying to reveal Dorian's existence any longer.

"Sure," I said. "See you tomorrow."

Brixton gave Max a fist bump before leaving.

"He doesn't want you to see where he lives," Max said.

"That's what that was about? Is it that bad?"

"Only the fact that the apartment is in a rundown building. I checked in on him there a few times after he got into trouble. It's a nice enough place. His mom is a painter, and keeps the house full of art and books. But most of his friends have houses. He's kind of touchy about it."

"You mentioned when he got in trouble—"

"You want some tea?"

"I'd love some."

Max went to the kitchen and put water in the kettle. It was both ornate and simple. And *old*. An embossed Chinese dragon wrapped around the iron kettle.

"Where did you find that?" I asked. "It's beautiful."

"It was my grandmother's kettle."

"It's your grandmother in this photo?" I indicated the black-and-white photograph in a simple bamboo frame. In the photo, the woman stood in front of a cabinet of brass jars. I remembered Max saying his grandparents had been apothecaries in China. Her lips were unsmiling, but the photograph captured a mischievous smile that could be seen in her eyes. I could tell why he liked the photo.

"It was taken in China," Max said, "before she came here with my mom. The other is of my wife."

"Your wife?" I croaked. He wasn't wearing a wedding ring, but not everyone did. I had already been feeling foolish about my feelings for the man, and now I had even more reason to do so.

"Chadna passed away shortly after we were married."

"I'm so sorry, Max."

"It was a long time ago. Shortly after she finished medical school. Chadna was the one who saved me from the immature ideas I had about magic as a child. It's because of her that I straightened my life around."

I gave him a moment, but he didn't seem to want to say more. "I wasn't kidding when I said this house is perfect," I said, changing the subject. "It's rare to find such an uncluttered space." I couldn't remember seeing anything so purposefully sparse in the last century.

Max turned off the kettle as it began to steam, then removed two handleless porcelain teacups from the cupboard, along with a box of loose leaf tea.

"If you have one teapot," he said, pouring hot water over tea leaves, "that will do you quite well. How much does he lack himself who must have a lot of things?"

"You're quoting Sen Rikyū," I said. At that moment, I wished more than anything that I had been in Max's house under other circumstances.

Max tilted his head and looked up from the tea. "How did you know that?"

"One of the few books I've kept in my trailer over the years is a book of quotations about tea. It reminds me to live in the moment and appreciate what I have in front of me." I didn't add how many years I'd had to read about tea and learn that lesson, but here in this house I found myself wanting to tell Max everything. It was a dangerous impulse, especially after hearing him talk about his scientific wife and dismissing the teachings of his grandmother. It was foolish of me to hope we could share something. Yet in this sanctuary he'd created for himself, I was more drawn to him than ever. I pulled myself back from that dangerous ledge and changed the subject. "You were going to tell me about Brixton."

"I wasn't, actually."

"It sounded like you were."

"You're too damn easy to open up to, Zoe. Do you know that?"

"I feel the same way." Our eyes locked and I lost all sense of time and place.

Max cleared his throat. "Breaking and entering, and assault. That's what Brixton did."

That startled me back to the present. "He's just a kid. How can whatever he did count as assault?"

"He beat up a guy who was harassing his mom. His stepdad was out of town for a while and this guy was hitting on his mom—close to harassment, but not enough for a restraining order." Max sighed and looked out the window. "Brixton was only twelve at the time, smaller than he is now. He knew he was too little to do anything to the guy if the guy could see it coming, so he broke into his house one night and beat him up, telling him never to touch his mom again."

"That sounds more heroic than criminal."

"The guy ended up in the hospital with several broken bones."

"Oh."

"Nobody liked it, but the guy wanted to press charges."

"Did he go to juvenile jail, or whatever it's called?"

Max shook his head. "Community service, but he's got a juvenile record now."

"You felt sorry for him, like he got a bad deal."

"I saw myself in him." He paused as he finished making the tea and handed me a cup. "I could see what was coming. I thought getting caught up in the system might push him into doing *more* bad things, because he saw that what he thought was a good deed was met with getting arrested."

"Were you right?"

"Yes and no. His mom isn't much of a disciplinarian. That friend of his, Veronica, keeps him in line more than his mom."

"I thought he said he had a stepfather."

"He's not around much."

"You said you saw yourself in him," I said, wondering what he'd meant a minute before.

"So," Max said, suddenly very interested in his tea leaves, "Brixton told me Blue woke up. I'm glad to hear it."

"Yeah, except that now she's being arrested."

"At this point, she's only being questioned. But that's why Brixton came over. He didn't know I was off the case. He was upset and thought it was my fault."

"So she's not under arrest?"

"I told you I'm off the case."

"Surely you know what's going on, though."

"I'm on leave, Zoe. I told you I play things by the book. I'm here in my sanctuary, not following up on cases that aren't my own."

Max's cell phone rang.

"Liu," he said. He listened for a few moments, his face stoic. "Sure. I know where she is. I'll bring her." He clicked off.

"What was that about?"

"Blue is asking for you," he said. "She says she'll talk, but only if you're the one she talks to. She says you saved her life."

I gripped the teacup. How did Blue know? And what had she told people?

"Why would she say that?" Max asked.

"I visited her. I've always wondered if people in comas can hear what people say to them. Maybe she heard me." I was used to leaving out details that would make people think I was crazy, but I hated lying to Max. Maybe I really should leave Portland before it was too late.

Max nodded, but his expression remained skeptical. "She's still at the hospital under observation, with a guard checking on her regularly. They're waiting for us."

I wanted to take my own car to the hospital to be alone with my thoughts, but Max said he had something to tell me before we got there. He insisted we ride together. I slid into the passenger side of a sleek black sedan. It suited him.

"What was it you wanted to tell me?" I asked.

"Blue Sky isn't her real name."

"Yeah, I kinda figured that."

"It's the real name on her identification," Max said.

"You mean she officially changed her name?"

200

"Not exactly. After we started looking into her, I discovered the truth. Since you're going to talk with her, you should know the truth going into this."

"I thought you didn't believe she was a killer either."

"Instincts aren't the same as facts, Zoe. You should know what you're agreeing to when you speak with her."

"What are you trying to tell me?"

"Blue's real name is Brenda Skyler. Ten years ago, she faked her own death."

TWENTY-FOUR

"You came," Blue said. Her voice was weak, but she was sitting up in the hospital bed. It had been adjusted so she could talk without getting out of bed.

I was being allowed to speak with Blue alone, on the condition that the conversation was being recorded. I wasn't sure why she would talk to me but not the police, but I was going to find out. "Of course I came. You know we're being recorded, right?"

"They told me." She held up her finger to her lips, then turned over her palm. There was something in her hand. It was the tincture dropper that had fallen into her bed after I'd given her a few drops. She handed it to me. "Thank you," she said, "for coming to visit me. The nurse told me you were the last person to come visit me before I woke up, even though the police think I'm the one who killed—" She broke off and gave me an earnest look. "I didn't do it."

"Why did you want to see me?"

"They told me Brixton was staying with you. That was the first thing I thought of when I woke up. He was supposed to stay with me. How is he?"

"Concerned about you."

"But he's all right?"

"He's good." Sure, he'd snuck out in the middle of the night and broken into a police lab ... but he was well-fed and healthy.

"Does he think—he doesn't think I did this, does he?"

"No, he believes in you. You're the one thing he talks about more fondly than anything."

She blinked back tears. I started to get up, but she grabbed my hand. "I asked for you because life is too short to waste time doing things one doesn't want to do. I know, now, that the truth has to come out, but I'll be damned if it's going to be on someone else's terms. I want to tell it to someone who understands."

"You barely know me."

"I know what you're doing here," she said.

My pulse quickened. "I don't know what you mean."

"Portland is the perfect place to reinvent oneself."

"I'm not—"

She laughed, then cringed. "Owe, I've got the damnedest headache."

"Let me get a doctor. I don't think you're up for talking." I didn't like the direction this conversation was going. I needed an excuse to get out of there. I had the strongest impulse to hook up my trailer to my truck and never look back.

"Wait, I want to get this off my chest," Blue said. "I can see it in your eyes. You're a kindred spirit. Someone who's here to start fresh. Was it a bad breakup? No, you don't have to tell me. That's the whole point of starting fresh."

I let out a sigh of relief. "Something like that. I've been living out of my trailer for a long time. But when I got to Portland…"

"It feels like home, doesn't it?"

"It does."

"I'm glad my instincts were right about you. You seem like you're too young to understand what it's like to feel so desperate that you need to flee your entire life, never looking back but always wondering if it's right over your shoulder. But you're an old soul. I hope you'll understand."

I wished I could tell her how right she was. That I could tell her I understood running more than she thought.

"You look like you want to say something," Blue said.

I shook my head. "You should probably start telling me what the police want to know, before they decide I'm not a good interrogator and they should do it themselves."

"I don't know where to begin."

"I already know," I said, "about Brenda."

"Ah. I suppose you want to call me that now."

"Not if you prefer Blue."

I was in no position to judge. After all, Faust was the name I'd chosen for myself after realizing what I'd become.

"I was going to tell you myself, but I guess they beat me to it." She ran a hand through her wild gray hair. "If you can believe it, I used to have perfectly coifed hair and not a gray hair in sight. I paid obscene amounts of money to have my hair dyed, straightened, and styled."

"I can't picture you without your untamed curls. They suit you."

"I agree. My old life didn't suit me in any way imaginable."

"Lawyer?"

"Lawyers always get a bad rap, don't they? Don't people think of any other profession that would be a drag?"

"So you weren't a lawyer?"

"No, you were right." She laughed. "I was a lawyer. Sort of. I went to law school straight out of college because it's what was expected of me. It never occurred to me that I could do something different with my life. I met my husband during law school. He was the charming guy all the women in our class fell for—handsome but with a little bit of quirkiness that showed in his imperfect nose, smart enough to do well at school without having to study all the time, confident enough to be a good public speaker and to flatter women in just the right way. I should have known he was too perfect."

"Things like that usually are."

"He wasn't as smart as we all thought. He was cheating on tests. The worst part was, after I found out, I *helped him*. I thought I was in love. I, however, took the code of ethics seriously. I couldn't bring myself to take the bar exam, because I knew I was morally compromised. For him. He knew he had me. We got married right after law school. He did a clerkship for a judge, during which I helped him with a lot of the work without anyone knowing. After the clerkship, he started his own private practice. It was early in his career to do so, but he was charming enough to pull it off—with my help. I couldn't legally practice law, but I helped him with research and cases, as a legal assistant. I played the part. I know I was fooling myself, thinking I was being ethical by not being a practicing lawyer myself. He was a master at psychologically manipulating me. It took years for me to see it. Years during which I blindly followed his lead."

"What happened to change your mind?"

205

"He knew me. He knew I was a good lawyer who did everything ethically except for lying about the work I did for him. He knew he could only push me so far and that I'd never do anything I knew to be *morally* wrong. "

"But he would."

"There were some of his cases," she said, "where he didn't ask for my help. He didn't even tell me he was working on them. I could see why. They were worse than I could have imagined. When I found out, I kept the knowledge to myself. But I knew what I had to do."

"You left him?" I asked.

"If only it had been that simple. He kept meticulous records. One of his files was a fake record of everything illegal I had supposedly done—without his knowledge, of course. He'd been keeping the records as insurance, in case he ever did push me too far. A few years before I found out the extent of his crimes, I had a brief moment of clarity during which I thought about leaving him. It was induced by one too many martinis—an indulgence that used to get me through my days with him—so I stupidly told him I might leave him. That's when he showed me the file."

"What was in it?"

"Falsified records about things he claimed I had done that would send me to jail. He had the gall to pretend I'd actually done these things and that he was being a faithful husband by protecting me and not turning me in. Spousal privilege and all that." She scoffed. "If I left him or told any 'lies' about him, he would no longer feel obliged to cover up my crimes."

"That's awful." What was even worse was that after everything I'd seen in my life, I could imagine him getting away with it.

"I knew, then, that I could never leave him. Not safely. I started putting away money. We spent so lavishly that it was easy to save a hundred dollars here and there without him noticing. It added up. But I didn't yet have a plan. I was a broken woman then. I couldn't see any way out. I still believed his only crime was in what he was doing to me—manipulating me into doing his work for him. He'd never physically abused me, so I told myself I wasn't being abused, even though I was. It would have been easier if he'd hit me."

As screwed up as that sounded, it made sense. Her husband had known how to push her just to the brink but not over the edge.

"Once I found out he was breaking the law to help corrupt clients, that's when I had the idea to disappear."

"But you knew you couldn't leave him without repercussions."

"Even if I'd gone to jail myself," she said, "that would have been okay, as long as I brought him down with me. But knowing him, I'd have ended up serving a life sentence while he came off looking like a saint for caring for a deranged wife for so long. I wasn't left with many options. But by then, I had saved up a decent amount of money that he didn't know about. Not a great deal of money compared to what we were used to spending, but what did I care about that? I never cared about the clothes or the spa treatments. I'd always wanted to do something like I'm doing here in Portland."

She paused to take a sip of water. Her hand shook as she did so.

"Do you need a doctor?" I asked, helping her raise the glass to her parched lips and then set it back on the side table.

"Hell, no. I've been asleep for days. It's just taking me a little time to wake up. Where was I? Oh, right, taking charge of my life." She clapped her hands together. "I'd wasted too much of my life with that bastard. I wasn't going to let him ruin the rest. Without him knowing, I collected my own evidence—real evidence—that he was falsifying documents for crooked clients. Sent the evidence to the proper authorities, left a suicide note, then drove my car into Lake Michigan."

"You died that day."

"Brenda Skyler died that day. Blue Sky was born."

"Max said it was smart of you to take a name so similar to your own. That way you'd recognize it and respond when people addressed you."

"*Max*, huh." Her eyes twinkled. "I know that look."

"You were explaining how you faked your death," I said, feeling the color rise in my cheeks. "How did you pull it off? And please tell me your husband didn't get away with his crimes."

"I met a lot of interesting people while we practiced law together. I was able to get a fake ID pretty easily, then got a real one once I moved to Oregon. As for my husband—" She paused and gave me a conspiratorial grin. "The bugger got disbarred and served five years in jail. The last I heard, he was selling men's suits in Detroit. I, on the other hand, have been living exactly the life I wanted to. No more working fourteen-hour days. No more dieting. No more playing hostess to people I never liked. No more straightening and dying my hair. No more manicures."

She paused to pat her ample belly and show me her calloused hands with short fingernails.

"I eat without starving myself," she said. "I use my hands to garden and collect wildcrafted plants, and opened the teashop to make enough money to live simply while doing something I love."

"I suppose it's illegal to fake your own death," I said. "But why is that important now?"

"That's not why they want to arrest me," she said.

"I know." I suddenly felt very awkward, knowing I was the one who found the poison attributed to Blue, which I was now certain had been planted to frame her.

"They have this crazy idea," she said, "that Charles was *blackmailing* me about my past. They think that's why I killed him."

TWENTY-FIVE

"WHAT, *WHAT*?" I SAID. "Blackmail?"

Blue looked taken aback. "I thought you said you already knew why they were arresting me."

"I do. Because of the poison and stolen items at your house."

"What are you talking about?" Blue said, trying to get out of bed but realizing she was still attached to an IV. "There are stolen goods and poison at my house?"

"Don't try to stand," I said.

"Did anyone get hurt?" She gave up fiddling with the IV and stared at me. "Oh, God, Brixton. You said he was okay, right?"

"Brixton is just fine."

Blue rested her head against the pillow and crossed herself. "Thank God for that. Anyone else?"

"Just you."

"I drank something, didn't I? Things are still a bit fuzzy."

A nurse stepped into the room. "That's enough for today."

"I'm fine," Blue said. "I want to know what's happening."

A detective followed the nurse into the room.

"I agreed to tell you what you wanted to know to fill in the blanks of my past," Blue snapped at the detective. "But you're not telling me everything. I have a right to know the charges against me."

"Thank you, Ms. Faust," the detective said. "We've got what we need."

"What do you mean?" None of this made any sense.

"*Thank you*, Ms. Faust," the detective repeated. "Your service in the interest of justice is greatly appreciated."

I held Blue's gaze for a moment before walking out the door.

I found Max in the waiting room. "What's going on?" I asked.

"Not here."

We walked in silence to his car.

"Blackmail?" I said. "You think Charles Macraith was blackmailing Blue? Why would you think that?"

Max drew a deep breath, his hands taut on the steering wheel of the car, looking straight ahead at the concrete parking garage. "I shouldn't have anything to do with this case."

"I might know something," I said before I could stop myself.

His head snapped toward me. He was so close to me I could smell peppermint on his breath. "If you know something, you should tell Detective Dylan."

"He won't believe me."

"Why would *I* believe you?"

"Isn't poison a strange choice for a killer these days?" I asked.

It used to be a lot more common for people to poison each other. Before modern toxicology, it had been easy to get away with it. Many fatal poisons could easily be confused with diseases of the day. Arsenic was such a popular way to kill someone and disguise the death as being from natural causes that it acquired the nickname "inheritance powder." But these days, poison was a strange choice, especially when it was such a diluted form.

This didn't make sense on so many levels. If Dorian and Brixton hadn't stolen the vial, I was confident the lab would have come across the mercury and isolated the other toxins. The killer hadn't stabbed Blue, so the lab *would* have been looking for poison in her case, unlike with Charles Macraith. It wouldn't have gone undetected. Which didn't seem worth it, since there wasn't enough poison to kill.

"I can't figure you out," Max said. "Why can't you answer a simple question with a simple answer?"

"It wasn't a simple question."

"So you have to answer it with another question? Why don't you just tell me what you're getting at."

"If you tell me what's going on with the blackmail."

"Why do you care? Detective Dylan isn't pursuing you as a suspect. You can get on with your life."

"I suppose 'justice' isn't a good enough answer?" I asked. I couldn't tell him about Dorian, the dying gargoyle, for whom I needed to solve the case in order to retrieve the book that I hoped could save him.

"One of the reasons I'm good at being a cop is because I know human nature. Justice is a damn good reason, but *only* if it accompanies something more personal."

"Brixton cares about Blue," I said, "and I care about Brixton."

"He got to you, huh?"

"You're telling me he hasn't gotten to you?"

"That was different."

"Why?"

"Because I saw myself in him." Max looked away and started the car, but didn't make a move to back out of the parking space.

"You mentioned that before. What did you mean by it?"

He hesitated for a brief moment. "Only that you were never a fourteen-year-old boy."

"I had a brother. He was impetuous like Brixton. He—" I broke off. My hand flew to my locket. I hadn't meant to let it slip out, but it was too easy to let my guard down around Max.

"I'm so sorry, Zoe."

"Why?"

"You used the words *was* and *had*."

"You picked up on that, huh?"

"Good cop skills, remember." He tried to smile but failed.

"It was years ago."

"I'm even sorrier to hear it, then. It's never easy to lose someone you love, but it's especially difficult when they're taken too young."

"We're supposed to be talking about Blue."

"*We're* not supposed to be talking about anything." He leaned back in the seat of the car and shook his head. "You're supposed to go talk to Detective Dylan about whatever it is you think you know about the case."

"It's only an observation."

"Your observations have been pretty good so far. Blue probably wouldn't have been found in time if you hadn't suspected something and gone to see her."

"A lot of good I did her."

"The evidence still would have pointed to her, regardless of when we found her. But because of you, she pulled through."

"Thanks for being a good liar. I doubt there was enough poison in her system to kill her."

213

"What do you mean?"

"That's what I wanted to tell you. Ever since you told me the poison was stolen from the lab, I've been trying to think more about what I smelled." It wasn't exactly a lie. Omitting facts he didn't need to know was hardly the same thing.

"You placed the scent?"

"I told you it reminded me of something I couldn't put my finger on. I realized what it was. It smelled like an old Chinese herbal remedy ... that had been tainted." I tried to think of a way to mention the mercury, but there was no good way to do it. It was odorless.

Max shook his head. "I know a thing or two about Chinese herbs. You're off base."

"You learned from your grandmother."

"I did." His lips tightened as he said it.

"She wouldn't have exposed you to toxins. To anything dangerous."

He opened his mouth and took a breath to speak but decided against it.

"You admit I have a point," I said.

"Maybe. It's too bad you didn't think of this *before* the sample was stolen. This could have helped the lab guys narrow things down."

"I know," I murmured. I wondered if there was a way for the vial to be "found." It wouldn't be able to be used as evidence, but successfully prosecuting the culprit was less of a concern of mine than finding Dorian's book and making sure Blue wasn't unjustly convicted. Would the police even consider testing something that was lost and then found? Maybe there was a way we could plant the vial in the grass near the lab, making it look like the thief dropped it ...

"Zoe?"

"Yes?"

"I lost you for a minute."

"Sorry. I'm distracted. I've got a lot on my mind."

"Tell me about it. Let me drive you home."

"There's something else I've been thinking about," I said as he maneuvered out of the parking garage.

"Tell it to Dylan."

"Let me run it by you first."

He sighed and kept his eyes on the road, flipping on the windshield wipers as a misty rain began to fall.

"You guys are looking into some blackmail angle about Blue's past—"

"I can't talk about it," Max cut in.

"I know. That's fine." It wasn't fine, but I could deal with that later. "What I mean is that you might be ignoring the real motive."

"Which is?"

"Those antiques of mine that were stolen. I've been spending a little bit of time cataloging, and some of the things might be even more valuable than I previously realized."

"Mmm hmm."

"Is that the cop sound for a noncommittal answer?"

"We've been looking into all the angles, Zoe. You don't have to play detective. We know what we're doing."

"But the alchemy book—" I broke off when I saw Max's hands tighten on the steering wheel. His expression had changed. A wall had gone up. This wasn't like the other information he was withholding. He was hiding something.

TWENTY-SIX

THE LIGHT RAIN HAD turned into a full-blown rainstorm by the time Max dropped me off at my house. Gusts of windswept rain crashed against the car, making it difficult to have a conversation, which was fine by me. I didn't trust myself to speak. Max *couldn't* be involved. Not only because he was a detective, but because of what my gut was telling me. The question was whether I should believe my instincts.

As I entered the house, I discovered the rain wasn't only falling outside. Hearing dripping water, I went straight to the attic room that I had been hoping to turn into my business workspace.

I found Dorian there, placing buckets and bowls under the leaks.

"*Il pleut des cordes,*" he said. "You caught up with the boy? Were you able to speak with Blue Sky?"

I filled Dorian in on what had happened that evening with Brenda Skyler, a.k.a Blue Sky.

"You have learned nothing helpful!" Dorian said, jumping up from where we sat on the hardwood floor in between the buckets of rainwater. A drop of water fell on his head. He swore.

"Moving into an old house during the wintertime might not have been a wise decision," he said, pushing one of the buckets under the new leak with his feet. "*Merde. Mon pied.*"

"Your foot?"

"It is nothing."

But as he spoke, I could see his foot rested at an awkward angle. It wasn't bending like the rest of his body. It was solid stone.

"Dorian—"

"I said it is nothing!" he snapped.

If he didn't want to talk about how quickly his body was turning to stone, I wouldn't force the issue. What I needed to do was figure out how to help him.

My eyes searched the beams of the sloping ceiling. "The tarp is secure. Where are all these leaks coming from?"

"Modern construction is not the same as the solid buildings from the old days."

"This house is about a hundred years old."

"*Exactement,*" Dorian said. "Modern."

We couldn't live like this. I needed to keep calling contractors until I found one who hadn't heard about the recent murder that was making people wary to work on the house. I didn't care about any of the cosmetic upgrades I had originally been interested in. For now, what we needed was someone who could make the house habitable.

I had to figure out what to do with Dorian while someone fixed the house. Because of his deteriorating life force, it wasn't a good idea for Dorian to turn himself to stone and pretend to be a decorative stone object in the house. I would have to lock the basement door and have Dorian stay there during the day while a handyman made stopgap fixes to the rest of the house.

But the house was the least of my problems. I was no closer to figuring out who was framing Blue and where Dorian's book was. I'd tackled memories from the past that I wasn't yet ready to face, all to help the little gargoyle, but I had little to show for it beyond the amorphous feeling that I might be close to understanding more about the book's coded illustrations.

"There is a haunted look in your eyes, *mon amie*," Dorian said.

I looked up at the dripping beams. "Speaking with Blue brought up memories I didn't want to think about."

"Come. We have done as much as we can to protect the room from water. Have you eaten dinner?"

I shook my head.

"I will cook."

Despite the fact that it was Dorian who was dying, I was the one who couldn't remain calm through our dinner of roasted chickpeas in a cayenne spice mix with cabbage braised in mustard and cumin seeds. I hated feeling helpless. I had grown accustomed to being lonely, but I was good at taking care of everything that had to get done. I could grow my own food from seeds, turn plants into healing remedies for the ailing, fix the engine of a truck on a desolate country road, and learn new languages and adapt to local customs. What I *couldn't* do was unravel the mysteries I'd encountered that week: Who killed Charles Macraith and why? Where was Dorian's book? What did the pages I'd photographed mean?

My unrest became unbearable when Dorian brought out a beautiful apple tart he made for dessert. It reminded me of food I'd eaten as a child on special occasions.

"The food was not good?" he asked.

"It's what the apple tart made me think of. You don't know the story of where I'm from. Before you knew of me in Paris."

"From your accent, I know you are American."

"I was born in Salem, Massachusetts."

"The same city as the famous witch trials. Oh! You do not mean—"

"I do."

"*Mais non*. This is terrible." Beneath his horns, his forehead creased with concern. "I did not know."

"You had no way to know the foods you cooked tonight would remind me of it."

"They burned you?" His black eyes widened.

I shook my head. "It didn't come to that." I took a deep breath. Dorian had told me his story. I wanted to tell him mine.

"By the time I was sixteen years old," I said, "the witch trials were going strong. I wasn't a witch. Therefore I thought I had nothing to hide. It was a foolish assumption."

"You were already an alchemist?"

"I was known as a 'simpler'—someone who understands how to use plants more than most people. Because I understood the cycles of nature, people said the plants 'spoke to me.' They said it was witchcraft."

"*Mon dieu*."

"By the time I realized what was happening, hysteria had taken over. I was going to be arrested and tried with those poor women."

"Were any of them witches?"

"I don't think so. But really, I knew so little at the time. I had led a sheltered life. Difficult, but sheltered. I came from a family of farmers in Salem Village, growing oats and rye in the rocky soil. It was a deeply religious community, one where you didn't dare speak out of line. If it hadn't been for Thomas …" I removed my locket necklace and held it in my hand for a moment before handing it to Dorian. "My brother was the one who saved me. He was only fourteen at the time, the same age as Brixton, but things were different then. We were expected to grow up more quickly. That's a miniature portrait of Thomas on the left side of the locket."

"Such a serious boy."

I pushed past my urge to cry. "He helped me escape to London, by boat. I was so hesitant to leave my mother and sisters that Thomas insisted on coming with me. As the only son in the family, he was expected to take over the farm, but he was willing to give up his whole life to help me escape my fate."

Dorian returned the locket.

"The trip to London used all of our money. This was the 1690s. A fourteen-year-old boy and a sixteen-year-old girl with no family and no formal training didn't have many options for employment. With my skills, I was able to make simple plant mixtures that helped people. It was enough to survive. It was also enough that alchemists took notice of my abilities. An alchemist used a tincture we had sold to track us down. When he found out it was I, not Thomas, who had used plants in such a way, he was wary. Female alchemists were quite rare. His associate, Nicolas Flamel, was more open to the idea. Nicolas and his wife took us in and agreed to train me."

"The famous French scrivener and bookseller," Dorian said. "Yes, I know of him. He and his wife Perenelle turned lead into gold and gave much money to charities in Paris. When wandering the streets of Paris during the night, I would often walk by their graves. But wait—the dates on their headstones were before the Salem Witch Trials."

"They discovered the Elixir of Life. When their graves were exhumed, they were found to be empty. They faked their deaths because the world was not yet ready to know the secrets of alchemy."

"Something you believe as well."

"I do. For many reasons. It takes rigorous study to truly understand alchemy. There are no quick fixes, which is what people would want. The Flamels knew that well. After faking their deaths, Nicolas and Perenelle moved to an estate in the French countryside, assuming new identities. It was there that I studied with them for several years. Thomas came with me and became a gardener. Then the plague came.

"It was the early 1700s. The plague hadn't been entirely eradicated in Europe. Before the Black Death killed much of the population of Marseille in 1720, it swept through the countryside where we were living. Thomas fell ill.

"I had been studying alchemy for nearly ten years, but as the study of alchemy goes, ten years isn't a very long time. I hadn't yet been expected to transmute base metals into gold or extend life. But when Thomas fell ill, and my usual herbal remedies failed to cure him from the plague, I was desperate. I threw myself into finding the Elixir of Life, hoping I would be able to share it with Thomas because of our strong familial bond. The Flamels told me that transferring the immortality of the Elixir of Life from one person to another couldn't be done, and that even the most clever of alchemists had never understood why. They suggested I spend Thomas's last days keeping him company. I didn't listen. I didn't know if it would work, but I had to do *something*. Everyone had told me I had a gift. My connection to plants was considered alchemy, so I thought I could use my plant knowledge to create the philosopher's stone and in turn use it to create the Elixir of Life. I'm human like anyone else. I wanted that quick fix. I worked so hard and slept and ate so little that I was often delirious. I didn't know what I was doing by then. I thought I might have been getting close when Thomas died."

"*Je suis desolé, mon amie,*" Dorian said. "I am so sorry, Zoe."

"If I had listened to the Flamels, I would have spent my time trying to heal Thomas through the means I already knew, or at least to have spent more time with him before he died. You can understand why I abandoned alchemy for many years after that. I left the Flamels and wandered for years, barely surviving. I didn't realize that I had indeed discovered the Elixir of Life until my hair turned white but the rest of me didn't age."

"How could you not know you had discovered it?"

"Alchemists speak in riddles. There was no way for me to know what the philosopher's stone looked like. Some alchemists suggest that it's not even a stone, but a powder or a liquid. The Greek alchemist Zosimos described it as a 'stone that is not a stone.' The Flamels told me that no alchemist can know what it is until they find it for themselves."

"*Alchemists,*" Dorian said, his snout flaring.

"Because I hadn't taken any of my research with me, I wasn't sure which of my transformations was 'the one true thing.' It was only my love for Thomas that had made me focused enough to discover alchemy's deepest secrets. Once I realized what had happened to me, I returned to the Flamels. But where their house had been—" I broke off, the memory of the landscape as clear as if it had happened that day. I saw the blackened land. I smelled the sodden ash.

"I found only charred ashes," I said. "The house had burned to the ground. I couldn't tell if they had died in the fire or escaped.

The nearby villagers couldn't tell me anything. The other alchemists I knew who also knew the Flamels had died by then, so I wasn't able to find out what happened to them."

"I thought you said they were immortal."

"The Elixir of Life doesn't stop violent or accidental death. It only stops the progression of aging. It's why I adopted the food habits I have now—if I was potentially going to live forever, I wanted to feel healthy."

"The Flamels might be out there somewhere."

"I don't know, Dorian. I tried to find them, but it was as if my whole life with them had been an illusion. I found no evidence of their existing after they faked their deaths in Paris."

"They were careful."

"Too careful. I never saw them again."

TWENTY-SEVEN

THE NEXT MORNING, I willed my eyes to focus on the woodcut illustrations from Dorian's book. The longer I stared at them, the more they blurred together. The twisted birds, the desolate landscapes, the fragments of Latin text that spoke vaguely of alchemy but didn't include nearly enough steps.

I took a brief break to fix myself a bowl of date and cinnamon oatmeal, as much for warmth as energy. In addition to rainwater, the house was leaking enough cold air that I couldn't shake a chill. I was seriously considering moving back into my trailer until I got the house fixed up. As I held the bowl cupped in my hands for warmth, there was a knock at the door.

Brixton stood in the doorway, a small paper bag in his hand.

"Don't you have school?"

"It's Sunday. But it's cool. You've got enough going on that I don't think you're senile or anything."

"Thanks. I think."

"So can I come in or what? It's freezing out here."

The rain had stopped but a cold wind was blowing. Brixton was dressed in his usual jeans, t-shirt, and hoodie, but it was cold enough that he'd also bundled in a bomber jacket.

"Sure," I said, "but it's not much warmer inside the house. And I thought your mom would want to spend time with you, now that she's home."

He rolled his eyes as he came inside. "Where's Dorian? I bought him something."

"He's upstairs dumping out the buckets of rainwater we collected last night, courtesy of the leaking roof."

"Do you need help with the tarp? I'm a good climber."

"I've got a professional coming over later today, hopefully before the rain comes back."

"How'd you find someone to come to a haunted house?"

"I don't think superstition would keep rational adults from a good job."

"It's not just superstition. We *told you* the place was haunted. That's why I came to check it out the first day I met you."

"You really believe that? Why weren't you afraid to stay in a haunted house?"

He shrugged. "I think it would be cool to see a ghost."

"Sorry to disappoint you."

"It could still happen. I've only been hanging out with you for a few days. The strange lights didn't appear that often."

I froze. "*What* strange lights?"

"The people who sold you the house didn't tell you? I thought they had to, like, legally tell you that stuff."

"*What lights*, Brixton?"

"That's why the house was empty for so long. Because nobody wanted to move into a haunted house."

"It was empty because there was a legal disagreement between the heirs."

"That's not what I heard. But it doesn't matter what I heard. It's what I saw. What *everyone* saw. Weird lights coming from this place. At first people said there must be homeless people crashing here. But whenever they sent the cops out here, they could never find a soul. Pretty freaky, right?"

Pretty freaky indeed. So *that* explained why everyone I called already knew about the house I was talking about. *What was going on here?*

Even if I believed in ghosts—and I'd never seen one in over three hundred years—I hadn't seen anything strange at the house. Various creaking noises, sure, but that was to be expected in an old house.

Dorian appeared on the stairs. He stepped more slowly than usual, holding the railing. At the sight of the limping creature, I forgot about Brixton's ghost story.

"I brought you Stumptown beans," Brixton said. "These are the ones I told you about that are wicked good."

"*Tres bon*," Dorian said, taking a bag of coffee beans from Brixton's hands when he reached the bottom of the stairs. "*Merci*, my young friend."

"Aren't you too young to be drinking coffee?" I said to Brixton.

He gave me a look that reminded me I was over three hundred years old. Come to think of it, Brixton had never asked me how old I was. He'd asked me about gold and transformations, about being immortal, and about food, but he hadn't specifically asked about my age. At fourteen, he must have felt like he'd live forever, so a formula to live forever wouldn't have been of much interest. But gold for a poor kid? And food for an eternally hungry kid? Those were things he could relate to.

"Brixton, how old do you think I am?"

"My mom told me I was never supposed to answer that question if I knew what was good for me."

Dorian laughed, then retreated into the kitchen with his coffee beans.

"It's okay," I said, "I promise I won't be upset."

Brixton studied me for a few moments. "I dunno. I know you're old."

"Thanks."

His face reddened. "You told me I should guess!"

"I was kidding! Make your guess."

"Not cool, Zoe. Not cool. Anyway, you're like, at least ten years older than me. Maybe... twenty-six?"

"Not bad." I had been twenty-eight when I accidentally discovered the Elixir of Life. If that hadn't occurred to Brixton, it was a conversation for another day. "Twenty-eight."

"I think Mr. Strum is around your age."

"Your teacher?"

"Yeah, maybe you two should be hang out. I mean, when all this is over. All he ever does is work, and you two are like the only cool old people I know. Max is all right, too, but he's a cop. And he's ancient—he's like forty."

It was oddly refreshing to be considered "old." Looking young did have its advantages, but it had almost as many disadvantages. It was difficult to be taken seriously as a young woman. The "woman" part of the equation had become easier over time, as society became more accepting of women being equal, but the "young" part had gotten worse. It used to be that someone was considered an adult at sixteen, the age that I fled from my home with my brother. It wasn't unusual for people like me and my brother to be on our own and have already learned a trade. By twenty-eight, it was expected that you had come far in mastering a skill. Nowadays, it was more likely that a twenty-eight-year-old would be finishing graduate school or trying out different professions.

"Blue isn't cool?" I asked.

"Nah. Blue is mom-cool. That's different."

"That was nice of you to bring Dorian coffee," I said, suppressing a smile. I didn't think he was working an angle like he was before, but I couldn't figure out where the gesture had come from.

"Yeah, well, he said he was having trouble staying awake, so, you know..." He shrugged and looked down at the floor.

"It was really thoughtful, Brixton."

"Whatever."

Dorian stuck his head out of the kitchen. "Espresso, Brixton?"

"Americano. Six sugars."

And that explained why he liked coffee. Diluted and with plenty of sweetness.

"I need to take care of a few things," I said. "Are you two okay on your own?"

They both gave me a look that *really* made me feel three hundred.

"Sheesh, I was just being nice!"

As I headed to the basement, I heard Brixton explaining to Dorian, "It's an expression that means she's annoyed."

"Ah, so."

———

I'd found a handyman who said he could be here later that morning. He couldn't hear very well, so I hoped he got the address right—and that he wouldn't leave after he realized what house it was. Now I had to get everything into the basement that I didn't want the handyman to see. I began by cleaning up the mess I'd made, so there would be space to move things into the room without having them covered in gray slime.

I didn't have time to properly unpack my crates. *Still.* One day at a time.

Instead of unpacking my crates and moving them into the basement, I decided it made the most sense to seal them back up so the handyman wouldn't go poking around. Most of the items inside were the objects I'd collected over the years that I sold online, but a few of them were more personal alchemy items I'd saved for myself. The items wouldn't reveal my secret to anyone who didn't already suspect anything, but I didn't want anyone raising questions.

I hadn't checked for online orders in a couple of days, so I went upstairs and opened my laptop. There wasn't yet any furniture in the room that would become my home office. I hadn't had a proper office before, only a small table in my trailer with my laptop computer plus the storage unit, so I hadn't ever acquired office furniture. Sitting on the water-spattered hardwood floor, I scrolled through a couple dozen emails, half of them spam.

Most people I'd met since the turn of the century would have been bombarded with many more emails and social media messages after staying offline for a couple of days. Though I was often tempted to stay in touch with many of the people I'd met on my travels, I had to be practical. The whole reason I moved on was because people couldn't learn who I was. I couldn't create an online presence. Though it was often painful at the time, it was for the best.

All I had was the email address I used for my shop, Elixir, which was a generic email that didn't contain my name. Even my email was lonely.

Since I only sold a small collection of high-end items online, I didn't have frequent sales to fulfill. The items I sold hadn't cost me much when I bought them, so along with the compound interest on my savings, selling a few items a month kept me afloat. But now that I'd plunked down most of my savings to buy and fix up this house, I had to step up my sales. Maybe even start *marketing*. I shuddered at the thought.

I hadn't had any new sales since the last time I'd checked, which was fortunate. It meant I didn't have to waste time rooting through crates and could devote my time to helping Dorian. I hoped the handyman would be able to stabilize the worst parts of the house quickly. I shut my laptop and went downstairs.

At the dining table, Dorian and Brixton sat across from each other, a crystal on a gold necklace chain in Dorian's hand. In an outstretched arm, he held the chain so the crystal swayed back and forth in a rhythmic cadence.

I knew where the crystal had come from. I sighed as I looked over at the crate I'd sealed up, now open with its contents spilling out on the living room floor.

"Dorian, what are you—"

"Do not interrupt us! He will forever think he is a chicken!"

"Um …" What did one say to that?

"I'm not hypnotized, Dorian," Brixton said.

Dorian frowned. "You are not?"

"No."

"Not even a little?"

"I don't think so."

I snatched the crystal from Dorian's hand. "What are you two doing?"

"You tell her," Brixton said. "It was your idea."

"It is a good idea," Dorian said. "Once she has thought it through, Zoe will agree."

"That means I'm not going to like it, doesn't it?"

"You said the detectives are keeping information from you," Dorian said. "Information that is vital for solving the case, clearing Blue's name, and retrieving the book that can save my life."

"I haven't even deciphered the pages I photographed yet," I said.

"Yes, but with the entire book it will be easier."

"I know. That's why I agreed to go to Blue's house with you, against my better judgment. What does that have to do with hypnotizing Brixton?"

"We wish to learn what the detectives know."

"By turning Brixton into a chicken?"

"I am teaching him to hypnotize people. I know of this skill from the magicians my father worked with. Once I impart my knowledge, Brixton can hypnotize the new detective and he will tell us many things."

"That's a terrible idea," I said, "for so many reasons." I knew of the varied skills of Jean-Eugène Robert-Houdin. When I had seen him perform, I had been impressed by the range of illusions he had perfected. In addition to his automated "orange tree," a mechanized tree that hid many wonders, he took advantage of modern ideas that interested the people of the mid-1800s. He used "ether" to make his son float into the air, hovering high above the stage. And using "second sight," he would read the minds of audience members. Jean-Eugène

Robert-Houdin was such an accomplished man that it was no wonder Dorian had the confidence to think he could teach Brixton to hypnotize a detective.

"Even if you *could* teach Brixton to hypnotize someone on our timeframe," I said, "you realize there's no way you could get a detective to agree to sit there while Brixton mesmerizes him with a crystal."

"You think I have not thought of this?" Dorian said.

I crossed my arms.

Dorian crossed his own arms and stared me down. His black eyes could be unnerving. I was glad he was on my side.

"The crystal is only phase one," Brixton said. "It's the easiest way to hypnotize people. Once I master it, then he'll show me how to hypnotize people without them knowing I'm doing it."

"Nobody," I said, "is hypnotizing anyone. Dorian, put everything back into the crate and seal it up. Brixton, you're welcome to stay here, but a handyman will be here to patch up the roof and look at the pipes shortly, so Dorian will need to be down in the basement. I need to run a few errands—"

"I have made a shopping list," Dorian said.

"I expected nothing less."

"It is on the fridge. You cannot miss it."

"I'll stop by the market. I'm also getting a lock for the inside of the basement door, so you can lock yourself in there while there are strangers in the house. No hypnotizing. Agreed?"

"It wasn't working anyway," Brixton said.

Dorian pouted for another few seconds before giving in. "Agreed."

———

I've never gotten used to modern supermarkets. I don't mind picking out my own items, as opposed to having a shop clerk select things from behind the counter, the way things used to be done. But small specialty shops have always made much more sense to me. Nobody can be an expert at everything. I liked that there was a revival of specialty shops going on in towns like Portland.

Today, however, I found myself at a sprawling supermarket with harsh fluorescent lighting. I'd be able to get all the items on Dorian's shopping list as well as a lock for the basement door. There was something to be said for convenience.

In the produce section, I saw a familiar face. His unshaven stubble remained unchecked and was growing into a scruffy beard.

"Ivan," I said, greeting Olivia's friend next to a pyramid of tangerines. "Nice to see you."

"*Dobrý den*," Ivan said. "It is Zoe, is it not? Lovely to see you."

I forced myself to keep smiling, even as I felt my blood turn cold. I gave an excuse about being late for an appointment and rushed off.

At the checkout counter, I felt myself shaking. I had never heard Ivan speak before, since he was always with the talkative Olivia. I'd seen him reading a book in a Cyrillic language, but hadn't wondered exactly where he was from. But his accent was unmistakable.

Ivan was Czech, from Prague. The center of alchemy.

The missing connection to alchemy had been in front of me this whole time.

TWENTY-EIGHT

PRAGUE HAD BEEN THE center of alchemy in the late 1500s and early 1600s. Alchemists flocked to Rudolph II's Court, establishing it as a center of alchemical innovation. The king of Hungary and Bohemia invited over two hundred alchemists to Prague, and the impact has lasted to this day.

Rudolph was before my time, but I had visited Prague many times. I knew it well, and I could identify a Prague accent. Ivan had one.

Being from Prague itself wasn't enough to make me worried. Olivia had given me the missing piece of information about Ivan, without realizing she'd done so. When she was bemoaning the fact that her own nephew had given up academic pursuits, she had told me that Ivan was a professor of chemistry who had retired early due to fading health and frequented the teashop promoting good health.

Olivia didn't know what that convergence meant. But I did. Alchemy was a precursor to modern chemistry. Ivan was a chemist from the center of alchemy who was ill and wanted to cure himself.

I felt certain I was onto something, but I was missing some piece of the puzzle. I tried to think back on when I'd first visited Portland and found Blue Sky Teas. Had Ivan seen me then? Even if he had, so many things still didn't make sense. Finding Dorian's book could have been a crime of opportunity, but how would he know I was an alchemist in the first place?

Nearly dropping my bag of groceries, I sprinted to my truck and drove like a mad woman on the way home.

Thankfully, Brixton had gotten bored and left, allowing me to speak freely with Dorian. I didn't want Brixton to get any ideas about dealing with a murderer himself. With how much he cared for Blue, I didn't doubt for a minute that he would act rashly.

"*Mon dieu!*" Dorian exclaimed upon hearing my theory. "This makes perfect sense!"

"We need to learn more about him."

"Google?"

"Google."

An Internet search told us that Ivan Danko had been a well-regarded chemistry professor in Prague before he retired early for medical reasons.

"Listen to this," I said. "One of the courses he taught was a history of alchemy as a predecessor to modern chemistry."

"This is uncommon, no?"

"Very uncommon. Alchemists who were also scientists have almost always had to hide the alchemical side of their research. Isaac Newton was incredibly secretive about the alchemical experiments he conducted."

"*The* Isaac Newton?" Dorian asked.

"Oh yes. Newton carried out more alchemical experiments than anything else. He wrote all about them, too, but most of those works were never published. Newton himself felt the world wasn't ready for the power of alchemy."

"*Mon dieu.*"

"I wonder," I said, "if, like Newton, Ivan became ill while doing his own alchemy experiments."

"I must question him," Dorian said.

"Um, no. That's not going to happen."

"I am not a pet! I am Dorian Robert-Houdin!" His wings flew open, crashing into the wall and taking a large swath of plaster with it. His mouth hung open, shocked at what he'd done. He was losing control of his body.

"I didn't mean—"

The doorbell sounded. Wonderful. I hadn't had time to install the lock on the inside of the basement door. At least the handyman was half deaf, so hopefully he hadn't heard a French voice shouting.

Dorian folded his wings as best he could, glowering at me the whole time. "I will be in the basement," he whispered. He puffed up his chest, grabbed three paperback novels from the coffee table, and limped down the stairs.

I greeted the handyman and got him to work patching the roof. As soon as I was certain he'd be occupied for a short time, I installed the new lock on the inside of the basement door so Dorian wouldn't have any unexpected visitors. Home handiwork wasn't one of my talents, but the installation wasn't bad. It wasn't pretty, but it was functional.

While the handyman worked, I had a chance to do more research on Ivan, but there wasn't much more to learn. He didn't have an online presence after leaving his university several years before.

Two hours later, the handyman had finished patching the worst hole in the roof and taping the worst leaky pipes. He said the roof should hold for now, but he'd need to pick up supplies for further patches, and that I really needed to hire a proper roofer and plumber. I gave him a bag of ginger cookies to take along with his payment, and scheduled another appointment with him later in the week. It was the only dessert Dorian had cooked that Brixton hadn't liked, and there was no way I was going to eat three dozen cookies.

I knocked on the basement door. My knock was met with no response.

"It's me," I called out.

A few moments later, the lock slid open and Dorian peered out at me.

"We need a special knock," he said, "to be sure it is you."

"Can't you just listen for my voice?"

"Interesting point. Yet a knock is more dramatic. That must explain why it is employed in fiction."

"You're enjoying the detective novels, then?"

"They are most entertaining—and also enlightening."

"Enlightening?" That couldn't be good.

"I have had an inspired idea," he said. "I will tell you about it as I prepare lunch."

I followed Dorian into the kitchen as he began cooking. He banished me to the far corner of the kitchen, where I jumped up to sit on the pristine counter. The cleaning crew who had cleaned the house before my arrival hadn't been able to clear away the years of grime as well as Dorian had. I watched as he created a *roux* out of olive oil, flour, and broth, transforming an oily, clumpy mixture that looked like clay into a creamy sauce that made my mouth water.

"These books from the library," Dorian said as he whisked, "it is interesting how they are all unique and stand the test of time, yet, at the same time, there is a common type of resolution."

I eased down from the counter and poked my head out the kitchen door to look over at the assortment of books strewn across the room on the coffee table. Agatha Christie, Ellery Queen, Dorothy Sayers, Arthur Conan Doyle, Margery Allingham.

"In this resolution," Dorian continued, "the hero of the story has put together facts in his mind—using his *little gray cells* as Poirot would say—to reveal that the killer is someone we already know, and one of the least likely suspects."

"Dorian—"

"This person," he said, "we now know to be Ivan."

"This isn't fiction."

"*Mon dieu.* Art imitates life. Life imitates art. This is why we must do what they do in the books. We must bring all the suspects together for a dinner party at which all will be revealed."

"I don't think so."

"But you *must* think so."

"Why is that?"

"Because it is already done."

My skin prickled. "What do you mean it's already done."

"While I was trapped in that dank room, I shared my plan with Brixton, via text message."

"Wait, how? You don't have a phone. You can't even use a phone screen with your fingers."

He pulled a Blackberry out of the apron pocket. "Brixton got this for me from his friend Ethan. I can punch the keys with my fingers."

"You told Brixton you thought Ivan was a murderer?"

"It is not nice to keep secrets from the people we are working with."

"He's fourteen!"

"I explained the plan to ensure he would not run off and do anything stupid before the dinner party. What are you doing?"

"I'm calling Brixton to tell him to forget whatever you told him."

"It is too late, Zoe."

"Why?"

"He has already emailed all the guests. The teashop regulars were overjoyed to be invited over to a home-cooked housewarming meal tonight from 'great chef Zoe.'"

TWENTY-NINE

I SPENT THE AFTERNOON preparing the house for the dinner party. There's nothing like the combined fear of knowing a murderer might be coming over for dinner—along with your new neighbors. Surrounded by moving crates in my leaky house, I wasn't sure which was scarier.

The party was to take place that night, just hours after Brixton invited everyone. Didn't these people have lives? I supposed it was the same human curiosity that made people crane their necks to get a better look at a car accident. Whatever plans people had, they had cancelled them so they could be here. I wasn't surprised. They were curious about me, had heard about my cooking, and had the natural human pull toward the macabre. And here I was throwing a housewarming party with gourmet food at the haunted house where a murder had taken place.

In addition to our suspect, Ivan, Brixton and Dorian had invited five other teashop regulars: Brixton's teacher Sam, Sam's aunt

Olivia, Olivia's friend Cora, Brixton's mom Heather, and because the instigators claimed they were being responsible, Detective Max Liu was the final member of the guest list.

The plan was for Dorian to cook the meal ahead of time and for Brixton to serve the meal, leaving me free to sit with the guests and help steer the conversation where I wanted it to go. I would also be on high alert for any hint of poison. Between my keen ability to detect the poison and our quest for justice and a cure for Dorian, I was confident in the plan. Somewhat confident. Okay, at least I knew it wouldn't be a disaster that ended with someone dead. I admit I was desperate.

Brixton enlisted the help of Veronica and Ethan to clear the worst of the weeds from the front yard, promising them a tasty snack plus cake to take home. Though the dinner party guests would be arriving after dark, I wanted to at least have the tall, wild grass pulled away from the path leading to the front door.

I had to run a couple of errands, so Brixton's job was to make sure the kids stayed in the yard and didn't come into the kitchen without warning. I'd rigged curtains in the kitchen so it was impossible to see in from the outside, including a curtain that blocked the herb garden's glass window box, but couldn't do anything about the swinging door leading from the living room to the kitchen.

After cooking, Dorian was going to turn to stone, playing the part of the antique stone gargoyle he originally was. I would have felt more comfortable with him hiding, because returning to life from stone was becoming increasingly difficult for him, but he insisted he wanted to be present to see what was happening.

By four o'clock Sunday afternoon, when the kids came in from the yard for a much-deserved snack, the house was beginning to look like I envisioned it would when I bought it. Between the weeded front yard and the few boxes I'd unpacked, I allowed myself a moment to appreciate the transformation. I'd been so focused on my frantic search for a cure for Dorian that I hadn't had many moments to step back and enjoy what was in front of me.

"Wow," Brixton said, rubbing the soles of his sneakers on the welcome mat.

"Is this stuff from Paris?" Veronica asked.

"Some of it is. I lived there for a few years."

She ran past me to the mantle, where I'd set up a display of antique alchemical items I found deep in my storage crates: two hermetic vases, a spirit holder, matrix vase, and in the center, a philosopher's egg. Honestly, I sometimes think the secret language alchemists created had as much to do with trying to outdo each other with clever names than with conveying information. The pelican made sense, because the glass vessel resembled the bird's beak. A snake was self-explanatory too. But a matrix vase? I was pretty sure that the motivation behind names had at least as much to do with guy trying to be cool as it did a spiritual connection to laboratory supplies.

I stood back and looked at the display. Rooting through the crates, I selected two brass apothecary boxes that would go nicely.

The curated display was my contribution to the plan. Dorian had initially suggested that once I gathered everyone together, I should lock all the doors and declare that I knew who the killer was, somehow forcing Ivan to confess. I countered with the idea that we let things unfold more naturally by placing alchemical objects on display in the living room to provoke a reaction from Ivan. Much more sensible than kidnapping people and making unsubstantiated accusations. I hoped it would work.

The boys made a beeline for a different section of the room. They headed straight for the dining table. Two large loaves of homemade bread, one a nut loaf and one a simple Parisian-style baguette, dominated the center of the table on a wooden cutting board from Marseille. A Spanish platter of nut cheeses sat to one side of the bread, its twin platter loaded with a pile of savory scones. Poking out from the baby lettuce leaves in a wooden salad bowl from Lisbon were tangerine wedges, thinly sliced roasted beets, and toasted almonds. I smiled to myself, watching the boys eat. I was glad I'd been able to unpack the special serving items I'd had in storage for too long.

Veronica ran her fingers along the carvings on the mantle before joining us at the table. I was glad Dorian was hiding for the time being; otherwise I had no doubt Veronica would have run up to a Dorian statue and patted it on the head. Dorian didn't care about eavesdropping on the kids, so he was brushing up on his Poirot deductive skills in the basement before the kids departed and he could finish preparing the evening meal.

"Thank you, Ms. Faust," Veronica said as she sat down.

The boys grunted in between bites of food.

"I can't thank you enough for helping with the yard," I said, pouring them ice water with fresh mint leaves.

"No problem, Zoe," Ethan said. "I should be thanking you. Now Brixton owes *me* a favor."

Veronica kicked him under the table. "Can't you do anything out of the goodness of your heart?"

"That hurt! I totally came, didn't I?"

"Remember," Brixton said, "she's paying you in cake too."

Veronica and Ethan stopped glaring at each other, and they departed half an hour later with chocolate cake. Dorian would have been horrified at the brevity of the meal, but he had to finish cooking.

"Sorry, man," Ethan said to Brixton in a low voice as he left.

"What was that about?" I asked, closing the door behind Veronica and Ethan.

"He thinks I'm staying longer to help out so you won't press charges for that day I met you last week."

Had it only been a week? Before coming here, months could go by without much happening. I would tend to my small herb garden and go on long walks wherever I had parked my trailer. I'd stay for a short duration of time, ranging from a week to a year, careful to never put down roots. Occasionally I became immersed in something I didn't plan on, but this had been the longest week I'd experienced in decades.

"I couldn't tell him the truth," Brixton continued, "that I'm helping you catch the guy who framed Blue and is keeping Dorian from getting better."

"*You* aren't catching anyone. Remember what we talked about. Anything bad starts to happen and you run out the door and call for backup."

"I'll go get Dorian," Brixton grumbled, knocking on the basement door. "Hey, why isn't he answering. Do you think he's okay?"

"He doesn't respond to knocks on the door unless it's a coded knock you worked out in advance."

"Oh. So how are we supposed to get him?"

"Just call his name. He'll recognize your voice."

Brixton's summoning worked, and the gargoyle and his assistant spent the afternoon preparing dinner.

The guests began to arrive at five minutes after seven. At the sound of the doorbell, I nodded at Dorian.

He limped to the side of the fireplace and gave me a curt nod. He pulled back his shoulders, stretched his wings, and squatted into a pose resembling a watchful stance on a perch. Dark, cracked lines covered his soft gray skin. Dorian was once again stone. I shivered and pulled the door open.

THIRTY

HEATHER HELD A BUNCH of long-stemmed snowdrops. The winter-blooming white flowers were held together with twine.

"Thanks for the invitation." She grinned and handed me the flowers. "And for looking after Brixton while I was painting." She had shoes on her feet tonight, but in spite of the cold she wore only a light shawl over her white cotton dress.

"He's a great kid."

"I think helping you around the house is really good for Brix. There's my baby!" She squealed and enveloped Brixton in a big hug.

"Hey, watch it!" Brixton extricated himself from his mom's hug and straightened his collar. "I should have stayed in the kitchen."

"Look at you. A tuxedo! We can't afford—"

"It's just a rental," I said, "and I'm taking care of it."

Dorian was enthusiastic about the idea of hosting a proper English manor house dinner party. That meant Brixton's role was that of the butler-slash-server, which of course required a tuxedo.

Finding one at the last minute had been one of my errands that afternoon. I hadn't expected Brixton to go for it, but he'd taken to the idea. So much so that he took a picture of himself in the tux and texted it to his friends.

"Such a handsome young man," Heather said, taking over for Brixton's clumsy attempts to straighten the collar.

"*Mom.*"

The doorbell rang a second time. Rather than opening the door, my butler retreated into the kitchen. I wasn't sure what Brixton thought a butler was supposed to do, but clearly opening doors wasn't one of his presumed duties. I opened the door and found Max standing on the porch. He smiled and handed me a mason jar filled with tea leaves. His face was unreadable, but he looked sexy as hell in black slacks, black and white wingtip shoes, a slim gray dress shirt, and black leather jacket.

Olivia, Sam, and Ivan arrived before I closed the door. Sam held a bottle of red wine and Ivan raised a bottle of Becherovka, a Czech liquor I was quite fond of that tasted of cinnamon and ginger. Sam had the same sad smile I remembered from the first time I'd seen him, and I wondered if his aunt had bullied him into attending when he'd had other plans.

"Cora sends her regrets," Sam said.

Olivia clicked her tongue. "That woman has been in mourning for her daughter for too long."

"People grieve differently," Max said.

Brixton saved us from an awkward conversation by backing out of the kitchen. He held a silver platter with seven crystal glasses of sherry. I hated the stuff, but Dorian insisted that it made the dinner party more authentic.

"Aperitif?" Brixton said.

Heather squealed, then whispered to me, "You're such a good influence on him, Zoe. I can never get him to study for vocab tests."

I wasn't entirely sure "good influence" was the best way to describe our relationship over the course of the past week. Especially since he was currently carrying a tray of alcohol.

"Brixton, my man," Sam said, "you clean up nicely. Looking quite dapper tonight."

"Thank you, Mr. Strum," he said, doing his best impression of a British accent and not failing too terribly.

Everyone laughed. Brixton joined along. He'd done a better job at breaking the ice than anything I could have planned.

"Where is this French boyfriend of yours?" Sam asked. "I expected he'd be here. Veronica told me after class that he's, quote, 'dreamy.'" He laughed. "I have no idea what counts as 'dreamy' these days, so I wanted to see for myself."

"He's only a friend," I said, feeling all eyes on me, "and he's not big on parties. Anyone need another drink?"

"I just handed out the first ones," Brixton said, squinting at me like I'd lost my mind.

"Right." Right. Why had I made up that stupid lie?

"Interesting gargoyle statue," Max said.

I would have been thankful for the change of subject except that I wondered if he recognized Dorian from the other night.

"He's a replica of one of the gargoyles of Notre Dame in Paris," I said. "In case you were wondering why you recognized him."

"Isn't it heavy?" Heather asked. "I thought I caught a glimpse of him in your kitchen before."

"I haven't yet found the right place for him."

"I know what you mean," Heather said. "I'm always moving my artwork around until I find the perfect spot where the light hits a painting just right. At least canvas isn't as heavy as stone."

"He's a handful," I said, "but I can handle him."

From there, I talked of Paris, which kept the group interested for some time. I had to stay on my toes not only because I was watching Ivan, but because most of my memories of Paris were from before everyone in the room was born. I'd occasionally slipped up over the years, but since people never believed I could have been alive centuries ago, they assumed I was "eccentric" when I covered up my mistakes by explaining I was an avid reader who got lost in the stories.

Once we finished our drinks, only Heather wanted a second glass of sherry. The rest of the group opted for wine or seltzer water.

I purposefully didn't bring up the alchemy display as we mingled before dinner. I wanted to gauge Ivan's natural reaction. Instead I tried to keep conversation light—until Olivia brought up the death of Charles Macraith.

"We should raise a glass to our departed comrade," she said.

We clinked glasses awkwardly, before an even more awkward hush fell over the group.

"Has anyone heard how Blue is doing?" Sam asked. "I can't believe it. Max, do you know more—"

"I'm not on the case. Besides, we're here to welcome our new neighbor. Let's not worry about all that tonight."

"Are you all ready for the first course?" Brixton asked.

Ivan laughed. "You have gone from an English to a Russian accent."

"Crap, I was thinking of the wrong movie character."

"Language," Sam snapped, then grimaced. "Sorry, a teacher's force of habit."

"Remember to carry the bowls one by one, Brixton," I said.

He rolled his eyes before disappearing into the kitchen. He came back carrying two bowls of pumpkin bisque, one in each hand. A splash of soup fell to the floor as he served Olivia and his mom. When he returned for the next round, he carried a single bowl.

By the time we moved on to the main course—ratatouille, which Dorian had selected because it was a dish that tasted even better when prepared in advance since it allowed time for the flavors to transform each other—Ivan still hadn't commented on the alchemical display in the living room. I'd even given him the seat with the most direct view of the items. Perhaps he wasn't feeling well. I noticed his hand shaking as he picked up his fork.

"Where did you learn to cook, Zoe?" Sam asked.

"For someone so young, this is quite impressive." Olivia smiled at her backhanded compliment.

"I've learned from people all over the place."

"She traveled all around the country in her trailer," Brixton said from his position standing next to the kitchen. He shuffled his feet back and forth. Being a proper butler must have been more difficult than he'd imagined.

"Really?" Olivia said. "Were you a college dropout?"

Sam elbowed his aunt.

"I've always been someone who learns more from experience," I said. "I've traveled to most of the states in my trailer over the last few years. I'm a bit of a history buff. That's why I got into collecting all the antiques I've got in the living room."

"I recognize the brass medicine container," Max said. "That's got to be centuries old."

I smiled. "That's one of my favorites."

"Quite an expensive hobby," Olivia said.

"I sell them," I said. "Most of them, at least. Never my favorites." I caught Max's eye and my heart fluttered a little. I cleared my throat. "I've got a business selling these things. That's how I make a living. I find old things like alchemy laboratory supplies that some people find interesting." I looked at Ivan as I spoke.

"That's what brings you to Portland?" Sam asked.

"My online store is called Elixir. I can run it from anywhere, but when I got here, I—"

"Fell in love?" Olivia finished for me. It was an innocent enough statement, but her eyes darted between me and Max as she said it.

"So," Max said, clearing his throat. "The house is looking good."

"There's still a lot to be done."

"If I didn't already have two jobs," Sam said, "I'd offer to help."

I hadn't counted on them all being so polite. Even Olivia's normally snarky tongue wasn't especially bitter that night.

"Dessert?" Brixton asked, clearing the ratatouille plates.

While plates were cleared and the chocolate soufflé brought out, I excused myself. Maybe I wasn't evoking the right response from Ivan because I hadn't put the right kind of items on display.

It took me a few minutes to find the books I was looking for, two old alchemy texts that I'd unearthed from deep in my crates. By the time I came down the stairs, the group was finishing dessert.

"What do you say, Max," Ivan was saying. "Shall we break out the Becherovka?"

"Sounds good to me."

"Ivan," I said, returning to the table with the books. "I thought you might be interested in these books."

"The soufflé was delicious," Heather said. "But I thought you were a vegan."

"This is a vegan soufflé," I answered curtly. My focus remained on Ivan, watching to see his reaction to the books. The problem was, he didn't seem to have any reaction at all.

Heather and Olivia took their wine glasses to the living room while I cleared space on the table to set the two books.

"You're not supposed to leave the table," Brixton said, his eyebrows pressed together.

His mom gave him a questioning look.

"It's okay," I said. The sentiment was Dorian's doing, no doubt. To be a proper English manor house mystery, all the suspects had to remain sitting around the table, or sitting in a circle in the drawing room, or some such artificial circle.

"Ah!" Ivan said, as soon as he'd opened the first book to its title page. "I did not realize what this was. My eyesight is not as good as it once was."

"I thought I saw you looking interested when I mentioned alchemy," I lied. "Have you studied the subject?"

"My field of study is chemistry, but you must know from your love of history that alchemy was a precursor to chemistry." His eyes lit up as he spoke.

Max shifted uncomfortably, then got up to open and pour the Becherovka. *What was going on?*

I nodded. "I've always thought these old books are so much more beautiful than the laboratory items on the mantle."

Olivia scoffed from the couch, then resumed a conversation with Heather.

"Those are alchemical vessels on your mantle?" Ivan asked.

"I believe so," I said, trying not to show my confusion at Ivan's reply. Surely he knew what they were. But unless he was an extremely good actor, his surprise was genuine.

"I have only seen woodcuts and museum re-creations. Your pieces are much smaller than I imagined alchemical vessels would be."

"These are alchemy books?" Sam asked.

I nodded.

"Max!" Ivan called. "You would be interested in this."

Max returned to the table with the open bottle of Becherovka.

"You're interested in alchemy, Max?" I asked. I knew this party had been a bad idea. Nothing was turning out like I wanted.

"There's a similarity in the tools of alchemists and apothecaries," Max said, loosening his collar.

"Such a fascinating subject," Ivan said, resting the book on the table and flipping through the pages. "I never realized it until I began research for a chemistry book. Ah! This book, now I remember why it is familiar. I have seen a copy only once before, in the Klementinum in Prague. If I recall, it provided historical context for the work of John Dee. It is not widely available. Wherever did you find it?"

"I spend a lot of time at estate sales and flea markets," I said, mulling over Ivan's answer. He wasn't expressing interest in the aspects of alchemy that I would have expected for my theory. He seemed genuinely interested in the historical figures of alchemy, not the practical aspects of the alchemy. And why was Max so nervous? I had to do *something* to find out what was going on.

"Shortly after I began my research for my book on the history of chemistry," Ivan said, "the focus changed. I discovered connections to alchemy I hadn't realized existed."

I grabbed my cell phone and pulled up one of the photographs I'd taken of *Not Untrue Alchemy*. "Have you ever seen this?"

He studied the screen for a few moments. His face contorted, moving from interest to confusion to awe. His voice changed too. "Where did you find this?" The soft-spoken man was gone, a fiery zealot in his place. I wasn't the only one who noticed the change.

"I knew it!" Brixton shouted.

Everyone stared at the fourteen-year-old butler.

"It was you," Brixton said, pointing at Ivan. Tomato sauce covered the cuff of the sleeve. Everyone turned to stare at him.

"Brixton," I said, glaring at him and attempting to stop myself from throttling him, "this isn't what we—"

I caught a glimpse of Max out of the corner of my eye. He looked every bit as angry as I felt.

"You're the one," Brixton said, "who hurt Blue and took Do—I mean, took Zoe's books!"

"What?" Ivan sputtered, looking from Brixton to Max. "I don't understand. You think *I* had something to do with Blue's accident and what happened here?"

"Brixton," Max said sharply. "You need to stop."

"Nobody else had reason to steal Zoe's books," Brixton said.

Ivan turned to me. "You have more alchemy books, and they were stolen?"

"Including a very rare book that I'm betting isn't in the Klementinum or any other library—it's the book that includes this page you're so interested in."

Max ran his hands through his hair and took a large swig of his drink.

"If the page on your phone is like the rest of the book," Ivan said, "this is a phenomenal book. Max, have you any leads to get it back?"

"I'm not on the case, remember?" Max's jaw was set so tightly that it affected his speech.

"Max," I said. "What's going on? What aren't you telling us?"

"You really think I had something to do with these tragedies?" Ivan asked. He gripped the edge of the table. Sweat coated on his forehead.

"Well this *is* interesting," Olivia said. "Pray, do tell, Max. What *are* you keeping from us?"

"Are you all right, Ivan?" I asked.

"The excitement…" He wheezed as he spoke.

"Maybe you'd better—" I began, but it was too late. Ivan slumped over, dead to the world. I only hoped he wasn't truly dead.

THIRTY-ONE

THE TINCTURE I'D GIVEN to Blue was in the pocket of my raincoat, hanging on the back of the door. Was it possible there might be a few drops left?

"Call 9-1-1!" Max shouted as he loosened Ivan's collar.

Before anyone had time do so, I pressed the liquid to Ivan's lips. At that moment I didn't care about what my guests might think. I had to try and save Ivan. I knelt down next to him, feeling relief as I felt him breathing. Confusion quickly followed. I hadn't detected any poison. How could I have missed something?

Ivan awoke with a gasp, causing Max to stumble backward.

"What the hell?" Max said. "Ivan, are you all right?"

Ivan groaned. "Did I faint? Please, everyone, put your phones away. This is nothing to worry about."

My attention had been focused on Ivan, but now I noticed that everyone except for Max, who'd been attending to Ivan, had their phones out to call the paramedics. They stood staring for a few moments; then everyone began to speak at once.

"We should still call—" Max said.

"It had to be that liquor—" Olivia whispered to Sam.

"Brix, honey, go see if he needs help," Heather said.

"You want help standing up?" Sam asked.

"Enough!" I said. "Party's over. Ivan says he's all right. It's his decision if he goes to a hospital. Ivan?"

"Thank you, Zoe. I'll be fine. This happens to me sometimes."

"Rest here for a bit, Ivan," I said as I picked up my guests' jackets. "Thank you all for coming."

"You can't kick us out," Brixton said. "I haven't even served tea and coffee yet!"

"Come on, folks," Max said. "Zoe's right. Let's give Ivan some space."

Olivia pursed her lips. While throwing her shawl over her shoulder, the tassels hit Max in the face. I didn't think it was an accident.

I felt safe with Max, no matter how suspicious he was acting. My instincts had served me well over the years, but I hadn't encountered many murders either. I put my hand on Max's elbow, holding him back before I showed Sam, Olivia, Heather, and Brixton to the door. Brixton didn't want to leave. His mom seemed disinclined to force him, so I insisted. I didn't want him there for what was going to follow either.

"What the hell did you give him?" Max asked as soon as I closed the door. "I can't just pretend I didn't see that."

"You think I gave him an illegal drug?" That was too much.

"Ivan," Max said, "how do you feel?"

"It's a simple herbal remedy," I snapped.

257

"Then why did it work so quickly? That's not how things work."

"If you hadn't noticed, I'm good at working with herbs."

"Then you won't mind if I see what you gave him."

"This is ridiculous!" I said.

"Leave it be," Ivan said. "My recovering quickly has nothing to do with anything Zoe gave me. This happens to me sometimes. I'm fine. I want to know what you were all talking about before I fainted."

Max shook his head and looked up at the cracked ceiling. "You, my friend, have been a person of interest in this investigation. Personal feelings aside, I had no choice but to look into your movements while I was the investigating officer."

"Me?" Ivan said. "Even if you think this of me, how could I? These past weeks, my health has been worse, as you can see evidence of tonight. That's why I haven't been at Blue Sky Teas as much as usual. I can barely hold a cup of tea these days. My doctor will confirm this."

"Why didn't you say anything when I saw you?" Max asked.

"I didn't know it was an interrogation! It's embarrassing, Max. I'm only in my fifties, but my body has other ideas. It thinks I'm an old man."

"I put a call in to your doctor," Max said. "He was out of town and we couldn't reach him to—" He broke off with a start.

"What are you staring at?" I asked. "Find something else you think is illegal and you want to report?"

He rubbed his eyes. "I could have sworn I saw the gargoyle statue move. That Becherovka must be some strong stuff."

"Why don't you two come into the kitchen." I gave a sharp glance at Dorian as I held open the swinging door for Max and Ivan. "I'll put the kettle on and make us all some tea."

"Zoe," Max said softly as he stepped through the doorway, "I'm sorry I reacted automatically when I saw you give something to Ivan. I'm trained to notice these things."

He was so close to me that I smelled the subtle scents surrounding him. He must have gardened in his yard earlier that day. His large brown eyes were downcast. I believed he was truly sorry, but that didn't mean I trusted him. Or that I trusted myself around him.

"How about I make the tea you brought, Max." I busied myself filling the kettle.

"Ah," Ivan said, "that'll make me good as new. In the meantime, Max can continue explaining why he thought I was involved in this madness."

"I was afraid," Max said, "when Zoe told me that one of the valuable books of hers that was stolen was an alchemy book, that you might have been involved."

"That's why you've been acting so odd this whole time?" I asked.

"I hated that I had to investigate a friend, but it goes with the job." He paused, looking at the espresso maker Dorian had purchased. "I thought you said you didn't drink coffee."

"It's for entertaining."

He nodded, but his eyes lingered on the open bag of coffee beans and the folded copy of *Le Monde* underneath it. He was a detective. It was natural he'd be observant. He could tell someone had made coffee recently and that someone who wanted to read a French newspaper was comfortable around my house. My lie about a French "friend" to cover up for Brixton was building on itself. Max now suspected my "friend" stayed over. My attempt at a simple life was nowhere in sight.

Max remained curt for the rest of our short conversation, clearing up that neither Ivan nor Max had any reason to want Dorian's stolen alchemy book. By the time I saw the two of them to the door, I wondered why I thought I could ever have a normal life.

———

It took longer than I would have liked to awaken Dorian from his stone pose. I had to shake his shoulders so vigorously that I was afraid I might break off a chunk of stone. Finally, he stirred.

"*Mon dieu*. I cannot believe we were wrong about the Czech professor! It was a perfect theory. Perfect!" He tried to flap his wings. It took a few seconds for his wings to respond to the flexing of his shoulders.

"Not exactly perfect," I said. "We were desperate, which blinded our better sense. We convinced ourselves about a far-fetched theory because we desperately wanted to find your book."

Dorian wriggled his toes and fingers. He continued to have difficulty moving his left foot, but the reversal of his life force hadn't yet progressed further. He looked from his claws to me. "Where does that leave us?"

"I don't know, Dorian. I wish I knew."

"I will clean up," he said, not meeting my eyes.

"You don't have to—"

"I am stiff from standing still. Washing dishes will be good for me. You will work on the book pages?"

Though I had come to the conclusion that I would need the full book to unlock *Not Untrue Alchemy*'s secrets, what the gargoyle needed was hope. Even if there wasn't anything else I could do, at least I could give him hope.

"I'll study the pages," I said. "Maybe if I read them right before bed, my subconscious can work something out that has eluded me so far."

I brought the printed pages with me to bed, along with a glass of water with lemon. I couldn't concentrate, but it wasn't because of my fatigue. Knowing Ivan was most likely not a killer or thief, I now wondered if I could ask him for his help. Though I'd studied alchemy for a longer period of time than Ivan, my focus was less academic and more specialized. His interest in alchemy was the exact opposite. I had no doubt I was better at turning plants into tinctures, salves, and balms than Ivan, but there was a good chance he was better at understanding alchemical texts.

Once I'd made the decision to contact Ivan the next day, I fell into a restless sleep. I dreamt of alchemists in Prague.

A man with a long, pointed white beard appeared before me in the dream. I recognized him as the great scholar John Dee. The man had lived before me but was a legend to alchemists. We stood on the Charles Bridge in Prague, which in my dream was crowded with merchants from an earlier century in place of the hordes of tourists of today.

Dee beckoned to me. I followed him across the stone bridge. The fog became thick, swarming around us. I called out, but no sound came from my throat. I tried to run, but although my feet moved, I made no progress crossing the bridge. The fog overtook me. I could no longer see Dee or anything else. Fog had never frightened me, but in my dream, I had the strongest sense that I should be very afraid. Something dangerous lurked in the fog.

Almost as suddenly as the fog had swallowed me, the cloud lifted. But instead of scholar John Dee, charlatan Edward Kelley stood before me, balancing on the edge of the bridge. Kelley held a vial of mercury in one hand and wore a smirk on his face. As he steadied himself, the liquid metal bounced from side to side in its glass prison. Kelley caught my eye and winked. The man had fooled many people, including John Dee.

In his hubris at taking his eyes off the ledge, Kelley lost his balance. His shout pierced my ears, as if echoing against invisible walls that held me in place. He splashed into the water below.

My feet were my own again. I ran to the edge of the bridge and looked into the black water below. Instead of Kelley below me, the figure drowning in the water was Isaac Newton. He held the figurine of a dragon in his hand. His head sank beneath the water, yet he held the dragon tightly in his hand, keeping it above the dark waters.

As I reached out to him, I lost my footing. I would have fallen in myself had it not been for a hand steadying my shoulder. Without turning, I knew his touch. It was Ambrose.

As I turned to face him, Ambrose swallowed the substance of a glass vial. It was the vial of mercury Kelley had held in his hands. I tried to stop him, but he was now far away from me. His face contorted, as if feeling the effects of the mercury, then suddenly relaxed. He hadn't been poisoned after all. He smiled. It was the loving smile I remembered. I reached out to him, but a thick fog swooped in between us. There was nothing I could do to reach him. I reached for my locket, but it wasn't around my neck as it always was. Panic rose within me. The fog that carried Ambrose away was coming for me.

My arms fought to escape the confinement—until I realized they were fighting against tangled sheets, not ropes of fog.

I was awake.

I felt for my locket, damp with the sweat that covered my body. My heart was racing, but I breathed a sigh of relief. I didn't usually dream so vividly, yet I had done so multiple times that week. Perhaps I hadn't been ready to return to alchemy after all.

I took a sip of water from the glass on my bedside table, thinking over the dream.

Prague achieved a pinnacle of alchemical enlightenment a century before I was born. I had visited the city many times, but not while its most famous residents had lived there. My hazy dream world had melded memories of my own with legends I had heard of in its alchemical heyday.

The city of Prague holds an important alchemical legacy because it straddled the old ways of "magic" and new scientific methods. At the cusp of the Scientific Revolution, Rudolph II—a.k.a the Holy Roman Emperor, the King of Bohemia, and more—became a controversial leader because of his fascination with alchemy. Rudolph II's Court in the late 1500s to early 1600s hosted hundreds of alchemists, including John Dee—but not Edward Kelley. In an ironic twist of fate, Rudolph imprisoned Kelley not for being the charlatan that he was, but for failing to share his secrets for creating gold. The king never doubted Kelley's gold transformations were real.

Rulers like Rudolph wanted to control alchemists because they believed the alchemists could truly turn lead into gold, which would wreak havoc on currency values—unless the rulers controlled the gold themselves. It came to be commonplace for rulers to grant licenses to alchemists to practice. They couldn't have "just anyone" turning lead into gold.

Alchemists also needed patrons to have the resources they needed to pursue their intellectual curiosity. It wasn't gold or immortality that most alchemists were interested in—it was science. They were trying to understand the world around them, and they did make many breakthroughs that led to modern chemistry. Only long after his death was Isaac Newton publicly revealed to be an alchemist. He practiced alchemy in secret, and for years after his death the scientific community hushed up the secret that he had practiced alchemy, fearing of the impact of his scientific discoveries would be lessened. Newton's favorite substance was antimony: the Black Dragon. That's what he'd been holding in his hand in my dream.

I pushed the damp sheets aside and found the photographed pages of Dorian's book. I picked up a page that had an image of the Black Dragon, which symbolizes death and decay. Death and decay were a natural part of alchemy and of life in general, so I wasn't disturbed by the existence of such an image. What I had found fascinating and disturbing about the image was the rendering of the flames coming out of the dragon's mouth, which is why I had photographed it. I hadn't, however, photographed the opposite page, which would have held an explanation of the woodcut.

I shoved the troubling image into the drawer of the bedside table and finished the glass of water. Shedding so much sweat during my dream had left me parched.

The dream had pulled me in opposing directions: past and present, scholar and charlatan, mercury and antimony, poison and healing.

I don't believe dreams are magic any more than I believe alchemy is magic. But I do believe my subconscious was trying to tell me two things.

First, the mercury and other elements used by alchemists was for a purpose, unlike the poisonous mixture that had been used on Charles and Blue. *It wasn't gold or immortality that most alchemists were interested in—it was science.* The experiments of alchemists were dangerous *but pure.* The poison I was dealing with here in Portland was impure.

Second, this dream was fundamentally different from the "dream" I'd had after being poisoned. It was a hallucinogenic effect I'd experienced that day.

I had it wrong. We weren't looking for an alchemist who had stolen Dorian's book. We were looking for a poisoner who had killed Charles Macraith.

THIRTY-TWO

IN THE MORNING, I found five text messages from Brixton on my phone. I felt bad that I hadn't thought to check the previous night. I texted him back that everything was fine, but we didn't know who had framed Blue. I asked him for Ivan's email address. It was a school day, so hopefully he'd be awake and heading to school. His last text message had come in at two o'clock in the morning, so I wasn't sure.

Two minutes later, Brixton texted me Ivan's email address—along with a passive-aggressive text thanking me for keeping him in the loop the previous night.

———

After a quick oatmeal breakfast to warm up, I met Ivan in Washington Park. He received my email on his phone and told me where he was, inviting me to join him. He said I could find him at the park's International Rose Test Garden. I wasn't sure why he would be at a rose garden in the dead of winter. Unlike the lush cemetery grounds

I'd walked through earlier that week, the barren landscape of a winter rose garden gave me a cold, foreboding feeling. Dark clouds hung low in the sky, but the rain held off for the moment.

Ivan stood next to the brittle branches of a row of roses, their thorns more prominent for the absence of leaves and flowers. Though he wore a fedora, thick scarf, and a coat with the collar turned up, he was easy to spot. He was the only person there.

"You wonder why I come here in winter?" he asked.

"You appreciate the solitude?"

"It reminds me," he said, "that death is natural. My body is failing me, but I do not wish to feel sorry for myself. Sometimes," he paused and ran his fingers over the gnarled remnants of a rose bush, "I need a reminder."

"Would you like to talk somewhere inside, where it's warmer?" The chill in the air penetrated my coat. I could take it, but it didn't seem to be a good place for someone with failing health.

"The air is good for me." Ivan rubbed his hands together and shook out his shoulders. "Shall we walk?"

We walked side by side through the desolate rows of branches that had once been beautiful roses. I hadn't yet figured out what I should say to Ivan. I had to strike the right balance between getting the help I needed from Ivan and not revealing why I needed it, or why there was such urgency.

"I've been thinking about the woodcut illustrations you showed me," Ivan said as we entered the Shakespeare Garden. "They are unlike anything I have come across in my research."

"It's an interesting puzzle, isn't it? I was hoping you could help me figure out what the book is about."

"I miss an academic challenge, but would it not make the most sense to wait until the police have recovered the book itself?"

"I'm anxious to get started," I said. "It's the one mystery around me that I feel like I have some control over."

"This," Ivan said, "I can understand. Helplessness can lead to despair. Did you bring the images?"

I removed the printouts from my inner jacket pocket. Ivan took them from me. He stopped walking and examined them in silence. I couldn't tell if the frustration evident on his face was because of the tremor in his hands or what he saw in the images.

"What do you know of the history of the book?" he asked.

"I only found it recently, so when it was stolen I hadn't yet discovered its origins."

"And you found it—"

"In Saint-Gervais," I said, sticking to the truth as much as possible. That was the French town where Jean Eugène Robert-Houdin had been living when he brought Dorian to life. "I wouldn't be able to find the seller again. I didn't realize at the time what a find it was."

"That is unfortunate. Also unfortunate that someone stole it by accident, not realizing what they had."

I nodded but didn't speak for a few moments. Had it really been an accident? A crime of opportunity, that happened to result in the most precious item in my new house being stolen? That was too big a coincidence, wasn't it? Whoever took it had to know of its worth. The question was whether the thief took it for its monetary value— or if they wanted it to bring creatures like Dorian to life.

"*Non Degenera Alchemia.*" I pointed at the photograph of the title page. "Strangely convoluted, don't you think? Even for an alchemist."

Ivan laughed. "*Not Ignoble Alchemy.* Yes, very unnecessary. But alchemists have never been known for their simplicity. There are *hundreds* of words used to describe prima materia. Hundreds! The sun, the moon, water of gold, shadow of the sun, the garden, lord of the stones—the list goes on and on. No, it's not the obfuscation that I find fascinating about this book. What's most interesting here is that the book does not list an author."

The absence of an author wasn't common, but wasn't itself enough to signal that something was especially strange about the book. But along with the bizarre illustrations, I wondered why the author hadn't at least used a pseudonym.

However, that wasn't the most interesting thing Ivan had said. He translated the book's title as *Not Ignoble Alchemy*, whereas I'd translated *degenera* into *untrue*. That was an approximation, as any translation is. And my ecclesiastical Latin wasn't the best. *Degenera* could also mean something closer to degenerate or ignoble. But even if I'd done a sloppy translation of the title, that didn't help.

"I wish it was real," Ivan said. He spoke so softly that the wind nearly carried away his words before I heard them.

"I examined the book. I've been working with antiques for long enough that I know it's real. Hundreds of years old." Based on the style of Latin, and my observations of the book itself, it wasn't created before the Middle Ages, but dating the book could help me uncover its secrets—if I got it back.

"You misunderstand me." He pulled his scarf more tightly around him as the wind picked up, careful not to lose hold of the photographs in his hand. "I meant that I wished the theories expressed by the alchemists of history were true accounts of what could be accomplished with alchemy. That they could stop death."

Unlike the rose bushes that surrounded us, Ivan wouldn't return to life with the spring. "Even if it were true," I said, feeling my locket through the fabric of my sweater, "would you really want to live forever? It sounds lonely. So very lonely."

269

"That's not a sentiment I'd expect from someone your age. But you're right. Forever? No, I don't wish that. Right now, I would settle for living to my sixtieth birthday. Blue's teas have been part of the changes I've made to spend my last years as happily as possible. A few more years of good health is all I ask. That would be enough time for me to complete the book I've been working on."

"Related to alchemy?"

"About the intersecting history of alchemy and chemistry that scholars have missed. Isaac Newton is the focus of many books on the subject, and so are other famous alchemists, but many others have been forgotten. I suppose you could say I'm writing about the unsung heroes of science. Max and I have talked about it at length at Blue Sky Teas."

"That's why he was worried you might have done something drastic to get your hands on my alchemy books."

"He's seen me on some of my bad days, desperate to complete the book but thinking I would not have time… Come, let's continue our walk and mull over the meaning of these strange illustrations. You didn't come here to hear the problems of an old man."

"Maybe," I said, "but I don't see any old men around here."

"Ha! I knew I liked you from the moment I saw how you held your own with Olivia. She's not as bad as she seems at first—" He broke off. "Aha! I know what it is that was bothering me about these illustrations. I wonder if the person who carved these woodcuts did not realize the final image would be flipped once printed."

"You think they're accidentally backwards?" What had that made me think of? I took the stack of photographs from his hand and flipped through them. "That's not the only reason these illustrations are creepy."

"No," Ivan agreed, "but that is the thing that stands out. One cannot tackle all research problems simultaneously. You start with the ones that are easiest to identify, and then peel back the layers—"

"Ivan! I don't think this was an accident."

"They are clearly backward—"

"Because it's *backward* alchemy." The fear I had been keeping at bay returned head-on. I looked up at the dark sky that was threatening to burst. "The title, as you translated it, is *Not Ignoble Alchemy*. I had translated it as *Not Untrue Alchemy*. Those two things aren't different on their face, but there's a subtle difference. Something ignoble exists, but dishonorably. I think we're looking at alchemy's 'death rotation'—that's why it's not only the counterclockwise motions that make the images look off. The distorted animals in these illustrations are *dead*."

"To symbolize the death rotation of backward alchemy. Very clever."

"But working backwards isn't possible," I said.

"I've read about some alchemists who tried it because it was quicker, but none of them claimed to have been successful, unlike the many alchemists who claimed to have succeeded at proper alchemy. Perhaps that explains the absence of an author identifying himself."

I couldn't tell Ivan what I had meant by my words. It was, of course, physically possible to follow the steps of alchemy backwards. But it wasn't right. It wouldn't lead to transformation and creation. Only death.

Earth, air, fire, and water. Calcination, dissolution, separation, conjunction, fermentation, distillation, coagulation. They all have a phase in alchemy, but the death rotation turns the process on its head. No good could come of it. Everything it created would eventually be undone.

"Sacrificing one element for another to complete a transformation," I said, feeling numb from the realization more than the cold. "Rather than striving for perfection, those alchemists were circumventing it. That would explain why any such transformations would deteriorate over time…" The full impact of what this would mean for Dorian was sinking in. If I was right, I could work with the book—but to do so, I needed that book.

"This *is* an interesting puzzle you've brought me," Ivan said. "It is delightful to speak with someone who feels so passionately about a theoretical exercise. I hope the book is returned to you soon so we can uncover more of its secrets. Do you realize the implications this book could have, if we're right?"

I realized, then, that this was much bigger than Dorian and myself. Not in the way Ivan thought. This wasn't about a theoretical history. There were real alchemists out there who had performed alchemy's death rotation. I had proof. It wasn't only Dorian this was affecting. Gold itself was crumbling.

I hadn't connected Dorian's deterioration with the thefts of gold statues from European museums, but now that I knew what I was dealing with, it was obvious. The journalists were wrong. There were no brazen thieves who broke into high security museums and left gold dust in their wake to taunt the authorities. *There weren't any thieves at all.* The gold statues were crumbling on their own. Turning to dust. The life force of the gold statues was fading—just as Dorian's was.

THIRTY-THREE

AFTER MEETING WITH IVAN, I was so distracted that I nearly forgot I was going to stop at the library. I was now making daily trips there to get enough books for Dorian to read to stay awake. He spent several hours each day cooking, but I couldn't keep him cooking twenty-four hours a day. As it was, the fridge didn't have any more room for anything else.

Picking up the heavy bag of books from the truck, I lugged the mystery novels Dorian had finished reading into the library. Before picking out a new batch of books, there was something else I needed to do. I knew very little about backward alchemy. Nicolas Flamel had mentioned it to me only once, to say it was a force not to be used. The reason I remembered it was because of the ferocious look on his face when he'd spoken the words. He had spoken not with the calm voice I had come to know from my teacher. It had been a warning he didn't want me to forget. Because of that, I hadn't ever pursued the subject, not even when I was trying to save Thomas's life.

At a computer terminal, I looked up the library's alchemy books yet again. They were scattered across different sections of the library. It took me some time to track down the relevant tomes and surround myself with them on a long table. I was parched and hungry, but I had to figure out what was going on.

I searched through the books for hours, but only found the vaguest of references to backward alchemy and the death rotation. Whatever I was going to find out about Dorian's book, it wasn't going to be through library books.

———

I hadn't realized how much time had passed. By the time I reached home, it was after dark. Dorian was busy cooking dinner. I wasn't sure why; the fridge was already overflowing.

I wasn't yet ready to talk to Dorian about what I'd learned. Without the book, what I'd learned wasn't going to do us any good.

Brixton was having a hard time dealing with Blue's arrest, so I thought I'd kill two birds with one stone, getting rid of some of the food while checking on him. Max had said Brixton didn't want me to see where he lived, but I thought it was worth the risk to see him. Brixton hadn't been returning my text messages, but I found his address easily enough online. I was glad for that immediate result, but scared for what this level of online information meant for my future.

Heather opened the door of the apartment. Wet green, brown, and white paint covered large swaths of her arms.

"I thought you two might like some pie," I said, holding up two sweet potato pies of the six Dorian had baked.

"That's so sweet of you! Abel is out of town, though. I couldn't possibly eat so much pie. Do you mind if I give one to the neighbors?" She welcomed me inside and took the pies from me, setting them on a rickety card table that served as the kitchen table and grabbing a paint-stained towel to wipe paint from her hands and arms.

The apartment wasn't what you'd call spacious, but they had made good use of the space. In a corner of the living room next to a large window, an easel held the canvas Heather had been working on. I was surprised by how masterful it was. A sea of trees filled the canvas, the perspective so close that neither the sky nor the ground was shown. As I looked more closely at the trees, I saw eyes looking out.

"Feel free to share the pie with anyone you'd like," I said, "but I meant you and Brixton."

Her eyes narrowed in confusion.

"He's not home?" I asked.

"He told me he was staying over at your house tonight."

I froze. It was one thing for Brixton to be late coming home from school. That was bad enough with a murderer on the loose. But lying to his mom about where he'd be *all night* was something different altogether. Brixton was desperate to save Blue from a murder conviction. We hadn't been right about Ivan being guilty. What would Brixton do to save Blue? Where was he and what was he up to?

"Heather," I said slowly, feeling the full extent of my worry creep through me, "Brixton isn't at my house."

Heather frowned. "He told me he was working on a gardening project for school, with Veronica and Ethan. He said you were helping them so they'd all be staying over at your place."

"You didn't think to call me to confirm?" I asked.

"I trust Brix." But as she said the words, her body tensed.

"Maybe you misheard him," I said, "and he's at Veronica's or Ethan's house?"

Heather's shoulders relaxed. "That must be it. He knows I don't approve of Ethan." She rooted through an oversize handbag, not bothering to wipe the remaining paint from her hands. She pulled out an old-model cell phone and scrolled through the contacts. Putting the phone to her ear, she tapped her foot while she waited. The seconds dragged out.

"Voicemail!" she said. "Ethan's phone went to voicemail. I guess I'll have to call his parents. I've got their number here somewhere…"

While Heather rooted through a stack of papers in a secretary desk next to the door, I stayed out of the way on the other side of the room, again looking at her painting. It was as if the eerie eyes in the middle of the impressionistic trees were watching me.

I pulled my eyes away from Heather's alluring painting and watched her speak on the phone to Ethan's father. She flipped the phone shut and stared at me.

"He said the boys were at your house."

"Same lie," I murmured. "They coordinated. Why didn't you tell Ethan's father they weren't at my house?"

She bit her lip and shrugged. "Let me try Veronica. There has to be a logical explanation for this. Maybe they're over there."

Veronica's cell phone went straight to voicemail. Heather called her parents, who were under the impression that Veronica was staying at Brixton's apartment, as she frequently did when she was younger. They hadn't thought anything of it when she said she was going to do so to work on a school project.

I could hear the voices of both of her parents on the line, their voices growing louder as they realized their daughter wasn't where she said she'd be. I couldn't make out their words, but Heather cringed. "Yes, but—no, I don't think—I really don't think—" She was barely getting a word in between the two irate parents. Her eyes grew wide in horror before she snapped shut the phone.

"They said they're calling the police," Heather said, biting her lip.

"Because some teenagers aren't where their parents think they are?"

"They're like that."

"I doubt the police will take them seriously," I said, pulling out my phone.

"Then who are you calling?"

"Max," I said into the phone. "It's Zoe Faust. Yeah, I'm sorry to bother you, but is Brixton hiding out at your place? He told his mom he'd be at my house, but he's not. He's been avoiding me. I know he's upset about Blue." I listened to Max for a moment. "I'm sure he'll turn up. I'll keep you posted."

I hung up and looked to Heather.

"It's only eight o'clock," Heather said. "Maybe they'll be home soon?"

"What worries me," I said, "is why would they make up the story about staying over at someone else's house, if they were planning on coming back at all tonight?"

Normally I wouldn't have been too worried about three teenage friends lying to their parents. There were any number of things they could have been doing that they didn't want their parents to know about. But with how worried Brixton was about Blue, I had a bad feeling about what they might have been up to. Dorian had

277

been giving Brixton ideas about investigating. What if he had enlisted the help of Veronica and Ethan to help him clear Blue?

I suggested to Heather that she check Brixton's usual haunts and headed out to do my own investigating. It was after nightfall, so it couldn't hurt to pick up a creature who could see in the dark to help me search.

———

Dorian agreed with my assessment. So much so that he wanted to search without me, thinking I would slow him down.

"I'm going with you," I said. "I think I know where they might be. Remember that spelunking hat Brixton had?"

"You think they are in the tunnels."

"I do."

"I know a back way to get there, going underground close to here. Why are you looking at me like that? I have been exploring this new city. The tunnels here do not have the same morbidity as the catacombs under Paris, but there is a certain *je ne sais quoi.*"

Since I wasn't capable of sleeping in, these late nights were getting to me. I made myself a simple yet energizing smoothie elixir in the blender with lettuce, ginger, chia seeds, and chocolate.

Knowing I'd be climbing up and down ladders and through who-knows-what, I left my long coat at home. To combat the effects of the chilly night, I opted instead for bundling in a wool turtleneck sweater, thick wool socks, and matching green hand-knitted gloves and hat a woman in Houston had made me after I helped her start a vegetable garden.

I knew that small sections of the tunnels were accessible to the general public on guided group tours. Tourists and history buffs met at a Chinatown restaurant, outside which an innocuous metal door in the sidewalk opened up to reveal a ladder leading to the tunnels below. But that was far from the only entrance to the tunnels. We entered through a metal grate I would never have noticed if Dorian hadn't pointed it out. It turned out the bundling wasn't necessary. As soon as we were underground, the temperature was in the sixties.

The tunnel we entered reminded me of caves I had once hidden in: nearly complete darkness with only a tease of light, a low ceiling to bump your head on if you weren't careful, and the smell of dust and desperation.

I was about to flip on my flashlight when the tunnel was illuminated from above, casting eerie shadows across the jagged stone walls, thick wooden beams, and dusty floor.

"I found the light switch," Dorian said. "This section of the tunnel is used by some tour companies."

We followed the lights a few dozen yards until the tunnel ended in two rooms.

"I think this is a dead end," I said.

"*Mais non*. I have been this way before."

He pushed gently on what looked like a section of rock just like the rest of the wall. It was, in fact, a wooden door covered in a false coating of rock.

There were no lights strung up in this section of the tunnels. We clicked on our flashlights. In the harsh glare of the flashlight beams in the darkness, every rock transformed into a malevolent creature.

A light up ahead flickered. It wasn't from our flashlight beams.

"Dorian," I whispered, grabbing his arm and shutting off my light. "Do you see that?"

"*Oui*." He switched off his flashlight.

In the darkness that surrounded us, the light up ahead shone brighter than ever. The light came from around a corner, and it wasn't a solid light. It flickered, as if from a fire. Had homeless people snuck in here for a warm place to stay and lit a fire? I didn't smell smoke, though.

We crept closer, staying out of sight. People were speaking, but I didn't recognize the muffled voices.

I let go of Dorian's arm so I could feel my way along the wall without tripping. In the darkness, I couldn't see him. I knew he was smart enough to stay out of sight, so I wasn't worried about that. But it would have been nice to know he was close for whatever we might find.

The stone walls were strangely warm under my fingertips. I stepped closer.

Something was off about the voices.

Music began to play. It didn't drown out the voices. This wasn't the random sounds of people talking and playing music. I groaned to myself. It was a *movie.*

I peeked around the corner.

An old-fashioned movie projector beamed a James Dean movie onto a relatively flat wall. Sitting on blankets on the ground were Brixton and Ethan, with Veronica in between the boys with an additional blanket resting on her shoulders. In front of them were three open bags of popcorn and several old-style glass bottles of soda I didn't know still existed. Three spelunker hats lay askew next to the blankets.

"Good movie," I said, stepping into the room. "But everyone is looking for you."

Veronica screamed and jumped into Ethan's arms. Popcorn scattered across the floor. Ethan scowled at me—and Brixton scowled at Veronica, who wasn't moving from Ethan's arms.

"OMG!" Veronica said. "You gave me a heart attack, Ms. Faust!"

———

Once the kids were safely at home, I had time to think about what I'd seen. The kids hadn't merely found an old, boarded-up entrance to a section of tunnels once used for transporting goods. The door had been purposefully *disguised*. Whoever had done that wanted not only to keep people out, but to make it look like that section of tunnel didn't exist. I began to wonder why someone would want the tunnel to remain hidden.

THIRTY-FOUR

THE NEXT MORNING I was so groggy I was sure that even a strong green tea and a fruit smoothie wouldn't fully rouse me. I was wrong. Shuffling down the stairs, I was given a fright that raised my senses to a state of high alert.

Dorian's body contorted at an unnatural angle, his head hanging upside down with his hands and feet stretched out. I rushed to his side.

"Are you all right? Can I help?"

"You can position my hips," he said.

"What?"

"The lady on the video says my hips should be the highest part of my body. But since people do not have wings, do you think wings count?"

My laptop computer sat open on the coffee table, the screen displaying a video of a yoga class.

"Yoga?" I said, relaxing. The gargoyle wasn't dying. He was contorting.

"I thought it might help keep my body moving." He moved from downward dog to cobra pose. "*Zut.* This is quite unnatural."

I burst out laughing.

"Yes," Dorian said, righting himself. He stretched his shoulders as he stood up straight. "I can see you agree."

"I'm sorry," I said. "I'm sleep deprived. Is the yoga helping?"

He shrugged. "I can still shrug, so it is not hurting. At what time does the library open? Can you get me more books before you meet with Ivan today?"

As we fixed breakfast, the phone rang.

"Zoe, it's Heather. Brixton has run off again. He, Veronica, and Ethan didn't show up at school today."

"What is it?" Dorian whispered, watching my reaction to the phone call. I shook my head.

"Since they ran off last night," Heather continued, "and were just goofing off, the police think they're just ditching school. But ... I don't know. I don't like what's been going on. I have a bad feeling."

I did too.

I thought back to that false door we'd gone through. The one that was clearly there to disguise the fact that anything was beyond it. While the kids were having their movie night, had they seen something they weren't supposed to see?

After I got off the phone with Heather, I tried Max. He didn't answer his cell phone. I didn't see him at Blue Sky Teas, either, which Cora was keeping open. As I headed to his house, wind whipped around me, blowing dark clouds overhead. I turned up the collar of my silver coat.

My repeated knocks on the door went unanswered. I was almost back to the sidewalk when I heard a noise behind me. Turning, I saw a bleary-eyed man standing in the doorway.

"*Max?*"

He wore a bathrobe and looked like he hadn't shaved in days. And what was he doing asleep at nearly nine o'clock? The wind was picking up. A gust blew open his bathrobe. I found myself surprisingly disappointed that he was wearing pajamas.

"This better be important," he said, cinching the belt of the robe.

"It is. Put the kettle on. I'm coming in."

———

Twenty minutes later, Max was showered and shaved and we stood together in the warm kitchen, a storm raging outside. Heavy rain beat against the kitchen window box that contained his indoor herb garden.

"I should call this in," he said.

"Call in *what* exactly? That we have *a bad feeling*? The kids went missing last night and they were fine."

Max looked out the window, his jaw firmly set. "Tell me again what you know."

"I suspected Brixton and his friends might have been exploring off-the-grid sections of the tunnels when I saw Brixton's spelunker hat."

"Why couldn't they be a little older so their dares involved sneaking into each other's bedrooms," Max said mostly to himself.

"When I found them last night, they weren't in a normal section of the tunnels."

"You mean they'd gone past the tourist section, through one of the boarded-up doors."

"That's what I thought at first."

"What do you mean that's what you *thought at first*?"

"The door I went through wasn't a boarded-up door. It was a *hidden* door. It had been made to look like it was stone, to blend into the rest of the wall."

"How did you find it?"

I hesitated. It was Dorian who had found the door. "I heard the movie playing. I followed the sound."

Max nodded. "Could you find it again?"

"I think so."

"Then let's go."

———

After several wrong turns, we found the hidden section of tunnel.

Max swore. "I've searched here so many times … I never found this."

"You've searched here?" I pushed open the door in the same way Dorian had done.

Max shook his head at the fake stone.

"What were you—" I continued, but Max held up his hand for me to be quiet.

We walked in silence for several minutes, falling into step beside each other. Max set the pace, alternating between walking slowly and hurrying. Whenever he saw an object like an old wooden chest or a break in the walls that might have been a door, he stopped to examine it, then quickly moved on. I understood the unspoken motivation. If the kids had been taken against their will, we needed to find them quickly. Only when we reached the dead end room where the kids had been watching the movie did Max speak.

"Damn," he said. "There's nothing here."

"What did you think you'd find?"

"You asked me earlier why I was searching the tunnels. Remember I told you I fell through a trap door chasing people I thought were involved in a girl's death?"

"When you saw the monster." I shivered at the memory.

"Don't remind me about my vivid imagination."

I hoped that was all it was …

"I was following a smuggling investigation that led me here," Max continued. "That's why I think it's possible that the kids may have seen something they weren't supposed to when they were down here."

"What were people smuggling?" I asked.

"It's an ongoing investigation, Zoe. I can't just tell you whatever I want to."

"No," I said. "You just lie around your house drinking twelve-year-old scotch."

"I wasn't—"

"I smelled it on your breath when I got to your house. That's something I'm sure anyone would have smelled, regardless of their herbal skills."

He sighed. "I had a bad night last night. I'm no good at sitting on the sidelines."

My flashlight flickered. "I could have sworn I put new batteries in this."

"I don't want to get caught here in the dark. Not after what I've seen. Let's get out of here."

We made our way back the way we came. Max walked especially quickly. I wondered if he was thinking of monsters.

When we reached the entrance through which we'd climbed down, the sound of the rain echoed as it pounded on the metal door above. We were now in a section of the tunnels with electric light and earthquake-reinforced walls. Two empty soda cans littered the dusty floor. Max clicked off his flashlight.

The string of electric lights was dim compared to the harsh flashlight beam, but it was reassuring to be in a section of tunnel that felt like civilization.

"This is private, dry, and well-lit," I said. "Tell me what you know about this smuggling operation. If Brixton and his friends saw something—"

"There's been a resurgence of interest in herbal remedies in recent years," said Max, "especially in places like Portland."

It was one of the reasons I felt comfortable here. People wouldn't look twice at a young woman growing strange herbs in her yard.

"But herbs aren't illegal," I said. "They're not regulated by the FDA."

He hesitated. "We think it's tainted herbal remedies."

"You didn't think to mention this before?" I felt my body shake with anger. "That's why you were so suspicious when I detected poisons!"

"Herbal poisons aren't a common type of poison to use to kill someone," Max said. "You were new to town and knew a lot about herbs and poisons…"

If only we had been able to tell each other what we knew. "I understand why I might look suspicious, but why would someone sell herbs that were poisonous? That hardly seems like a good business model."

"The most educated guess we've pieced together is that these are tainted herbs coming in from China. The smugglers wanted to capitalize on this new herbalism craze, but they didn't know much about herbs themselves. They bought a large, cheap shipment from criminals, hoping to turn a quick profit without paying any taxes. And the tunnels were the perfect place to store the supplies. They didn't realize the herbs were tainted with poison until Anna became ill and killed herself. After that, they pulled back. We haven't seen anything lately."

"You think Charles Macraith was involved in it?"

"He had a work injury last year that made it impossible to work."

"I know," I said. "He told me my house was his first real job in a while. He'd been hired by the agent who put the house on the market just to do a walk-through to make sure prospective buyers wouldn't fall through any holes in the floors and sue her. He wasn't up for more than that while he recovered. The real estate agent is the one who gave me his name."

"Charles had to have been hurting for money because of his loss of work," Max said. "Sure enough, when we looked into him, we found a large sum of cash at his house."

"That's why you think Blue blackmailed him. Because she was hiding from her past, and she only accepted cash at the teashop so she would have access to large amounts of untraceable money."

"It fits."

"How does it fit?"

"He was known for being the kind of guy who inspires confidences," Max said. "You haven't been here long enough to know it, but even though Portland is a big city, its neighborhoods like ours have small-town characteristics—including the gossip. The community Blue created at her teashop fostered a lot of friendships, but Charles never gossiped about anyone. That's the kind of person people open up to, sometimes unwisely."

I had to bite my tongue. That was exactly why I had hired Charles Macraith in the first place.

"But it still doesn't make sense," I insisted. "Blue knows all about herbs. She would never buy tainted herbs. Even if I could believe she'd do something like that, she knows too much to buy and sell tainted herbs."

"I agree. I've known Blue for years. But that's the way the facts point."

"Except that she's under arrest, meaning it's someone else on the loose who's taken the kids."

"We don't know they've been taken," Max said. "They lied to their parents last night. All the facts point to the conclusion that they're playing hooky today."

"That's not what your gut says."

"No," he said. "It's not. The thing that's bothering me most is that I can't put my finger on *why* I think that."

"I know why," I said, the reason dawning on me. "Their parents were irate last night. There's no way the kids would do something stupid so soon after their last escapade. Something else is going on."

"I'm half-tempted to pull Sam out of school to get him to help us search the tunnels for the kids," Max said, "since that's where you found them last time. He teaches a section of his class on local history, including information about the Shanghai Tunnels. The students get really into it."

I frowned. "Brixton said he took them on an underground tour that involved sections of the tunnels not included on the tourist tours."

"That can't be right," Max said. "He wouldn't have taken them anywhere off-limits."

"He's the 'cool young teacher' who loves his students. Of course he would. But what I'm wondering is what *else* he knows."

"You're suggesting Sam is somehow involved in this?"

"I don't know what I'm suggesting," I said. "Something isn't right, though."

"I know. I feel the same way. I hate that I can't trust my own gut anymore. Ever since I saw that monster." He winced. It could have been from his injury, but my guess was that it was his chagrin for believing he'd seen a monster.

"I don't think you saw a monster," I said. The pieces clicked into place. Tainted herbs. My dream that had been hallucinogen-induced. The timing of the arrival of Dorian and his book. "When you saw 'the monster' the first time, it was on the smuggled herbs case, right?"

"What does that have to do with it? It was the fall that disoriented me—"

"I think," I said, "you were given something tainted with a hallucinogen."

There *wasn't* another creature like Dorian. Max had only equated the two after he caught a glimpse of Dorian. I let out a huge sigh of relief.

"You're *relieved* that I was drugged?" Max began to pace.

"The police never determined if there were drugs in the dead girl's system, right?"

"It was determined to be suicide. The family had the body cremated before I was on the smuggling case, before I could see the two might be connected. So you're right. We never learned if there was a hallucinogen in her system."

"Did the lab test for hallucinogens in the poison you found at Blue's—"

"God, Zoe, I'm not even on this or *any* case anymore!"

We stared at each other for a few moments. The close air of the tunnels felt stifling.

"Fine," I said. "I'll find Brixton and his friends on my own. Have a nice life drinking good scotch alone in your house."

Max groaned. "Wait. Fine. Tell me more about what you were thinking about Sam. I didn't know he was such an expert on the tunnels."

"I was thinking he could have found tunnels nobody else knew about," I said. "But I'm grasping at straws now. Forget I said anything. There's nothing to connect him to this. Lots of locals are interested in the tunnels."

But Max wore a strange expression on his face, caught between concern and anger. "Not everyone has a pile of medical bills for a sick aunt who raised him. That's why Blue took him on at the teashop, to help him supplement the money he made as a teacher."

"I knew about that. But lots of people need money. They don't go around poisoning people."

"Not only that. Olivia was in the hospital at the same time last year as Charles Macraith."

"And both with bills they couldn't pay?" I asked, remembering what Olivia had told me about Sam taking on the second job at Blue Sky Teas to help with the bills.

Max nodded, his face looking hollow in the dim light of the tunnel.

"Wait, where are you going?" Max asked as I started up the ladder.

"Sam is teaching and Olivia should already be over at Blue Sky Teas since she's helping keep it open. I'm going to look around their house." I'd dropped Olivia off at her house earlier that week. I didn't remember the house number, but I'd remember the barren rose bushes and pink shutters.

Max swore. "Zoe, you can't go breaking into people's houses. I need to get a search warrant."

I paused on the stair ladder to look over my shoulder. "You think you have enough to get one?"

He didn't answer immediately.

"I thought so." I continued climbing the stairs back to civilization.

"Zoe!"

Without pausing, I called over my shoulder, "If he's using the tunnels, he's got to have maps somewhere. I'm going to find them."

THIRTY-FIVE

DORIAN NARROWED HIS EYES. "You want me to climb into this suitcase?"

"It's a duffel bag. And yes. I promise it won't be for long. You want to help Brixton and me find your book, don't you? I don't know how to pick a lock. You have to come with me."

The gargoyle grumbled several words of French that weren't fit to repeat as he climbed into the duffel bag. Sam and his aunt Olivia's house wasn't too far from mine, but I wouldn't make it carrying the heavy bag of gargoyle. I'd need to take the car. I didn't like the idea of driving my distinctive car to a house I was breaking into, but I didn't see any other choice.

It was a good thing I'd added extra chia seeds and cocoa powder to my smoothie that day. I needed the extra energy to lift the heavy bag and place it in my truck. I tried to lift it gingerly, but it hit the door frame as I raised the bag onto the passenger seat.

"Oomph."

"Sorry, Dorian."

Things would have been much easier if we could have waited until nightfall, but there wasn't time. If the kids weren't playing hooky, we needed to find them, and the tunnels were our best lead.

"Wait here," I said as I parked down the street from Sam and Olivia's house.

"Where would I go?" was the muffled response from inside the duffel bag.

I did a quick circle of the house and found a side door. I let out a small sigh of relief. Even though the neighbors appeared to be at work, it was all I needed to be caught with a gargoyle picking a front door lock.

I carried the bag to the side of the house and unzipped the bag.

Dorian made quick work of the lock with his claws. I'd seen some thieves at work before, and those claws were better than lock picks.

A vase filled with the white flowers I'd bought for Blue was displayed prominently on Olivia's mantle.

My cell phone buzzed in my pocket. Max's name flashed on the screen. It was best if he didn't know what I was doing. The phone went back into my pocket.

"I do not see my book," Dorian said.

"No, but take a look at this." I picked up a poster tube labelled "world map." I popped off the top and looked inside.

Rolled inside a laminated map of the world, tightly rolled thinner sheets of paper were visible. I pulled them out.

"The tunnels," Dorian said.

My cell phone buzzed again. This was getting ridiculous. I pulled the phone out to turn it off, but along with Max's name across the screen, I noticed something else. He had called *five times.*

I must have missed some of the calls while I was lugging the heavy bag with Dorian inside.

I picked up the phone, but I'd just missed him. I had a voicemail waiting for me. Dorian's eyes grew wide as he watched me listen to the message.

"Zoe," Max's voice said. "If you're where I think you are, get out of there. I tried to get hold of Sam to see if he would voluntarily help us with his knowledge of the tunnels. But he wasn't at school. He called in sick today, Zoe. He could be anywhere."

I hung up the phone, feeling my pulse race.

"We need to go, Dorian. *Now*."

"Uh, Zoe. A young man is approaching the front door."

"I have to put this poster tube back where I found it." I moved quickly as I did so, scanning the room to see if there was anything else we'd moved. I spotted papers strewn on the entryway table.

"Zoe—"

"One second."

"You do not have one second."

My ears pricked with the sound of a key turning in the door.

Dorian pounced. Not on Sam, but on the door. He reached it right as the deadbolt began to open. With his strong hand, Dorian held the handle of the deadbolt, keeping it from opening.

Sam twisted his key from the outside. "Come on ..." he said. He must have thought the door was stuck.

I moved as quietly as I could toward the desk we'd disturbed. I put all the contents back, then nodded at Dorian. He held up his free hand, asking me to wait.

"Come on," Sam said again from behind the door. He gave the doorknob a shake, then pulled out his key. We heard the sound of

295

his keys rattling. While he searched for the right key, Dorian and I took our chance.

We ran out the back and hurried around the side of the house. There was no time to get Dorian back into the bag. I peeled off my jacket and tossed it on top of him, then peeked around the corner of the house. Sam was shaking his head as he opened the front door.

We didn't stop running until we were inside the truck. I was glad I had the foresight to park my truck down the street instead of in front of the house.

———

When we reached the hidden entrance to the tunnels, I dropped the bag at my feet, unable to hold it any longer. I had made Dorian crawl back inside the duffel bag for our walk from the truck to the entrance.

Making sure there was no one around, I pulled open the iron grate.

"Hurry," I said to the duffel bag.

"*Grâce à Dieu*," Dorian stepped out of the bag. He glared at it with a look of disdain before coming to his senses about his exposed location and darting into the tunnel.

I climbed down after him, closing the grate behind me. Dust from the tunnel floor wafted up to my nose, causing me to sneeze. My shoulder ached as if I'd been carrying a boulder. Which, essentially, I had been.

I handed him a flashlight, but he shook his head. I spread out the map of the tunnels on the surface of a dusty wooden trunk, shining the light onto the sketch.

"I think we're here," I said.

"*Oui*," Dorian agreed.

"You don't happen to have a photographic memory, do you?"

"Unfortunately, no. But I have explored the tunnels on my own and I see much better in the dark. I will lead."

Dorian scampered ahead. Though he moved quickly, one of his legs dragged behind, giving him an awkward gait. My flashlight bounced off the gargoyle, showing me that his whole leg up to his knee joint was now a solid mass of stone.

I tucked the map under my arm and hurried to keep up with the limping gargoyle. The temperature in this section of tunnels must have been close to seventy degrees, but I felt myself shaking. It couldn't have been the temperature making me shiver. It couldn't have been poison, either. I had fully recovered from the effects of the small amount that had affected me.

I knew what it was: *fear*.

THIRTY-SIX

AT A JUNCTURE IN the tunnels, Dorian turned and looked back at me.

"This way," he said.

A few minutes later, we reached the door that had been purposefully disguised. What we hadn't known until we found the map was that beyond that door there was a *second* disguised door. What looked like a load-bearing beam of wood was in fact a cleverly disguised entry to a hidden set of tunnels.

It was the perfect setup for Shanghaiers. If someone happened to discover their first false door, the interloper would carry on straight ahead, never thinking to look for *another* hidden passageway.

The two-foot section of thick wood stood directly next to the stone wall. It looked innocent enough, but we knew from the map that there had to be a way to make it move. It wasn't a structural part of the tunnels at all. It was a narrow opening.

I pressed against the wood from one side, and then the next. It didn't budge. I pushed it forward. Nothing. I grabbed the sides and pulled. That didn't work either.

"Perhaps there is a trigger mechanism," Dorian suggested.

"It could be in one of the stones." Dorian tapped on them with his fingers. "You are taller. Try the ones above."

I handed the map to Dorian so I could work the stones with both hands. I tried each of the stones surrounding the beam, quickly at first, and then more methodically after quick pushes didn't do the trick. I was now sweating from apprehension. I peeled off the bulky sweater I was wearing over a cotton blouse.

"*Mon dieu*," Dorian whispered. "Why does it not open? And why must you touch your necklace after you press each stone?"

I hadn't realized I was doing it, but he was right.

I pushed on the highest stone I could reach, then turned and rested my back against the wall.

"You know what the locket means to me," I said. "I can't lose someone else I care about."

"Your brother. Brixton reminds you of him, *n'est pas*?"

"I suppose he does." I clenched my fists in frustration. "Why won't this open!?" I whirled around and banged my fists against the stone wall. Pain shot through my forearms, but I didn't care.

Dorian pulled me away.

"It will not help anyone for your arms to be bloodied," he said.

I sighed and slumped down against the beam.

"Turn off the flashlight," Dorian said.

"We're not giving up—"

"No, but the shadows from the light confuses things. I can see better in the dark. I will look to see if there is a mechanism we have missed."

The darkness that enveloped us was complete. I saw nothing, and heard only my own breath and the light sound of claws tapping on stone.

"The other man in the locket," Dorian said softly, "you are thinking of him as well?"

I didn't answer immediately. As I listened to Dorian tapping on stone, the darkness gave me the courage to speak. "His memory was what I was running from," I said, "when you first saw me in Paris, helping the *Commandant*."

"He died because he had not found the Elixir of Life you had found?" Dorian continued to examine the wall as he spoke.

"The opposite, actually." I laughed ruefully in the darkness. "It was *because* he found the Elixir of Life that he died in the manner he did."

"*C'est vrais?*"

"It would have been better had he died of old age. A natural death, I could have handled. I would have grieved, but it would have been a natural death. Not like what happened."

"Did he die of the plague, as your brother did?"

"It's worse than that."

"*Merde*," Dorian said. "My claw is caught in the stone." He paused, and a rustling sound filled the darkness. "Ah! It is free."

"Is it the lever?"

"No. Nothing has moved. Yet the map shows clearly that this is the second door!"

"Maybe we're looking at this in the wrong way." I clicked on the flashlight, this time shining the light toward the ceiling. "If it's a mechanism that triggers the door, it doesn't have to be part of the door itself. It could be anywhere around here."

I stood up to take a closer look at the wooden beams running across the low ceiling. I methodically traced each of the beams. Four metal objects shone as the light passed over them. The simple hooks looked like they had been placed there to hold oil lamps to illuminate the passage.

But one of them was different from the rest.

I stepped closer to get a better look. I know metals. This particular hook wasn't solid zinc iron alloy like the rest. It had been painted black to look like the other hooks.

I reached up and tugged on the hook. I was rewarded by the sound of a latch clicking.

"You have found it!" Dorian said. He scurried to the thick beam and shoved. This time, the beam gave way, revealing a narrow passage of darkness. He hurried inside, carrying the map and my sweater with him.

"Wait a second," I whispered. "We don't know if it will close behind us and trap us. We need to find the mechanism on the other side, so we can get back."

Dorian pointed to a visible lever. "On this side," he said, "they have no use for disguise."

"Let me see the map," I said, taking it from Dorian's outstretched hand. "Damn. There are two branches of this tunnel."

"We shall split up?"

"I don't think that's a good idea."

Dorian snatched the map back, grumbling to himself as he studied it. We followed the narrow passageway for several dozen yards before the tunnel forked. I shone the flashlight in both directions.

"To the right," Dorian said softly, consulting the map, "is the shorter distance."

"Both directions go on for quite some distance," I whispered, "so the right is as good a choice as any."

I clicked off the light and took a deep breath. "We should be careful from here."

"Agreed. Give me your hand. I will lead you through the darkness."

In spite of myself and the situation, I laughed. I was being led by a living gargoyle through a secret section of tunnels underneath Portland. I remembered Brixton saying "My life is too weird." I could relate.

"This is amusing?" Dorian asked.

"You've heard the expression that someone laughs so they don't cry?"

"*Oui.*"

"This is one of those situations."

We walked in silence, in the cavernous darkness, for at least twenty minutes. Dorian periodically whispered for me to duck or to be careful as I stepped forward. As we walked further into the tunnels, the air grew close and stifling. Dorian maintained a firm grip on one of my hands to lead me. With my other hand, I felt along the wall. The only sounds were our light footsteps and the sound of my heartbeat.

Dorian's hand was neither rough nor smooth, neither warm nor cold. It felt like I was holding an ocean-worn rock, warmed to the temperature of its surrounding environment.

As we rounded a corner, the air quality shifted. I saw no light, but I felt a gentle breeze.

"Where are we?" I whispered.

"*Zut!* We have reached the end!"

"The end?"

Dorian pulled me further. I hadn't switched on the light, but a dim light spread out before us. We stepped forward into a room with a metal grate above. Light poured into the room from above. As my eyes adjusted, I became aware of a rhythmic sound.

I groaned. "The river. We're somewhere along the Willamette."

"It appears this is another disguised entry point."

"I can't reach the grate," I said. "If I lift you up, you should be able to reach it."

He nodded, and I cupped my hands to boost him up with his good leg. By holding him on my shoulders, he was able to reach the grate.

"Rusted shut," he said. "This has not been used in many years."

"We went the wrong way."

"Come," Dorian said. "There is no longer the need to be quiet as we retrace our steps."

Using the flashlight this time, we were able to move more quickly. Still, it wasn't fast enough. I held the flashlight in one hand and my locket in the other.

"We will find them," Dorian said. "Have faith."

"Faith doesn't save people."

"You are a good person, Zoe Faust. Whatever happened, it could not have been your fault."

"You're wrong. Because of me, both Thomas and Ambrose died. That's why I first gave up alchemy and ran from everything—including myself."

"What you told me of your brother was not your fault. Failing to save someone from the plague is not your fault."

"But that's not what happened to Ambrose." I clutched my locket more tightly. "I should never have let him talk me into practicing alchemy again."

"What happened that is so terrible?"

"I already told you that after Thomas died, I left the Flamel's house, unaware I had discovered the Elixir of Life." I walked more quickly than Dorian, so he wouldn't see my face as I spoke. "After I knew what I had become and returned to the Flamel's house to find it burned to the ground, I felt as if I was cursed. I didn't think I deserved to live, but I at least wanted to help others. I used my herbal skills of plant alchemy to do so. I was never good at making gold, so I sold healing tonics to survive. I gave away more than I sold, so I barely survived. I could never turn my back on a needy person. There were so many of them …"

I tried to shake off the memory of so much suffering. Though I had helped many people, there were so many more I couldn't save.

"The man in the locket was someone you could not help?"

"Ambrose," I said. "When I met him, I was an emaciated wreck, curing others while I lived on boiled meat and potatoes, barely surviving myself. I had learned that I was nearly as human as everyone else—feeling sick when I ate poorly, bleeding when cut, blistering when burned—but I hadn't felt worthy of healing myself. Not until I met Ambrose. He was a fellow alchemist, so he recognized me for what I was."

"Ah!" Dorian said. "So the tragedy is that he found the Elixir of Life, yet still died?"

"Worse. It won't make sense unless you know what he did for me. When we met, though Ambrose was a practicing alchemist, he hadn't yet found the Elixir of Life. I fell in love with him, and he with me. He helped me realize my life was worth living. That's when I began to eat a plant-based diet, which helped me heal my body and feel alive again. I believed my life was worth living again, so I wanted to feel alive in every way. We worked together for many years, happy in our shared alchemy lab. But he had a son. Percival."

"The son did not approve of you?"

"I didn't approve of Percival. Ambrose was devoted to his son, but I saw him for the mean-spirited man he really was. Ambrose tried to get Percival interested in alchemy, but Percival is a perfect example of why the world isn't ready for alchemy's secrets. Percival was only ever interested in quick fixes. He took opium to excess, and ate and drank with a similar indulgence. He never held a job for long, because he always knew his father could make him gold. Whenever I tried to broach the subject with Ambrose, he wouldn't hear of it. He would believe nothing bad about his son. Ambrose was the most brilliant alchemist I've ever met, but Percival was his weakness."

"This is what I understand it is to be a parent."

"Maybe so. I should have seen it coming. Maybe then I could have prevented it."

"What happened?"

"Working together in our laboratory—me working with plants to create healing elixirs and Ambrose working with metals to create the philosopher's stone—we complemented each other and increased each other's learning. Ambrose created his own philosopher's stone that led him to the Elixir of Life. In spite of my protestations that it wouldn't work to transfer it to another, Ambrose tried to transfer it to Percival. When it didn't work, Percival became irate. Cutting corners, he tried to create it for himself, envious that his father and I would live while he would die. Percival continued to age, becoming a bitter old man who wasted away and died. Ambrose couldn't take it. Knowing he'd caused his son so much pain and that he would go on living—Ambrose went insane."

305

"*Mon dieu.*"

"I tried to get him help, but he was taken away and placed in a mental institution. He couldn't live like that. He killed himself."

"I am so sorry, Zoe. But you should also realize you are lucky to have found Ambrose at all. To have found that even briefly, for this I am envious."

"Believe me," I said, wiping away a tear with my sleeve, "you don't need to be envious of my life."

"I have never met another like myself. My father was the only one who knew my true self. The blind men I worked for believed me to be a man, like them. They believed me to be disfigured, and this is why I wished to stay out of sight from others."

Guilt washed over me. I hadn't considered that Dorian's life had, in some ways, been lived in even more isolation than my own. "We've both lived lonely lives."

"Yet," Dorian said, "I still wish to live."

We walked in silence for a few minutes, the weight of Dorian's words hanging in the air.

"How much further do we have to go?" I asked.

"*Merde,*" Dorian whispered.

"What is it?"

"Quiet," he whispered sharply. "Turn off your light."

I clicked off the light. "What do you see?"

"Wait here."

"We're not splitting up."

"I shall be back momentarily."

"Wait—"

"There are two more passageways I see," Dorian said, "*neither* of which are marked on the map, yet there is light ahead. Remain here."

I crossed my arms and waited impatiently as Dorian's footsteps faded.

A few minutes later, he still hadn't returned. I began to tap my foot anxiously. Where was he?

A faint tapping noise sounded. I stood still. The noise continued. It wasn't caused by my fidgeting.

In the darkness, I wasn't sure which direction Dorian had gone, so I couldn't tell if the sound was coming from the same direction. Keeping the light off, I edged forward, following the sound.

As I crept forward, the noise grew louder. It sounded like someone hitting metal. Or maybe someone's bones being hit with a piece of metal.

I gave up stealth in favor of speed. I turned on my flashlight and ran toward the sound. I ran for minutes, down the narrow passageway of heavy, dusty air. I nearly tripped on a pile of boxes stacked on the side of the narrow tunnel. My lungs heaved, but I kept going.

The tunnel jogged left at a sharp angle. As I rounded the corner, two lamps illuminated a larger section of tunnel. Jail cells lined one wall. Brixton, Ethan, and Veronica were trapped in one of the cells.

On the outside stood a woman in a distinctive red shawl. It was Olivia.

THIRTY-SEVEN

VERONICA STOPPED BANGING ON the iron bars of the jail cell as soon as she saw me. After a few seconds of the harsh sound echoing through the tunnels, the sound ceased. All was silent.

Olivia raised an eyebrow at me, while the kids stared open-mouthed from behind the bars of the Shanghaier's cell.

I mentally kicked myself. Everything that applied to Sam Strum also applied to his aunt Olivia. Olivia needed money for her medical treatments. Olivia was at the hospital at the same time as Charles Macraith. And sharing a house with her nephew, she would know about his local history research findings about the Shanghai Tunnels.

"Well," Olivia said, "are you going to just stand there, or are you going to help me rescue the children?"

"*Rescue* them?" I repeated.

Olivia pursed her lips. "Did I give you too much credit by thinking you were an intelligent young woman?"

"Mr. Strum locked us up," Brixton said.

"It was so creepy!" Veronica added.

"Wait," I said. "*Sam* locked you up?"

"Give the lady a prize," Ethan said. He stood with his back against a brick wall on the far side of the cell, mimicking a casual stance that was betrayed by the nervous twitches of his hands.

Veronica elbowed him. "Ms. Faust is here to help—um, aren't you?"

"I am," I said, eyeing Olivia.

"She's not working with her nephew," Brixton said.

"I didn't know what Sam had done," Olivia said sharply. "Are you going to just stand there, or help me unlock these cell doors?"

"Where's Sam?" I asked.

"He wouldn't hurt them," Olivia said. "He just needed them out of the way. You don't have to worry about him. He won't be back."

I wasn't so sure. Regardless of what I thought, we had to get ourselves out of the tunnels. We were so far from fresh air that I didn't know what would happen if we stayed there too long.

I joined Olivia at the metal door. "What have you tried so far?"

"Brute force. It didn't work."

I looked at my cell phone. No reception.

"Mr. Strum took the key with him," Veronica said.

I tugged on the door. "What happened?"

"The last time we were here exploring—" Brixton began.

"Spelunking," Ethan cut in.

"Yeah, spelunking," Brixton said, rolling his eyes. "Well, we found some evidence that looked like there was modern Shanghaiing going on. Well, not Shanghaiing, exactly. Smuggling, though. That's almost as cool, right? There was like a truckload of boxes from China. We thought Mr. Strum would think it was cool, 'cause of his interest in this stuff. So this morning when we got to school, we went to find him before classes started."

"To tell him about what we found," Veronica added.

Brixton gripped the bars. "He was totally into it. Said we should all ditch school today so we could show him what we found."

"We thought he was cool!" Veronica said, stamping her ballet flats on the dusty cell floor. "A teacher ditching with us. That was going to be, like, the best story ever. Instead, he locked us up in here! Right after we showed him the hidden boxes! I couldn't believe it. We totally thought it was a joke at first."

As she spoke, I knelt down to examine the lock.

"When we saw that it wasn't," Brixton said, "I tried to hypnotize him."

I glanced sharply at Brixton.

"I, uh, read about hypnosis online," Brixton said. "But anyway, it didn't work. He left us here."

"Does anyone have a pocketknife?" I asked.

"Tried it already," Ethan said, and Olivia held up a broken pocketknife.

Where had Dorian gone off to? He would be able to pick the lock, but he couldn't reveal himself openly. If only I had the map he'd run off with, I could have made my way out of the tunnels to get help. The tunnels stretched on for miles in so many directions that I wasn't confident I could find my way out without the map.

"Olivia," I said, "how did you end up here?"

"After Sam left for the high school this morning, he came back to the house to grab a key. I didn't think much of it until I looked out the window and saw the children in the car. I knew something was wrong. He'd been acting strange lately. I thought it was because

310

he was tired from working two jobs. But when I saw what he was doing this morning, I began to put the pieces together ..."

"So you followed them."

"I don't drive, you know. But I suspected where they were going. I took the bus to a tunnel entrance I knew about from Sam, and used the stories he'd told me to find my way here."

"Could you find your way back to get help?"

She hesitated. "I followed the sound of Veronica banging on the bars with a brick. But without a sound to follow on the way back ..."

"How did *you* find us here?" Ethan asked.

"Brixton's mom called me, worried after she got a call that you were ditching school."

"Why didn't you guys call Max?" Brixton asked.

"I did. I told him my suspicions about Sam using the tunnels for smuggling tainted herbal supplements. He said he needed a search warrant to search Olivia and Sam's house ..."

"You broke into their house?" Brixton said. "Wicked."

Olivia clicked her tongue.

Another, louder click sounded a moment later. Everyone froze.

"Sam?" Olivia called out, her body tensing. She wasn't nearly as confident in her assessment of Sam as she wanted us to believe.

There was no reply.

"You see?" she said hesitantly. "He's not here. He's not going to hurt anyone."

I could have pointed out that Sam had killed not once but twice—the first time accidentally killing Anna West, the second time deliberately murdering Charles Macraith, and a third death was only foiled because I'd found Blue in time—but I held my tongue.

"I don't like it down here," Veronica whispered. She tugged at the sleeves of her sweater, then wrapped her arms around herself.

"You found Sam's map of the tunnels?" Olivia said to me. "Why didn't you bring it with you?"

"I had to leave it behind."

Olivia threw her arms into the air, her shawl stirring up dust. She coughed before speaking. "We should split up. That way one of us should be able to find our way out of here and get help."

"We shouldn't split up," I said. "We can't be sure Sam isn't coming back."

"I told you," Olivia said, "he wouldn't hurt them."

"Only imprison them."

"He only did this to help me!" she said. "I knew he had gotten extra money to help pay for my experimental treatments abroad, but I thought it was Blue who was paying him generously because she knew about our money troubles. He never meant to hurt anyone! He would never have hurt anyone on purpose. He couldn't have known he'd been lied to and given tainted herbs."

Ethan put two fingers in his mouth and whistled. "Can we focus here?" The normally unfazed boy was visibly rattled.

"I have an idea," I said. "Give me one second."

I retraced my steps into the darkened portion of the tunnel. I was hoping it was Dorian who'd made the sound in an attempt to draw me out into a private meeting. I walked forward a few yards until I was out of earshot.

"Dorian?" I whispered. "Dorian?"

Nothing.

I waited for a few moments, but didn't dare go forward for fear of getting lost.

"Dorian?" I tried one last time.

I sighed and walked back to the group.

"Well?" Olivia said. "What was your brilliant idea?"

"I thought I remembered which way to go," I said. "But I was wrong."

"Looks like we could use these," Brixton said, pulling a bag out of his backpack. It was filled with a dozen chocolate date balls. He took one and passed the bag around.

Dorian had made the dessert treats. He'd made an awful mess of the kitchen at the time, searching for flour that I didn't have. Instead of abandoning the ingredients he'd already mixed, he'd experimented without expectations and was able to create something even better than he'd initially envisioned. I breathed in the dusty air as an idea tickled the back of my mind. Giving up on expectations was exactly what I needed to do here.

"I've got it," I said, looking from the lock to the opposite side of the old jail cell door. The hinges were covered in rust. "Can I see that broken knife?"

Using the broken blade of the Swiss Army knife, I eased the pin out of the upper hinge. It made a horrid squeaking noise as it pulled out of its socket.

"No way!" Veronica said.

Ethan swore under his breath, mumbling something about how he should have thought of it himself.

"Mwmsm," Brixton said through a mouthful of dessert.

Olivia held the door as I removed the second hinge pin. Together, we swung open the door in the opposite direction than was intended.

Veronica leaped out of the cell and gave me a hug. "Thank you, Ms. Faust!"

"Now we can all get lost together," Ethan said.

The bright light of a flashlight came around a corner.

Veronica shrieked like a banshee, causing the boys to cover their ears.

Olivia and I stepped instinctively in front of the kids.

"He wouldn't …" Olivia whispered.

It wasn't Sam who came into view. It was Max. I let out a sigh of relief. Max's shirt was askew and his chest heaved. He must have been running.

"You're all okay?" he asked.

His eyes locked on mine while everyone spoke at the same time to say they were all right. I barely heard them. At that moment, I was no longer in a claustrophobic tunnel, surrounded by three teenagers and the aunt of a murderer, with a gargoyle somewhere in the shadows.

"Thank God," Max said, his eyes never leaving mine. He took a step forward and pulled me into a kiss. His lips tasted of licorice and spearmint. I found myself lost in the intensity of the kiss, something I hadn't felt in nearly a century. The feeling scared me. I wasn't afraid of Max himself, but the *idea* of Max. It was too much. We were too different. He was a skeptic who would never accept me if he knew the real me. I pulled back. As I broke away, the look on his face surprised me. The confident, stoic cop was *hurt*.

"Mr. Liu!" Veronica said.

Max cleared his throat. "It looks like everyone is all right."

"How did you find us?" I asked, clearing my own throat.

"An anonymous person left me a map of the tunnels with this section circled. It was accompanied by a note saying I'd find Brixton, Veronica, and Ethan here. Was that you, Olivia?"

"It wasn't me," she said.

"You don't have to protect Sam any longer," Max said. "We've got officers at the house arresting him."

"I only figured out what my nephew was up to this morning," she said, "and I have no idea who left you that map."

I knew the answer. I wondered how many Portlanders had noticed a stooped, child-size figure using a bulky sweater to cover himself as he ran through the streets, taking a great risk to rescue us from the cavernous tunnels deep beneath the city.

THIRTY-EIGHT

THANKS TO MAX, THE police had arrived at Sam and Olivia's house in time to find Sam packing hastily for a getaway. And thanks to Dorian, Max had the map to find us and lead us all out of the tunnels.

The kids were now safely at home with their parents, who'd left work when they heard what was going on. I was waiting at the police station to find out what was happening. I was torn. Part of me had wanted to return home to see Dorian, but the best way I could help Dorian was to learn what had happened to his book. If the police could break Sam, they might discover where he'd hidden it.

As I waited to hear what was going on, I thought about how it was his own guilty conscience that had done him in. If he hadn't acted, he would have been safe. The kids wouldn't have gone to anyone else with what they saw, and Sam could have gone home "sick" and disposed of the merchandise to cover his tracks, now that he knew the boxes had been discovered.

I knew about guilty consciences. But whatever blame I shouldered for the deaths of Thomas and Ambrose, it didn't include murder.

Max poked his head around the door of the waiting room. Was it my imagination, or was he blushing?

"Your idea to remove the rusty hinge pins to get everyone out of those old hidden jail cells garnered a round of applause," he said, "and Detective Dylan has agreed to let you watch the interrogation from another room."

I followed Max into a small room with a video screen.

Instead of sitting down, Max left the room, leaving me to contemplate the man on the video screen. Sam Strum looked at peace. Not *happy*, but as if a great weight had been lifted. It made sense, now, why he continued to go to the teashop that was a reminder of the innocent girl who'd died because of him. The sadness I'd seen in him that day had been his penance.

Max returned a minute later with two cups of tea.

"Are we waiting for his lawyer to arrive?" I asked.

"He's declined a lawyer," Max said. "Says he wants to get everything off his chest. All he asked for was his favorite tea from his house before he'd talk. One of the guys is getting it. That's what we're waiting on. Zoe, I—"

Another officer entered the room, causing Max to break off whatever he was going to say.

"Looks like they're about to get started," the officer said. "Took long enough to find that damn tea."

We watched Sam breathe in the steam from the tea. He smiled oddly before he spoke.

"I wasn't going to hurt Veronica, Brixton, or Ethan," Sam said. "It's important to me you know that. I was only going to keep them locked up until I could disappear. Then I was going to call in a tip so they'd be found."

"Why don't you start at the beginning," a voice from off camera said.

Sam nodded. "When my aunt got sick a couple of years ago, she couldn't live by herself. I moved in with her."

"That was a generous offer."

Sam shot a confrontational look toward the interrogator, but continued. "She'd essentially raised me, so it was the least I could do. Aunt Olivia doesn't have any children of her own, and she needed me. It was difficult for her, as she went through her cancer treatments. She'd had cancer before, and beat it. But this time was different. They didn't think she'd survive." Sam paused and ran his hands over his face.

"That's where you met Charles Macraith—at the hospital?"

"I knew him before, but that's where we got to know each other better. Aunt Olivia and I had been going to Blue Sky Teas ever since the first time she got sick. I'd seen Charles around there. We were friendly but not friends. But at the hospital … We got to talking about how he'd been out of work for so long that he was hurting for money. And me and Olivia? She couldn't work, so I took a second job at Blue's. It was enough for us to get by, but not enough to try an experimental treatment for her. I had to find a way to pay for that treatment. She was dying, you know? How could I not do absolutely everything I could?"

I knew that feeling. Sam's heart had been in the right place, at least at first. But he'd gone way too far. I shuddered. Max glanced at me. His hand moved toward me, but he immediately pulled it back. I pretended I hadn't noticed.

"So you and Charles came up with a plan," the detective prompted.

Sam shrugged. "Charles was the kind of guy people would open up to. He knew a lot of people from all the home renovation work he did. And people knew they could trust him. He was never one to gossip."

"Uh huh."

"We'd both seen how herbal remedies had been getting so popular. Olivia took some, to try to manage some of her side effects. I knew how expensive they were. There must have been a *tremendous* markup. So one day Charles and I were talking about our money problems and how expensive herbal remedies were, and he got all quiet. I mean, quieter than he usually was. Which was already pretty quiet. Then he said he knew a guy who could get us some Chinese herbal remedies in bulk. The guy had problems himself, so he was getting out of the business. He had all these unused, packaged herbal supplements that could help people. He was willing to sell them to us cheaply, and we could even take over a company he'd already set up, but we'd have to sneak the shipment into the country. It didn't seem too risky. I mean, herbs aren't regulated the same way pharmaceuticals are, since they're safe. That's what we thought. It was supposed to be easy." He paused to take a deep breath and have a sip of tea. "Nobody," he said through clenched teeth, "was supposed to get hurt."

"But then Anna—"

"You don't have to remind me. I'm getting to that. Because you need to know that was never supposed to happen. Charles and I scraped together the little bit of money we had to do this deal with the guy. I put in a higher percentage. Charles had the contacts on both ends, but what he didn't have was money. He worked on selling the various supplements. You have to realize neither of us understood much about these supplements. We trusted the guy who sold them to us. That was our mistake. Being too trusting." Sam took another deep breath.

Sam was justifying his actions, still believing he was in the right. That had to have been obvious to Detective Dylan, but he didn't aggravate Sam by saying so.

What Sam was saying also helped me understand what had gone on with the different experiences that I and others had with the tainted herbs. There were *different* herbal remedies that had all been tainted. A large shipment from China, and they didn't even know what they were getting. It was an idiotic plan, but I still felt a sliver of empathy for Sam. He'd acted irrationally because he wanted to help someone he loved.

"We didn't know the shipment he sold us was tainted," Sam said. "We didn't realize it until Charles's distributor told him they wouldn't take any more. Said there was something wrong with it. Nobody was dying, though. Not until Anna. She was a health nut. I had her in my class a couple of years ago, and I'd see her at Blue Sky Teas after school. When she killed herself—"

He closed his eyes and breathed in the scent of the tea he held in his hands. He brushed a tear from his cheek before speaking again.

"When I heard she killed herself, I didn't believe it. She'd been acting erratically in the weeks leading up to it, but I assumed it was boyfriend problems making her paranoid. Teenagers have a lot of drama. But when I talked to her mom, I realized she was taking a "brain booster" herbal formula that was supposed to help her focus on her schoolwork. She was responsible like that." He laughed, and more tears rolled down his face. "She didn't want to take any of the 'real drugs' some of the other kids were taking. Ironic, right?"

Ironic, indeed. I knew what had driven Anna to kill herself. Mercury poisoning, also known as "mad hatter disease." Hatmakers in the 1800s came in habitual contact with mercury, which was used to treat the felt in hat manufacturing. Many an alchemist had been poisoned by mercury as well.

"It wasn't your intent," Detective Dylan said.

"I told Charles, then, that we couldn't sell the rest of the tainted supplements. He'd been trying to find someone else to distribute them, but I said it had to stop. I thought he agreed with me, but when Zoe Faust moved into that house, I knew he had no intention of giving up."

Max glanced sharply at me.

"Zoe Faust was involved?" Dylan asked, sounding surprised himself.

"She has an online shop called Elixir, with all sorts of apothecary items. The guy we bought the herbs from called himself an apothecary. I knew there had to be a connection. Charles told me he was going to work on her house because he was ready to go back to work and make an honest living. But when I looked her up, I knew that he was lying to me. I mean, who on earth would buy that house to live in? It gives 'fixer-upper' a whole new level of meaning. I suspected Charles found a sympathetic partner to buy the house."

"Why would you suspect that?"

"Oh, didn't I say? Because that house was the first place where we kept the shipment. It was abandoned and had a huge basement. I helped Charles make a false wall in the basement to hide the boxes. He knew the house wasn't going to be occupied, because he was paid to do an inspection when they were ready to put it on the market. He said there was no way, with everything wrong with it, that anyone would buy it. That house was the perfect location to store the shipment, which was another reason we thought our plan would be easy."

The lights! That explained the "haunted house" lights people had seen in the house when it sat empty.

Sam's suspicion of me also explained how it wasn't a coincidence that Charles Macraith had been killed at my house the morning after my arrival, but at the same time the murder and theft had nothing to do with me or Dorian. It was both related to me *and* not related to me.

"After Anna died," he continued, "we got spooked. We didn't want anything to tie us to that place. I'm a local history buff and had done a lot of exploring in the Shanghai Tunnels under the city, including finding some that nobody else knew about. Those tunnels were originally built to transport merchandise to downtown shops from ships docked on the river, but they hadn't been used for that in ages, and only a tiny fraction of the tunnels are open for guided tours. I thought the unused tunnels would be an ideal place to move the boxes. Charles and I thought that there, nobody would find them. I'd taken some of my students on a field trip to the tunnels, but never to the section where we hid the boxes. And just to be safe, I stopped taking the students on field trips to far-flung sections of the tunnels altogether."

"An officer was injured in the tunnels recently."

"Max Liu," Sam said quietly. "I really was sorry about that. It was a lot more work than we thought to move so many boxes to their new hiding place. Someone got suspicious and called it in, I guess. I couldn't let Max see me. I had to pull the deadfall lever. It was nowhere near the section of tunnel we were using, so I wasn't worried about him or anyone else finding our shipment."

"And Zoe Faust?"

"I told you," Sam said, "she bought that rundown house. Charles must have lied to me about giving up the business. I thought she was going to be his new partner."

"That's why you killed him?"

"He had to be stopped, or more people would die. I did what I had to do to take care of Olivia, but I didn't want any more innocent people to die."

"The day of Mr. Macraith's death, what happened?"

"I took some of the tainted herbs—the same ones Anna had taken. I went to his house, making up an excuse that I thought I'd left something. I put the herbal mixture in his coffee. He drank coffee so thick I didn't think he'd notice."

"But he did?"

"No. He didn't. But it wasn't as poisonous as I thought it would be. I had to follow him to Zoe Faust's house to finish … To do what had to be done."

"Why'd you steal from the house? To make it look like a robbery?"

"I know about history. When I saw those antiques and books, I knew they would be worth a lot of money. I was still hurting for money, so I took them. I didn't think anyone would notice, but then I heard someone coming, and I dropped a couple of things on my way out the back door. I never meant it to look like a robbery, though. I thought Zoe would be arrested and you'd find evidence linking her to Charles. But you didn't. That made me wonder if I was wrong that they were working together."

"Tell me about Brenda Skyler. Who you know as Blue Sky. Why did you make an attempt on her life?"

Sam sighed. "That wasn't my first choice. When it was clear you weren't going to arrest Zoe, I tried to take care of Zoe like I did Charles."

My breath caught. Max reached for my hand and gave it a quick squeeze. I needed it more than he knew. I now understood why I had detected a strange odor in my trailer after Brixton found "poison" that was actually the spice asafoetida. I had dismissed the feeling at the time, thinking it was merely an unpleasant mix of scent bottles Brixton had broken. I was wrong. Sam had tried to poison me.

"But she didn't drink it," Sam continued. "I didn't want to hurt Blue, but something had to be done. If I went to jail, who would look after Olivia? She was doing better after the treatment, but the cancer had come back once already." He laughed and shook his head. "I know Aunt Olivia can be brusque, but she's a good person. She believes the best of people. She actually believed Blue was paying me enough for me to cover the cost of the airline tickets and experimental treatment for her cancer. And the reason Olivia wears that red shawl all the time is because of its sentimental value. It was given to her by a group of women who knit clothing for cancer patients."

"So you framed Blue—er, Brenda—to protect your aunt."

"I knew Blue was hiding something from her past, the way she wouldn't even use a credit card, so I figured she was the best person to blame."

"Where are the rest of the books that are still missing?"

"I sold them."

I groaned. I closed my eyes, images of Dorian trapped in stone filling my thoughts.

"I told you I needed money," Sam was saying. "I drove a few towns over and sold them to a pawnshop. The guy gave me a decent price for some of the items. I planted the rest at Blue's house. Like I said, I wished I didn't have to do it. I'm glad she's okay."

Detective Dylan grunted.

"Is that all?" Sam asked. The same strange expression I'd noticed earlier was back on his face.

"That'll do for now."

"Good," Sam said. He swallowed the last of his tea. "Very good."

"You can get up now."

"No," Sam said, "I don't think I can."

"Oh no," I whispered.

Next to me, Max tensed. "What is it?"

"The tea," I said. "The special tea he asked for. It's—"

On the screen in front of us, Sam Strum vomited across the table and fell forward, his head hitting the table with an excruciatingly loud smack.

"Poison," I finished.

THIRTY-NINE

I stayed up with Dorian, waiting for news about whether Sam would regain consciousness and be able to tell us more about where he'd sold the books he'd stolen. The police said they would investigate out-of-town pawnshops, but I didn't know if that would be soon enough. Dorian was running out of time.

While we waited, we learned that Sam had kept a container of poison disguised as tea, which he'd hidden in his fridge, explaining why I hadn't detected it when I was at his house. It was what he'd used on Blue and had tried to use on me.

Sam didn't make it through the night.

It was after midnight when I received a call from Max that Sam had passed away. Dorian limped to the kitchen to make hot chocolate. He was using blended cashews to create a creamy, comforting texture without dairy. While the mixture heated on the stove, he rooted through the fridge, settling on a plate of vegan éclairs he'd cooked earlier that week using whipped coconut milk to create the custard filling. French comfort food.

Sitting in front of the fireplace with Dorian, a cup of steaming hot chocolate in my hand, I watched the light of the fire flicker over the gargoyle's gray profile. The hardened stone progression was accelerating. Most of his left leg had now turned to stone. The same progression was beginning in his left arm. The fingers of his left hand hung stiffly, as if attached to invisible splints. The plate of éclairs sat untouched in front of him, slowly melting from the warmth of the fire.

"It is over for me," Dorian said, holding up his stiff hand in front of the fire. "I thank you, Zoe Faust, for trying to save me."

"It's not over," I said. "I don't accept that. I'll be back in a minute."

I found my laptop and brought it back to the living room.

"What are you looking for?" Dorian asked.

"Pawnshops."

"They will not be open in the middle of the night."

"No," I said, "but we can create a list of them. Since we can't tell the police about the urgency of finding out what happened to *Not Untrue Alchemy*, I don't know how soon they'll look into it. But there's nothing to stop us from calling shops ourselves in the morning. How many pawnshops could there possibly be?"

As it turned out, there were a lot of pawnshops. I'd done the impossible before, so I wasn't going to let that stop me. I moved to the couch to get comfortable for a long night.

The next thing I knew, I was lying down, listening to a tapping sound. Not rain. The noise was different. It was the sound of fingers tapping on a keyboard. I opened my eyes, sat up, and stretched. I'd fallen asleep on the couch.

The fire had gone out, but Dorian had pulled a blanket over me. Though the room was dark, I felt that the sun was rising. It was nearly dawn.

"*Bonjour*," Dorian said, looking up from his perch at the dining table. "I have created a spreadsheet. There are some *magnifique* computer programs these days. They have helped me narrow the search to eighty-four pawnshops you should try."

———

By the time I'd had a tepid bath, drank a fruit smoothie, and taken a walk to clear my head, some of the pawnshops were open.

Since the title of the book was written in Latin on the cover as *Non Degenera Alchemia* in a script nearly unreadable to most people today, I wasn't optimistic about finding a storeowner who remembered the book by its title. But I had to try. I figured if anyone remembered buying a set of rare, old books the previous week, I could follow up and show them a photograph of Dorian's book.

While I sat at the dining table and made phone calls, Dorian plied me with food and drink to keep me going. Plenty of tea to wet my parched throat, dried blueberries plumped in creamy millet cooked in almond milk as a mid-morning snack, homemade chocolate truffles as a pre-lunch pick-me-up.

It was mid-afternoon before my ears perked up at what I'd heard on the other end of the line.

"You remember the book?" I repeated, standing and motioning Dorian over to me. I put the phone on the speaker setting.

"I know books," the man said. "Used to be a rare book dealer, back in the day. Now *that* was a fulfilling job. Strange clients, sure, but in an eccentric way. Not like the creepy characters I see nowadays. One guy even tried to sell me a knife that had blood on it! Can you believe that?"

"Um—"

"I told him, you've gotta wash off that blood before I'll take it. Can't expect me to be cleaning up other people's messes."

"You *took it*?" I asked. I knew I should have been steering the conversation back to the book, but after a statement like that, the words were out of my mouth before I could think.

"Sure. It was a great knife. Strange that the guy never came back for it. I made me a couple hundred dollars off it."

"About the books—"

"Oh, right, I got off on a tangent there. Yep, I used to be a rare book dealer, back when you could make a living doing such a thing. I know there are some folks who still do it, but the money isn't there anymore."

"Uh—"

"What book was it you were asking about?"

"*Non Degenera Alchemia.* It looks like a seventeenth-century book. It would have been sold to you with a few other historical alchemy books."

"Right, that's why I remembered it. Alchemy. Strange subject. Most books I see on occult subjects are modern books pretending to be old, but these ones were truly antique. Yep, I bought three alchemy books from a young fellow who'd recently inherited them. He didn't want to get them back; wanted to sell them free and clear."

"Can you save them for me behind the counter?" I asked, beaming at a wide-eyed Dorian. "I can be there in two hours."

"Oh, I don't have them."

"Wait, you don't?"

"Nah. Like I said, they were a good find. A couple days ago, someone bought them all. If I'd known there would be other interested parties, I would have held out for more money."

"I'll give you a finder's fee if you help me locate the buyer so I can buy the books."

"Wish I could help you, but he paid cash and didn't leave a name."

Dorian's wings flew out from the side of his body, knocking over a chair.

"Everything all right there?" the pawnshop owner asked.

"Fine," I said, staring at Dorian's shocked face. "Thanks for your help." I clicked off the phone.

Dorian's body shook. "*Mon livre*," he whispered. "It is truly gone forever."

"There has to be another way," I said. "There has to be."

"I—" Dorian began, but was interrupted by a knock on the door.

"You'd better hide," I said. "I don't want you turning to stone. It's too risky. Go to the basement."

Dorian's face registered alarm. "I cannot seem to lower my wings."

The knock sounded again.

"Zoe?" It was Brixton's voice. "I'm here with Veronica and Ethan."

"One second!" I called. "Dorian, I'll help you down the basement stairs."

He nodded. I could see the fear in his watery black eyes.

After getting him into the basement, I opened the door for the kids. "Sorry, I was in the middle of cooking. Come on in."

Brixton raised an eyebrow as they walked inside.

330

"You went to school today?" I asked them, noticing their back-packs.

"Our parents said it was best if we went back to life as normal," Veronica said. "Did you hear about what happened to Mr. Strum at the police station?"

I nodded.

"I can't believe it," Brixton said. "I mean, if you can't trust someone like him, who can you trust?"

"It's like all anyone's talking about," Veronica said.

The entitled Ethan hadn't spoken, walking straight past his friends to the dining table, where he opened his laptop.

"I don't mean to be rude," I said, "but I've had a long day. Was there a particular reason you stopped by?"

"We thought you'd want to see this, Zoe," Ethan said.

"We could have texted you earlier," Brixton said, "but Veronica thought you'd give us some food."

Veronica elbowed him.

"Coming right up," I said, laughing at the resilience of youth. I returned from the kitchen with a platter of mini chocolate éclairs to find the three of them sitting around Ethan's laptop.

Veronica took an éclair and beamed at me. "Show her, guys."

Ethan turned the laptop around, showing me the screen. The browser was open to the website of an antiquarian bookshop based in Seattle. It showed a photograph of Dorian's book.

"How did you—" I began.

"Ethan is good at finding stuff online," Brixton said, not trying to hide a wide grin.

"I get bored during class," Ethan said with a shrug. "Brixton said this book meant a lot to you, and we heard today that Mr. Strum had stolen your stuff and wouldn't be able to tell anyone what he'd done with it. I thought I'd make it my project for the day. I found it during fifth period."

"I don't know what to say, Ethan," I said. "*Thank you.*"

"I hope you've got a credit card with a high limit," Brixton said. "You do, right? For your business?"

"Why?"

"Look at the asking price," Brixton said, pointing at the screen. It was a figure far greater than I had access to. My elation from moments before disappeared.

"Won't the police get it back for her?" Veronica asked. She took another éclair as Ethan turned the computer back around to face him.

"They probably can," I said, looking at Brixton, "but it might take a long time to go through those channels."

Going through the legal system to retrieve stolen property from an innocent business person was going to be a nightmare. And one that would take far longer than Dorian had. It was going to be hard enough to use what Ivan and I had realized about the book to stop Dorian's deterioration. I had even less faith that I'd be able to reverse the effects once he'd turned completely to stone.

Brixton's smile faded. "More bureaucracy? Blue is still in jail, and you don't get your stuff back? This is totally screwed up. Maybe if we call Max—"

"I doubt there's anything he can do." I sat down at the end of the table and put my head in my hands. "But thank you, Ethan. Thank you all for trying."

"It's done," Ethan said, leaning back and smiling. He popped an éclair into his mouth.

"What's done?" Veronica asked.

"See for yourself, V," Ethan said, pointing at the screen.

"No way," she said. "You *bought it*?"

"Of course I bought it. What else is my dad's money good for if not to thank the person who saved us from that cell?" Ethan shivered as he spoke of it. "Do you want to drive to Seattle by seven o'clock tonight to pick it up, or should I ask them to send it by express mail?"

FORTY

IT WAS NEARLY TEN o'clock by the time I got home.

I made good time on the three-hour drive to Seattle, including having the good fortune to avoid the speeding ticket I deserved. Finding the book dealer's shop was another story, but he generously agreed to stay open later so I could retrieve the book. Ethan paid enough for the book that he really had no choice.

I was thankful for Ethan's generosity, but I knew I couldn't accept it. As soon as I got my alchemy lab into proper shape, I'd transmute some lead into gold. Either that or become a much better businesswoman.

Brixton had wanted to accompany me on the drive, but I thought it best not to subject him to my anxious mood and the high speeds I planned on testing out in my old truck. The speedometer went to one hundred, and although I'd occasionally driven fast on the open road, most of the time I'd had the truck it had been attached to my trailer. It was time to test my truck, and it came through.

I slammed the door of the truck and rushed to the house, cradling the book in my arms. I left Dorian doing yoga stretches while reading the newspaper—two forms of distracting movement were better than one. As I came through the door, he was nowhere in sight.

"Dorian?"

"*Aidez moi!*" The panicked voice came from the kitchen.

I found him standing on his stool, facing the counter. His wings were askew, one of them partially unfurled as stone.

"Can you move?" I asked.

"I am so glad you have returned. My fingers are too stiff to properly stir the batter for these crepes! There are lumps. Lumps!"

I smiled to myself. I'd gotten home in time.

"We have more important things to do than make crepes," I said. "Get down from there and come with me to the basement."

With what Ivan and I had pieced together about backward alchemy, I had a much better idea about what I should look for in the book. I didn't have as many ingredients in my laboratory as I would have liked, nor did I have a full understanding of backward alchemy, but tonight I was going to perform a quick fix. I never thought I'd hear myself say that again, but that was the very nature of backward alchemy's death rotation: sacrificing one element for another to skip the laborious process of true alchemy.

My vibrant herbs were the sacrifice. They had been lovingly cared for, which gave them power. Turning the pages of *Not Untrue Alchemy* with shaking hands, I found a section that suggested, in coded illustrations, how to use mercury to dissolve plants without going through the usual steps that required weeks or months.

For the next two hours, I crushed and extracted the essences of the fresh herbs, working backward by beginning with fire. The resulting ashes weren't the true salt that alchemists strive to achieve, but was none-the-less salt. Of the three essential ingredients of alchemy, mercury is the spirit, sulfur the soul, and salt the body. Salt was what I needed to save Dorian's deteriorating body.

I didn't know if this strangely transformed salt should be ingested or topically applied, so I tried both. While I dissolved the salt in a tea-like decoction, I also made a paste to cover Dorian's skin. The gargoyle eyed the gooey paste skeptically, so we tried the tea first.

At nearly the stroke of midnight, the stone pieces of Dorian's body began to shimmer. His stone leg returned to gray flesh, granule by granule. He was able to move, but the skin on his leg was a lighter shade of gray than it had been. He wasn't the gargoyle he once was.

He smiled and hopped up into my arms to give me a hug. Terribly undignified for a Frenchmen, and my back nearly gave out under the heavy weight of his stone body, but I wasn't complaining.

"I knew, Zoe Faust, that I could count on you."

I hugged Dorian back, happy he couldn't see the mixed emotions flashing across my face. Though relief was at the forefront, worry was close behind. The unnatural alchemy I'd performed to stop Dorian's deterioration was a quick fix that hadn't fully healed Dorian. It wasn't a real cure. There was much more I would need to do to discover the book's secrets and stop Dorian's body from once again becoming a stone prison.

"This isn't a cure, you know," I said, setting Dorian down. "There's more work to be done."

"You said this book is backward, and takes from other life forces?"

"There's still a lot I don't understand, but that appears to be the case."

His snout quivered. "Does this mean," he said slowly, speaking barely above a whisper, "that I am evil?"

"No," I said, shaking my head and feeling tears well up in my eyes. "It doesn't mean that. I don't yet understand what brought you to life, but the gargoyle you are—the gargoyle I know—isn't evil."

"Someone else did not have to die to bring me to life? Only the plants?"

I hesitated. "Nobody died for this temporary fix. That much I know. As for a permanent solution… I wish I knew, Dorian. I'll figure it out, though. I promise."

I knew I should be happy in the present moment. Dorian was safe. But for how long?

————

The following week was a blur.

Blue was out on bail. Charges had been filed against her for the illegal things she did to change her identity, but Max thought there was a good chance she'd only get probation.

When I stopped by Blue Sky Teas, Blue greeted me with a proposition. She'd heard about what a great cook I was, and also that I was underemployed. She made me an offer to bake vegan treats for the teashop. I happily accepted on the spot, without consulting Dorian. I knew he'd love the idea of yet another excuse to experiment with recipes, plus it could be his contribution to the huge food bills I was incurring.

Nobody could believe what Sam had done. Once people heard he'd done it for his aunt, they realized it made a certain kind of sense. But when they remembered his aunt was curmudgeonly

Olivia, it again made less sense. Olivia hadn't made an appearance at the teashop, so nobody was sure how she was doing.

Brixton was more dedicated to keeping Dorian's secret than ever, and he was enjoying the cooking lessons the gargoyle was giving him. I think he even appreciated the weeding he was doing for me. As we prepared the yard for spring planting, he peppered me with questions about plants and alchemy.

He, Veronica, and Ethan said they had given up their tunnel explorations, as well as every other type of dare they used to come up with for each other. I wasn't sure how long that would last, but I was pleased it sounded like the kids wouldn't get into too much trouble for a while.

Dorian was in denial that his health would again begin to deteriorate, so I was left to my own devices to decipher the book. Well, I wasn't completely on my own. Ivan was eager to help. Although he didn't know I was a true alchemist or that Dorian existed, he was happy to have found a fellow enthusiast of the history of alchemy. He'd been depressed after being forced into his early retirement, so he was overjoyed to have an ongoing alchemy project that would drive his passion to finish his book.

I was getting ready to return a two-foot-high stack of library books when Max Liu appeared on my doorstep.

Looking at him through the peephole, I paused with my hand on the doorknob. I pressed my forehead to the door and closed my eyes. *Should I open the door?* My heart beat a little quicker as I remembered his kiss. The electrifying kiss that I'd pulled away from.

He and I could never work. Rationally, I knew that. But that was my problem. I wasn't as rational as I wanted to believe. I tried to take a sensible course of action, living on the road, staying away from attachments, and giving up alchemy after it caused me so much pain. I'd once transformed myself accidentally, becoming an accidental alchemist. Maybe, just maybe, I was finally ready to transform myself on purpose. Here in Portland, I'd found a place that made me want to stop running from myself. I didn't know what would become of me, but I was open to the possibilities.

I took a deep breath, opened my eyes, and turned the doorknob.

"Peace offering," Max said, holding out a bundle of fragrant jasmine green tea. In his other hand he held a canvas bag with greens poking over the top.

"Peace offering for what?"

"I was way out of line the other day," he said. "First at your dinner party, and then in the tunnels. I was just so happy to see that you were okay—"

"I accept your apology for how you acted about my herbal remedy at the dinner party." I took the tea and ushered him inside, giving me a second to think. "As for what happened in the tunnels, there's no need to apologize."

"But your boyfriend..."

I let the question hang in the air for a moment. His assumption gave me the perfect excuse, but I no longer wanted it. "I was being serious when I said he's just a friend. Veronica has an overactive imagination. I have a friend who's French. That's it."

Max was smart. I thought it best to stick to the truth. By keeping things simple, I could do that.

"I was hoping that was true. In that case, could I cook you dinner?" He held up the bag with greens poking over the side and gave me an endearing smile that hovered between confident and shy. "I'm not nearly as good a chef as you are, but I feel bad about how your dinner party ended the other night. It's the least I can do."

I felt warmth rise in my cheeks. "I'd like that very much."

Max paused on our way to the kitchen. Something in the living room had caught his eye.

"What is it?" I asked. "Don't tell me there's something else falling apart in this house."

"You throw me off balance, Zoe," he said, breaking off with an embarrassed look on his face. "I mean that in a good way. It's your gargoyle statue. I could have sworn it scowled at me as soon as I made a move for the kitchen."

THE END

AUTHOR'S NOTE

Though this book is a work of fiction, *The Accidental Alchemist* is based on fascinating historical facts that were too good not to run with in fiction.

Dorian's "father," Jean Eugène Robert-Houdin, was a French stage magician who lived from 1805 to 1871. He's considered the father of modern magic, for donning formal attire and moving magic from the streets into theaters. The biographical information in the book is true—including the facts that Robert-Houdin was a clockmaker who stumbled across magic by accident, and that he was asked by the French government to avert a crisis in Algeria. He helped convince Algerian rebels called the Marabouts that his "magic" was more powerful than that of local Marabout elders, therefore impressing the Algerian mullah leaders and helping the French cause. Fiction takes over where Dorian enters his life; his autobiography does not include anything about bringing a stone gargoyle to life.

French architect Eugène Viollet-le-Duc (1814–1879) was a contemporary of Robert-Houdin. Viollet-le-Duc is famous for restoring Notre Dame Cathedral in Paris, not only repairing it but also bringing new life to the cathedral. It was he who added the gallery of gargoyles—technically "grotesques" or "chimeras" because they don't serve as functional water spouts.

I took the liberty of making the two men friends and having Viollet-le-Duc give a prototype stone gargoyle to Robert-Houdin as a gift. As far as history has recorded, no such exchange took place.

Nicolas Flamel was a fourteenth-century bookseller and scrivener in Paris. He and his wife Perenelle donated large sums of money to charity, which Nicolas claimed was gold he had acquired through alchemy. The two lived exceptionally long lives for their time, and when their graves were exhumed years later, no bodies were found.

Many early scientists were alchemists who practiced their craft in secret. Isaac Newton was one such scientist who carried out alchemical experiments secretly, and it's speculated that a nervous breakdown Newton suffered may have been caused by mercury poisoning.

———

The Accidental Alchemist is very much my "cancer book." The month after my thirty-sixth birthday, I was diagnosed with aggressive breast cancer. The Elixir of Life was a powerful idea during that time, as was life transformation in general. For National Novel Writing Month during the year of my cancer treatments, I wrote a draft that became *The Accidental Alchemist.*

I've always loved all things mysterious, and have been fascinated by gargoyles from an early age. I run the Gargoyle Girl blog of mysterious photography (www.gargoylegirl.com) and had toyed with the idea of writing a gargoyle as a minor character in a book or a short story. When I began jotting down notes about Dorian, he refused to stay in the shadows.

The cooking thread of the book emerged because my husband and I had recently moved from a tiny apartment to a house with a large kitchen and a little bit of land in the backyard. A passionate gardener, my husband planted an organic vegetable garden. I took cooking classes, wanting to take advantage of the biggest kitchen I'd ever had, as well as the herbs and vegetables we were growing. I didn't expect it, but I fell in love with cooking.

After my cancer diagnosis made me take charge of my health, I taught myself to cook vegan meals from scratch that were just as good as—and often better than—anything I'd eaten before. Through a combination of more classes and experimentation, I discovered tricks that transformed foods into decadent savories *without using bacon*. Once I'd done that, I knew I was ready to write a book involving cooking.

I hope you enjoy the transformations in *The Accidental Alchemist*. Recipes, like life, aren't set in stone, so definitely try out your own variations on the recipes I've included here. Since this book takes place during the winter, the foods in this book are seasonal winter foods. Next time around, it'll be springtime…

In the meantime, you can find more information, including how to get in touch with me, at www.gigipandian.com. I love hearing from readers.

RECIPES

Kid-Friendly Green Smoothie (Vegan)

Total prep time: Under 15 minutes
Makes 2 servings

Ingredients:
- 1 green apple or 1 ripe green pear (use an apple for a tart smoothie, or a pear for a sweeter one)
- 1 medium cucumber, peeled
- ½ ripe avocado, skin and pit removed
- 1 ½ cups frozen broccoli
  Tip: For creamy sweetness, frozen broccoli works much better than fresh.
- 1 tsp fresh ginger, peeled (or more to taste)
- 1 heaping tbsp cacao nibs or unsweetened cocoa powder
  Tip: If you use cocoa powder instead of cacao nibs, it will turn your green smoothie brown—similar to a chocolate milkshake.
- 1 heaping tbsp peanut butter or almond butter

- Approx. 1½ cups of coconut water
  Tip: You can find canned coconut water at health food stores, often in 11 fl. oz. cans that provide the perfect amount of liquid for this smoothie. If you can't find coconut water, substitute water plus a little bit of added sweetener of your choice.
- Optional: a few fresh mint leaves

Directions:

Chop the above ingredients roughly, then blend together in a blender. Add more or less liquid depending on how thick you'd like it.

Variations for a less sweet smoothie:
- Greens substitution: a few leaves of fresh kale instead of frozen broccoli
- Protein substitution: a heaping tbsp of hulled hemp seeds or 2 tbsp soaked chia seeds instead of peanut butter
  Tip: Unlike hemp seeds, chia seeds expand in water and benefit from soaking. Soak 3 tbsp dry chia seeds in ¾ cup water. Let sit for 10 minutes or longer, shake or stir the mixture to avoid clumping, then store in a sealed container in the fridge for up to a week.
- Liquid substitution: plain water instead of coconut water
- Additions: Lots of green vegetables work well in this smoothie, such as celery, spinach, and parsley—try out your favorites.

Cherry Walnut Oatmeal Cookies (Vegan)

Total cooking time: Under 30 minutes
Makes 12 cookies

Dry ingredients:
- 1 cup old-fashioned oats
- ¾ cup unbleached all-purpose flour
- ¼ cup coconut sugar or brown sugar
- 2 tsp baking powder
- 1 tsp baking soda
- ¼ tsp sea salt

Wet ingredients:
- ¼ cup maple syrup
- ⅓ cup olive oil
- 1 ½ tsp vanilla

Mix-in ingredients:
- ⅓ cup chopped walnuts (or substitute a favorite nut)
- ⅓ cup unsweetened dried tart cherries (or substitute chocolate chips or a favorite dried fruit, such as cranberries)
  Tip: Even if you're not a fan of plain dried cherries, try them here at least once because this flavor combination brings out the best in them.

Directions:

Preheat oven to 350. In a large bowl, combine the dry ingredients. In a smaller bowl, mix the wet ingredients. Stir the combined wet ingredients into the dry ingredients. Fold in the mix-in ingredients.

Place a sheet of parchment paper on a baking sheet. Form approximately 12 cookie dough balls with your hands, and place them on the baking sheet 2 inches apart. Bake for approximately 12 minutes.

Roasted Butternut Squash with Lemon Tahini Sauce (Vegan)

Total cooking time: A little over an hour
Makes a side dish for 4, or a light main course for 2
Note: This is a great dish to serve meat-eaters who are skeptical that hearty vegan foods exist. The creamy, flavorful tahini sauce is a crowd-pleaser.

Ingredients for squash:
- 1 large butternut squash
- 1 large white onion (or substitute a smaller yellow onion; white onions are milder)
- 1 tbsp olive oil
- ½ tsp dried rosemary
- ½ tsp dried sage
- Salt and pepper to taste
- Optional: ¼ cup raw pepitas, a.k.a shelled pumpkin seeds
- Optional: paprika, for garnish

Ingredients for tahini sauce:
- ½ cup tahini
  Tip: Tahini is a sesame seed paste. You can often find it in a jar in the peanut butter aisle or with Middle Eastern foods, but if you find it to be expensive or hard to find, you can always make your own from scratch. See www.gigipandian .com/recipes for a recipe to make tahini from scratch.

- 3 tbsp fresh-squeezed lemon juice
- ½ cup water
- ¼ tsp granulated garlic (for a chunkier sauce, substitute 2 minced garlic cloves)
- ¼ tsp sea salt (or more to taste)
- Optional: cayenne to taste

Directions:

Preheat oven to 425. Peel butternut squash and cut into ½-inch cubes, discarding the seeds. (*Tip: If the squash is difficult to cut, pierce with a knife and microwave it for a minute or two to soften it.*) Peel the onion and chop roughly. Toss squash and onion with olive oil, then spread out on a parchment-paper lined baking sheet. Sprinkle spices on top. Bake for approximately 40 to 50 minutes, stirring once after 20 minutes.

While the squash mixture is baking, prepare the sauce. Whisk all the sauce ingredients together, then taste to adjust for salt and spice levels.

Tip: You'll most likely have extra sauce. It's a versatile sauce, which also works well as a salad dressing. Pour into a lidded glass jar and it will keep in the fridge for a couple of weeks.

Tip: You can use more or less water, depending on preferred consistency, keeping in mind that the sauce will thicken in the fridge.

Optional touch for a tasty garnish: Toast ¼ cup raw pepitas in a dry skillet on medium heat for a few minutes, until they begin to pop.

Tip: Always watch toasting nuts, as they burn quickly.

To serve: Transfer squash mixture to a serving bowl, drizzle with tahini sauce, toss pepitas on top, and sprinkle with a dash of paprika.

For more recipes and tips, visit www.gigipandian.com/recipes.

© MICHAEL B. WOOLSEY

ABOUT THE AUTHOR

Gigi Pandian lives in the San Francisco Bay Area with an overgrown organic vegetable garden in her backyard. A breast cancer diagnosis in her thirties taught her two important life lessons: healing foods can taste amazing, and life's too short to waste a single moment. Therefore she writes the *Accidental Alchemist* mystery series while drinking delectable green smoothies and eating decadent home-cooked meals. Gigi was awarded the Malice Domestic Grant for her debut mystery novel. She does not apologize for loving kale. Find her online at www.gigipandian.com.